C000252673

About tl

USA Today bestseller **Mich**..... .... more than forty books. You can usually find her in her office with her laptop loving the fact that she gets to work in her pyjamas. Michelle loves to hear from her readers! Visit Michelle on Facebook at Michelle Celmer Author, or email at michelle@michellecelmer.com

Jamaican-born **Lindsay Evans** is a traveller, lover of food, and avid café loafer. She's been reading romances since she was a very young girl and feels there is a certain amount of surreal magic in that she now gets to write her own love stories. Contact Lindsay at LindsayEvansWrites.com

City loving, book addict, peony obsessive, **Katrina Cudmore** lives in Cork, Ireland with her husband, four active children and a very daft dog. A psychology graduate, with a MSc in Human Resources Katrina spent many years working in multinational companies and can't believe she is lucky enough now to have a job that involves daydreaming about love and handsome men! You can visit Katrina at katrinacudmore.com

Friends to Lovers

June 2024
One Kiss

July 2024
Pretend

August 2024
Always You

September 2024
A Little Surprise

January 2025
Something More

February 2025
Better Together

Friends to Lovers:

Pretend

MICHELLE CELMER

LINDSAY EVANS

KATRINA CUDMORE

MILLS & BOON

All rights reserved including the right of reproduction in whole or in part in any form. This edition is published by arrangement with Harlequin Enterprises ULC.

This is a work of fiction. Names, characters, places, locations and incidents are purely fictional and bear no relationship to any real life individuals, living or dead, or to any actual places, business establishments, locations, events or incidents. Any resemblance is entirely coincidental.

This book is sold subject to the condition that it shall not, by way of trade or otherwise, be lent, resold, hired out or otherwise circulated without the prior consent of the publisher in any form of binding or cover other than that in which it is published and without a similar condition including this condition being imposed on the subsequent purchaser.

® and ™ are trademarks owned and used by the trademark owner and/or its licensee. Trademarks marked with ® are registered with the United Kingdom Patent Office and/or the Office for Harmonisation in the Internal Market and in other countries.

First Published in Great Britain 2024
by Mills & Boon, an imprint of HarperCollins*Publishers* Ltd,
1 London Bridge Street, London, SE1 9GF

www.harpercollins.co.uk

HarperCollins*Publishers*
Macken House, 39/40 Mayor Street Upper,
Dublin 1, D01 C9W8, Ireland

Friends to Lovers: Pretend © 2024 Harlequin Enterprises ULC.

More Than a Convenient Bride © 2015 Harlequin Books S.A.
Affair of Pleasure © 2015 Lindsay Evans
Best Friend to Princess Bride © 2020 Katrina Cudmore

Special thanks and acknowledgement are given to Michelle Celmer for her contribution to the *Texas Cattleman's Club: After the Storm* series.

ISBN: 978-0-263-32483-9

This book contains FSC™ certified paper and other controlled sources to ensure responsible forest management.

For more information visit: www.harpercollins.co.uk/green

Printed and Bound in the UK using 100% Renewable Electricity at CPI Group (UK) Ltd, Croydon, CR0 4YY

MORE THAN A CONVENIENT BRIDE

MICHELLE CELMER

To Best Friends

One

Julie Kingston stood and waited in the crowd, her heart overflowing with pride as her best friend and colleague, Lucas Wakefield, prepared to cut the ribbon marking the opening of the new, state-of-the-art Wakefield Clinic. It seemed as though the entire town of Royal, Texas, had shown up to mark the occasion.

The town's original free clinic once stood directly in the path of the F5 tornado that had ripped through Royal last October. In the blink of an eye, all that had remained of the structure was the concrete foundation. Patients from all over the surrounding counties had lost an important lifeline in the community.

Lucas, who had been a regular volunteer there despite his duties as chief of surgery at Royal Memorial Hospital, hadn't hesitated to donate the money to rebuild, using some of the proceeds from the sales and licensing of surgical equipment he'd invented several years ago.

Humble as he was for a multimillionaire, he'd intended to keep his identity as the donor a secret, but someone leaked the truth, and the news spread through Royal like wildfire. The town council had immediately wanted to rename the clinic in his honor. But of course

Luc had protested when he'd heard about plans for the Lucas Wakefield Clinic.

"This clinic doesn't belong to me," he'd told Julie when she'd tried to convince him that he was being ridiculous. "It belongs to the people."

"This is a huge deal," she'd argued time and again. "You donated millions of dollars."

He gave her his usual, what's-your-point shrug, as if he truly didn't understand the scope of his own good will. For a man of his wealth and breeding he lived a fairly simple life. "It was the right thing to do."

And that was Luc in a nutshell. He always did the right thing, constantly putting the well-being of others first. But finally, after much debate, and a whole lot of coercing from his mother, Elizabeth, Julie and his colleagues in the Texas Cattleman's Club, he relented, allowing the use of his last name only.

Julie smiled and shook her head as she thought back on it. Lucas was the most philanthropic, humble man she had ever known. And at times, the most stubborn, as well.

Luc looked out over the crowd, and when his eyes snagged on hers she flashed him a reassuring smile. Despite his dynamic presence, and easy way with his patients and coworkers, he despised being the center of attention.

To his left stood Stella Daniels, the town's acting mayor. To his right, Stella's new husband, Aaron Nichols, whose company R&N Builders rebuilt the clinic. In the six months since the storm, the town's recovery had been slow but steady, and now it seemed as if every week a new business would reopen or a family would move back into their home.

"I'm so proud," Elizabeth Wakefield said, dabbing away a tear with the corner of a handkerchief. Julie knelt beside the wheelchair Elizabeth had been forced to use since a botched surgery a decade ago left her paralyzed from the waist down. In the months since Julie came to Royal last October, Elizabeth had contracted a multitude of infections that led to numerous hospital stays, and she now required permanent, round-the-clock care from a registered nurse. Though she was a beautiful and proud woman, she looked every one of her sixty-eight years, and a recent hospital stay for viral pneumonia had left her weak and vulnerable. Originally Luc forbade her from attending the ribbon cutting, but she insisted she be there. After much debate, he eventually caved, and it was more than clear to Julie where he inherited his stubborn streak.

"You have every reason to be proud," Julie said, patting Elizabeth's frail arm. "You've raised your son to be an amazing man."

"I wish his father could be here. From the day Luc was born he insisted that his son was destined for great things. It still breaks my heart that he didn't live to see how right he was."

Julie took her trembling hand and gave it a gentle squeeze. "He knows."

The mayor completed her brief speech and handed Luc a pair of gold-plated scissors. With a quick swish of the blades the ribbon drifted to the freshly laid grass, and a round of applause erupted from the crowd. Luc's club brothers crowded around him to congratulate him and shake his hand, but Julie hung back, still clutching his mother's hand. Elizabeth looked proud but tired. The simplest of activities exhausted her.

"We should get you home," her nurse, Theresa, said. Too sleepy to argue, Elizabeth nodded.

"Shall I call Luc over?" Julie asked. "So you can say goodbye?"

"Oh no, don't bother him. I'll see him at home later tonight."

Julie kissed her papery cheek and said goodbye, then joined her friends Beth Andrews and Megan Maguire several feet away.

"She doesn't look so good," Beth said as Theresa wheeled Luc's mother toward the parking lot to the van Luc had custom-built for her. When it came to taking care of his mother, he spared no expense.

A stab of sadness pierced Julie's heart. In the six months since she'd moved to Royal, Julie had come to consider Elizabeth a dear friend. She was the closest thing Julie had had to a mother since her own mother died giving birth to her sister, Jennifer. Her father waited to remarry until after she and her sister had left home, and though he dated, he'd never brought a woman home to meet his daughters. He traveled extensively, so they were raised by nannies and the other house staff. Homeschooled by tutors.

And when he was home? Well, she didn't like to think about that.

"I don't suppose you'll have any free time to volunteer this week," Megan said. "Just an hour or two? Someone left a cardboard box of three-week-old puppies on the doorstep. They need to be bottle-fed every hour or so and I'm ridiculously understaffed this week." Manager of the local animal shelter, she was known for taking in strays. Animals and humans alike. She had certainly gone out of her way to make Julie feel welcome when she arrived in Royal. Her significant other, as well as Beth's, were members of the Cattleman's Club with Luc.

It was shaping up to be a very busy week, but Julie could always make time to help a friend. And sadly, this would probably be the last time. "Of course," Julie said. "Just let me know when you need me."

Megan sighed with relief. "You're a lifesaver!"

They stood chatting for several minutes, before Julie heard a familiar voice say, "Good afternoon, ladies."

She turned as Luc joined them, smiling brightly to hide the deep feeling of sadness that seemed to radiate from the center of her bones. She could tell by the way he tugged at his tie that he was already irritable. No sense in making him feel even worse.

"It's a wonderful thing you've done," Megan told him, and Beth nodded in agreement.

"Thank you, ma'am," he said, pouring on the Texas charm. Though he was her boss, and they had never been more than friends—best friends, but just friends—that drawl sometimes gave her a warm feeling inside her bones.

"Can I give you a lift home?" he asked Julie. Her apartment was within walking distance from the clinic, and it was a sunny and pleasant day for a stroll, but she suspected he was looking for any excuse to leave.

"If you wouldn't mind," she said, playing along, noticing a look pass between Megan and Beth, as if they knew Luc was eager to escape.

"Good to see you ladies," he said, nodding cordially, that hint of Texas twang boosting his charm somewhere into the stratosphere.

Julie followed him to his car, his stride so much longer than hers she practically had to run to keep up.

"What's your rush," she said, though she already knew the answer.

"Damn," Luc muttered, pulling at his tie as if it were a noose. "Why does everyone have to make such a big deal about it?"

Seriously? "Because it *is* a big deal, doofus. You're a hero."

"It's not as if I built it with my own two hands," he said, using his key fob to unlock his Mercedes. "I just wrote out a check."

"A ridiculously enormous check," she reminded him as he opened the door for her. He'd also remained involved through the design stage and the construction process, to be sure that everything was built to his exact specifications. Whether he wanted to admit it or not, this was, in many ways, *his* clinic.

As they drove through town, sadness and regret leaked from every pore. In the six months she'd been here, Royal had become her haven. The US felt like more of a home to her now than her native South Africa, and now she had to leave. She had no idea where she would go, or what she would do, and she had little time to figure it out.

Silence filled the car, and as they pulled into the gated community where she was currently staying, Luc said, "You're awfully quiet. Would you like to talk about it?"

"Talk about what?" she asked, dreading the inevitable conversation. But Luc could always tell when she was upset. She could swear that sometimes he knew her better than she knew herself.

"Whatever is bothering you." He parked outside her condo and turned to her. "Did I do something to upset you?"

"No, of course not." She'd hoped to put this off a little while longer, so as not to dampen his special day, but there was so much concern in the depths of his eyes, it seemed only fair to tell him now.

"So, what is it?"

As her brain worked to find the appropriate words, tears burned the backs of her eyes. Maybe the parking lot wasn't the best place to do this.

"Can you come inside for a few minutes? We need to talk."

His brow furrowed, he killed the engine. "Of course. Is everything okay?"

No, not at all. "Let's talk inside."

Gentleman that he was, Luc took her keys as they reached her door and unlocked it for her. He didn't even do it consciously. It was just his way. His mother, born and bred in Georgia, was old-fashioned when it came to matters of social grace. He claimed that from the day he was born, she'd drilled him with proper Southern manners.

Whatever she'd done, it had worked. He was one of the most courteous men Julie had ever known. In all the time they had been friends and worked together, he'd never said a harsh word, or once raised his voice to her. Or to anyone else, for that matter. He had such a commanding presence, he never had to. People took one look at those piercing hazel eyes and that *GQ*-worthy physique, heard the deep baritone voice, and spontaneously bent to his will. Women especially.

As they stepped inside the apartment, afternoon sunshine and fresh spring air poured in through the partially open window in the living room. Luc shrugged out of his suit jacket and dropped like a lead weight onto the sofa, looking far too masculine for the floral printed chintz. The furniture, which was too formal and froofy for her taste, and not all that comfortable, either, came with the apartment. Expecting good news when she'd filed to renew her visa, she'd been tentatively window-shopping in her spare time for furniture more suited to her. She wouldn't be needing it now. Not here, anyway.

She wasn't even sure where she would live. Other than a few distant aunts and uncles, she had no family left in her hometown. And when her father had passed away, his wife, whom Julie never had the pleasure of meeting, sold off the entire estate before the body was cold.

Julie had so much to plan, and so little time to do it.

She set her purse on the coffee table and sat beside Luc, fisting her hands in her lap. There was nothing she hated more than giving good people bad news.

Luc unknotted his tie, tugged it off and tossed it over the sofa arm on top of his jacket. Relaxing back against the cushions he undid the top two buttons of his dress shirt. "Okay, let's hear it."

She took a deep breath, working up the nerve to tell him. "I heard back from immigration yesterday."

One brow rose in anticipation. "And?"

Just say it, Jules. "My application to renew my visa again was denied."

In a blur of navy blue Italian silk and white Egyptian cotton, Luc was on his feet. "*Denied*? You can't be serious."

Tears pricked the corners of her eyes. Now was not the time for a messy emotional display. She'd learned years ago that crying only made things worse. "According to your government I've overstayed my welcome. I have two weeks to pack up my things and get out of the US."

"How is that possible? You're on a humanitarian mission."

"Technically I'm on a work visa."

"I still don't see the problem. You're still my research assistant. Gainfully employed. What changed?"

"Remember how I told you that in college I attended several protests."

"I remember."

"Well, what I didn't tell you is that I was arrested a few times."

"Were you convicted?"

"No, but I was afraid that if I put it down on my application I would be denied."

"So you left it out?"

She bit her lip and nodded, feeling juvenile and ashamed for having lied in the first place. But she would have done almost anything to come to the US and help her best friend. Now that one serious lapse in judgment was coming back to bite her in the rear. "I screwed up. I thought that because the charges were dropped, and it was a peaceful political protest, it wouldn't matter anyway. I was wrong."

"There has to be something we can do," he said, pacing the oriental rug, brow deeply furrowed. "Maybe I could talk to someone. Pull some strings."

"The decision is final."

His chin tilted upward. "I can't accept that."

She rose from the sofa, touching his arm, stopping him in his tracks. "You don't have a choice. It's done."

He muttered a curse, one he wouldn't normally use in the presence of a female, and wrapped his arms around her, pulling her close. She rested her head against his chest, breathed in the scent of his aftershave. It wasn't often that they embraced this way, and she found herself dreading the moment he let go.

The stubble on his chin brushed her forehead as he spoke. "There has to be something we can do."

There was one thing, but it was too much to ask. Even of him. *Especially* of him. "At this point all I can do is accept it. And move on."

He held her at arm's length, and she could see the wheels in his head spinning. But this was one situation all his money and influence couldn't fix. "Where will you go?"

"South Africa for a while, until I can find another research assistant position. Maybe in Europe, or even Asia."

"I'll do whatever I can to help. I'll write such a glowing recommendation people will be clamoring to hire you."

The problem was, she didn't want to work for anyone else. She used to love moving from place to place, meeting new people and learning new cultures and customs. Now the only place she could imagine living was right here in Royal. It was the first place in her travels that had genuinely felt like home. The first place in her life really.

There had to be something she could do.

Two

Luc sat at the bar at the Cattleman's Club swirling a double Scotch, watching the amber liquid tornado along the sides of a crystal tumbler, still reeling from Julie's news. And wracking his brain for a way to fix this, to keep her here in Royal where she belonged. Where she wanted to be.

She was the only person in his life—aside from his mother—who truly understood him. Who knew what made him tick. In fact, there were times when he wondered if she knew him better than he knew himself. These past few months, with the stress of seeing his hometown devastated, she was the anchor that had kept him grounded. She had been there to support him during his mother's past two hospital stays, which seemed to stretch longer each time she was admitted. Julie sat with her on her breaks, read to her when she was too weak to hold a book in her own two hands. He never even had to ask for her help. She just seemed to sense when he needed her, and she was there.

Drew Farrell, a fellow club member, and the owner of Willowbrook Farms, slid onto the stool beside him at the bar. In blue jeans, worn boots and a dusty cowboy hat, he looked more like a ranch hand than a man responsible for breeding multiple Triple Crown–winning horses. And though he dealt regularly with an elite and prestigious clientele, he couldn't be more down-to-earth. He was that guy in town everyone liked. Well, everyone but his neighbor Beth Andrews, who, up until the storm, had it in for Drew. But now, by some strange twist of fate, they were engaged to be married.

The complicated nature of relationships never ceased to amaze Luc.

Drew gestured to the bartender for a drink, and within seconds a bottle of his favorite brew sat on the bar in front of him. "What's the score?" he asked Luc.

It took Luc a few seconds to realize Drew was referring to the game playing on the television behind the bar. He'd been so lost in thought he hadn't even noticed it was on. "No idea," he said, taking a sip of his drink.

"I'm sorry I missed the ribbon cutting at the clinic. I had a client in town looking to buy one of my mares."

"No apology necessary. If there was any way *I* could have gotten out of it, I would have."

"Is that why you look so down?"

Luc ran his thumb around the brim of his glass. "Nope."

"Anything I can do to help?"

He shook his head. "Nope."

"Maybe it would be better if I left you alone," his friend said, grabbing his beer and making a move to get up.

"No," Luc said, realizing that he was being unnecessarily rude. And frankly, he could use the company. "I'm sorry. I just got some bad news today."

"It must have been pretty bad to put you in such a foul mood."

"Julie's request to extend her visa was denied."

Drew's eyes went wide with disbelief. "No way."

"I couldn't believe it, either." Nor was he willing to accept it. But when it came to plausible ideas to stop this from happening, he was coming up short.

Drew shook his head, expression solemn. "After all she's done for this town since the storm, they should be giving her a medal, not kickin' her to the curb."

Luc's thoughts exactly.

"What are you going to do?" Drew asked.

At this point there wasn't much Luc could do. Despite her objection he'd made a call to his lawyer, who had confirmed what Julie had told him. It was a done deal. "Let her go, I guess."

"Dude, you can't do that. You can't give up on her."

"I'm out of options."

"I'll bet there's one thing you haven't considered," Drew said.

"What's that?"

"You could marry her."

Marry Julie? His best friend? Drew was right, he hadn't considered that, because it was a ridiculous notion.

"Julie is like me," he told Drew. "She's very focused on her work. Neither of us has any plans to marry."

Drew rolled his eyes, as if Luc was a moron. "It wouldn't have to be a real marriage, genius. But it would be enough to keep her in the country."

A pretend marriage? "Not only is that a preposterous idea, it's illegal. We could both get in serious trouble. We could go to prison."

Drew grinned. "Only if you get caught."

Luc could hardly believe that Drew of all people

was suggesting he break the law. "And if we do get caught, what then?"

He shrugged. "Volunteer in the prison infirmary?"

Luc glared at him and Drew laughed.

"I'm kidding. Besides, it would never come to that. No one in this town would ever question the validity of your marriage."

Confused, Luc asked, "Why is that?"

"Are you kidding? You two are inseparable. Or at least, as inseparable as two workaholics can be. Most married couples don't spend as much time together as you two do."

"We're colleagues. It's part of the job description."

"It's more than that. You just...I don't know, *fit*."

"Fit?"

"People have been waiting for you guys to hook up. And there are others who think that you must already be knocking boots."

Annoyed that anyone would make that assumption, Luc said, "People should mind their own damn business."

Drew shrugged. "Small towns."

That didn't make it any less irritating. He and Julie didn't have that kind of relationship, nor would they ever. Yeah, he may have had the hots for her when they first met, but he had been reeling from his ex-fiancée, Amelia, abruptly calling off their engagement, and Julie had just come out of an emotionally rocky relationship herself. Before they'd had a chance to get over their former significant others and explore a physical relationship together, they had become pals instead. She was his buddy, his confidante. He would never do anything to jeopardize that. "We're just friends, and that's all we'll ever be."

Looking exasperated, Drew said, "Dude, it doesn't matter. You would be married in name only. Consider the alternative."

He had, a million times since she'd hit him with the bad news. Although the term *bad news* didn't quite measure the depth of his feelings when he imagined her leaving. Living thousands of miles away. Who would he talk to? Who would remind him to pick up his dry cleaning, or share late-night Indian takeout with him in the break room on those evenings when they were both too jammed to leave the hospital?

There had been nights like that for weeks after the storm, performing surgery after surgery. Some successful, some not. While volunteering for Doctors Without Borders, he had seen his share of heartbreaking situations and managed to stay detached and objective for the most part. A disaster in his hometown was a completely different story. Without Julie to lean on, to keep him grounded, he would have been a wreck. She was his anchor, his voice of reason.

Did he love her? Absolutely. But that was very different from being *in* love. And finding a new research assistant would be a nightmare. Julie knew his work inside and out. Training someone new would take more time and energy than he cared to expend.

"I obviously don't want her to leave," Luc said. "But if we were caught and something happened to her, I would never forgive myself."

After she was gone they could keep in touch through email and social media. They could even video chat on their computers or phones, though it wouldn't be the same as having her there. But was defrauding the government and risking both her freedom and his the answer?

"I'm telling you, no one is ever going to know," Drew insisted. "Even if the truth comes out, you're a local hero. Can you name one person in town who would turn you in?"

He made a good point. And even if there was an investigation, he and Julie knew each other as well as any married couple. He had no doubt they would pass any test with flying colors. The question was: How would Julie feel about it? She was the one with the most to lose.

"I guess it couldn't hurt to bring it up and see what she thinks," he told Drew.

"Great. I suggest a small- to moderate-sized ceremony and reception at the club and a long relaxing honeymoon somewhere tropical."

A wedding was one thing, but leaving Royal? That was out of the question. "I wouldn't have time for a honeymoon. I'm needed here."

Drew laughed and slapped him on the back. "Dude, you're a brilliant and devoted physician and, yes, this town needs you, but *everyone* needs a break now and then. No one will blame you for wanting a honeymoon. When was the last time you took time off? And I mean *real* time."

Luc tried to recall, and came up blank. It had definitely been before the storm. And probably quite some time before that. A year, maybe two. Or three. He'd traveled all over the world volunteering with Doctors Without Borders. That was how he'd met Julie. Their duties had taken them to many exotic and unfamiliar destinations, but it had been no vacation. Maybe they could use a break…

Luc shook his head. He and Julie married and taking a honeymoon? Until today the thought had never even crossed his mind. And it wasn't that he didn't find her appealing, both mentally and physically. Any man would be lucky to win her heart. He'd found her so appealing when they first met, it had been a little difficult to be objective. Practicing medicine in a developing country, the accommodations weren't exactly lavish. It wasn't uncommon for all the volunteers, male and female alike, to share living quarters, where modesty took a backseat to practicality. He was used to seeing his colleagues in various stages of undress. But in the case of Julie, he would often find his gaze lingering just a little longer than most would consider appropriate. But if she'd noticed, or cared, she'd never called him out on it. The issue was exacerbated by the fact that Julie didn't have a bashful bone in her body. In his first week working with her he'd seen more skin than the first two months he'd been dating Amelia, his college sweetheart and ex-fiancée. She'd had enough body hang-ups for half a dozen women.

But he would never forget the day he'd met Julie. He had just arrived at the camp and was directed to the tent where he would sleep and store his gear. He stepped inside and there she was, sitting on her cot, wearing only panties and her bra, a sheen of sweat glistening on her golden skin, her long, reddish-brown hair pulled into a ponytail. He froze, unsure of what to do or say, thinking that his presence there would offend her. But Julie hadn't batted an eyelash.

"You must be Lucas," she said, unfazed, rising from

her cot to shake his hand while he stood there, caught somewhere between embarrassment and arousal. It was the first of many times he'd seen her without her clothes on, but that particular memory stood out in his mind.

He and Julie had seen each other at their best, inventing surgical tools and techniques that they knew would change the face of modern surgery, and at their worst, unwashed and unshaven for weeks on end covered in bug bites from every critter imaginable. They had been to hell and back together, and they always, under any circumstance, had each other's back. Was this situation any different? Didn't he owe it to her?

It was becoming less of a question of why, and more of a question of why not. "You really think this could work?" he asked Drew, feeling a glimmer of hope.

"You would have to make it convincing," Drew said.

"Convincing how?"

"Well, she would have to move in with you."

Of course as a married couple they would have to live together. He and his mother had more than enough space, and four spare bedrooms for her to choose from. "What else?"

"In public you would have to look as if you're in love. You know, hold hands, kiss...stuff like that."

There was a time when he'd wondered what it would be like to kiss Julie. A real kiss, not her usual peck on the cheek when she hugged him goodbye. How would her lips feel pressed against his? How would she taste?

The tug of lust in his boxers caught him completely off guard. What the hell was wrong with him?

He cleared his throat and took a deep swallow of Scotch. "I could do that."

"No one else can know it's not real. We keep it

right here, between us," Drew said. "You know you can trust me."

Trusting Drew wasn't the issue. He knew that any one of his club brothers would lay down their life for him. The whole idea hinged on Julie's willingness to break the law and play house with him for heaven only knew how long. And her willingness to play the part convincingly.

It was something he would have to investigate thoroughly on his own before bringing it up to her. Talk to his attorney about the legalities. Make a list of the pros and cons.

"I'll talk to her," he told Drew.

"Who knows," Drew said with a sly grin, "you two might actually fall in love."

That's where Drew was wrong. If Luc and Julie were meant to fall in love, meant to be a couple, it would have happened a long time ago.

Julie sat in her office the next day, eyes darting nervously from the work on her desk to the clock on the wall. She was due to meet Luc in the atrium for a late lunch in fifteen minutes. Seeing her best friend had never been cause for a case of the jitters, but this was different: this had her heart thumping, her hands trembling and her stomach tied in knots. She was planning to ask Luc a favor, the biggest and most important favor she had ever asked him. Ever asked *anyone*. But if there was a single person on the planet she could count on to come through for her, it was Luc. More so than her own sister, who could be flighty at best. It sometimes took her days or even a week to answer a text or email. Sometimes she didn't answer at all.

Luc was truly the only person in her life who she could count on unconditionally. And if everything went as she hoped, she would be able to stay in the country indefinitely. Worst case, Luc would laugh in her face, and she would be on her way back to her native home, where she had only distant family left and no friends to speak of.

In the event that Luc said no, she would spend the rest of her time in the US tying up loose ends regarding the research on Luc's latest invention. She had reports to file and interviews to transcribe so that the switch to his new assistant would be a smooth one. Though the idea of someone else finishing her work left an empty feeling in the pit of her stomach.

The sudden rap on her office door startled her out of her musings. She looked up and was surprised to see Luc standing there. She checked the clock. She still had ten minutes to spare.

"Can I come in?" he asked. He wore scrubs under his lab coat, meaning he must have had a surgery scheduled that morning.

"Of course," she said, gesturing him in. "I thought we were meeting in the atrium. Did I get the time wrong?"

"Nope." He stepped into her office, which wasn't much larger than a small walk-in closet, and as he did, she felt as if all the breathable air disappeared from the room. It would explain the dizzy feeling in her head, the frantic beat of her heart.

What was wrong with her? She'd never been nervous around Luc. The truth is, she never got nervous about much of anything. Especially Luc. Everything about him, from his slow, easy grin and low, patient voice to his dark, compassionate eyes, naturally put people at ease. He could be intimidating as hell when he wanted to be. She'd seen it. But unless the situation warranted it, he chose not to be.

"I wanted a minute to talk in private," he said, snapping the door closed behind him. He crossed the two steps to her desk and sat on the edge. She could be mistaken, but he looked a little uneasy, which wasn't like him at all.

"There's something I need to ask you," he said.

What a coincidence. "There's something I need to ask you, too."

"Why don't I go first," he said.

Now that she'd worked up the nerve, she couldn't back down. "I think I should go first."

"What I have to say might impact what you have to say."

All the more reason to say it right now. The last thing she wanted was to make a huge deal about this. If she made a fool of herself, so be it.

It sure wouldn't be the first time.

Three

Luc was watching her expectantly, and she knew that the longer she dragged this out, the harder it would be. What she was about to ask him was no small favor. She wouldn't blame him at all if he said no.

Okay, Jules, you can do this.

Hoping he didn't hear the slight quiver in her voice, notice her unsteady hands or the erratic flutter of her pulse, she said, "I may have come up with a way to stay in the country. But I need your help."

His brow rose expectantly. "What kind of help?"

Her heart lodged in her throat, so when she opened her mouth to speak, nothing came out. For several seconds she sat there like a fool, the words frozen in her vocal cords.

Wearing a quirky smile, Luc asked, "Are you okay?"

Yes and no.

She was being silly. He was her best friend. Even if he said no, it wouldn't change anything. Hopefully it would only be slightly humiliating.

Come on, Jules, just say it.

Gathering her courage, she said, "You know that I really don't want to leave the US."

"And I don't want you to leave," he said.

"Royal has become my home. I feel like I belong here."

"You do belong here." He said it as if there were no question in his mind. "And you know that I'll do anything I can to help. As a matter of fact—"

"Please, let me finish." Earnest as he appeared, he might want to take that back when she told him her plan. "I've looked into every possible avenue, but there's only one way I've come up with that will assure I can stay."

She paused taking a deep, empowering breath. Then another.

"Are you going to tell me," he asked, looking mildly amused. "Or do you want me to guess?"

Oh, for Pete's sake, just say it, Jules. "We could get married. Temporarily of course," she added swiftly. "Just until I can earn my citizenship. Then we can get a quickie divorce and pretend it never happened. I'll sign a contract or a prenup. Whatever makes you most comfortable."

Luc blinked, then blinked again, and then he burst out laughing.

Wow. There it was. Her worst nightmare realized.

"You're right," she said, quickly backtracking. "It was a ridiculous idea. I don't know what I was thinking." She shot to her feet, when what she really wanted to do was curl up in the fetal position and wallow in shame. "Let's forget I said anything and go have lunch."

She tried to duck past him, and he wrapped a very large but gentle hand around the upper part of her left arm.

"Just hold on a minute," he said in that firm but patient way of his. From anyone else it would have come off as condescending. "It is *not* ridiculous. Not at all. I'm laughing because I came here to suggest the exact same thing."

It was her turn to blink in surprise. Did he mean that, or was he just trying to make her feel less stupid. "Seriously?"

"But it is a legally and morally gray area. I wasn't sure if you would be willing to risk breaking the law."

Desperate times required desperate measures. "I'm willing if you are."

"We can't risk anyone else knowing the truth."

"I won't tell if you don't."

"Drew knows. He's the one who suggested it. But we can trust him. And I won't lie to my mother."

Julie had never known Drew to be anything but a stand-up guy. If Luc trusted him, so would she. And she would never expect Luc to lie to Elizabeth, nor would she want him to.

Julie had no one else to tell, except her sister, Jennifer, who probably wouldn't care anyway. When she married her husband, an older, wealthy man she'd met on a trip to New York, he became the center of her life. She quit college and set her sights on being the perfect trophy wife. Between charity balls and country club brunches with the other trophy wives in her elite social circle, she had little time for her nomadic, unsophisticated sister.

Though she had never actually met Jennifer's husband—nor did she care to—her sister's description of him gave Julie a bad feeling. He sounded very controlling, like their father. But now was not the time to dredge up those old memories. She had promised herself a long time ago that she would never look back in regret, but instead learn from her past and always move forward. Always strive to better herself. Marrying Luc, though completely unexpected, would be just another leg of her journey.

"Having second thoughts already?" Luc asked, and she realized she was frowning.

"No, of course not. Just wondering what happens next."

"Drew suggested we have the ceremony and reception at the club and we have to do it soon."

"How soon?"

"How's this Saturday afternoon looking for you?"

This Saturday? That was only five days away. She knew absolutely zero about planning a wedding, but less than a week sounded ridiculously fast. "Is it even possible to put a wedding together that quickly? And what about immigration? Don't we have to have an interview or something?"

"My attorney is taking care of all of that. And as for the wedding, we'll keep it simple. Close friends only. Very informal."

"I don't even know where to start."

"All you need to do is find a dress. And a maid of honor. I'll take care of the rest."

Of all her friends in Royal, Lark Taylor was the closest. They'd met during the first few weeks of the cleanup efforts and became fast friends. She was a nurse in the intensive care unit at the hospital. They often took coffee breaks together, and sometimes went out for drinks after work. She was planning her own wedding to Keaton Holt, a longtime Cattleman's Club member, so perhaps she could give Julie a few pointers.

"We'll have to kiss," she heard Luc say, and it took her brain a second to catch up with her ears.

"Kiss?"

"During the ceremony," he said.

"Oh…right." She hadn't considered that. She thought about kissing Luc and a peculiar little shiver cascaded down the length of her spine. Back when she first met him, she used to think about the two of them doing a lot more than just kissing, but he had been too hung up on Amelia and their recently broken engagement to even think about another woman. So hung up that he left his life in Royal behind and traveled halfway around the world with Doctors Without Borders.

A recent dumpee herself, she'd been just as confused and vulnerable at the time, and she knew there was nothing worse for the ego than a rebound relationship. They were, and always would be, better off as friends. In her experience, it was usually one or the other. Mixing sex and friendship would only end in disaster.

"Is that a problem?" Luc asked.

She blinked. "Problem?"

"Us kissing. You got an odd look on your face."

Had she? "It's no problem at all," she assured him, but if that was true, why did her stomach bottom out when she imagined his lips on hers. It had been a long time since she'd been kissed by anyone. Maybe too long.

"We'll have to start acting like a married couple," he said.

"In what way?"

"You'll have to move in with me."

She hadn't really considered that, but of course a married couple would live together. Having separate residences would raise a very bright red flag. Since Julie left home, when she wasn't volunteering abroad, she'd lived alone. She liked the freedom of answering to no one but herself, of doing what she wanted to do, when she wanted to do it. That would be hard to give up.

As if Luc read her mind, he added, "Nothing in our relationship is going to change. We only have to make it look as if it has."

But by pretending that it changed, by making it look that way to everyone else, wasn't that in itself a change?

Ugh. She never realized how complicated this could be. She could already feel the walls closing in on her.

"Look," he said, and this time he was the one frowning. "If any of this makes you uncomfortable, we don't have to do it. I want you to stay in the US, and I'll do whatever I can to help make that happen, but if it's going to cause a rift in our friendship, maybe it's not worth it."

"I'm just used to living on my own. The idea of changing that is a little intimidating. But it is worth it. And I don't want you to think that I'm not grateful. I am."

"I know you are." He smiled and laid a hand on her forearm, and the feel of his skin against hers gave her that little shiver again. What the heck was going on? She never used to shiver like that when he touched her. She was sure it was due only to the stress of her situation.

What else could it possibly be?

"It's bad, isn't it?" Julie looked up at Lark, her maid of honor, in the dressing room mirror at the Cattleman's

Club. Julie was on her third attempt of giving herself "smoky eyes." But she looked more like a cheap street walker than a bride.

"When it comes to eyeliner and shadow, especially for someone as naturally pretty as you, I think less is more," Lark said, which was her kind way of telling Julie to give it up.

"Oh my God, what a mess," Julie said, swiping at her eyes with a damp cloth. It had looked pretty simple in the instructional video she'd found online, but her technique lacked a certain…finesse. Which is why she never wore the stuff.

Her father had lived by very traditional values and as teens, Julie and her sister had been forbidden to use makeup of any kind. Or wear pants. Dresses and skirts were the only acceptable attire for a female in her father's home, and Julie had played the role of obedient daughter very well. It was easier not to make waves. She concentrated on her studies and getting into a good college. She never did develop the desire to wear makeup, but after eighteen years of wearing only skirts and dresses, she swore she would never wear anything but pants. Yet here she was now in a newly purchased, off-white, silk shift dress, which she had to admit hung nicely on her athletic frame. But with her raccoon eyes Luc was going to take one look at her and run in the opposite direction.

Her sister, the queen of all things girly and impractical, would have been a big help right about now but she wasn't answering calls or texts. If it was anyone but Jennifer, Julie might have worried, but that was typical for her sister. She was either completely distant and unreliable, or smothering Julie with her sisterly love. There was no middle ground.

"I suck at this," she said.

"Maybe just a little mascara and liner," Lark suggested, with a sympathetic smile. "Would you like me to help?"

Julie looked up at her with pleading, raccoon eyes. "Yes, please."

Lark worked her magic and she was right. Julie was lucky to have been blessed with smooth, clear skin, and just a touch of liner and mascara and a little clear gloss on her lips subtly enhanced her features.

"You're a genius," she told Lark.

"And you look beautiful," Lark said, smiling and stepping back to admire her work. "Lucas is a lucky man. And forgive me for saying, but it's about darned time you two tied the knot."

Julie had heard that same remark from a dozen people since she and Luc made the announcement earlier that week. "It doesn't seem...*sudden*?"

"I always suspected you and Luc had something going—I think everyone has—but you're a very private person, so I didn't want to ask. I figured that if you wanted me to know, or needed to talk about it, you would tell me."

If there had been anything to tell, Julie probably would have.

There was a rap on the dressing room door and Lark's sister Skye stepped into the dressing room. She looked surprisingly healthy for someone still recovering from a near-fatal car crash during the tornado. Luc had performed an emergency cesarean to save her unborn child, and her injuries had been so severe she'd been in a coma for four months. Until Skye was well enough to care for her daughter, Lark had taken responsibility for Baby Grace, who was the sweetest most adorable infant Julie had ever seen.

"It's time," Skye said, then sighed wistfully. "You look beautiful. Luc is a lucky guy."

Julie took a good look at herself in the mirror, spinning in a circle to get every angle. Not half-bad.

Though she usually kept her hair pulled up into a ponytail, she'd worn it down today, in loose, soft curls that tumbled across her shoulders. She'd even put on her mother's diamond earrings. It was the only thing of her mother's that she had left. In his grief after she died, Julie's father had removed every trace of his wife from their home. Photos, personal items, anything that reminded him of her. Julie had only been four at the time, but she remembered sitting on her parents' bed, crying as she watched their housekeeper clear out her mother's closet, shoving her clothes into black trash bags.

Between his wife's death and having a newborn infant to care for, her father seemed to forget that he had another child who was mixed up and lonely and desperate for the unconditional love and affection her mother had always given so freely. Within weeks of her death he'd hired a nanny and began traveling extensively. He had never been what anyone would consider an attentive father, but after her mother's death he had become virtually nonexistent.

Julie breathed deep to ease the knot of sadness in her chest, the burn of tears behind her eyes. Now was not the time to think about her less than ideal childhood. God forbid she start crying and ruin her makeup.

"How are you doing?" Lark asked. "You nervous?"

Julie shook her head. This wasn't going to be a real marriage, so what reason did she have to be nervous?

Though they wouldn't be married for long, she had insisted on a prenup. To protect not just his interests, but her own, as well. She'd never been the type to flaunt her wealth, but with the inheritance her father had left her and her sister, and a little savvy investing, Julie was pretty much set for life. A simple, no frills life, but that was fine with her. She didn't need much.

"So, are you ready?" Lark asked, and Julie turned to find her and Skye watching her expectantly.

After one more quick glance in the mirror, she nodded and told her friends, "Let's do this."

Four

With so little time to plan the wedding, Drew had volunteered to put a guest list together for Luc. But now, as Luc stood with Drew at his side, waiting for the ceremony to begin, scanning row upon row of guests idly chatting, he was beginning to think that had been a bad idea. It seemed as if half the town was there.

He leaned in close to Drew and said in a harsh whisper, "This is your idea of small and intimate?"

"Just helping to make it convincing," Drew said with a wry smile. It was obvious to Luc that he was thoroughly enjoying himself. "Are you nervous?"

"Of course not." What reason did he have to be? This was nothing more than a business arrangement between friends. In fact, he felt exceedingly calm. A little bored even.

"All grooms get nervous," Drew persisted.

"But I'm not a real groom, am I?"

"Look around you. This sure looks real to me. Besides, you can't argue with a marriage license."

Okay, so maybe he was a real groom, but not in the traditional sense. They would be married, but not really married. Together, but not really together.

Luc glanced over at his mother, who sat in her

wheelchair in the front row, an encouraging smile on her face. When he told her about the marriage she was beside herself excited, even when he explained the true nature of the situation.

"It's just a way to keep Julie in the States," he'd explained.

"Of course it is," she'd said with a twinkle in her eyes, as if she knew something he didn't. If she believed it to be anything more than a friend helping out another friend, if she had her heart set on Luc and Julie falling in love, she would be sorely disappointed.

Stella Daniels, who was officiating, touched Luc's shoulder and said softly, "Words cannot express how happy I am for the two of you. And forgive me for saying this, but it's about damned time."

He kept a smile planted firmly on his lips, but he felt a distinct twinge of guilt. He'd heard many similar remarks this past week, and as much as he hated the idea of lying to everyone, he and Julie had no choice.

The music started and everyone turned to the doorway where Lark stood, carrying a small bouquet of miniature yellow roses—Julie's favorite color.

Here we go, Luc thought, his stomach bottoming out.

Okay, so, maybe he was a *little* nervous.

Lark made her trip down the aisle, but Luc's attention remained fixed on the doorway, anticipation tying his stomach into knots. Then the "Wedding March" started and Julie appeared in the doorway, and all Luc could think was *wow*.

Rarely did he see Julie with her hair down, and in all the time he'd known her he couldn't recall ever seeing her in a dress. Cut several inches above the knee, it was just long enough to be tasteful, but short enough to showcase her toned, suntanned calves and a little bit of thigh...

Whoa, he thought, as his pulse picked up speed. This was Julie he was gawking at, his best friend. But damn, who could blame him? She looked stunning and sexy and as his eyes met and locked on hers, he experienced a distinct tug of sexual attraction. Bordering on red-hot lust.

Talk about getting caught up in the moment. If this kept up he was going to need a serious attitude adjustment.

Everyone stood and she started down the aisle, walking alone, holding a single long-stemmed yellow rose, looking cool and composed, as if she did this sort of thing all the time. This may have been a "pretend" wedding, but in that moment it couldn't have felt more real to him, and despite her cool exterior, when Julie faced him and he took her hands, they were trembling.

Stella began the ceremony, but he was so focused on Julie, the mayor's words all seemed to run together. It was almost as if he was really seeing Julie for the first time. And though he'd been to more weddings than he could count, as they recited their vows, he realized he'd never really grasped the gravity of the words. Real marriage or not, as he slid the platinum band on her ring finger—she'd balked at the idea of a diamond—he pledged to himself that as long as they were married, he would honor those vows.

Then came the part he'd been most anticipating. The kiss to seal the deal. They had to make it look convincing. Too chaste or formal and it might make people suspicious; too passionate and Julie might crack him one. Probably not here at the wedding, but later, when they were alone.

There was another possibility. One he hadn't truly considered until just now. What if he kissed her, and he liked it? So much so that he wanted to do it again. And even more intriguing was the possibility that she might like it, too.

"You may kiss the bride," Stella said, and Julie's pulse jumped as Luc, seemingly in ultra slow motion, bent his head. The entire ceremony had been a bit surreal, as if she were standing outside of her body watching herself. But this? This was very real.

Her chin lifted in anticipation, and she began to wonder if this was something they should have rehearsed ahead of time. No one's first kiss should have an audience, yet here they stood with dozens of pairs of eyes planted firmly on them.

Oh boy, what had they gotten themselves into?

Luc reached up, his hand gently cupping her cheek, and her knees went weak. His lips brushed softly across hers, seeming to linger undecidedly between obligation and curiosity, and a sound, like a soft moan, slipped unexpectedly from her lips. Without realizing she'd even moved, her hands were on his chest and curling into the lapels of his suit jacket, pulling him closer. If it hadn't been for the sudden round of applause, and the hoots and howls from their guests, she would have gone right on kissing him. As their lips parted and she looked up into his eyes, she could see that he was equally perplexed. And as lame and juvenile as it sounded, she heard herself saying softly, "Wow, you're really good at that."

A wry grin tipped up the corners of his lips. "So are you."

Her kissing skills, and his, were irrelevant. So why the shiver of pleasure? The weak-kneed feeling of anticipation? There was nothing to anticipate. They were married and she was a legal resident. As devious plans go, this one was playing out exactly as they'd expected. The hard part was over.

With all the handshaking and hugs, the walk back down the aisle took so long that when they finally made it to the room where the reception was being held, people were already sipping very expensive champagne and nibbling on the appetizers catered by a restaurant in town that had reopened its doors just last week. Though she distinctly remembered Luc saying it would be small and intimate, it looked to Julie as if nearly every member of the Cattleman's Club and their significant others were in attendance.

She looked up at Luc. "Small and intimate, huh?"

"I put Drew in charge of the guest list," he said, nabbing two glasses of champagne from a passing waiter and handing one to her. "So if you have a bone to pick, it's with him. And forgive me for saying it, but you look positively stunning."

Forgive him? His words made her feel dizzy with pleasure. "If it wasn't for Lark's help, you would have married a raccoon."

He regarded her with a curious expression.

She laughed and shook her head. "Never mind."

Somewhere behind her Julie heard the sharp tink of metal on glass and turned to see Skye tapping her champagne flute with the tines of her fork. Her husband, Jake, mirrored her actions, then several other guests joined in, all turning to look at Julie and Luc as if they were waiting for them to do or say something.

She heard Luc mumble something under his breath, and asked him in a hushed voice, "What are they doing?"

"They want us to kiss."

Julie blinked. "Kiss?"

Luc shrugged. "It's tradition."

And he couldn't have warned her about this? So she could at least prepare herself. "I've never been to an American wedding. You're saying we have to kiss? Right now? In front of all these people?"

"If we want them to stop."

Considering the rising decibel level, if she and Luc didn't kiss, someone was bound to shatter something. Besides, it had been so nice kissing him the first time. One more time wouldn't hurt, right? Who was she to question the tradition.

"Well, if we have to," she said.

Luc bent his head and brushed a very brief and chaste kiss across her lips, but the tinking didn't stop.

"You can do better than that," someone shouted.

Her heart did a back-and-forth shimmy in her chest. Oh boy, this could wind up being a very long evening.

Luc gazed at her questioningly, his eyes saying it would be best if they appeased the crowd. Julie shrugged, whispering, "We have to make it look real, I guess."

She tried to play it cool, but on the inside she was trembling as Luc cupped the back of her head, his hand sliding through her hair, fingers tangling in the curls. And if that didn't feel nice enough, his kiss nearly did her in. When his tongue swept across her lower lip she felt it like an electrical charge, as if every cell in her body came alive all at once. But then it was over and she had to fight the urge to toss her champagne glass aside, grab the lapels of his jacket and pull him in for more.

It must have been sufficient for the guests, because the tinking faded out, only to start up again a few minutes later, instigated this time by Paige Richardson, who stood beside her brother-in-law Colby.

Colby was Aaron Nichols's partner in R&N Builders, which was almost single-handedly responsible for rebuilding the town after the tornado. And though Julie knew him to be a friendly and outgoing, all-around nice guy, the deep furrow in Colby's brow said something was troubling him.

The tinking rose to an unreasonable level and Julie could swear that every single guest had joined in.

She looked up at Luc, who appeared as amused as he was apologetic. "I have the feeling we're going to be doing a lot of kissing today."

"So do I." And what a hardship that would be. *Not.* And even if he was the worst kisser on the planet, her citizenship depended on it. It was her obligation to make this marriage look as real as possible. Because if she were to be discovered, and someone proved the marriage was a sham, she would go down hard and take Luc with her. That was not an option.

Before he could make a move, to change things up a bit, she set her empty champagne flute down, slid her arms around his neck and kissed him first. A no-holds-barred, knock-him-on-his-butt kiss that jump-started her pulse and made her tingle in places she didn't even know she could tingle. His arms went around her and he tugged her against him. He cupped her behind and rocked his pelvis against her stomach. She gasped against his lips when she felt the thick ridge behind his zipper. Obviously he was just as into this as she was, and not at all shy about letting her know it. If not for his suit jacket, everyone else would probably know, too.

This time when they parted he was wearing a wry, sexy smile, and whispered, without a trace of contrition, "What can I say. I'm a guy."

This was a side of him she'd never seen before. Playfully sexy and a little risqué. She wanted nothing more than to be alone with him, and at the same time felt thankful for their guests. Until they both had time to settle down, being alone together might be a bad idea.

No, not *might*, it *would* be.

As the evening progressed, each subsequent kiss was more brazen and more ardent than the last, his touch as bold as it was scandalous.

It went on like that for a good hour before, to Julie's disappointment, the kiss requests finally began to taper off until they stopped altogether. People began to leave, until only their core group of friends remained.

Though Julie had already had far too much champagne, she headed to the bar for another drink and Beth followed her. "This has been so much fun," she told Julie.

"I think so, too."

"Your sister couldn't make it?"

Julie had texted her, called her and sent her a detailed email about the situation, but still no reply. Her husband traveled extensively for business and Jennifer often accompanied him, occasionally for weeks at a time. "I couldn't get ahold of her. They're probably out of the country."

"That's too bad."

Julie shrugged. "It was awfully last-minute."

"It certainly was. Which brings me to my next question. What was it like making out with your best friend?"

Julie just stood there, mouth agape. Did she mean—?

"Drew told me. We don't keep secrets from each other."

Now Drew, Beth, Luc's mother and her sister all knew the truth?

"Don't worry, I won't tell a soul," Beth assured her. "And for what it's worth, you gave a very convincing performance."

And Julie had relished every moment. Much more than she meant to, or should have. "He's a good kisser."

Beth grinned. "So I gathered. I'll bet he's good at a lot of things."

Her suggestive grin left no question as to what she was implying. And Julie knew she was probably right. She was dying to know how it would feel, their bodies intertwined, his weight pushing her into the mattress…

A ripple of heat coursed through her veins and she could feel her cheeks growing hot. Definitely not something she should be thinking about. "I'm sure he is," she told Beth. "But I'll never find out."

"The way Luc looks at you, I get the feeling you won't have a choice."

No choice? "What is it you think he'll do? Tie me down and make passionate love to me?"

Beth's smile widened. "One can hope."

Oh God, she was right. If Luc wanted Julie in his bed, restraining her wouldn't be necessary.

Ugh, *no*. She was not going to sleep with him. The combination of champagne and all that kissing was screwing with her brain, flooding it with hormones, or pheromones, or some other kind of mones. They were friends and that's all they would ever be.

"Where are you two going for your honeymoon?" Beth asked.

"Nowhere. Luc has a new patient to evaluate this week. A little boy who needs spinal surgery. Besides, you know how he is about leaving the hospital for any extended amount of time. Or his mother. She's still weak from her last hospital stay."

"Most new brides would expect to be put first."

Julie shrugged. "I guess I'm not like most new brides. I can't expect him to rearrange his whole life just because we're married. I wouldn't want him to."

Luc's ex-fiancée had been one of those women. Like any young resident, Luc had been required to work insane hours. It was part of the job. Amelia demanded more attention than he was able to give, which was what ultimately caused their split. The way Luc described her, she was spoiled and snotty, always wanting things her way. Even if she had married him, Julie doubted it would have lasted.

"A lot of women go into a marriage thinking they can change their spouse," Beth said.

"That's ridiculous. If you don't love the person for who they are, why marry them in the first place?"

Beth grinned. "Luc is a lucky man."

Julie wasn't sure what she meant by that, and she didn't ask. Drinks in hand, they rejoined the others.

Luc, Colby and Whit Daltry, owner of Daltry Property Management, were discussing the hospital, and how much money it would take to rebuild the damaged portion. Stella and her husband, Aaron, were discussing baby formula options with Lark and Skye, who both had plenty of information on all things baby. Paige, who Julie noticed had been avoiding her brother-in-law like the plague all evening and pretending not to see the looks he kept shooting her way, sat silently.

Beth took her seat at the table where they had all congregated, and for a minute Julie stood there watching everyone, soaking it all in, a feeling of peace and happiness warming her heart. The town, the people… they were so familiar to her now and so accepting. This was, without question, home.

"Come sit down," Luc said, holding out his hand for her to take. She twined her fingers through his, intending to sit in the empty chair beside him, but Luc had other ideas. He tugged her down onto his lap instead, and up went her heart, right into her throat. He slipped one arm around her and settled his palm against her stomach, his thumb grazing the underside of her breast as he did, and the other hand came to rest on her bare knee. What if that hand were to slide up the inside of her thigh under her dress? Would she stop him? *Could* she?

She glanced over at Beth, whose smile seemed to say, *I told you so*.

She realized just then, with no small amount of anticipation, that if Luc decided he wanted her, there wasn't a damned thing she could do about it.

Five

They didn't get home until eleven—it was a little weird to think of Luc's house as home—and they were both bushed. It had been a long and exhausting evening spent in a near-constant state of arousal, but now it was time to shut it down. The wedding was over and they were back to being friends.

Luc walked her to her bedroom door, which was directly across the hall from his own. She expected a hug and a kiss, even if it was just on her cheek, but she got neither.

"Well, good night," he said, shutting the door to his room firmly behind him.

She stood in the hallway alone, wondering what just happened. After having his hands on her all evening, that was the best he could do? He could just walk away without even acknowledging it?

What if he was having second thoughts? What if he realized he didn't want to be married? He'd been exceedingly quiet on the drive home—there was that word again…*home*. He could be in his room right now, pacing the floor in a panic, thinking that maybe they should get the marriage annulled.

There was no way she could fall asleep with this

hanging over her. She had to know what was going on in his head, before she let herself get too comfortable.

Was she really home, or wasn't she?

Taking a minute or two to think it over, she devised a genius plan to engage him in a conversation. Once she got him talking, she could spring her suspicions on him and see how he reacted.

Feeling confident that she was doing the right thing, she rapped softly on his door. He opened it several seconds later wearing silk pajama bottoms slung low on his hips, his chest bare.

Oh good Lord.

She had seen him bare chested plenty of times in the past, but it occurred to her that she had never actually *seen* him. Only now did she really notice and appreciate the lean muscles of his torso. The sprinkling of dark hair that circled his navel and disappeared under his waistband. Wide chest, above average pecs. He was beautiful.

He hadn't even touched her and she was feeling all tingly again.

He leaned against the doorjamb. "Everything okay?"

"I'm sorry to bother you, but I wondered if you could unzip me. My dress, I mean."

His brow rose. "Seriously?"

Was that such an odd request? "Yes, seriously. I can't reach it."

He folded his arms, looking amused. And sexy as hell. How had she not noticed before how insanely gorgeous he was? Had she been wearing blinders all these years?

"So what you're telling me is that if I weren't here

to unzip you, you would be stuck in your dress indefinitely?"

She blinked. "Well...no, but—"

"If you're going to make up an excuse to come to my room, you could be a little more imaginative, don't you think?"

Boy, did he have her number.

"You were so quiet on the way home I was afraid something was wrong," she said. "I thought that maybe you were having second thoughts about this."

"Then, why didn't you just say that?"

Because...well, she didn't exactly know why. She'd never had a problem being totally honest with him before they were married. Maybe this time she was afraid of the answer she might get. But she had to know.

"So, are you?" she asked him.

"Am I what?"

"Having second thoughts?"

He shook his head and said, "Nope."

She waited for more, for some sort of assurance everything was fine, but he just stood there looking at her. *Oooookay.*

"You were very distant on the ride home. Then we got here and, well..." Why was this so hard to say? He wasn't helping matters, standing there all sexy and gorgeous, his eyes locked on hers.

"We got here and what?"

"We're married now. I figured you would at least hug me good night or something. Maybe a kiss on the cheek?"

"You don't want me to do that."

"I don't?"

"Nope."

"Why not?"

"Suffice it to say, I'm a little...overstimulated."

Oh, this was interesting. Now they were getting somewhere. "So, you're turned on."

He trained his eyes on her and...*whoa*. The heat smoldering in their dark depths could have burned a hole through her dress. That was a definite yes. Her heart flip-flopped, making her pulse race and her mouth go dry.

"You want the truth?" he said.

She nodded.

He leaned in just a little closer. "I wanted everyone to leave the reception so I could lock the door, strip you naked, spread you on the table and lick wedding cake off every inch of your body."

"*Every* inch?"

He grinned. "*Every* inch."

She knew there was a reason she should have wrapped up the leftover cake and brought it home.

"However," he added, "friends don't do that."

"Some friends do. And I'm pretty sure I read somewhere that we have to consummate the marriage to make it official and legally binding."

"And I'm pretty sure you just made that up."

Yes, she had made it up. But she needed to kiss him again, feel his hands on her. Right now. Without her clothes getting in the way. It was their wedding night for heaven's sake. Hadn't she earned the right to jump his bones? Just this once? Would that really be such a terrible thing? Their friendship was solid. It would take a lot more than one night of sex to come between them. Or even two or three nights.

His pajama bottoms did little to hide the erection

pushing outward as if it was reaching for her touch. And oh, did she want to touch him.

One strategically placed hand and he would be toast. Not to toot her own horn, but she knew her way around the male body. He wouldn't be able to resist her, and he damn sure would walk away thoroughly satisfied. "So, you don't think we should sleep together?"

"I didn't say that."

What did he want her to do? Get down on her knees and beg? "You didn't *not* say it, either."

"It's been an emotional day, and we've had a lot to drink—"

"Oh, I get it. Say no more. I would never want you to, you know, embarrass yourself."

His brows jumped upward. He knew she was up to something, and clearly he was enjoying the game just as much as she was. Verbal foreplay was highly underrated.

"Embarrass myself how?"

"You're worried about your performance. Alcohol can make things a little, well, limp."

He glanced down to his crotch, then back up to her. "That's obviously not the case."

No, it wasn't. *And enough playing around already.* She was ready to get to the good stuff.

"Are you sure?" She reached out and wrapped her hand around his hard-on through his pajamas, giving it a firm squeeze. Holy cow, he was *big*.

Luc groaned and leaned into her hand, clutching the doorjamb in a white-knuckled grip, his eyes never leaving her face. He was hers, no question.

"I guess you're right—everything seems to be in working order. But just to be sure…" She slipped her hand under his waistband and around his erection, skin against skin, giving it a couple of slow strokes, teasing the tip with the pad of her thumb. "Feels good to me."

His eyes turned black with desire. She almost had him. Most men would have caved by now, but Luc had a steel will.

"You're positively sure you want to do this?" he said.

At this point, how could he even ask her that? Wasn't it obvious that she wanted him? "Without a doubt."

"You're not worried that it will change things between us?"

"One time? It's not as if we're going to make a habit of this." She squeezed and felt him pulse against her palm. "Besides, we spent half the day making out and now I'm standing here with my hand in your pants. If something was going to change, wouldn't it have already?"

"So what you're saying is, the damage is already done?"

"In a manner of speaking." He was making a bigger deal out of this than was warranted. But he was a planner. He liked to think ahead, plot out his every move. Which, she supposed, was why he was such an accomplished surgeon. She, on the other hand, was more of a live-in-the-moment, fly-by-the-seat-of-her-pants girl. They sat on opposite ends of the spectrum. He was all about duty and honor and doing the right thing. She believed in trying new things and taking chances. Living life to the fullest and going where the wind took her.

Tonight, the wind was blowing her in the direction of his bed.

Knowing Luc the way she did, she knew exactly

how this would play out. He would caress her as he slowly removed her clothes, taking his time. Her pleasure would be his main priority because that's the kind of man he was. Always putting the needs of others before his own. She would let him take his time, and when they were both good and worked up, she would take over. If this was going to be the only time they slept together, she planned to give him a night that he would never forget. And if they decided to do it again, well, that was okay, too.

That was her plan at least, but Luc was playing by a totally different set of rules. He looked at her as if he were a hunter stalking its prey, and then he lunged and went all caveman on her. One second her feet were on the ground, and the next, she was hanging over his shoulder, which was more than wide enough to accommodate her. She gasped and clutched his back, dizzy with desire and a little disoriented as he kicked the door closed and carried her across the room to his bed. And there was nothing gentle about the way he tossed her down on the comforter.

Who was this man and why was she just now meeting him? And how, after all these years of friendship, could she have pegged him so wrong?

He knelt on the mattress beside her, his hand resting on her inner thigh, and all she could think was *more*. He slid the hand up under the hem of her dress. His fingertips grazed the crotch of her panties, no more than a tickle. She sucked in a breath and her thighs parted, straining against the skirt of her dress.

He pulled his hand away and her back arched, her body seeking out his touch. "Did I mention how sexy you look in this dress?"

"Thanks. I don't usually wear them," she said, the words coming out all breathy and uneven. She couldn't seem to pull enough air into her lungs. What happened to all the oxygen?

"I'm going to buy you a dozen more."

If this was the reaction she got when she wore a dress, maybe that would be a bad idea. Or a good one. She wasn't sure. Suddenly everything felt backward and upside down.

He was back under her dress, tugging her panties down. There was nothing slow about the way he undressed her. Or gentle. Then he took his pajama bottoms off…

Yikes. He wouldn't be the only one walking away satisfied. This was going to be fun.

She tried to push him onto his back but it was like trying to move a brick wall. She wound up on her back instead, and when she reached out to touch him, he pinned her arms over her head, a move that would normally trigger a sense of panic. He wouldn't let her take control, which both frustrated and aroused her. But she knew deep in her heart that she was safe with him. She usually felt threatened by sexually aggressive men, but she *wanted* him to dominate her. She trusted Luc, so she did something she had never done before. She dropped her guard and let go, let him be the one in charge.

It was as cathartic as it was exciting. And Luc held nothing back, stroking here, kissing there. Licking and biting and flipping her around until she felt like a pretzel, so he could explore every inch of her body. He knew exactly what she liked, what she needed, without her having to say a thing. Besides, she was too busy gasping and moaning to form intelligible words. He teased her relentlessly. And every time she thought she was getting the upper hand, he turned the tables on her again. She'd orgasmed twice, and was headlong into number three when he rolled her onto her back and settled over her.

He didn't ask her if she was ready, or if she was having second thoughts. They were both too far gone for that. He parted her thighs with his knee and thrust inside her. She savored the sweet stretch of her body accepting him, his weight pressing her into the mattress as he eased back, then thrust again. And again, picking up speed, but with more hip action this time. Pretty much all she could do was wrap her legs around his hips and hang on for the ride. Pleasure rippled through her in hot waves, her body clenching down around him like a vise as orgasm number three took hold.

After that things got very fuzzy. And rowdy. And a little loud. He asked a lot of questions, too. "Do you like this?" "Does this feel good?" He must have told her a dozen times that she was beautiful, that she was the sexiest woman he'd ever seen. "By leaps and bounds," he said. And he wasn't shy about telling her what he wanted, and exactly how she should do it. "Touch me here, lick me there. Faster. Slower. Just like that." She'd never been with a man so chatty during sex. Or bossy. But the best part by far was watching him reach his peak, seeing him completely let go, knowing that she was the one making him feel that way.

When it was over, and they lay there in a sweaty tangle, she couldn't seem to wipe the smile from her face, until she realized, with considerable horror, that she hadn't given a single freaking thought to birth control.

Luc lay with Julie, his leg resting between hers, one arm under her neck, the other draped across her stomach. "I guess an annulment is out of the question now," he joked, and without warning Julie shot up in bed, nearly dumping him over the edge onto the floor—the *hardwood* floor—and spewed a string of expletives.

Luc sat up beside her. He put a hand on her shoulder and she jumped, as if she'd forgotten he was there. "It was a joke, Julie."

"Oh my God," she said, looking panicked, the color leaching from her face. "I can't believe we did this. How could I be so stupid?"

But it had been some of the best sex he'd ever had, and she had seemed to enjoy herself, too. "Don't you think it's a little late to be having second thoughts?"

She looked puzzled, then said, "I'm not having second thoughts. At least, not in the way you think."

"In what way, then?"

"This is probably a dumb question under the circumstances, but did we just have unprotected sex?"

Is that what this was about? "Relax, you're not going to catch anything from me."

"I know that," she said. "But unless you're sterile, we could have bigger problems."

Whoa, wait a minute. "I thought you were on the Pill. You told me you were."

Her eyes went wide with indignation. "When did I say that? I *never* said that."

"A couple of years ago. You were complaining that it made you nauseous."

"Which is why I *stopped* taking it."

Aw, hell. He should have asked. He was a doctor, after all. He knew better than to assume. Which is why he always kept condoms on hand. They were in the drawer in his bedside table, not two feet away. "This is my fault. I should have checked with you first."

"No, I'm just as much to blame. It never even crossed my mind." She dropped her head in her hands. "How could I be so careless? I don't want a baby. Definitely not now, maybe not ever."

"Before you get all panicked, stop and think about where you are in your cycle."

She took a deep breath, looking so tense she could have snapped like a twig. It took her several seconds to collect herself, then she said, "I'm due to start my period in a couple of days. A week tops."

"Then, we're probably fine. The odds are pretty slim that you would conceive so late in your cycle."

"Is that your official medical opinion?"

"It is." There was a sprinkle of optimism in his tone for good measure. And on the bright side, it wouldn't be long before they knew for sure.

"You're right," she said, sounding a little less freaked out. She rested her head on his shoulder. "I'm sorry I got so upset."

He put his arm around her shoulder, drawing her closer. "No apology required."

She was quiet for a moment, then said, "Just so you know, I don't usually sleep with men on the first date. But since our first date was our wedding, I thought I could make an exception."

"I understand."

She smiled up at him. "That was really good, by the way. The sex, I mean."

"Was?"

She looked confused.

"There is no 'was.'" He lay back and pulled her on top of him. "We're just getting started."

Six

Julie woke slowly the next morning to the sound of water running. Her first thought was that the leaky pipe under her bathroom sink had finally burst. Eyes too heavy to open, she reached over to grab her phone off the bedside table, but it was gone. Not just her phone, but the table itself wasn't there. She pried her eyes open only to realize that this was not her bedroom. Not even her apartment. She lived with Luc now, and the sound of the running water was coming from his bathroom. Then she recalled last night and a smile curled her lips.

Best. Sex. Ever.

She had always assumed, because Luc was so reserved and practical, that he would be the same way in bed. Boy, was she wrong. Hours later she still felt limp as a dishrag and sore in places she didn't know could get sore. If she knew he would be that good she would have jumped him years ago. Just thinking about it was getting her all worked up again. Then she remembered that they forgot to use a condom the first time and her heart sank a little. But Luc was right, the odds were low she would get pregnant. And if she had, they would deal with it. At least they were married. Right?

She sat up and looked around for her phone, finding it in her purse on the floor beside the bed. It was 8:00 a.m., which was early even for her. Sundays were the only days she allowed herself to sleep in. She typically dragged herself out of bed around ten, went for a run around the track at the high school, then showered and sometimes met Lark for brunch. But not today. She looked at the platinum band on the ring finger of her left hand. She was a newlywed. A married woman.

That was going to take some getting used to.

The water shut off, and a minute later she could hear Luc humming to himself—one of those country songs he loved so much—while he shaved. She'd only ever heard him hum when he was in a good mood. And why wouldn't he be after last night?

He would be out of the bathroom any minute now and she really should go to her own room, lest she be tempted to pounce on him. But she wanted to see him. She wrestled with her options, but before she could make a decision, the bathroom door opened and Luc stepped out. And boy was she glad that she stayed. He wore a towel slung low on his hips, his dark hair damp, his face cleanly shaven and smooth. Droplets of water clung to his chest, rolling down his pecs and over those wonderfully ripped abs.

She usually looked like a beast in the morning, her hair askew, pillow creases on her cheek, and she imagined the liner and mascara had smeared under her eyes for that charming raccoon effect, but he'd seen her looking worse.

"Good morning," he said, looking surprised to see her awake.

"G'morning. You're up early."

He shrugged. "Habit."

He was usually at the hospital by 7:00 a.m. to start his rounds, but this was Sunday, not to mention their honeymoon. Technically speaking.

He sat on the edge of the bed beside her and kissed her forehead. If he was put off by her appearance he didn't say so. "Sleep well?"

"Like the dead." When she had finally gotten to sleep, which hadn't been until 3:00 a.m. or so. In typical man style he'd fallen asleep before her, about a half an hour earlier. For a long time she'd lain there wrapped up in his arms, listening to his slow even breaths, wishing they could hit Rewind and relive the night all over again. "How about you? Sleep well?"

"Great. How are you feeling this morning?"

How was she feeling? "A little sore, actually. You gave me quite the workout."

"Jules, I don't mean physically."

She didn't think so. "I'm not having regrets, if that's what you mean. Are you?"

"Nope. I do feel a little guilty for not feeling guilty, if that makes any sense."

"I know exactly what you mean."

"Are you sorry that we can't have a honeymoon?" he asked.

"Not at all. You have responsibilities. We both do. In fact, I was thinking about going into work for a while today."

"You can't."

"Why not?"

"Because I read somewhere that a marriage isn't official unless the newlyweds spend the day after their wedding together."

Oh, so they were going to play this game again. "Did it say what we have to do?"

"We have to have sex again. Then lunch, and maybe a walk in the park. Or we could combine the two and have a picnic, weather permitting."

That sounded like fun. "What then?"

"More sex, of course."

Of course. "And after that?"

"A candlelight dinner."

"Then more sex?"

"Obviously." He shot her one of those steamy smiles. "And we should get started right away. You know, to make it official."

He hooked the edge of the covers and slowly eased them down, revealing her breasts, which were covered in love bites, then her stomach, then the tops of her thighs. *Here we go again*, she thought, struck by how natural it felt. How comfortable she was with him, as if they had been sleeping together all along. And at the same time it felt exciting and new.

His hand, which was still warm from his shower, came to rest on her thigh, then trailed slowly upward, his touch light, it was barely more than a tickle. Her legs parted, giving him space to play around, but they were interrupted by a firm rap on his bedroom door. He mumbled a curse, removed his hand and pulled the covers back up over her.

"I'll make it quick," he said.

He grabbed his robe from the foot of the bed and tugged it on as he walked to the door. Julie sat and held the blanket up to cover herself.

It was his mother's nurse. She glanced over, saw Julie in the bed and quickly averted her eyes. Julie was surprised Luc had opened the door wide enough to let her see inside.

"I'm sorry to bother you, Mr. Wakefield, but I thought you should know that your mother is running a low-grade fever."

A look of concern transformed his face. "How high?"

"Only 99.8. She said that she feels fine, and not to bother you, but I thought you should know."

For the average healthy person a temperature that low wouldn't have been a big deal, but Julie knew that any sign of systemic infection had to be addressed immediately. Elizabeth had barely gotten over the last illness and her body was still weak. Another infection this soon, even something as simple as the common cold could spiral out of control and become deadly.

"Did you check for sores or wounds?" he asked the nurse.

"She wouldn't let me."

Luc sighed and shook his head. "I'll be down there in a minute. And tell her that *I* told you to check her."

"Yes, sir," she said, and he closed the door, mumbling to himself about his mother being stubborn.

Ever look in a mirror? Julie wanted to say.

"You realize she saw me," she told him.

"I know she did." He stepped into his closet for clothes, seemingly unconcerned.

"What if she tells your mother?" Julie called after him.

"So what if she does?" he called back.

"Didn't you tell her that this isn't a real marriage? That we're still just friends."

"I seem to recall you telling me last night that to

make the marriage official we had to have sex." He stepped out wearing jeans and pulling a T-shirt over his head. "Didn't you?"

"You know damn well I made that up to get you into bed. You were being very…uncooperative."

His brows rose. "Is that what I was doing?"

"Don't change the subject. You don't think it will confuse your mother?"

"Her body may be failing her but as you know, her mind is sound."

That was putting it mildly. "I know. I just… I respect her and I don't want her to think I'm slutty."

"For having sex with your husband?"

She shot him a look. "You know what I mean. It might upset her."

"What is she going to do? Ground me? Besides, we're two consenting adults. Married or not, it's still not hers or anyone else's business what we do in bed."

"You know you're impossible."

"I have to go check on her," he said, but he was smiling.

"I'm going to take a shower."

"When I get back we're going to finish what we just started," he said, grinning suggestively as he walked out. If she hadn't already been aroused, that would have definitely done the trick.

She had been a little worried that this morning might be awkward, or involve misplaced guilt and needless justifications. There was nothing more depressing than to wake up with a man and hear why the fantastic sex you had the night before was a mistake. That had happened to her once, and was the precise reason she didn't sleep with men on the first date.

The only thing that seemed to have changed with Luc was that now they both knew what the other looked like naked. *Totally* naked. Up close and *very* personal.

And if he was okay with his mother realizing what was going on between them, who was Julie to question it?

Elizabeth, it turned out, had a small scratch on the back of her thigh that had become infected. Because she had no feeling below the waist, she'd had no idea it was there. Which is why daily physical exams, especially after she'd been moved in and out of her chair frequently, were so critical. With such poor circulation, the smallest scratch could become a festering wound overnight.

Knowing she was bound to get worse before she got better, Luc stayed with her, and they never did get to finish what they'd started. But as she told Beth last night, she didn't expect him to drop everything when she snapped her fingers. Besides, he had just done her an enormous favor; the last thing she had the right to do was demand his attention. In fact, without the threat of deportation looming in the future, this was the most content and happiest she'd felt in months. Any uncertainty she'd had about her future was gone.

She was confident that it would be smooth sailing from here on out.

Luc spent his first day as a husband not in bed having phenomenal sex with his new wife—sex he never planned on having—but instead carefully monitoring his mother's condition. He felt guilty that he'd had to cancel his and Julie's plans, but not only had she not complained, or acted the least bit perturbed, she spent most of the day with him at his mother's bedside. Her temperature continued to rise, slowly but steadily all day, even after the nurse cleaned and dressed her wound and administered ibuprofen and intravenous antibiotics. He was considering hospitalization when finally, around eight that evening, her fever broke. He checked on her several times during the night, and by Monday morning her temperature was holding steady in the normal range and her wound seemed to be healing well.

"I think I need to hire a new nurse," he told Julie that morning. She sat on the edge of his bed, looking adorably mussed, watching him get ready for work. She had offered, for his own peace of mind, to stay home from work and keep an eye on his mother and the nurse. Which was a bit like needing a babysitter to watch the babysitter. "This could have been prevented if she had only done her job. I've stressed to her, more than once, that the physical exams are critical. And my mother knows better. If the nurse can't handle her—"

"Your mother really likes this nurse."

"That isn't my concern." Her safety and physical well-being were the only things that mattered.

"It should be your concern," she said in a tone so sharp it nearly took him back a step. "How would you feel having some stranger inspect every inch of your body twice a day, day in and day out? And don't you think there would be times when you just wanted to say to hell with it and take a break? Maybe her nurse was being more compassionate than negligent. She made a mistake."

He tugged on his shirt and buttoned it, saying, "A mistake that could have cost my mother her life."

"And I'm sure she's learned her lesson."

She damn well better have.

Julie was quiet for a minute, then said, "I've mentioned my nanny Ginise, haven't I?"

"That was the nice one, right?"

"Did I ever tell you why my dad fired her?"

He shook his head, looking thoughtful. "I don't think so."

"I'm sure I told you how strict my father was."

He nodded. From all the stories Julie had told him, to say her father was strict was putting it mildly. She and her sister were practically prisoners in their own home.

"Nanny Ginise was hard-nosed when he was around, but when he was gone, she really loosened the leash. She let me and my sister go to friends' houses and use the phone. She let us go without tights on hot days. She let us drink soda and eat candy. Nanny Ginise gave us the freedom to be kids. Which is eventually what got her fired."

"What happened?"

"One of my friends from school was having a pool party. I begged my father to let me go. All of my friends were going to be there, including boys—though I didn't tell him that—but he still said it was out of the question. I cried and pleaded but he wouldn't budge. But the day of the party he was away on business and wasn't due back until the following night. Nanny Ginise let me go. She even bought me a two-piece bathing suit to wear, since all the other girls would be wearing them and I wanted to fit in. I mean, what thirteen-year-old girl doesn't?"

He flipped his collar up and looped his tie around his neck. "Naturally."

"Well, my father came home early, and Nanny Ginise had no choice but to tell him where I was. He charged over to my friend's house, which was just up the road. The fact that I defied him was bad enough, but when he saw what I was wearing, and that there were boys there, he went ballistic. I had never seen him so furious. He pulled me out of the pool by my hair."

Luc's eyes went wide. "In front of everyone?"

She nodded. "He wrapped me up in a towel and dragged me home. I was mortified, and as if that wasn't punishment enough, I wasn't allowed to leave my room for a month. I was a prisoner. He even made me eat my meals in there."

That wasn't strict, that was abuse. He knew her childhood was bad, but he hadn't realized just how bad. "How could he treat his own children that way?"

"Our mother's death really hit him hard. I'm still not sure if he was trying to shelter us, or if he just resented us."

"Why would he resent you?"

"For being alive, when she wasn't. It took years for me to accept that it wasn't my fault. That it was his problem, not mine."

The idea that she grew up so miserable made his chest ache. "And Nanny Ginise, what happened to her?"

"Fired on the spot. Two days later we had a new nanny. Ms. Fowler, a retired headmistress of a private girls school in Wales."

"What was she like?"

"Horrible. She'd followed our father's rules to the

letter. And came up with quite a few of her own. She believed that teenage girls all had lusty and indecent thoughts and therefore should not be left alone to their own devices. She forbade us from closing our bedroom doors, and walked right in without knocking whenever she felt like it. If she caught us doing something she considered inappropriate she gave us the switch."

"The switch?"

"Yeah, it was this stick she carried around with her all the time."

Luc blinked. "Are you saying that she used to hit you with it?"

"All the time. Damned thing hurt like a bitch and left nasty welts."

Jesus. Luc actually felt sick to his stomach. "Did your father know?"

"Of course. He was all for corporal punishment."

And it just kept getting worse. "Did he hit you?"

"Me *and* my sister. But she got the worst of it. I learned to drop my head, keep my mouth shut and be as invisible as possible. Jennifer was outspoken and defiant. I remember a time, not long before I left for college, when she snuck out of the house in the middle of the night to meet a boy. Our father caught her. There was hardly a spot on her that wasn't black and blue. He grounded her to her room for weeks."

Luc sat down on the bed beside her, at a loss for words. "I don't even know what to say. I knew your childhood wasn't ideal, but I had no idea it was that bad."

"I didn't tell you to make you feel sorry for me. I just want you to try to see things from your mother's point of view. She's a prisoner in a body that constantly betrays her. I think the nurse was just trying to cut her a little slack, like Nanny Ginise did for me and my sister. There was no malicious intent. And I know she feels horrible about it."

Wow, talk about a convincing argument, and she spoke of it so matter-of-factly, as if it had happened to someone else. And yes, sometimes he forgot what his mother must go through. How difficult and unpleasant her life could be. Years ago, before her surgery, she was active and independent. Now she relied on others for most of her needs. That couldn't be easy for her. "You're right," he told Julie. "She meant no harm. If my mother is happy with her, then I'm happy."

"Thank you. You're a good man. And an even better son."

"I don't know about that," he said.

She smiled. "I do."

He couldn't help himself. He had to kiss her. He leaned in and she met him halfway. He was enjoying this arrangement, and found himself thinking about her, far more than he should have.

The kiss didn't last long. Julie patted his shoulders and said, "You need to get to the hospital. You'll be late for rounds."

She was right. Typically he looked forward to work, but today staying home in bed with Julie sounded much more fun. "Maybe tonight, if all goes well—"

"Yes," she said with a saucy smile, knowing exactly what he was going to say before he said it. It looked as if he wasn't the only one with sex on the brain. And if he didn't finish getting dressed and get his ass out of there, he might not make it to the hospital at all. It had been a long time since he'd been so hot for a woman he wanted to play hooky from work.

He stood, knotting his tie, then pulled on his suit jacket. She sat on the bed watching him. "Are you sure you're okay with staying home today?"

"I have my laptop," she said. "I can work here. I have some numbers to crunch. And phone calls to make. And your mom mentioned something about a few rounds of poker."

"For God's sake don't let her talk you into playing for money."

Julie laughed. "She's a cardsharp, I know."

"And she's ruthless."

He grabbed his wallet and keys from the basket on the chest of drawers, hesitating another second. Damn, he really didn't want to go. If it weren't for the new patient he was seeing this morning, he just might stick around for a while, have one of his residents do rounds for him.

"I'll see you tonight," he said. He considered kissing her goodbye, but once he got started he wouldn't want to stop. "Call me if there's a problem."

"I will."

He was almost to the door when Julie said, "Hey, Luc."

He turned to find her kneeling on his bed. Then she dropped the covers to flash him.

Her breasts were full and firm. Not large by modern standards, but they fit her just right and he couldn't wait to get his hands on them again.

With that saucy smile, she said, "Have a nice day, dear."

Oh, he definitely would. And an even better night.

Seven

Luc made it to work with five minutes to spare, stopping in the cafeteria for a cup of coffee on his way up to his office.

"Cutting it close today," his secretary, Ruth, said, looking at the clock. She was used to him being on time, or most days, a little early.

"Busy weekend," he told her.

"I'll bet. It was a lovely wedding. You two looked so happy, and so in love."

It sounded as if they'd done a pretty good job fooling everyone. But the happy part? That was real. His best friend was here to stay. What more could he ask for?

"Tommy James was admitted last night," she said.

"No problems?"

"Not that I've heard."

"How is the rest of my day looking?" He was hoping to get home at a decent hour tonight. Maybe even a little early. One of his favorite upscale restaurants had reopened in the past week and he thought maybe he would take Julie for a nice dinner.

Oh hell, who was he kidding. To heck with dinner. He wanted to get her back in bed and finish what they'd started.

He shrugged out of his suit jacket. Ruth took it from him and handed him his lab coat. "You have a procedure at 9:15, and a staff meeting at 11:30. In the afternoon you have several consultations. And a meeting at 5:00."

He pulled it on and she clipped his ID onto the pocket. It had been their morning routine for as long as he'd been chief of surgery. A position that was as much about politics as it was medicine. Ruth, who had been in hospital administration for three decades, had been his saving grace.

"So how does it feel?" she asked him, straightening his collar.

Puzzled, he asked, "How does what feel?"

"Being *married*."

Better than he thought it would. In fact, it was pretty damned fantastic so far. Friendship and sex without the complications. Who wouldn't want that? And it was really good sex.

No, it was *fantastic* sex. And he couldn't wait to get home so they could do it again.

"It's good," he said, and left it at that. "If Julie calls, page me immediately. My mother had an infection over the weekend. Julie is staying with her today."

Ruth clucked and shook her head. "I'm so sorry. I noticed at the wedding that she looked tired. Poor Elizabeth, she's been through so much."

And every infection seemed to suck more of her strength, more of her spirit. As a physician, he knew her time was running out. Her body could handle only so much before it gave out for good. But as her son, he wanted her to live forever.

"She pushes herself too hard," Luc said.

"She's a proud woman."

More stubborn than proud if you asked him.

Luc left his office and checked on the five surgical patients in his care, each in different stages of recovery. Knowing the parents would have a million questions for him, as he would if his son were going in for major surgery, he saved Tommy James in the pediatrics ward for last.

The boy had come in as a referral from a colleague in Houston that Luc had known since med school.

"This is right up your alley," he'd told Luc when he called last week. The five-year-old had congenital lumbar spinal stenosis that had begun to cause him considerable pain, and in the past few weeks he had begun to lose feeling in his legs. It was a rare condition for a child but using techniques he'd perfected himself, with Julie's help of course, Luc could correct the problem by fusing the spine. The parents would be hard-pressed to find a physician more qualified than him to do the surgery.

Because it was congenital, this was quite possibly a temporary fix. As Tommy matured, the stenosis, which started in his lumbar spine, could gradually work its way upward into the thoracic, then cervical spine. This might be one of several surgeries he would need to stabilize his spine before adulthood. But other than his back being less flexible, he would live a long, productive life. Just not as a gymnast. And he would have the bonus of impeccable posture.

Luc stopped outside the patient's door, where a nurse stood updating his chart on her laptop.

"Is he all settled in?"

"Yes, Doctor. He was pretty uncomfortable so I gave

him pain meds. He's sleeping now and his vitals are good. He seems like a real trooper. He always has a smile on his face, even through the pain."

Kids were resilient. It was the parents who were typically the toughest to deal with. "Are the parents in there?"

"His mother stepped out to get coffee. She should be back in a minute."

"And his father?" Luc asked.

"Not here. And from the sound of it, he won't be coming to Royal."

"That's a shame." Luc knew that having a chronically ill child could devastate the soundest of marriages. He'd seen it all too often. But to not be there for your child who's having major surgery? What sort of man was this boy's father?

Though he had studied the chart thoroughly, he gave it another quick look to be sure that nothing had changed before he stepped into the boy's room.

He was indeed asleep, and though he looked small and fragile—all skin and bones—his color was good. Luc checked his vitals again, then he eased him onto his side to see his back, and checked his feet. Despite the loss of feeling in his legs, his circulation was still adequate. There wouldn't be any permanent damage.

He heard someone behind him and turned, his usual greeting on the tip of his tongue and ready to go...then froze when he saw the woman standing there.

The spark of recognition was instantaneous, but it took another ten seconds to determine that his mind wasn't playing tricks on him. That it really was his ex-fiancée, Amelia, standing there holding a cup of coffee and a gossip magazine. The woman who'd shredded his heart like confetti and ate it for breakfast without batting an eyelash.

"Amelia," he said, more a statement than a question, and regretted it the instant the words were out of his mouth. But it was too late now.

She flashed him a weak, tired smile. "Hello, Lucas. How have you been?"

Meeting new patients could be hit-or-miss, yet of the dozens of scenarios he might have imagined, this one didn't even come close to making the list.

She hadn't really changed all that much. She was a little thicker around the middle, and a little older. The stress of her son's condition showed in her face, in the fine lines at the corners of her eyes.

For a good ten seconds he was at a loss for words.

You're the physician, he reminded himself. The one with the upper hand. And she was just the mother of the patient. Nothing more. He had to keep this professional. Yet he heard himself saying, "Should I assume this isn't a coincidence?"

"Yes and no. Tommy's doctor in Houston told me that he knew another doctor with more experience in this sort of surgery. I had already made the decision to come when he told me who and where the doctor was located. Of course then I knew it was you."

"And you came anyway?"

"It's not about me."

She was right. Nor was it about him. And he had no right to question her motives.

Keep it professional. "Why don't we talk about the surgery."

"Okay."

He went into surgeon mode, describing the procedure and recovery in layman's terms, feeling a bit like a robot. It was the same speech he'd used countless times before, but now it felt stilted and awkward.

"His doctor explained all of this in great detail," Amelia said. "He said permanent paralysis was a possibility."

"That is a possibility, but given your son's age, and the fact that he's in otherwise good health, I don't foresee any complications," he said.

Of course there were no guarantees. Complications could arise, but Luc was confident the surgery would go smoothly. Besides, she didn't have much choice at this point. "No surgery comes without risks. But without the procedure, the spinal column will continue to narrow. Then you'll be looking at paralysis, loss of bladder and bowel function. Excessive pain."

"I know all that," she said, looking conflicted. "I just needed to hear it from you. Of course he needs the surgery. And I trust that you'll take good care of him. How soon can you do it?" she asked.

"It would be next week at the soonest."

Her mouth fell open, eyes went wide. He knew that look as well as if he had seen it yesterday. "*Next week?* But he's in pain! I assumed you would do it right away."

He sighed quietly. That was Amelia, always expecting things to be done her way. "I'm already booked up this week and most of next. I have to check with my secretary, but I think I can squeeze it in either next Thursday or the following Tuesday."

"You can't do it *any* sooner?"

"Thursday or Tuesday. That's the best I can do."

She nodded slowly and said with a weak smile, "So, no special treatment for the ex-fiancée, huh?"

Is that what she'd expected? Special treatment? "I have a busy schedule," he told her. "Until the surgery we can control the pain and at this point there's no danger of permanent damage. But he will have to stay in the hospital so we can monitor him."

"If that's the case I'm staying here with him. In the room," she said, her chin lifting a notch, as if she were trying to challenge his authority, when there was really no need. This combative attitude was unnecessary. As her son's surgeon, his patient was his main priority.

"You'll have to talk to your son's nurse about hospital policy," he told her. "But I'm sure it won't be a problem."

"There is something else I wanted to ask you, that, uncomfortable as it is, I feel needs addressing."

He made a point of checking the time on his watch. He was already running late. "Okay."

"I need to be sure, because of our past, that you don't see this as a conflict of interest," she said.

Several years ago it might have been. But after getting over the initial shock of seeing her again, the only thing he felt was a medical obligation to care for his patient to the best of his ability. As he always did.

And she was nothing more to him than the mother of his patient.

"There's no conflict," he said, and he could see the instant she noticed the ring on his left hand.

"Oh. You're married," she said, sounding surprised.

"Yes, I am."

"Anyone I know?"

"No."

She paused, as if she was expecting him to give her

a name, or details, and when he didn't, her smile wavered. "I'm very happy for you.

"In case you're wondering, I'm divorced now. For almost two years. He traded me in for a younger model," she said, bitterness dripping from her words. "They moved to San Antonio and are expecting a baby. He sends Tommy gifts, and calls occasionally, but he never comes to see him."

None of Luc's business. He was her son's doctor, not a confidant.

He checked his watch. "Is there anything else—?"

"Leaving you was the biggest mistake I ever made," she blurted.

Oh, what he would have given to hear those words six years ago, but it was too late to turn back. He was happy with his life just the way it was. He didn't love her anymore. He hadn't for a long time. Maybe all along he'd only been in love with the idea of her, and deep down she had never been what he needed.

Julie was, though. And he did need her. More than he'd ever realized.

"I'll talk to my secretary and see about scheduling the surgery," he told Amelia. "In the meantime I'd like to run some tests."

She looked up at him with big blue eyes that used to melt him on the spot, and he felt nothing. Not a single damn thing. He was beginning to wonder what he had *ever* seen in her. Had he changed so much since then?

It was clear now that all these years he'd been wondering what-if had been a waste of time. Now he knew. Even if she hadn't dumped him, he seriously doubted they would have lasted very long. Her narcissism would have eventually driven him away.

"You don't want to talk about it," she said. "I get it. Just let me say that I'm really sorry for the way things turned out. I know I hurt you. I hope someday you can forgive me."

He might have laughed if he wasn't so appalled. Same old Amelia, thinking she was the center of the universe, and he refused to take the bait.

"I'm ordering tests today. I'll let you know when I get the results." Or more likely, he would tell one of his residents, who would then notify her. The less contact he had with her the better.

"I really am sorry," she said softly, looking genuinely apologetic, but she was six years too late. He turned and walked out without another word.

Julie set up a folding table and chair to make a small work space for herself at the foot of Elizabeth's bed where she could keep an eye on her while the nurse, who had been up most of the night, took a few hours to nap. Luc had spared no expense on his mother's home care. The room was as efficient and well equipped as any hospital room Julie had ever seen, yet it lacked that sterile atmosphere that was inevitable in a hospital setting. But if his mother's health continued to fail her, Luc would have to consider hiring another nurse for the overnight shift.

As fragile as Elizabeth was now, Julie was a little nervous being even temporarily in charge of her care. She was too emotionally invested in the relationship to be impartial. Elizabeth was her mother-in-law, but more than that, she was becoming a good friend. A bit like the mother that Julie never had.

When Julie and Luc first discussed their childhoods,

she had asked him about growing up without a father. Did he feel resentful or cheated? Had he ever wished his mother had remarried?

My mother gave me everything I could have possibly needed, he'd said. *We took care of each other.*

They still did. Julie wished she could have been so fortunate, that there had been someone in her life who always had her back, who loved her unconditionally. Wasn't that what everyone wanted? What everyone needed to feel whole? Luc had brought her closer to that feeling than anyone in her life ever had.

"Are you in love with my son?"

The sound of Elizabeth's voice startled her. She looked up from her laptop and saw that her mother-in-law was watching her. "You're awake. How do you feel?"

The older woman's shoulders lifted in a shrug and she smiled weakly. "Eh, I've been worse."

Her strength of character, her resilience, never ceased to amaze Julie. She could only hope that faced with similar circumstances, she would handle her condition with equal poise.

"So? Are you in love with my son?" she asked again.

"He's the most important person in my life."

"But that isn't what I asked, is it?"

Julie hesitated. Luc was right, his mother was sharp as a tack. "Elizabeth—"

She held a hand up to stop her. "No, no. You don't have to explain. You feel what you feel. I know how that is. But a mother can hope, can't she?"

Julie picked her chair up and moved it closer to Elizabeth's bed. "I'm honored that you feel that way, that you would want me in your son's life, and I wish things were different. I really do. What Luc and I have is very special, it's just not…" She struggled for the words to explain.

"Luc was my miracle baby," Elizabeth said. "Did I ever tell you that?"

Julie shook her head.

Elizabeth smiled wistfully. "His father and I had been trying for five years to have a child."

"Wow, that's a long time." For her and Luc's dad it must have felt like forever.

"Back then there weren't as many options as there are now, but we did everything we could. I was young enough to keep trying, but Luc's father was seventeen years older than me. He felt as if he was getting too old. I was his second wife and he had two grown boys when I met him, so he'd been through it all before. I couldn't blame him for his feelings. But, as these things sometimes happen, when we finally made the decision to give up, when I resigned myself to the fact that I would never have a child of my own, I got pregnant."

"Luc doesn't really talk about his father."

"He doesn't remember him. But they're so very much alike. My husband was a simple man. He believed in hard work and family, and giving back to the community."

"That does sound like Luc."

"We used to own one of the largest ranches in the county. He always hoped his boys from his first marriage would want to take over, but they had no interest in the family business. Or me for that matter. That ranch was his life and out of respect I wanted to keep it running, keep it in the family, but then I had my surgery and everything changed. I couldn't keep up with the day-to-day operations, and like Luc had no interest in ranching. I knew he was meant for greater things. The proceeds from the sale of the business paid for medical school."

"Luc said his dad had a heart attack."

"A massive coronary," she said, looking so sad, even all this time later. "They found him out in the field, his horse at his side. They told me that it was instantaneous, that he never suffered. I always took comfort in the fact that he died doing what he loved most.

"That's why I believe in seizing the moment. Living as though every day might be your last."

"I was in love once," she told Elizabeth. "I met him at university. I thought he was the love of my life."

"But he wasn't?"

She shook her head, the pain of that time still as real and sharp as a slap in the face.

Elizabeth frowned. "If you're uncomfortable talking about it…"

"It's not that," Julie said. It was just embarrassing to admit she had been so desperate for love. So gullible.

"You have to bear in mind how I was raised," she told Elizabeth. "I had no positive male influence in my life. My sister and I grew up believing that nothing we ever did was good enough."

"Oh, honey," Elizabeth said, patting her arm. "You've done amazing things with your life. You've dedicated yourself to helping people. You should be proud of your accomplishments. No matter what anyone else thinks."

That was easier said than done. "I try, but there's always that small part of me that says it's not enough.

That I could be doing more. That I'll never quite measure up."

"Inner demons," Elizabeth said with a sigh. "There's nothing more difficult to face than your own overinflated expectations. Believe me, I've been there."

Julie certainly had her share of those. "I found most men intimidating at that time, but there was something so different about him. He was so gentle and kind. He filled a place in my heart that had been empty for so long. I was able to set my fears aside. I was convinced he would never hurt me. At first."

"But he did."

She nodded. "Things started to gradually change. Little things at first. He became more critical and more demanding. He wanted all of my attention. He resented my friends, my professors, my homework. But I was so desperate for someone to love me, to accept me, I was blind to what was happening, to the way he was gradually tearing down my self-esteem, shrinking my world until I was totally dependent on him. By the end, he controlled nearly every aspect of my life."

"Love makes us do foolish things," Elizabeth said, and something in her eyes said she was speaking from experience. "Especially when we're vulnerable. The important thing is that you got away."

"It took every bit of courage I had to walk away from him. I was miserable for months. He had me convinced that I needed him. But as time passed and things moved into perspective, I was disgusted with myself, and embarrassed that I let it go as far as it did. I felt as if I should have known better. The first time he called me stupid I should have walked out the door." She paused, shaking her head. "No, not walked. I should have run for dear life."

"It's not your fault," Elizabeth said. "You were vulnerable and he took advantage of you. He was a predator."

"And he was damned good at it. I haven't been in a serious relationship since. I still don't trust my own instincts."

"Do you trust Lucas?"

"I do." With her life. He was the only person she trusted unconditionally

"You believe he would never hurt you?"

She could see where Elizabeth was going with this, and though Julie hated to disappoint her, there was no way around it. "Not purposely, no. But Luc and I will never be anything but friends. I love him. I can't imagine what I would do without him. Hands down he's the most important person in my life."

"I know he feels the same way about you."

That didn't change anything. "I'm sure as a mother, you want what's best for Luc," Julie said.

"Of course."

"Even if we were in love, he deserves someone without all the emotional baggage. It would be unfair to lay that all on him."

"Everyone has emotional baggage, Julie. *Everyone.* Even Luc."

Yes, well, some had more than others. Elizabeth didn't realize that Julie was doing both her and Luc a favor. She didn't know the first thing about being a wife. Or a daughter-in-law, for that matter.

"I wish things were different. I don't doubt that Luc would be an exceptional husband. In fact, I *know* he would be. It's my role as his wife that I'm not so confident about."

"Shouldn't Luc be the one to make that decision?"

As far as Julie was concerned, he already had. "I can't force myself to fall in love, and neither can he."

Eight

The nurse returned from her nap a few minutes later to check Elizabeth's vitals and gently suggested that it was time for her to rest. Julie gathered her things and went back to her bedroom, where she set up a work area at the small desk under the window overlooking the rolling green lawns and sprouting flower beds of the estate.

She opened the window and breathed in deeply. Spring was in the air. When she'd arrived in October, everywhere she looked there was devastation. It seemed as if now, slowly but surely, the town was waking up to the world, and life in Royal was returning to normal. Or what she perceived to be normal. Displaced families were back in their homes, and every week shops and restaurants had begun reopening.

She needed to get out more and explore the city. If this was to be her permanent home, she needed to get to know it better. And the people. That was the worst part of growing up so sheltered. The lack of community, missing that feeling of belonging somewhere. But things were different now. *She* was different.

She smiled to herself, thinking, *This is home*. This was exactly where she was meant to be.

Taking one last deep breath of cool fresh air, she closed the window, opened her laptop and got back to work. Sorting data took every bit of her attention and concentration, so it was no surprise that she didn't hear Luc walk in the room. When he spoke her name, she nearly jumped out of her skin.

"Didn't mean to startle you," he said, but he knew as well as she that when she was immersed in work, startling her was inevitable. "How's the research going?"

"Great." She looked over at the clock, surprised to see that it was barely after four. She couldn't remember the last time he'd left the hospital before seven in the evening.

Her first thought was that something must have been wrong. "Is everything okay?"

"Fine," he said, shrugging out of his jacket, which he then tossed over the footboard of her bed. "Why wouldn't it be?"

"The time, for one. You're home so early."

He loosened his tie and pulled it off, then started unfastening the buttons on his dress shirt. "I told Ruth to clear my afternoon. That I had something I needed to do."

Something that required he take his clothes off, because that's what he was doing. And why was her bedroom door closed? "What do you need to do?"

A sexy grin tipped up the corners of his lips. "You, of course."

What the advance lacked in creativity, he made up for with red-hot sex appeal. He unbuttoned his shirt, slowly exposing a band of smooth, defined chest with just a sprinkle of crisp black hair.

Nice.

"You know, I almost stopped to pick up Mardi Gras beads on the way home," he said.

Huh? Why would they need those?

Seeing her confused look, he said, "You don't recall flashing me this morning?"

Oh yes, she had done that, hadn't she. She never dreamed that a quick peek at her breasts in the morning would motivate him to cancel his afternoon appointments and rush home three hours early.

Damn. She must be doing something right.

"We never had our postwedding sex-a-thon. Unless you don't want to," he teased, his shirt halfway down his arms. Big, thick, delicious arms she wanted to feel wrapped around her.

"Oh, I want to," she said.

"Then, why are you sitting over there?" he asked, and the hunger in his eyes made her heart flutter.

"I'm enjoying the view."

"You'll enjoy it more on the bed."

She'd never known him to be impatient, but rather than wait for her to get up on her own, he walked over to her chair and scooped her up, then tossed her onto the bed.

He did seem to enjoy manhandling her, and weirdly enough, she liked it.

Bare chested and beautiful, Luc climbed up with her, kneeling on the mattress, straddling her thighs. "So, about this shirt."

She looked down at the totally unsexy but comfortable T-shirt she'd thrown on this morning. "What about it?"

"It needs to go."

No problem. She made a move to pull it over her head, but he said, "Allow me."

He grabbed the front of her shirt in his fists and gave it one good tug. She gasped as the fabric came apart in his hands.

"Better," he said, looking satisfied with himself. He was literally tearing her clothes off. And she *liked* it.

He unfastened her jeans and tugged them off, though she had the feeling that if he could have torn the denim, he probably would have ripped those off of her, too. But now he was eyeing her bra, and thank goodness for the front clasp or he may have tried to rip that off, too.

Of course the panties were the next to go. Had she been wearing socks he would no doubt rip those, as well.

Luc sat back to admire his work. "You're perfect," he said, his eyes raking over her. He cupped her breasts, rolling her nipple between his thumb and forefinger. He knew from their wedding night how crazy that made her.

"Tell me what you like," he said, pinching hard enough to make her gasp. "I'll do anything."

"Anything. Everything." *Just keep touching me.*

His brow lifted. *"Anything?"*

The look in her eyes must have said it all. She wasn't sure what she was getting herself into, but she didn't care. In the past she never would have suggested such a thing. She would never leave herself so exposed. The ramifications would have scared her to death. Amazing what trust could do.

And boy did he "do" her. And kept on doing her.

For two solid hours. Until he'd established an up-close-and-personal relationship with every inch of her body.

"I need to rest," she finally said, limp and draped across the bed, her head hanging over the side of the mattress. The comforter lay on the floor, the bottom sheet had come loose and was halfway off, and the top sheet was…well, she wasn't sure where that had gone.

"Finished *already*?" he asked, but his smile said he was teasing her.

"Aren't you supposed to roll over and go to sleep?" she said.

"You don't want me to do that."

She did and she didn't.

Her stomach rumbled and she realized that not only was it dinnertime, but she'd skipped lunch today.

"No more sex until you feed me," she said.

"We could go out. We never did get that candlelit dinner I promised you."

"Would I have to get up and get dressed?"

"I highly recommend it."

That sounded romantic and all, but putting on clothes and fixing her hair was just too darned much work. "Or we can make sandwiches and eat in bed."

"Are you sure you don't want to go out?" he asked, looking as if he was still raring to go. Did he ever get tired?

Her legs were so weak from being overextended—she hadn't realized her feet could go that far over her head—she wouldn't make it to the front door. "Some other time."

"Sandwiches it is," he said, hopping off the bed. *He actually hopped.* Then he pulled his slacks back on, walked to the door and, wiggling his eyebrows suggestively, said, "I'll be back. Don't start without me."

Not a chance.

She must have dozed off, because he was back in what seemed like seconds, a tray propped on one palm.

"Dinner is served," he said, setting it right on the bed.

She dragged herself into a sitting position, noticing that he was hiding something behind his back. "Whatcha got?"

"Let's call it dessert."

"Can I see what it is?"

He held up a squeeze bottle of chocolate syrup, wearing that lascivious grin, and all she could think was, *Oh boy, here we go again.*

The rest of the week flew by. Luc and Julie tried to make time for one another, but life kept getting in the way. Luc had hoped to spend Sunday with Julie, but she had already promised Megan she would volunteer for the pet adoption fair, to find homes for the animals displaced in the storm.

The following Monday Luc was sitting in the cafeteria catching up on his reading while he ate a late lunch, when someone sat down across the table from him. He glanced up from the medical journal, expecting to see a colleague sitting there.

It was Amelia.

He cursed silently. He had no other patients in Pediatric, and hadn't seen her since the consultation last Monday. To be honest, he hadn't given her much thought, either. But that hadn't stopped her from seeking him out. She'd come to his office several times hoping to "catch him" and he heard that she'd objected rather firmly when his resident came to check in on Tommy in Luc's place.

As careful as he'd been to avoid her, here she was anyway, invading his space. Other than information about her son's care, he had nothing to say to her.

"Someone has been avoiding me," she said in a sing-song tone. Her smile said she thought she was being cute, when in reality, it was just annoying.

"Is there something I can help you with?"

Her smile wavered. "I saw you sitting here so I thought I would stop and say hi."

"Hi," he replied, knowing that wouldn't be the end of it. He recognized that determined look on her face.

"It would be nice if we could talk."

Nice for her maybe. As far as he was concerned they had nothing to say to each other. "I have an extremely busy afternoon."

"You know you can't stay mad at me forever, Luc."

He wasn't mad, just disinterested in whatever she had to say. She seemed hell-bent on getting him to concede his feelings, but the truth was, he didn't have any. At least, not the kind she expected him to have. "As Tommy's surgeon, it's critical that I remain impartial. I'm sure you can understand."

"I just want to talk," she said. "I've missed you. Haven't you missed me even the tiniest little bit?"

His blank expression had her frowning.

"You're playing the tough guy. I get it."

"I'm not *playing* anything," he said. "I'm just trying to eat my lunch in peace."

"No need to get snippy," she said, in the voice one

might use while addressing an impatient child. "I'm just trying to be polite."

Had she used that tone with him six years ago? And if she had, how did he stand it?

He looked across the table at her. *Really looked.* He wondered what it was about her that he had found so appealing. She was attractive, in a debutante sort of way. Never a hair out of place, her makeup applied to perfection, her clothes designer and expensive. And he had been a penniless college student, working two jobs, struggling to keep up with her high expectations. Which seemed ridiculous now when he considered the generous weekly allowance her father provided. And if that wasn't enough, all she had to do was ask and he would supply her with yet another credit card.

Her parents thought that Luc, the lowly son of a rancher, wasn't good enough for their precious daughter. But Luc knew he was destined for great things, and he was proud of all that he'd accomplished. He wondered what her parents would think of him now, and realized he didn't really give a damn. But he sure had back then. Amelia wanted the prestigious role of a surgeon's wife, but not the work and sacrifice it would take to get there. But like any other young resident he'd had to pay his dues, and Amelia had no patience to wait around for him.

"So, how is your mother?" she asked him. "I heard that she's been ill."

"She's recovering."

"She must get lonely in that big house all by herself. Maybe I could come visit her someday."

Not a good idea. His mother never liked Amelia. *That girl is too big for her britches*, she used to say.

There was nothing his mother liked less than pretension, and Amelia's nose was—as his mother liked to say—locked in an upright position. His mother's wheelchair made Amelia feel awkward, as if by going anywhere near it she might catch something.

In all the time he'd dated her, he couldn't recall Amelia and his mother having any more than a five-minute conversation. So why the need to talk to her now? And what did she know about his "big house"? Had she been snooping into his personal life?

He wondered where he would be now if she hadn't run off with someone else. He'd been too proud to beg her to come back, but he'd wanted to. Those first few months afterward he'd been beside himself. It was only after he met Julie that he began to feel whole again. She was the one who filled the empty place in his heart. Just by being a good friend.

"My mother isn't well enough for visitors," he told Amelia. "Her immune system is too vulnerable."

"I'm sorry to hear that," Amelia said. "Maybe some other time."

Doubtful.

"Please send her my regards."

When he was away from work, Amelia was the furthest thing from his mind. And why would he think about her when he had Julie? Even though they weren't a real couple, she was everything he could ask for in a woman, and a wife. And especially a lover. Pleasing her, making her feel good, was by far his favorite part of the day. There was only one thing missing. After sex, she always went back to her own room to sleep. If he had his way, she would be sleeping in his bed. Even if it was only temporarily.

"Just the man I wanted to see," Luc heard someone say, and turned to see Drew walking toward him, swooping in like an angel of mercy to save him. He looked from Luc to Amelia, one brow raised slightly. "I hope I'm not interrupting."

"Not at all," Luc said, pushing to his feet, picking up the tray with his half-eaten lunch. "I'm finished."

With his lunch *and* with Amelia. He didn't introduce her to Drew, nor did he say goodbye when he walked away. Maybe now, after this chilly conversation, she would take the hint and leave him alone.

He dumped the contents of his tray in the trash on their way out of the cafeteria and asked Drew, "What brings you to the hospital?"

"I dropped off fresh flowers at the gift shop for Beth, then came in here for a soda. Then I saw you and, frankly, you looked like maybe you needed rescuing."

Now, that was a true friend. "Drew, you have no idea."

They stopped at the main bank of elevators. "Is that her?"

"Is that who?"

"Your ex."

Luc blinked. He'd made it a point not to say anything to anyone about Amelia's being in Royal. Not even Julie. "How did you know she was my ex?"

"Amelia...is that her name?"

Luc nodded.

"Well, she's been kinda broadcasting it all over town."

Disbelief stopped him in his tracks. "She's doing *what*?"

"Word is spreading fast."

Fantastic. Just what he needed. But was he surprised? Not really. Amelia loved to be the center of attention. And he'd bet anything she was pinning him as the bad guy. "What has she been saying?"

"She's making like you guys are getting chummy. At least, that's what I've heard."

He cursed and shook his head. "Nothing could be further from the truth. Today was the first I've seen of her in a week. And it wasn't by choice, believe me."

"Yeah, you looked pretty uncomfortable sitting there with her. What does Julie think about her being here?"

"Like I said, I haven't told anyone."

Drew looked pained. "Please, tell me you're joking."

"I prefer to leave work at work. Amelia is the mother of my patient, nothing more. She has nothing to do with my personal life."

Drew's expression said that Luc was a sad and pathetic man. "Dude, I hate to be the one to break it to you, but in a marriage, it doesn't really work that way."

"But we're not really married, are we?"

"No, but she is your best friend. I thought you guys told each other everything."

Well, almost everything. And he could see Drew's point. If Amelia was broadcasting the details of their past relationship, Julie was bound to hear it from someone. He didn't want it to appear as if he was hiding things from her. "I'll talk to her tonight."

"Smart move. The way it's spreading, it's only a matter of time before the entire town knows."

Luc cursed under his breath. He should have known that Amelia was up to something. He should have expected it.

Hadn't she done enough damage? Caused him enough pain. He was going to put an end to whatever she thought she was doing.

Nine

Julie met Megan and Lark for lunch at the Royal Diner. There was a real camaraderie among the three of them, a sense of genuine respect and friendship. Only recently, as she'd grown so close to these women, did Julie realize all that she'd missed out on being so sheltered as a child, and having that inherent lack of trust. But it was never too late to start living.

"The adoption fair seemed to go well," she told Megan after the waitress took their orders.

"And we're still bursting at the seams. It's like that every spring, plus we're still feeling the aftereffects of the tornado. We have a lot of animals coming in, but not so many getting adopted back out. I don't suppose you would be interested in a puppy or a kitten? Or better yet an older cat or dog?"

Julie had never had a pet before. Her father forbade animals of any kind in the house, and at university, with a full class-load, there hadn't been time. After that she'd moved around so frequently, spending months abroad, owning an animal, even something as benign as a goldfish, had been impractical.

Her condo in Royal had a no-pet policy, so adopting had never been an option. But she no longer had that obstacle, did she? She wondered how Luc would feel about adopting a small dog or even a cat. He spoke fondly of the various pets his family had owned in their ranching days, so she knew he liked animals.

"Maybe I'll come by and take a look," she said. "After I talk to Luc about it, of course."

"Speaking of," Megan said. "How is he holding up?"

"He's good." It had been touch and go with his mother all last week, but now she was infection free, eating better than she had in months and growing stronger every day. As they drew closer to April, and the days grew warmer, Elizabeth had been spending time outside in the gardens with her nurse.

"It must have been a shock for him," Lark said.

"Not really," Julie told her. "It's just a part of her condition."

"Condition?" Megan asked, looking confused. "I thought her son was the patient. Is Luc treating her, too? And wouldn't that be a conflict of interest?"

Julie frowned. *Her* who?

"Far as I heard he's only treating the boy," Lark said. "Which is bad enough if you ask me."

There were obviously some crossed wires here. "I'm a little confused."

"And that's perfectly natural," Megan said. "I would be, too, if Drew's ex showed up."

Drew's ex? *Wait, what?*

Before she could ask what the heck they were talking about, she noticed Stella approaching their table.

"Hello, ladies! Isn't this fantastic." She gazed around the diner. "It's so inspiring to see things getting back to normal in our little town."

"Are you here for lunch?" Lark asked her.

"Would you like to join us?" Megan chimed in. "We're giving Julie some much needed moral support."

They were? And what exactly did she need support for?

Stella sat in the empty chair next to Julie and with eyes full of sympathy said, "I heard she was in town. How are *you* holding up?"

She who? "Guys, I'm really confused."

"Of course you are," Stella said gently. "Who wouldn't be under the circumstances."

"No, I mean I'm confused right now, by this conversation. I must have missed something, because I'm lost. Who are we talking about?"

"Amelia," Stella said.

"Amelia who?" The only Amelia that she knew of was the one who'd broken Luc's heart. The one he was still hung up on all these years later. They couldn't possibly mean...

The three women exchanged a look, and Megan said, "I'm sorry. We just assumed Luc had told you."

Julie was beginning to get a very bad feeling. "Told me what?"

"His ex-fiancée, Amelia. Her son is Luc's patient."

Amelia was here, in Royal? Julie's stomach did an odd little flip-flop and a rush of heat flooded her cheeks.

As his wife, she should have known that. Even as his fake wife, a heads-up would have been nice. Weren't they supposed to make this marriage look legitimate?

"I guess it must have slipped his mind," Julie said. Though technically Luc was her boss, it wasn't often that their paths crossed at the hospital. On the average day, she rarely left her office. And though she had seen a picture of Amelia from six years ago, she had no clue what she would look like now. She could have passed her in the hall and not even known it. "We're both pretty busy. Some nights we don't even see each other."

Maybe Amelia and her son had just arrived and he'd forgotten to mention it. And maybe seeing her again, talking things over with her, would give him the closure he needed. So really, this could be a good thing. Right?

"When did she get here?" Julie asked them, forcing a smile, trying her best not to come off as the jilted wife.

The women exchanged another look and the bad feeling grew.

"Last Monday," Stella said.

For reasons that escaped her, Julie's heart plummeted to the pit of her belly and her appetite disappeared. She had been in Royal for more than a week?

"I'm so sorry you had to find out this way," Lark said. "We all just assumed you knew."

As Luc's wife, she should have known. But as his friend and employee, since that's all they really were, he was under no obligation to tell her anything. He had his life and she had hers. But he'd put her in a difficult situation.

She wracked her brain for a way to backpedal, to make herself look at least a little less pathetic, but trying to explain something she had no real answer for would only make things worse. Maybe Luc was trying to protect her feelings, or maybe he figured she wouldn't care either way.

You're rationalizing, and for no good reason, she told herself. It was what it was. An arrangement. After all that he'd done for her, how could she complain? If he wanted to talk about it with her he would in his own good time. And if he didn't, that was okay, too.

"He probably just didn't want to upset you," Megan said. "Her showing up so soon after the wedding. Maybe he felt hesitant to tell you."

"Or maybe he's so over her that he didn't feel the need to say anything," Lark added.

Julie appreciated their efforts, but they were only making things worse. "Can we maybe not talk about it anymore?"

"Of course," Stella said with manufactured cheer. "Hey, did you guys see in the paper that the coffee shop is set to reopen next week? And construction on the hospital will begin next month. I'm not sure if it's possible, but I'd like to have the new city hall building completed by the first anniversary of the tornado. We've come so far already in our rebuilding efforts."

"It's definitely starting to look like home again," Lark said.

The rest of the meal was awkward to say the least. No one brought Amelia up again, but considering the occasional sideways glances and sympathetic smiles from her friends, the subject was clearly on everyone's mind.

It would have been easy for her to make some sort of excuse and leave the diner, but Julie forced herself to sit there and pick at her salad, pretending to follow the conversation, when inside she was all jumbled up. She wondered how much time he'd been spending with Amelia. He'd come home very late from the hospital the past two nights. Could he have been with Amelia? Had they rekindled their romance? Was it possible that he was sleeping with her?

The thought made Julie sick to her stomach, though it shouldn't have. They never said they wouldn't see other people. Julie had just assumed, in the spirit of making their marriage look legitimate, and because they were intimately involved, that they wouldn't. And though she wanted to put it out of her mind and let it go, her brain went into overdrive instead.

She picked at her food and sipped her sweet iced tea, when what she really needed was something big and alcoholic. Anything to loosen the knots in her chest, to sooth her bruised pride.

The lunch seemed to go on forever, but Julie refused to be the first one to leave.

Claiming she had more establishments to visit, Stella left first, and then Lark got a call from the hospital and had to rush back to work, leaving just Julie and Megan.

"Julie, I am so sorry," Megan said the instant they were alone. "We never meant to embarrass you that way. We just…"

"Assumed that as his wife Luc would have told me. I would have thought so, too."

"I'm sure he had a good reason for not saying anything. And I'm sure nothing is going on between them."

"Are you sure? Really? If nothing was going on, why would he hide it from me?" She heard herself and shook her head with disgust.

"As your friend, husband and boss, he should have had the courtesy to tell you. You have every right to be angry with him."

At this point Julie wasn't sure what she was feeling. Or what she *should* feel. If the tables were turned, would she have done anything differently?

Yes, she would have. She would have told him the truth. She wondered how she could be so blind to what had been going on around her. Had she just been lulled into a false sense of security? And why hadn't anyone told her?

"What exactly have you heard about her?" Julie asked Megan.

Megan hesitated. "Maybe you should talk to Luc about it."

Oh, she would, but first she wanted the entire story, or as much as Megan could tell her. "I want to know what you've heard. I thought she was married."

"Divorced."

Swell. "What else?"

Looking pained, Megan said, "I heard they've been spending a considerable amount of time together. But that could just be talk."

She doubted it. "How much longer will she be here?"

"I really don't know. Her son is having spinal surgery, so as long as it takes him to recover I guess."

At least a week, maybe a little longer. That wasn't too bad. "Did Luc do the surgery yet?"

Megan shook her head. "And I have no idea when he's supposed to do it. Soon, I would imagine."

Not soon enough as far as Julie was concerned. The faster they left, the better. Unless it was already too late. Maybe he'd fallen back in love with her. Which would mean what for Julie? Divorce? Deportation? Or would she simply have to share him until she became a legal citizen?

What a horrifying thought.

For the rest of the day Julie walked around with a knot in her chest. And though she had no right to, she felt angry and betrayed. She went back to the hospital and tried to work, but she couldn't concentrate worth a damn. What she wanted to do was confront Luc, but she was still too hot under the collar. She needed time to cool off and put things into perspective. Convince herself that technically, Luc had done nothing wrong.

She left work early and headed for home, wondering how much longer she would actually be calling this grand place home. Would Luc move Julie out, and bring Amelia and her son in? Or would they all live there together as one big happy family? The idea made her shudder.

She wandered the house aimlessly for several minutes, confused and scared, her thoughts too jumbled to be rational, wondering what her next move should be. Should she confront Luc, or let him tell her in his own good time? And what if she didn't like what he had to say?

She wound up in the den, with its ceiling-high stone fireplace and panoramic windows, staring blankly into the afternoon sunshine, feeling as if the perfect life she'd had just this morning had completely fallen apart.

"You're home early," she heard Elizabeth say, and turned to see her wheeling her chair into the room. "How's my favorite daughter-in-law today?"

She said it with a smile so filled with love and genuine affection, Julie burst into tears.

An emergency surgery came in just as Luc was about to leave the hospital, so by the time he finally did get home it was after eleven. He went straight to Julie's room to tell her about Amelia, but she was already asleep.

"Julie," he called softly, but he didn't get an answer. He considered waking her, but he figured the news would be much better received after they both had a good night's sleep.

His stomach rumbled, reminding him that he'd skipped dinner, so he went down to the kitchen for a snack. He foraged though the fridge and found a pot of leftover stew.

"You're home late," he heard his mother say, and turned to see her wheeling herself into the kitchen. She was in her pajamas, but clearly hadn't been to bed yet.

"What are you doing up?" he asked her. "You know how important it is that you get your rest."

"Where have you been?" she asked.

"The hospital."

"Doing what?"

He frowned. What did she think he would be doing? "I had an emergency surgery. Why? Is something wrong?"

"Come here," she said, gesturing him to her.

He set the pot on the stove and walked over to her.

"Down here," she said, and he leaned over, thinking she wanted to give him a hug. Instead she whacked him upside the head.

Hard.

"Ow! Jesus," he said, seeing stars, rubbing the pain away. He could say with confidence that her strength was definitely coming back. "What the hell was that for?"

"Amelia is here," she said, and her tone said she wasn't at all pleased about it.

"Yes. Her son is my patient."

"And you didn't think this was something your wife might have liked to know?"

Aw, hell. "I was going to tell her tonight when I got home. I take it she already knows?"

"Of course she knows! The way people talk around here, how long did you think you could keep it a secret?"

"I wasn't keeping it a secret." He just hadn't brought it up.

"And the way she found out…" She pressed her lips together in a thin line, shaking her head. "What were you thinking?"

"I honestly didn't think it was a big deal—"

"Not a big deal?" she shrieked, her eyes wide, and he backed up a step, just in case she took another swing at him.

"—until today," he finished. "Drew warned me that Amelia has been all around town making noise like she and I have some sort of relationship, but it's not true."

"That's a little hard to believe, all things considered," his mother said.

Did she actually believe the lies Amelia had been spreading? And if she did, had Julie believed them, as well?

"How did Julie find out?"

His mother explained that she'd been out with her friends when the subject came up, and that everyone knew but her. "The poor thing was beyond humiliated."

He cursed under his breath. He never meant for it to go this far. He should have known Amelia would do something like this. "I intended to tell her tonight."

"Well, you're too late. And you owe her an apology."

"Of course I'll apologize."

"Not only are you a lousy excuse for a husband, you're not a very good friend, either."

Damn, she really was furious. "You don't think that's a little harsh?"

"Not in the least. Honesty and trust are the basis for any relationship. Platonic or romantic. You lied to her."

Technically, he hadn't, but he knew what his mother would say, because he'd heard it a million times growing up. A lie by omission was still a lie. "As I said, I didn't think it was relevant. I had no idea Amelia was spreading rumors."

"The poor thing sobbed on my shoulder."

He blinked. "Amelia?"

"No, you idiot. Julie."

Julie *cried*?

Julie?

In all the years he'd known her, through the worst conditions and situations, he'd never so much as seen her well up. She had tenacity, and nerves of steel. She really must have been humiliated to get that upset. And he felt like a louse for putting her in that position. His mother was right. He was an idiot. And a sad excuse for a spouse. And an even worse friend. Had he honestly believed that by avoiding Amelia, she would have no impact on his life? Or Julie's? This was Amelia they were talking about; he should have known better.

"Are you still in love with her?" his mother asked.

"Julie?"

She rolled her eyes. *"Amelia."*

The fact that she would even ask that question was a clear indication of just how far out of hand this had gotten. In retrospect, all this time later, he wasn't sure if he'd ever loved her. If it had instead been a case of extreme infatuation. "I do not love her. I have no feelings for her whatsoever. I didn't intend for any of this to happen."

"But it did happen, and you need to fix it."

He intended to. First thing tomorrow he would talk to Julie.

Ten

After tossing and turning most of the night, Julie dragged herself out of bed at the crack of dawn, relieved to discover that Luc was still sleeping. She'd heard him come in last night, but feigned sleep when he opened her bedroom door. Late as he was, it didn't take a genius to know where he'd been. And whom he'd been with.

She knew they needed to talk about it, but she needed to get her head on straight first. It was weird how quickly things could change. One minute everything was fine and going as planned, the next she didn't have a clue what to expect. But it wasn't Luc's fault, or hers. Neither of them could have anticipated this happening. But if he wanted Amelia, Julie wouldn't stand in his way.

If Luc were to divorce her so soon after the wedding, the immigration people would be suspicious to say the least. She needed to formulate a plan, an exit strategy that wouldn't involve deportation though the idea of staying Royal had lost its appeal. It would be too humiliating. There was nothing for her in South Africa. Maybe she could move closer to her sister, find a new job.

She sat in her office at the hospital, staring blankly at her laptop, her mind moving in so many directions at once, she couldn't make sense of anything. And she dreaded the moment Luc walked through her office door wanting to talk, because she had no idea what to say to him, or how she was even supposed to feel.

Several minutes had passed when she heard a knock on her door. Her heart raced up to her throat and her knees went all soft and squishy.

Here we go.

She took a deep breath and looked up, expecting to see Luc, but when she saw who was really standing there, her heart plummeted to the pit of her stomach. She'd seen that face before, in a photo Luc used to carry in his wallet. For all she knew it was still in there.

Amelia looked so harmless, her skin pale, her hair flat and lifeless and in need of washing, Julie almost felt sorry for her. Having a child with a chronic illness had obviously taken its toll on her.

"Hi, there," she said, looking nervously around the office. She spoke with one of those adorable Southern accents, and despite looking a little run-down and tired, she was still a very beautiful woman.

"Hello, Amelia, I'm Julie."

"You know who I am?"

Unfortunately.

Julie rose from her chair and crossed to the door, reaching out to shake her hand. It was small and delicate, just like the rest of her, but her grip was firm.

"I hope I'm not interrupting anything," Amelia said. "I just had to meet the woman who finally got a ring on Luc's finger."

The way Julie understood it, Luc had been more

than ready to settle down with Amelia. It was she who ran off with someone else. Which obviously hadn't worked out very well for her.

"Have you got a minute?" Amelia asked her. "Can we talk?"

"Come in." As much as Julie wasn't looking forward to this, she knew that it would be best to clear the air. Since Luc didn't seem inclined to talk to her about it, she could hear it straight from the source. At least here, in her office, she had the upper hand. Amelia was in her territory.

Amelia stepped inside. Julie shut the door and gestured to the chair across her desk. "Sit down."

Amelia hesitated, looking conflicted. "Are you sure? I know this is awkward…"

Not as awkward as it would be if they didn't talk. "I'm sure. Please, sit."

Amelia sat on the very edge of the seat, as if she might jump up at any second and bolt for the door. Julie returned to her chair and sat.

"I understand there's been talk," Amelia said. "I wanted to clear the air. I'm not sure what Luc has told you…"

Not a single damned thing, but she didn't tell Amelia that. When in doubt, change the subject. "First, how is your son?"

At the mere mention of her boy, her face lit. "Antsy. Ready for his surgery, but still a little scared. He knows his recovery will be slow and painful. But he can't wait to get on his feet again so he can play with his friends. He's crazy about baseball, and for a five-year-old he's really good, too.

"The last few months, as he's become more and

more limited physically, have been very hard for Tommy. Tommy's father, my ex-husband, rarely sees him. He never could forgive me for giving birth to a less than perfect child."

"I'm sorry to hear that," Julie said, feeling sympathy for the boy. She knew too well what it was like to grow up in a single parent home. Though her father, at best, was never more than half a parent. *At best.*

"He traded me in for a younger model," Amelia said with a weak smile. "I guess that's what happens when you marry for money and social standing."

The admission surprised Julie, and it must have shown.

"I don't deny that I've made many mistakes," Amelia said, head held up proudly. "My only regret is how it's affected my son. After all he's been through, he deserves better. He deserves a father who gives more than a monthly check."

"He has you," Julie said. "What more could he possibly need?" She would have given anything to have her mother back, for her parents to trade places. For her father to be the one who died.

Tears welled in Amelia's eyes. "My gosh," she said, dabbing at them. "You are just so sweet. I want you to know that when I came here I had no idea that Luc was married. He's a lucky man."

"I'm the lucky one," she said, and it was true. It was a wonderful thing he was doing for her and she couldn't lose sight of that. Even if he did fall back in love with this adorable woman. Who would blame him?

"I hear a bit of an accent there," Amelia said, cocking her head slightly. "Where are you from?"

"South Africa. But my parents were from Wales originally."

"Were from? They're not with you anymore?"

"No."

"Mine are alive and kicking," Amelia said with a sigh of exasperation. "And still trying to tell me how to run my life."

"I'm sure they mean well."

"No, they're just nosy and controlling. They always have been. I swore that when my Tommy was born, I would allow him to grow up to be whatever he wants to be. Play with the friends he likes regardless of their social standing, marry the girl he loves even if she's penniless. All of the things I never had. I'll even let him go to public school if that's what he decides he wants."

It sounded as if she and Amanda had quite a bit in common when it came to family. "My sister and I went to a private girl's school," Julie told her. "I hated it. I never felt as if I fit in."

"And I fit in too well. I was an entitled, spoiled brat. If not for my Tommy, I probably still would be, but having him has taught me so much about what really matters, you know?"

Julie could only imagine.

Amelia relaxed back into her seat, looking a bit less as if she might bolt. "How did you and Luc meet?"

"We were both volunteering for Doctors Without Borders."

"Oh, you're a doctor, too?"

"No. Currently I'm Luc's research assistant."

"Research for what?"

"Luc's medical inventions and surgical techniques.

They've made him quite famous in the medical community." And very wealthy.

"What is it that you do exactly?" Amelia said, looking genuinely interested.

"I conduct interviews, collect data and statistics."

"So you must see him a lot."

"Actually, no. As chief of surgery for the hospital, he's always on call. There are days when I barely see him."

Amelia scrunched up her nose. "Don't you hate that?"

"That's just the way it is," she said. "The way it's always been. But I work long hours as well, so I can't really complain." Nor would she ever feel the need.

"I used to hate that Luc's career meant more to him than I did. I was so jealous. At the time, I was used to getting what I wanted, and he did try to accommodate me. Looking back now, I have to wonder why he stuck around as long as he had. Why he wasn't the one who dumped me. I was such a bitch sometimes."

Julie had no answer for her. But she was guessing it was because he loved her, and he was willing to overlook the not-so-perfect stuff.

"He's still mad at me," Amelia said, eyes lowered. "I feel so bad for the way I treated him and I was really hoping we could put the past to rest, but that doesn't seem very likely. He won't even talk to me."

"Just give him time. I'm sure he'll come around."

"I appreciate the encouragement, but I think it's misplaced. And you're probably the last person I should be confiding in about this. To be honest, I'm not even sure why you're talking to me. If the situation were reversed, I wouldn't talk to me. Or if I did, I would tell me to stay the hell away from my husband. Why aren't you, by the way?"

Because he isn't really my husband. "You two clearly have unresolved issues. It's in both your best interests to deal with them so you can move on."

"That's all I want."

Julie wasn't sure she believed that. She didn't not believe it, either. Luc had always described Amelia as cold, heartless and manipulative. To Julie, she just seemed sort of…pathetic.

"How is his mom doing? I heard that she's been sick. It must be difficult for him, as close as they are."

"It is."

"Do you get along with her?"

Julie hesitated and Amelia cringed.

"Am I getting too personal? I'm sorry if I am. I'm just curious. Too curious for my own good, my daddy used to claim."

"Yes, we get along. I consider her one of my closest friends."

"She hated me—but I didn't like her, either. She and Luc were very close and I was threatened by that."

Elizabeth was as down-to-earth and easygoing as her son. It was hard to imagine her *hating* anyone. And Julie had always considered his close relationship with his mother a good thing. She'd certainly never felt threatened or jealous.

Amelia must have read her mind. "I don't blame her for not liking me. I was different back then. I was very much into appearances. Her disability made me uncomfortable and I'm sure it showed. I'd never known anyone in a wheelchair. I had no idea how to act around her. I realize now how ridiculous it was for me to let her disability define who she was as a person. The idea of someone judging my Tommy based on his physical capacities makes my heart hurt. I feel as if I owe her an apology. I asked Luc if I could visit her. He didn't seem to think that was a good idea."

"Her health is compromised, leaving her vulnerable to infection. I'm sure that's the reason." Though to be honest, she really wasn't sure.

"And I'm sure that you're just saying that to make me feel better," Amelia said with a sad smile. "But I appreciate the effort. I guess some things just aren't fixable."

She genuinely seemed to want to rectify her past mistakes. Luc should at least give her the chance to explain, for both their sakes. "I'll talk to Luc and see what I can do, but no promises."

"You know," Amelia said, "you're not at all what I expected."

When Julie smiled, she really meant it. "Neither are you."

That morning, the instant he stepped through the hospital doors an hour later than usual, Luc was ambushed by half a dozen people needing him for one thing or another. Sign this. Initial that. Should it be the red or the blue pill? It was the major drawback of being chief of surgery. When he did finally get to his office, Ruth greeted him with one brow raised, looking from him to her watch, then back to him again. "Working a half day, are we?"

"I know, I was up late and slept through my alarm." All night, Luc had been attuned to even the slightest noise coming from Julie's room across the hall. When she woke he wanted to talk to her, but he never got the chance. The last time he looked at the clock it had been four forty-five and still dark. When he opened his eyes again, sunlight was pouring through the blinds and the clock said 7:38 a.m. He'd gotten up and checked Julie's room, but of course she was gone.

He took off his suit jacket and waited for Ruth to get up and retrieve his lab coat, but she just sat there. "Lab coat?" he said, expecting her to jump to attention.

She didn't.

"I'm very busy," she said, but she just sat there, arms crossed, glaring. She didn't look busy to him. She did look pissed off though.

"Did I do something to upset you?" he asked her.

"Like what?"

"I have no idea. That's why I'm asking."

"It wouldn't have anything to do with the fact that a week after your wedding you're hooking up with ex-girlfriends?"

"Hooking up?" He'd never heard her use the vernacular of a much younger generation. "Do you even know what that means?"

"I know that what you're doing is wrong," she said, chin tilted stubbornly. "How do you think this will make Julie feel?"

Pretty lousy if what his mom said was true. "Cancel anything I have before noon," he told Ruth, getting the lab coat himself. He had a lot of explaining to do, and he had the feeling it might take a while. "And for the record, I am not hooking up with Amelia. I've barely spoken to her."

"That's not what I've heard."

And he didn't have the time to sit there and explain. Ruth's feelings on the matter were the least of his worries.

He headed to Julie's office three floors up. He knocked on the door, hoping she was there.

"Come in," she called, so he opened the door...and got the shock of his life when he realized Amelia was sitting there with Julie.

Talk about awkward.

Or was it? Julie and Amelia looked completely at ease with each other.

"What the hell is this?" he asked, his tone sharper than he intended, feeling like the odd man out.

Julie looked at Amelia, and Amelia looked at her, and then both women burst out laughing.

Eleven

"We weren't laughing *at* you," Julie insisted to Luc several minutes later after Amelia left her office and they were alone.

"You looked right at me and laughed," he said, not sure who irritated him more, Julie or Amelia. Or maybe it was how cozy the two of them had looked sitting there together. This was not supposed to happen. Julie was supposed to dislike Amelia as much as he did.

"Not ten seconds before you knocked we were talking about how you would react if you walked in and saw us together," Julie said. "It's the timing that had us laughing. Not you."

It sure hadn't felt that way. He sat on the corner of her desk. "We need to talk."

"About what?"

About what? Was she joking? "For starters, what Amelia was doing here."

Julie shrugged. "We were talking."

Thanks, Captain Obvious. "I could see that. What were you talking about?"

"You, mostly."

Swell. Did he even want to know what was being said? Probably not.

"I should have told you that she was here," he said. "And that her son is my patient. And I know the fact I didn't looks suspicious—"

"*Luc*, stop. You don't owe me an explanation."

Of course he did. "We're married, I should have said something about her being here."

"This marriage is only pretend, remember?"

He was getting a little tired of her reminding him of that. Who was she trying to convince, him or herself? "Then, as your friend, I should have told you."

"I'm sure you had your reasons not to. Besides, I think it's good that you're finally getting a chance to settle things with her. You should have done it a long time ago."

"There's nothing to settle."

"For her there is."

"That's not my problem. And despite what you've probably heard, I have not been spending time with her. She, on the other hand, has been stalking me."

"I know. She told me."

He blinked. "She did?"

"Well, she didn't use the term *stalking*, but I know she's been trying to see you. All she wants to do is talk."

"You believe that?"

"Unless I hear otherwise from you, what reason do I have not to?"

He could think of a couple dozen. "You don't know her the way I do."

"People do change."

Not people like her. "She's the same old Amelia, trust me."

"How can you know that if you won't talk to her?"

He knew Amelia was manipulative, but to coax Julie over to her camp with a single conversation? That was quite an accomplishment, even for her. "As I said, I have no need or desire to discuss or settle anything from our past. Period."

"She's been through a lot. I really think that she's different now. Who knows, she may still be the love of your life."

Oh, good God no, she wasn't. "She is not the love of my life."

"Either way, it's okay with me if you spend some time getting to know her again. And if you decide you need to end our marriage—"

"Absolutely not." Was she serious? What kind of friend would he be? Besides, he would choose Julie over Amelia any day of the week. The trouble was making her believe that. Julie had never had a man in her life who hadn't disappointed her deeply in one way or another. It was almost as if she expected it, planned for it even. He refused to let that happen to her again. He wouldn't let her down, no matter what he had to do. "Until you get your permanent citizenship you're stuck with me. As long as it takes. I don't go back on my promises." He took her hand and squeezed it hard, his eyes locked on hers. "I mean that. I don't want this to come between us. You're the most important person in my life."

"It won't come between us."

"You promise?"

She smiled. A *real* smile. "I promise."

Somehow that just didn't seem good enough. There was something else going on here that he just couldn't seem to put his finger on. "Are you sure you're okay? My mom said you cried. You never cry."

Her cheeks blushed a vivid shade of pink. She never cried, and she blushed even less often. "I wish she wouldn't have said anything to you. It was really, really embarrassing."

"She was concerned."

"It was PMS, that's all. Every now and then it makes me emotional. And for the record, I do cry occasionally. I just don't let anyone else see it. It was just bad timing."

"So, if you have PMS, I guess that means you're not..."

"I'm not pregnant."

He waited for the relief to flow over him, but weirdly enough, he felt a twinge of disappointment instead. He wasn't ready to be a parent, and neither was Julie, but knowing there had been a slight possibility, it had gotten him thinking. But the timing couldn't have been worse. And he was completely overlooking the fact that, as she liked to point out, he and Julie were married in name only.

"I was thinking, if you're going to be seeing Amelia—"

"I'm *not*. I'm married to *you*, and until that changes I'm not *seeing* anyone else."

"I was just going to say, you should try to keep it on the down low."

Was she giving him permission to cheat on her? Did she really believe he would put her citizenship in jeopardy? Not to mention her dignity. And his own. And their *friendship*. What sort of man did she think he was? "It's not going to happen. Not now, not ever. I don't find her even remotely attractive."

"You can't deny that she's beautiful."

On the outside maybe. "As far as I'm concerned, she's nothing more than the mother of my patient. That's as far as it goes now, or ever will go. Amelia and I had our shot and she blew it. She doesn't get a second chance."

"I think she's really changed."

Somehow he doubted that. Amelia liked to manipulate, and she was good at it. He didn't doubt that she was manipulating Julie. Julie's instincts when judging a person's character had never been stellar, but she'd had Luc around a good majority of the past six years to give her guidance. She'd always listened to him before. Why not now? "Are you that eager to get rid of me?"

"Of course not," she said, laying her hand on his arm. Her skin was soft and warm. Whenever she touched him, something happened, something deep down inside of him shifted. He'd never been with a woman who could excite him the way she did, or frustrate him, while at the same time making him feel more at peace than he ever had in his life.

"I just want you to be happy," she said.

"Then, please trust me when I say to stay away from her. *That* will make me happy."

"Why?"

"She's not the person you think she is." Julie was too trusting, too nice to see Amelia for what she really was. Amelia would chew her up and spit her back out without batting an eyelash.

"We'll see," Julie told him, as if she knew something he didn't. Some significant piece to the puzzle that hadn't yet fallen into place.

Chumming up to him was one thing, but why would

Amelia befriend Julie? What did she possibly stand to gain? Or was she just screwing with his head, hoping to cause chaos? Anything to make herself the center of attention.

"What do you think of cats?" Julie asked, and the abrupt change of subject threw him for a second.

"I think they're delicious. Why?"

She laughed, and it was truly like music to his ears. He liked making her happy, seeing her smile.

"I'm being serious. Do you like them?"

"I don't *dis*like them. We had several at the ranch when I was growing up. But they were always more of my mother's thing."

She frowned. "Oh."

"Why do you ask?"

"The shelter is filled beyond capacity, and I've never actually had a pet, so I thought maybe a kitten...but it sounds like it would be a bad idea."

"Why not a dog? I like dogs."

"Let's be honest. Neither of us has the time for a dog. Our schedules are just too busy."

He couldn't deny that. "You're right. But a cat?" He made a sour face. "They're so...sneaky."

"Never mind. Like I said, it was just a thought."

She sure didn't put up much of a fight.

He shrugged apologetically and said, "Sorry."

"No, it's okay," she said, forcing a smile. And not a very convincing one. "I've gone this long without one. When I get my own place I'll have to find a pet-friendly apartment this time."

Though he knew it was inevitable, the thought of her eventually moving out didn't sit well with him. He liked having her there, knowing that she was just across the hall if he needed her, or if she needed him. Though he would much rather she be a permanent addition to his bed, even if all they intended to do was sleep. He'd gently suggested on more than one occasion that she stay the night in his room, but she never would. Their wedding night had been the only exception.

"I'm used to sleeping alone," she'd explained, but he had the feeling it was more than that. He just wasn't sure what. He'd begun to wonder if this friends with benefits deal they had going was a little more complicated than either had expected. Aside from the sex, their relationship hadn't changed, so why did everything feel so...different? Was he falling in love with her? For real? And if he was, what next? Did he take the chance and tell her? If she didn't share those feelings, he knew it would only drive her away.

That wasn't a risk he was willing to take.

Twelve

Julie believed Amelia when she said she only wanted to talk to Luc, but she seemed to be the only one in town who did.

"Everyone hates me," she told Julie that Friday, while they shared lunch in the hospital cafeteria. When Tommy slept, which was quite often due to the heavy dose of pain meds that he was on, Amelia would sometimes sneak away and visit Julie. She was the only friend Amelia had in town, and though they were an unlikely pair all things considered, they had quite a bit in common.

"I'm sure no one hates you," Julie said, though she, too, noticed Amelia getting the cold shoulder and more than a few suspicious looks. "Luc is a respected member of the community. People are just very protective of him."

"I noticed," Amelia said, moving her food around her plate, but not really eating much. With her son's surgery scheduled soon she was understandably edgy. "I'm getting sick of hospital food, so I went to the diner last night. But I got so many dirty looks I had to leave. Even the waitress gave me the cold shoulder. I had them wrap my food up and I took it back to the hospital to eat."

Julie hated that people would treat her that way when they didn't even know the full story. Didn't even know Amelia. Did no one care that she had a sick child? Why couldn't they cut her a little slack? "If they knew you like I do, they wouldn't act that way."

"They don't want to know me," she said. "I can see now that coming here was a mistake. After the surgery, as soon as Tommy is stable enough to be moved, I'm going back to Houston. I'm as big a joke there as I am here, but at least there I don't get sneered at every time I walk down the street. They're kind enough to do it behind my back. The poor little debutante with the sick kid whose husband couldn't keep it in his pants."

Julie cringed. "Ouch."

"I know. And my parents hold me personally responsible for tarnishing our family reputation."

That was just wrong, but Julie knew from experience how unreasonable parents could be. "How is your husband cheating on you your fault?"

"Oh, they didn't care about the cheating. That's just what husbands do, apparently."

"According to who?"

"Houston high society."

"That's crazy," Julie said.

"At first Tom, my ex, was very discreet, but I knew something was up. He'd work lots of late nights and went on weekend business trips. I fooled myself into thinking that I was imagining things. I was used to men fawning all over me. I was young and beautiful and rich, and I knew it. It was a blow to my pride to think that my husband, the man who was supposed to worship the ground I walked on, would stray.

"I was sure that fatherhood would settle him down."

"Did it?"

She shook her head. "It only seemed to push him further away. Tom was never there for our son, not even when he was an infant. Even less after he was diagnosed. All the money and status in the world wasn't worth my baby being treated that way."

"What did you do?"

"I got really, really angry. Then I said enough is enough and divorced him."

Julie admired any woman who had the courage to stand up for herself in the face of adversity.

"For what it's worth, I never would have had the guts to do what you did," Julie said.

"Humiliation is one hell of a motivator."

Julie told Amelia about her abusive ex, and how long it took her to screw up the courage to walk away. "He completely shredded my self-esteem. I was weak and pathetic."

"You were doing the best you could with the skills you learned growing up."

"That's just the thing. I never learned how to defend myself."

"That's my point. You were totally ill equipped to deal with the situation, but you still got away. You prevailed."

"Not as soon as I should have."

"Julie, I stayed for over *four* years."

"But you were married with a son. There was nothing keeping me from leaving. Nothing but my own cowardice."

"Don't be so hard on yourself," Amelia said. "You're one of the bravest people I know."

For a second Julie was sure that she was joking. Brave? *Her?* "How could you possibly think that?"

"Look at all the extraordinary things you've done. You've traveled all over the world helping people. You ventured off on your own and turned a terrible situation into something really good. That takes guts."

Julie had never really thought of it like that before. "I guess so."

"As crazy as my parents drive me, my mother especially, the idea of completely cutting them from my life is terrifying. I think about it all the time, but I could never actually do it. Despite everything, their opinion still matters to me. You don't seem to let anyone else's opinions color your judgment. If you did, you sure wouldn't be sitting here with me. The town pariah. I thought talking to Luc's friends and the people in town might give me some insight into how to relate to him. To make him listen to me. Maybe find some common ground. All I've managed to do is make a whole bunch of enemies."

"What those people think shouldn't matter to you. You know your intentions were good. That's all that's important."

A frown furrowed her brow. "I guess."

After lunch Julie went back to her office, feeling bad for Amelia. She believed it would be in Amelia's and Luc's best interest to talk, to settle the past so they could both move forward, but if Luc refused, there wasn't much Julie could do about it.

Or could she?

She wasn't duplicitous by nature, but if the situation called for it, and she truly believed it could benefit Luc, even she could be a little creative.

* * *

A few hours later Julie's phone rang and she was surprised to see Elizabeth's number on the screen. Her first thought was that it was her nurse and something was terribly wrong. And if she was calling Julie, Luc must have been unreachable. But when she answered it was Elizabeth's voice, and she sounded just fine.

"Something arrived for you today," she told Julie. "Can you get away from work? You should probably come home and open it."

It was an odd request, to say the least. "Who is it from?"

"I'm not sure, but I think it might be perishable."

It was probably something from her sister, who had finally called Julie to congratulate her on her "pseudowedding"—Jennifer's exact words. She'd probably sent chocolates or a fruit basket. "Can't you just stick it in the fridge for now?"

"It wouldn't fit."

"Can you open it for me and tell me what it is?"

"I wouldn't feel right opening someone else's package," she said. "You should come home."

Julie looked at the pile of transcripts from the interviews she'd conducted with spinal patients, and had been hoping to review that afternoon, but for whatever reason her coming home now was important to Elizabeth, and that was good enough for her. "Let me finish up what I'm doing, then I'll come home. Give me thirty minutes."

"See you soon!"

That was a little strange, but, okay. She finished what she'd been working on and headed home, surprised to find Luc's Beamer in the garage next to his mother's van. What was he doing home so early?

Julie let herself into the house, hung her keys on the rack next to the door and called, "I'm home."

"In here!" Elizabeth called back from the vicinity of the living room. When Julie got there, she saw Elizabeth in her chair, and Luc sitting close by on the sofa. He was dressed casually in jeans and a polo shirt, and next to him on the cushion was a brown cardboard box. It was around eighteen square inches and from what she could see, unmarked. The top wasn't sealed, either. Nor did it look like it ever had been. It would have been pretty easy for anyone to peek inside.

"You're home early," she said.

"I am," he agreed, wearing what she could only describe as a sly smile. "I had a few things to take care of this afternoon."

There was a weird vibe in the room. A feeling of expectation. She looked from him to his mother. "Is everything okay?"

"Fine," he said. So why were they looking at her that way? As if something was about to happen.

"So is that it?" she asked, nodding to the box.

"That's it," Elizabeth said. "Open it."

Julie eyed it warily. Was something going to explode or jump out at her? Was this some sort of gag gift? Because it sure didn't look as if had been shipped there.

"Come on," Luc said, sliding the box closer to himself to give her room to sit. If it were something volatile he probably wouldn't do that. Right? Of course, if he were the type of man to give his wife a box of some volatile substance, she wouldn't be married to him.

She sat gingerly on the edge of the cushion. He slid

the box to her, and feeling a little nervous still, she reached for the top. She tested the weight of it, and it was definitely too light to be a fruit basket. Bracing herself, she lifted the flaps, sure she was in for a shock. And boy, did she get one when she looked inside. Curled up in the bottom of the box, on a hospital baby blanket, lay a sleeping ball of fluffy, snow-white fur with an itty-bitty pink nose and black tipped ears.

"Oh my gosh, it's a kitten!" she said, but by their smiles, it was clear that they both knew exactly what was inside the box. "Did you do this?" she asked Luc.

"My mom and I went to the shelter today."

"But...you said—"

"Did you honestly think I wouldn't let you have a cat?" he asked.

Actually, she had. He'd said no, and in her world, no meant no. "But I thought you didn't like cats."

"I said I didn't dislike them. Would I rather have a dog, yes, but as you said, we don't have the time."

"It would probably be best if I watch him for you while you both work," Elizabeth said. "Until he gets bigger and knows his way around the house."

"He?" Julie said, lifting him gently from the box. He was so small and fragile looking. As she cuddled him in her palms, he blinked his little eyes open and looked right at her, making a soft mewling sound, as if he was saying hello.

"He is a very special kitten," Luc said. "One that no one else wanted."

Who in their right mind wouldn't want this adorable little ball of fluff? "Is there something wrong with him? Is he sick?"

"He's blind," Luc said. He moved the box out of the

way so he could scoot closer. "I guess it's common in white cats. There were a dozen or so other kittens available, but Megan said the little ones go fast. I knew you would want an animal who really needed a good home. We looked at the older cats first, then Megan told me about this little guy. The second I saw him I knew he was perfect."

"He is perfect," Julie said, rubbing her cheek against the softness of his fur, and he started to purr. A surprisingly loud purr to be coming out of something so small. "He's just so tiny and sweet. I love him."

"There's the added bonus of him not jumping up on things," Luc said, rubbing the kitten under the chin with his index finger. "Since he wouldn't know where to jump."

"He really can't see anything?"

"Megan said he won't respond to visual stimulation. Otherwise he's perfectly healthy. He'll need shots eventually, but that's about it."

"How old is he?"

"Eight weeks."

He was wide-awake now and fussing to get free, so she set him down on her lap, but he didn't stay there long. He sniffed around the sofa cushions for a few seconds, then leaned way over the edge, and before she could grab him, toppled over and landed on his back on the rug.

"Oh no!" she said, reaching for him, thinking he might be hurt, but he got up on his feet, shook it off and started sniffing around the coffee table leg. "Resilient little thing, isn't he?"

"What will you name him?" Elizabeth asked.

"I'm not sure. I'd like to get to know him a little better before I give him a name."

The nurse came in the room looking for Elizabeth. "I'm sorry to interrupt, but it's time for your PT."

"Already?" Elizabeth said with a sigh. To keep the circulation moving in her legs she had a daily physical therapy session. "It can wait a while."

Luc shot her a look. *"Mother."*

"Fine, fine, I'll go," she mumbled, wheeling her chair from the room.

"So you like him?" Luc asked, even though it was pretty darned obvious.

"He's adorable."

"His litter pan and food are in the utility room. I wasn't sure where you would want to keep them."

"In my room for now, I guess." She scooped the kitten up before he could get far, but he didn't want to be held and struggled to get free. She set him back on the floor and watched him sniff around. "This is the sweetest thing anyone has ever done for me."

"And I know just how you can thank me," he said his lips tipping up in a sly grin. She knew that look, and what it meant. And she was more than happy to oblige.

She leaned in and kissed him, and when he slid his hand behind her neck and under the root of her ponytail, cradling her head in his palm, she was toast. Luc knew just what to do to get her engine revving, and right now, her gas pedal was to the floor.

"Maybe we should take this upstairs," she said. "If you have time."

"I could be persuaded to take the rest of the day off. How about you?"

"I don't know, my boss is kind of a hard-ass."

Luc grinned. "I think he could make an exception just this— Ow!"

He winced in pain, and she looked down to see her sweet little kitten climbing his leg, nails out.

"Hey, you," she said, carefully extracting him from Luc's slacks, hoping that he hadn't ruined them. "Climbing up pant legs, not cool."

"Beth warned me that he can be very mischievous," Luc said. "She said that we have to keep a close eye on him until he's familiar with the layout of the house."

Considering how big the house was, that could take a while, and she could hardly imagine anything so small and sweet being mischievous. How much damage could one tiny kitten do?

It didn't take long to find out.

Thirteen

They took the kitten along up to Luc's bedroom, putting him on his blanket in his box on the floor by the bed. Luc had never been a cat person. As a kid he pretty much ignored the ones they had on the ranch. But he couldn't deny that this little guy was kinda cute.

When he first walked into the shelter he'd been overwhelmed by the volume of animals in need of homes, and picking one seemed a daunting task. He'd wandered the facility looking in cages. His mother had been no help at all. Had it been up to her they would have left the place with a couple dozen felines. It had been Megan who swayed him in the right direction.

He had been looking at the older cats, the ones who had been in the shelter the longest, when Megan suggested a kitten.

"I would think that kittens would be pretty easy to place," he'd said. "Julie would choose a cat no one else wants."

"I have just the thing," Megan had said, steering him to a cage in the kitten section. "Someone brought in a litter last week, and this little guy is the only one left."

The second he saw the little white fur ball he was

sure Julie would love him, and when Megan told him the kitten was blind, he knew it was fate.

Julie was so independent and capable, not to mention practical, it wasn't often that she let him do anything really nice for her. So when she asked him about getting a cat he lunged at the opportunity. Nothing meant more to him than making her happy.

And she seemed happy now. But they barely had a chance to get started in bed before the kitten climbed up the side to join them.

"Down you go," Luc said, scooping him up and setting him back in his box. "This is your bed."

They had just taken off their socks when he was up there with them again, so back in the box he went. And back up he climbed a few seconds later.

"This is not working," Luc said, dropping the kitten into his box again, this time not quite so gently. And back up he came like a spring, clawing his way up the comforter. "Do we have any packing tape?"

Julie shot him a look. "If you're thinking we're going to tape his box closed, think again."

Okay, bad idea. "We could lock him in the bathroom."

He got another look.

"Have you got a better idea?" Luc asked, putting the kitten on the floor this time. "Shoo. Go play."

When he didn't immediately spring back up, they both sat there waiting, watching the edge of the bed for his reappearance.

A minute or so passed and no kitty. "You think he got the hint?" Luc said.

"Seems that way," Julie said, then she looked behind them and started to laugh. "I take that back."

Luc turned to see that the kitten had come up the opposite side of the mattress this time and was sitting behind them. He yawned and licked his paws, content as could be.

Luc sighed and shook his head. "Ideas?"

"Let's wait a minute and see what he does. He's got to be tired from all the climbing."

They sat and watched while the kitten sniffed around the bed for several minutes, nearly toppling over the edge a few times. He made his way to the head of the bed, up onto Luc's pillow, where he curled up in a ball and promptly fell asleep.

"So now what?" Luc asked.

"It's a king-size mattress," Julie said. "There's room for everyone."

It was a little strange at first, making love with an audience, even if that audience was asleep, but eventually Luc forgot he was even there. They stayed on their side and the kitten stayed on his, while Julie "thanked" Luc.

Afterward, as they lay there together, Julie cuddled up against him, the kitten woke up, toddled over and joined them. He flopped down on his back, right on Luc's chest.

"This is the best gift anyone has ever given me," Julie said. She tickled the kitten's belly and he attacked her hand.

They played with the kitten for a while, and then Julie grabbed her phone from the bedside table to check the time.

"Are you getting hungry?" she asked Luc.

He eyed her warily. "When I said cats are delicious, I was kidding."

She laughed and gave him a playful nudge. "It's almost dinnertime. And it's Friday. We should do something."

"We still haven't had that romantic dinner out that I promised you. We could get dressed up and go somewhere nice, just the two of us."

"Or we could see if your mom would like to join us. We could go to the diner. And if she's feeling up to it afterward maybe we could take her to see a movie."

"Are you sure that's what you want?" he asked her.

"She's been stuck at home for almost two weeks now, and she's definitely well enough to leave the house. I would feel guilty going out and leaving her home alone."

Luc grinned and shook his head.

"Why are you looking at me like that?" she asked him.

"You're an extraordinary woman, Julie."

She blinked. "I am?"

He nodded.

"Why?"

"I offer to take you out to an expensive, candlelit dinner, and you would rather spend the evening with my mother."

"She's my friend. I want her to be happy. You know that it's only a matter of time before she gets another infection."

"I know," he said, his heart aching at the thought of losing her. "She's getting more and more fragile."

"So let's have fun with her while we still can."

"What are we going to do with him?" Luc nodded toward the kitten, who had curled up between them on the comforter and was sound asleep again.

"He can stay in here," she said. "As long as he has food and water and a litter pan he should be fine. And we keep the door closed. How much trouble could one tiny kitten get into?"

They had a nice dinner with Luc's mother, then took her to the theater to see the latest chick flick. Julie knew for a fact that Luc would have picked an action film any day of the week. Frankly, so would Julie, but his mother wanted to see a romantic comedy. It was after eleven when they finally got home.

"I'll help the nurse get her into bed," Luc told Julie. "You should probably go up and check on the fur ball."

She headed upstairs, opened the door to Luc's bedroom and switched on the light. "Here kitty, kitty. Mummy's home."

He wasn't on the bed sleeping, where she would have expected him to be, but then what did she know about having a cat? The most she'd ever had petwise was a caterpillar in a glass jar, until her father saw it there and flushed it down the toilet.

"Kitty, kitty," she called, checking all around the bedroom and the bathroom. "Come to Mummy."

She waited, but when he didn't come trotting out to greet her she frowned. "Where are you, you silly kitten?"

There was no sign of him so she got on all fours to look under the bed. From behind her she heard, "I don't know what you're doing, but I like the view."

She turned to see Luc standing behind her. "I can't find the kitten."

"He's got to be here somewhere," he said. "Did you try the closet?"

"Not yet."

Luc headed that way while Julie crawled over to check under the chest of drawers.

"Um, Julie? I found him."

"Oh thank goodness." She jumped up and darted to his closet door to join Luc. She looked inside and gasped. It was as if a hurricane had torn through. A dozen or so of Luc's clean, pressed dress shirts lay in piles all over the floor like an Egyptian cotton rainbow, while several others hung half on and half off the hanger. From the cuff of one, dangling a good two feet from the floor, hung the kitten, his claw snagged.

"Oh my gosh!" Julie dashed to his rescue, carefully unsnagging his nails and cuddling him to her chest. "You poor baby. How long were you hanging there?"

Luc just looked around, shaking his head. "What was that you asked? 'How much trouble could one tiny kitten get into?'" He spread his arms wide. "Here's your answer."

"He has been busy, hasn't he? On the bright side he'll probably sleep well tonight."

"So I guess I should have listened to Megan when she said that he's mischievous."

"I'm sorry. I hope he didn't ruin them."

"You'll make it up to me," Luc said, and she didn't have to ask what he meant. She helped him clean up the kitten's mess, then spent the next hour or so making it up to him, and what a hardship that turned out to be.

After making love again, he asked her to stay with him all night. She said no, he said please. She couldn't recall him using the word *please* any of the previous times he'd asked her and hearing the word spoken so earnestly, seeing the earnest look in his eyes…well, she just couldn't tell him no.

"Just this once," she said, settling back against the pillows. "But I'm used to sleeping alone, so I'll probably toss and turn most of the night. I apologize in advance if I keep you awake."

"It's a king-size bed, you won't even know I'm over here," he said, but nothing could be further from the truth. He never even made it onto his own side. He curled up behind her, his arm draped across her hip. And as if that wasn't crowded enough, the kitten, who was clearly exhausted after his adventure, curled up on the pillow above her head. She was annoyed, and utterly content at the same time. She closed her eyes, mentally preparing herself for a long restless night, and when she opened them again, it was morning. Not only had she not had a lousy night's sleep, she felt well rested and full of energy.

Luc was gone, but he'd left a note on the pillow. "Volunteering at the clinic until noon. How about lunch in the hospital cafeteria at 1:00?"

She looked at the clock, stunned to find that it was almost 10:30 a.m. She grabbed her phone off the bedside table and typed up a quick text.

Lunch sounds great, see you at 1:00.

He responded a few seconds later with a happy face icon.

She would have plenty of time to shower and make a trip to the pet supply store.

Speaking of pets…

She reached up over her head to pet the kitten only

to realize that he was gone. *Here we go again*, she thought. She pushed herself up out of bed and threw on the T-shirt and panties she'd been wearing the night before. She looked in the obvious places first. Under the bed, in the closet by his food dish, in the bathroom by his litter. But she couldn't find him anywhere. Had he snuck out when Luc left?

She checked everywhere, every corner and nook. She even checked under the covers, in case he'd been sleeping beside her when she flipped the blanket off.

Nothing. It was as if he'd vanished.

Where the hell could he have gone? she wondered, a feeling of panic building in her chest. How in the world would she find him? In a house this huge it could take days.

She was checking behind the curtains one last time, and was about to initiate a whole house search, when she heard a loud and very unhappy-sounding meow. But it seemed to be coming from above her head. She looked up to find the kitten clinging to the curtain valance on top of the rod, and now that she took a better look at the curtain panel, she could see teeny tiny holes where his claws had sunk in. The little imp had climbed all the way up, and apparently couldn't find his way back down. "You are mischievous," she said, getting up on her tiptoes to scoop him up. "Let's not go up here again."

She put the kitten in his box, grabbed the rest of her things and walked across the hall to her own room.

She set the box on the bed. "You stay here while I take a shower."

She didn't really expect him to obey, so it was no surprise when he escaped the box, tumbled down from the mattress onto the floor, got back on his feet and followed her into the bathroom where he started digging around in his litter. He may have been blind, but he had no trouble getting around.

Figuring he would be safe in there with her, she shut the bathroom door, locking him in. She undressed, turned on the water and stepped into the shower, leaving the door open an inch, so she could hear him if he got into trouble again. Though she wasn't sure what kind of trouble he could get into. There was really nothing for him to climb. The room was all tile and porcelain, which he couldn't get his claws into.

She was lathering her hair when she saw the shower door move, and looked down to see the kitten poking his head in. "You don't want to come in here," she said, but that was exactly what he wanted. He took a tentative step inside, and when the outer edge of the spray hit his fur, he stopped, looking confused. She thought for sure that he would turn tail and run; instead, he walked right under the spray, rubbing against her ankle with his soaked white fur, crossed to the opposite side, then sat down and started to clean himself.

What the heck? A cat who liked water?

She picked him up and set him on the bath mat, but before she could get the door closed, he was back in the shower. After one more failed attempt she managed to get him out of the shower and the door closed.

She finished, toweled them both off—which he didn't seem to appreciate much—then blow-dried her hair and got dressed. By the time she was finished, the cat had pulled another vanishing act. It took another few minutes of searching and this time she found him playing inside a canvas bag on her closet floor.

She carried him down to the kitchen where Elizabeth was sitting having her morning coffee and reading the newspaper. "Oh, there's the little guy!" she said, and Julie set the still-damp ball of fur in her lap.

"What happened to him?" Elizabeth asked, frowning up at Julie. "He's all wet."

"He took a shower with me."

Elizabeth's brows rose in disbelief. "Cat's don't like water."

"Someone forgot to tell him that."

Looking perplexed, she said, "That's odd."

Julie shrugged. "Maybe it has something to do with him being blind. Or maybe he's just weird."

"How was his first night home?"

Julie grappled for the right word. "It was…eventful."

She told Elizabeth about Luc's shirts, the curtain incident and finding him in her closet.

"He was probably bored," Elizabeth said. "Kittens need lots of stimulation."

"I'm going this morning to buy him some toys."

Looking excited, Elizabeth asked, "Would you like me to watch him for you while you're gone?"

"You don't mind?"

"Of course not. Take all the time you need."

"I do have several errands I'd like to run." He looked pretty harmless sitting there in Elizabeth's lap licking the water from his fur, but Julie knew what a little terror he could be. "But are you sure? He's a handful."

"I've had lots of cats. I'm sure I can handle it."

Julie hoped so. Shy of locking him in her room alone for the day, which seemed cruel, she really had no other choice. At least until he was bigger.

"Can we talk for a minute?" she asked Elizabeth, taking a seat at the kitchen table.

"Of course, honey. You can talk to me about anything, you know that."

She did, but this was different. "I need a favor. And it's a big one."

"As long as it doesn't involve me getting up and dancing," she joked. "Name it."

"Luc mentioned that you'll be at the hospital Monday for an iron infusion."

"That's right."

"Would you come to Amelia's son's room while you're there. Just for a few minutes."

She sighed. "Julie, I know you and she have become friends, and against my better judgment I've kept my opinions to myself, but—"

"I know you two didn't get along, and I know how Luc feels about her, but she really has changed. She knows she treated you badly and she'd only like the chance to apologize. She's been carrying around a lot of guilt—"

"Which was her own doing," Elizabeth said sharply.

"She doesn't deny that."

"Luc may be a grown man, but he'll always be my baby, and she hurt him deeply."

"She wants to make amends."

"Did she ask you to ask me?"

"No. But she's my friend and I want to help her. She asked Luc if she could visit you but he wouldn't allow it."

Up went Elizabeth's hackles, and in a cutting tone she said, "Who I do and don't see is not his choice."

Julie knew Elizabeth would feel that way, which is

why she'd brought it up. If she was going to persuade Luc to talk to Amelia, she would need Elizabeth on her team. Was it a little underhanded and sneaky? Maybe so, but Julie believed deep in her heart that Luc needed to settle things with Amelia, and this was the only way she could see to make that happen.

"If I didn't know better, I might think that you were trying to push the two of them together," Elizabeth said.

"If they're meant to be together, nothing I do or don't do will change that."

"That's very convenient for you."

Julie blinked. "What is that supposed to mean?"

"It's the perfect excuse to keep him at arm's length."

"It's not that," Julie said, though Elizabeth's words hit a little too close to home. "Whether he falls in love with Amelia, or some other woman, I just want him to be happy."

"Have you considered the possibility that Luc might be in love with *you*?"

She considered and dismissed it. But not to protect herself as Elizabeth implied. Julie was a realist. She knew that sex did not always equal love. Not the forever kind.

"I really feel that he needs this to move forward," Julie told the older woman. "With me or anyone else."

Elizabeth sighed. "I suppose you're right."

"So...you'll talk to her?" Julie said.

"I'll think about it," Elizabeth said. "But no promises."

That was all Julie could ask. "Thank you."

"I wouldn't do this for just anybody."

"I know."

"Even though you and Luc are married in name only, I think of you as my daughter."

"And I consider you one of my closest friends." Elizabeth smiled.

"Well, I should get going. I'd like to stop by the hospital and check on Amelia. Her son's surgery is Tuesday and she's getting nervous."

"You really do like her," Elizabeth said, looking perplexed. "And you trust her?"

"I do. She just wants to make amends."

The older woman nodded slowly and said, "I'll keep that in mind."

Fourteen

Having never had an animal before, there had never been a need to patronize a pet supply store. The sheer volume of available products was mind-boggling. Julie stood in the cat food aisle for a good forty-five minutes reading labels and looking up online reviews on her phone. The litter aisle was a nightmare as well, and the toy aisle even worse. There were a bazillion choices of every shape and size. How was she supposed to know what a blind kitten would like to play with? Even something as simple as picking out a collar took forever.

She made her selections to the best of her ability, nearly having a stroke when the cashier rang it all up and gave her the total. No wonder the shelter was always desperate for donations. Everything was so expensive.

With the kitten taken care of, Julie drove to the hospital. She had a few spare minutes, so when she got there, she made a quick detour to Tommy's room. Amelia sat in a chair next to her son's bed reading to him. She smiled brightly when she saw Julie, but the dark smudges under her eyes said it had probably been a long night.

She patted her son's arm. "Wake up baby, look who's come to visit."

With effort, Tommy opened his eyes, flashed her a sleepy smile and said, "Hi, Julie," so softly she had to strain to hear him.

"How are you feeling today," she asked him, but he had already fallen back to sleep.

"They had to up his pain meds again," Amelia said, concern darkening her features as she gazed down at her son. "Thank God the surgery is Tuesday. I never thought I would hear myself say this, but I'm actually a little homesick."

"Understandable considering the way people have been treating you."

"It's lonely. Tommy sleeps most of the time, and no one else around here talks to me unless they have to."

Not only did she look exhausted, but she'd lost weight, meaning she probably wasn't eating properly. The last time they had lunch she'd only picked at her food. "Have you been sleeping?"

"As much as I can. The nurses come in at all hours of the night to check on Tommy and I'm a light sleeper, so they inevitably wake me up. I'm only able to catch an hour or two here and there. I could swear that sometimes they do it just to mess with me."

"You need some uninterrupted sleep," Julie told her. "In a *real* bed."

"I can't leave the hospital. I don't want Tommy to wake up alone."

"You're no good to Tommy if you don't take care of yourself."

Her expression said that she knew Julie was right.

"Are you working today?" Amelia asked her.

"Nope, I'm meeting Luc for lunch."

"Speak of the devil," Amelia said, looking past her to the door. Julie turned to find Luc entering the room.

"Am I late?" she asked with a smile, but he didn't smile back. Now what?

"I have the results of the blood test from this morning," he told Amelia in his "doctor" tone, and the grim look he wore made Julie's heart drop.

Amelia must have sensed that something was amiss, that it wasn't just Luc being his usual bitter self, because her face paled a shade and she asked, "Is something wrong?"

"Tommy's white count is up," he said.

"What does that mean?"

"It could mean that he has an infection somewhere."

"Which means what exactly?" Amelia asked him, and Julie could see that she was struggling to hold it together, to be strong for her son.

There was genuine compassion in Luc's tone when he said, "If it remains elevated we may have to postpone the surgery."

The devastation on Amelia's face made Julie's heart hurt for her. "How long?" she asked.

"It's hard to say until we know what we're dealing with. Days, a week. Maybe longer."

Amelia looked so pale and distraught Julie worried she might lose consciousness. Julie wasn't a hugger by nature, but she felt compelled to do something to ease her pain, and Amelia readily accepted her embrace.

"I'm so sorry," Julie said. "I know this is frustrating, but I'm sure he'll be better in no time."

Amelia clung to her for several seconds, then let go and blinked away the tears that hovered just inside her eyelids. She took a deep breath, pulled herself up by her bootstraps, lifted her chin and asked Luc, "What's our next move?"

"I'm going to start him on a round of broad spectrum antibiotics, and do more tests. See if we can pinpoint the problem."

"You think that will take care of it?"

He hesitated, then said, "I'm cautiously optimistic. But if you would like to get a second opinion—"

"No," she said firmly, shaking her head. "If I didn't trust your judgment we wouldn't be here. Do what you think is best."

A look passed between Luc and Amelia, and they both smiled. Was he finally coming around?

Julie felt as if a weight had been lifted from her shoulders. For a few seconds anyway, before she felt a sudden and intense twinge of something unpleasant.

It was envy, she realized. She *wanted* the two of them to bury the hatchet, so why would she feel jealous?

Jules, you're being ridiculous.

She shoved the feeling deep down where it belonged.

"I'll stop by later this afternoon to check on Tommy," Luc told Amelia, and she flashed him a grateful, if not exhausted smile.

Amelia needed sleep. Badly.

"Can I see you alone for a minute?" Julie asked Luc, nodding toward the door, and he followed her into the hall. "Let's go down by the nurses' station."

When they were far enough away that Amelia wouldn't hear them, Julie turned to him. "In light of what just happened in there, I have a favor to ask."

He looked confused. "Something happened?"

"You and Amelia had a moment."

"We did? When?"

"Just a minute ago. You smiled at each other."

"I smile at a lot of people."

Now he was just being difficult. "There was a connection. Don't deny it."

He shrugged and said, "If you say so."

Did he seriously not see it?

"You mentioned a favor," he said, wiggling his brows at her. "Your office or mine?"

She couldn't help but laugh. "Not that kind of favor. I was hoping you could maybe say something to the nurses about the way they've been treating Amelia. I would, but I feel as if it's not my place to tell them how to do their jobs. But if you say something—"

"I'll talk to everyone," he said.

One less thing to worry about. "Thank you."

"We should get down to the cafeteria," Luc said.

"About lunch…" She looked from her watch to Tommy's room.

"Go," he said with a grin. "Amelia needs you. We'll have lunch another day."

"You're sure? Thanks for understanding."

He reached up and touched her cheek. "I hope Amelia realizes how lucky she is to have you as a friend."

Julie knew that she did. "How late are you working?"

Luc looked at his watch. "I should be home for dinner."

She pushed up on her toes to kiss him goodbye, aiming for his cheek, but Luc had other ideas. He cupped the back of her head and pulled her close, slanting his mouth over hers, and then kissed her in clear view of everyone at the nurses' station. And not a hospital hallway sort of kiss. This was a bona fide, just-wait-until-I get-you-home kiss.

Public displays of affection usually made her uncomfortable, but she could feel herself melting against him as he drew her closer. Until someone at the nurses' station wolf-whistled.

She pulled away and grinned up at him, her cheeks warm and her blood pumping. "That was nice. A little inappropriate considering where we are, but still nice."

"You're my wife. I can kiss you however and wherever I want."

"Is that how it works?"

"Damn straight." His eyes locked on hers, and the look he gave her was so supercharged with desire her heart skipped a beat. He was playing a role, that's all. They both were. But something in his eyes said he may have forgotten that.

"But I'm not really your wife," she reminded him.

He took her hand, grazing his thumb over her wedding band. "As long as this ring is on your finger, you're my wife. In every sense of the word."

He looked so serious, as if he really meant it, which was as confusing as it was terrifying. And yes, maybe a little exciting, too. Not to mention totally unrealistic. "Aren't we a little far into the game to be changing the rules."

"Maybe I don't like the rules anymore."

Her heart jerked violently, and then raced ahead double time. What the heck was he trying to say? Did this have something to do with her decision to sleep in his bed last night? Was she unknowingly leading him on? That had certainly never been her intention.

She took a step back and he let go of her hand. "I'd better go."

"Eventually we'll have to talk about this."

No they wouldn't, because they had already talked about it. It was a done deal. His friendship meant too much to her to risk losing over a misguided sexual relationship. Even if it was really fantastic sex. "I'll see you later."

Looking resigned, he said, "See you later."

She could feel his eyes boring into her back as she walked to Amelia's room, but she was too chicken to turn around and face him. She was terrified of what she might see. Maybe it would be wise to put a little distance between them. Perhaps Luc was becoming a little too comfortable with the physical aspect of their relationship.

Amelia stood next to her son's window, gazing blindly out the window, looking distraught.

"Everything will be okay," Julie said.

Amelia turned to her. "Deep down, I know that."

Amelia would feel so much better if she could get some uninterrupted sleep, and was able to take a long hot shower. Or better yet, soak in a hot bath with essence of lavender and lots of bubbles. Which Julie just so happened to have at her condo…

Before she could talk herself out of it, Julie pulled her key ring out and unhooked the key for her condo. She crossed the room and handed it to a confused Amelia.

"What is this for?" she asked Julie.

"My condo. I want you to use it as a home base while you're here in Royal."

She looked warily at her sleeping son. "You know

how I feel about leaving the hospital. What if Tommy wakes up…"

"He'll be fine. The nurses will take good care of him."

Amelia looked from her son to Julie, and back again. "I don't know…"

"Have you seen yourself in a mirror lately? You look terrible."

Amelia sighed, her shoulders sagging. "And I feel terrible. But he needs me here."

"Does he need you, or is it that *you* need *him*?"

Amelia frowned.

"Do you think Tommy doesn't notice how you look? He needs you to be strong for him. You can't do that if you're about to collapse."

Julie's words clearly hit home. "I guess I could sneak out for a little while."

Feeling relieved, Julie jotted down the address for Amelia, who typed it into the GPS on her smart phone.

"You know, you're going to be a great mom some-day," Amelia told her.

It was meant as a compliment, but it made Julie's heart hurt. She wouldn't be a good mother, because she would never have children. If she couldn't set aside her fears and let her guard down for Luc, her best friend, there was little hope left of her ever finding Mr. Right.

Fifteen

Late that afternoon, when Luc pulled into the garage, Julie's car was gone. He felt both disappointed and relieved at the same time. They needed to talk, to figure this marriage out. Despite his best efforts to adhere to their "plan," to think with his head, his heart seemed to be calling the shots now. He wanted Julie, in every way a man could want a woman. But her unwillingness to even consider discussing it didn't bode well for him. And she was so insistent that he and Amelia settle their past, he couldn't help but feel that she was hoping that he and Amelia would fall back in love. That would certainly save Julie the task of confronting her feelings. The difficult ones, that she kept buried deep. Her heart was like a fortress, and he wasn't quite sure how he would tear the walls down.

Or if that was even possible.

Luc let himself into the house, and found his mother in the family room, by the window overlooking the garden, reading a book. On her lap, curled in a ball, slept the kitten.

"Babysitting?" he asked her with a grin. He'd suspected she would enjoy the kitten as much as Julie did.

"Houdini," his mother said, and in answer to his confused look, added, "That's the kitten's name."

"Why Houdini?"

"He's an escape artist, and once he gets away, finding him is almost impossible."

"He's white, how could you miss him?"

"You'll see. And when you're searching for him, do yourself a favor and look up. That's where he prefers to be."

"Up where?"

"Anywhere he can reach. If he can get his nails into it, he starts climbing and doesn't stop until he reaches the top."

"Like what?"

"A bed, curtains, a pant leg. A *bare* leg—and you can bet that my nurse wasn't happy about that. It doesn't matter as long as it takes him vertical."

Luc frowned. "He's blind. That could be very dangerous."

"I tried to explain that to him, but you know cats," she said with an exaggerated shrug, "they never listen to reason."

He shot her a look.

She smiled. "On the bright side he has a very hard head."

"And how do you know that?"

"Every now and then he gets overexcited, takes off running and slams headfirst into something. Usually a wall or a piece of furniture. I won't lie, it's hard not to laugh, but he just shakes it off and keeps going. Then, bam, he hits something else. He'll do that three or four times in one spot, until he learns the landscape. I think he's mapping out the house."

"With his head?"

His mother shrugged. "Whatever works, I guess."

Luc wondered if cats were capable of using that sort of logic. "I don't suppose you know where Julie is."

"She's sitting with Tommy while Amelia naps, so he won't wake up alone."

"Where is Amelia?"

"At Julie's condo. She insisted that Amelia go there and take a nap."

Julie's condo? Hadn't she given it up when she moved in with him? She'd never actually said she would, but he'd just assumed...

He sighed and shook his head. Wrong again.

"Dinner will be ready at seven," his mother told him, in a tone that said being late was unacceptable.

Which gave him just enough time for a couple of beers at the Texas Cattleman's Club.

He turned to leave, but she stopped him. "There's something I wanted to ask you."

"About what?"

"I'm having my blood transfusion tomorrow and Julie asked me to stop in and see Amelia while I'm there. She said Amelia wants to apologize to me."

"Will you let her?"

"That's what I'm not sure about. I feel as if forgiving her would mean being disloyal to you."

A week ago, he may have thought so, too. But this wasn't about him anymore. He was finally at peace with their past. Didn't Amelia deserve the same?

"You should talk to her," he said. "I didn't want to believe it either, but she really has changed."

His mother gasped softly. "Don't tell me you still have feelings for her."

The idea made him chuckle, because other than sympathy for her and her son, he didn't feel much of anything for her. "Not at all. And I wouldn't consider your speaking to her as disloyal. In fact, I think it would be good for both of you."

"She broke your heart."

"Only because I let her." And now it looked as if he might be in a similar situation with Julie. Would he chase her down, only to have her break his heart? He'd been patient these past weeks, but his patience was wearing very thin. Either she loved him or she didn't. He needed to know if they had a future together.

When he got to the club he took a seat at the bar, ordered a beer and settled in to watch the basketball game playing on the television. He'd had three beers when his phone rang. It was Julie. But he had no idea what to say to her.

He ignored the call, turned the ringer off on his phone and ordered a scotch

The bartender, who knew he normally didn't have more than a beer or two, regarded him with growing concern. "Everything okay?" he asked.

"I should think that's pretty obvious," Luc said, swirling the scotch in his glass. Then he drained it in one swallow, set the glass down a little too forcefully and tapped the bar for another.

"Not until you hand them over," the bartender said, holding out his hand.

Without argument Luc dug his keys out of his pocket and dropped them in his hand. He was no stranger to the end result of drinking and driving. He'd seen it far too many times to make the same mistake himself. If he had to he would walk home.

Everything was getting a bit fuzzy, so Luc wasn't sure how long he'd been sitting there or how many drinks he'd consumed when Drew sat down at the bar beside him.

"Hey," Drew said, gesturing to the bartender for a beer.

"Hey," Luc replied.

Drew took a long pull on his beer when it arrived, then set it down on the bar and asked Luc, "You want to talk about it?"

"About what?"

"Whichever sorrows you're drowning with that scotch."

Trying to drown, and failing miserably. In fact, Luc felt even worse than he had when he walked in the door.

"You gonna make me guess?" Drew asked.

"I'm in love with Julie." He'd never said that out loud before, and hearing those words come out of his own mouth was a little surreal. So he said it again. "I am in love with Julie."

"Are you trying to convince me or yourself?"

He laughed bitterly. "Drew, I would give anything to go back to way things were before, when I didn't know what I was missing. When being her best friend was enough. But being with her has changed me, and now I can't change back."

"What makes you think you have to?"

"She doesn't love me."

"I don't believe that for a second."

"Okay, she isn't *in love* with me."

"Have you told her that you're in love with her?"

"She won't give me the chance. I tried to talk to her about it today and she refused to listen. She wants things to stay just the way they are now. I'm worried that if I push her too hard, it will only drive her away." He used to believe that he could think his way out of any situation but this one had him stumped.

"So what are you going to do?"

"If I knew that, I wouldn't be sitting here. Maybe I shouldn't do anything yet. Maybe I should give her more time. Just keep doing what we've been doing. Everything was perfect until I brought it up today."

"It seems to me that if things were perfect, you wouldn't have had to bring it up."

He'd be damned if Drew wasn't spot on. As close as Luc and Julie were, emotionally and physically, he wanted more. Being Julie's friend just wasn't enough now. But was he willing to risk their friendship?

Maybe he didn't have a choice.

Looking thoughtful, Drew said, "Maybe what you need to do is shake her tree a little, see what falls out."

"I'm not sure what you mean."

"Nudge her out of her comfort zone. See what she does."

"And how would I do that?"

He shrugged. "She's your wife. You know her better than anyone. You'll think of something."

Luc thought he knew her. Now he wasn't so sure. Maybe all this time he'd only been letting her see what she wanted him to see.

Maybe deep down he didn't know her at all.

Sixteen

Sunday was supposed to be Julie and Luc's special day, but he spent the majority of it in bed nursing a hangover. They had planned to have breakfast at the diner, then check out the recently reopened organic produce store to buy fresh flowers. After their food settled they would take a long walk in the park. Then maybe they would head back home for some afternoon "exercise." Later he would take her to dinner, then it was back home to make love again.

Instead Luc spent Sunday in bed nursing a hangover. It didn't take a genius to know why Luc had gone out and gotten hammered.

She knew that sleeping in his bed had been a bad idea. She should have listened to her instincts. She'd given him the wrong impression, led him on. She'd made him fool himself into believing that he was in love with her. But men confused sex with love all of the time, right? Or was it the other way around?

Either way, she would be sleeping in her own bed from now on.

She and Luc barely said two words to each other all day. She slept in her own bed that night, though she didn't do all that much sleeping. Luc didn't even try to talk her into staying with him, and when she kissed him good-night his lips felt so cold. So passionless. She knew that in a day or two he would realize what a huge mistake he'd almost made thinking they should take their relationship to the next level. He would realize that they were better off as just friends, then everything would go back to normal. Everything would be okay.

The kind of baggage Julie carried around wasn't so easily shed. And the idea of opening those bags and rooting through the traumatic events of her childhood made her feel sick to her stomach.

Monday dragged by, and every time Julie tried to see or call Luc he was too busy to be disturbed. He was still upset. She got that, but he was going to have to let it go at some point, so they could get back to being best friends. One day of the silent treatment had taken its toll. She missed him. She just wanted things to go back to the way they used to be. Friends with benefits. Hell, if it meant restoring their friendship to its previous, uncomplicated manifestation, she would even be willing to end their physical relationship. Though that would seriously suck.

Tonight, she decided. After dinner she would take him aside and offer to have that talk he wanted. Now that he'd had a few days to think it over, she was positive he would agree that it was best for both of them if they just kept going the way they had been.

The only bright spot of the day was when she stopped in Tommy's room to find Amelia next to her sleeping son's bed, tears in her eyes.

Julie's heart sank. Was his infection worse? Would they be postponing the surgery? "What happened?"

Amelia turned to her and smiled. "His white count is back to normal. They're going ahead with the surgery tomorrow morning at seven a.m.!"

Julie was thrilled for Amelia and Tommy, but her happiness deflated like a balloon when she realized what that meant for her and Luc. With such a delicate surgery on his schedule, the last thing Luc needed was to be distracted by their marital issues. That conversation they were supposed to have would have to wait.

The day of Tommy's surgery, Julie left Houdini in Elizabeth's capable hands and drove to the hospital early, intending to spend her morning waiting with Amelia in her son's room.

She'd heard Luc getting ready for work, but stayed in her room until after he left. She didn't want to risk a confrontation on this very important morning. Besides, after having two whole days to think about it, he would come around. She knew he would. He just needed time to realize the mistake he'd made letting his heart overrule his head. Then they could go back to being best friends.

Julie stopped in the cafeteria for coffee and doughnuts on the way up, and by the time she got to Tommy's room they had already wheeled him out for surgery. Amelia was sitting cross-legged on her air mattress, looking surprisingly well-rested and calm.

Julie handed her one of the coffees and offered her a doughnut. "I figured you could use this. One cream, two sugars, right?"

"You're a goddess," Amelia said, taking them from her. "How are things going?"

Julie sat in the visitors chair by the window. "Good."

"Luc came in to see me a little while ago," Amelia told her, and at the mere mention of his name Julie's heart dropped. It had been doing that a lot—pretty much every time she thought of him or heard someone say his name. "He explained what will happen during the surgery, and what to expect when Tommy is out of recovery," Amelia was saying, and Julie struggled to stay focused, but all she could think about was her looming conversation with Luc. "I'm still nervous of course, but I know that Tommy is in good hands. I'm more concerned about the pain he'll be in afterward, and the physical therapy he'll go through."

Speaking of being nervous…

She and Luc had barely talked since Saturday. What if he'd had enough? Would he back out on their deal and ask her for a divorce?

Of course he wouldn't. But it didn't hurt to prepare herself for the worst. Everyone should have a backup plan.

How could things go from blissful perfection to so unbearably confusing so damned fast?

Julie left briefly to get them lunch from the cafeteria, and when she came back, Amelia was beaming.

"You just missed Luc."

Down her heart went into her stomach again.

"How did it go?" she asked, even though Amelia's relief was explanation enough.

"The surgery was a success and Tommy is in Recovery and doing great."

"That's wonderful news," she said, hugging Amelia. With the surgery over and declared a success, it was time to talk to Luc.

After Tommy had been returned to his room and

settled in, Julie went by Luc's office, almost hoping he wouldn't be there. But he was. He sat at his desk, chair turned toward the window, his back to her, hands folded in his lap.

It took all of her courage to step inside and close the door, and if Luc was aware of her presence, he didn't let on.

"Hey," she said, so nervous that her hands were trembling.

"Hey," he replied, not turning around. Not even moving.

"Can we talk?"

He swiveled around to face her. He wasn't smiling. He wasn't frowning, either. His features looked frozen in a nonexpression, his eyes blank. "About what?"

"This thing happening between us."

"You mean love?"

She cringed.

He shook his head, looking so disappointed. "You can't even stand to hear me say it, can you?"

"It's not that. I just…"

"Don't bother trying to explain. I know you well enough to recognize when you're running away."

She could understand why it might look that way. But she didn't want to *go* anywhere. "I'm not, I swear."

"You just don't trust me."

Why would he think that? After all they had been through. "That's not true."

"Isn't it? Then tell me why you kept your condo?"

She bit her lip, unsure of how to answer, to make him understand.

"Speechless?" he asked. "Always have a backup

plan. Isn't that what you've always told me? I just never imagined you would need a backup plan from me."

To deny it would be a lie. And it sounded horrible when he said it like that.

He leaned forward in his chair. "I know you better than you know yourself, Julie, and maybe that's the problem. I got too close and now you're running scared. You don't trust me."

"I do, it's just… Can't we just go back to the way things were before? When we were best friends?"

He sighed and sagged back into his chair. "We can't unring the bell. And I can't go on pretending that everything is okay. Because it's not."

She felt utterly sick inside. "I don't want to lose you. You mean more to me than anything."

"Just not enough to love me."

He was breaking her heart. "Luc—"

He held his hand up to stop her. "Sorry, that was a low blow. It was uncalled for. Like you said so many times before, you feel what you feel. Or don't feel. And the fact of the matter is that I love you and you don't feel the same about me."

"If we could just talk about this—"

"There's nothing to say. My mind is made up."

Her heart dropped so violently she could barely breathe. It wasn't supposed to be like this. He was supposed to agree with her. He'd always been on her side, but now, when she needed him most, he was just going to do what? Divorce her?

"W-what are you saying?" she asked, her voice so wobbly her words were barely understandable.

"We can't be together anymore," he told her. "Not like before."

"Are you saying you want a divorce?"

"I made you a promise, one I intend to keep. We can go on living like a married couple, but it would be best if we saw each other as little as possible. That will be much easier if you take the spare room downstairs."

She could hardly believe this was happening. He was ending their relationship, just like that? "So that's it? We're not even friends anymore?"

"That's it," he said, that damned blank look on his face. He could have the decency to show a little emotion, to feel angry or hurt. *Something.*

"What about work? Are you firing me?"

"No, but I think that after you establish your citizenship, you should consider looking for another position. It would be easier on everyone."

Then what reason did she even have to stay in Royal? She'd had such grand plans for making Royal her home, and suddenly now they were unraveling around her. Maybe she would be better off in South Africa after all. Maybe it would give her the chance to make a new start.

Julie was a nervous wreck for the next few days, praying she didn't run into Luc, then feeling so cold and empty inside when she didn't. Luc was really good at making himself scarce.

How was it that just a week ago everything was fine. She was happy, he was happy. Why did he have to go and ruin everything?

That wasn't fair and she knew it. This wasn't his fault. It was all her. But she missed him, in a way she had never missed anyone. She woke up lonely and went to bed feeling sick. When she was able to sleep, which wasn't often, he tormented her in her dreams.

He preoccupied her mind until she could barely think of anything else.

What the hell was wrong with her? Why was she such a mess?

She tried her best to keep her feelings to herself, to put on a good face, but she must not have been very convincing because Amelia confronted her Sunday afternoon at the hospital.

Tommy was working with his physical therapist and making impressive progress, so Julie and Amelia went down to the cafeteria for lunch.

"I am not going to miss this hospital food," Amelia said, glaring with contempt at her overcooked burger and soggy fries. Julie pushed her tuna salad around the plate but couldn't make herself take a bite.

"You've been unusually somber this last week," Amelia said.

So much for putting on a good face. She felt like an empty shell, as if losing Luc had sucked everything she loved about life right from her. The days seemed to have no point. Food lost its flavor and not even sleep was an escape from the harsh reality of how horribly she had screwed things up. Why hadn't she just told Luc that she loved him?

Because it would have been a lie, and no matter how much she missed him, he deserved someone who could love him with her whole heart. Someone who trusted him the way she never could.

"I thought I would give you time to work it through before offering an ear," Amelia said, "but we have to leave tomorrow. Could you at least assure me that you're okay?"

Julie put her fork down, feeling hollowed out and cold. A nonperson. "To be honest, I'm not sure if I am."

Amelia's brow knit with concern. "Do you want to talk about it?"

She hadn't intended to tell Amelia about her pretend marriage, but there was no way to explain the situation without telling her the whole truth. Besides, *not* telling her seemed dishonest somehow. "If I tell you a secret, do you promise not to say anything to anyone. And I mean no one."

"Of course."

She took a deep breath and said quietly, so no one else would hear, "Luc and I aren't really a couple. We only got married to keep me from getting deported."

Amelia sat back, looking stunned. "I have a hard time believing that."

"It's the truth."

"You two are Royal's 'it' couple. Everyone talks about you. You're the blueprint for the ideal marriage. The fairy tale come true."

She'd had no idea people viewed her and Luc's marriage that way. It looked as though they had successfully pulled the wool over everyone's eyes. Which only made her feel more depressed and vacant.

"So, if you're just friends, your relationship isn't physical?"

"Well, it was. But not anymore."

"Something happened?"

Unable to even look at her food, Julie pushed her tray away. "He told me that he's in love with me."

Amelia looked confused. "And that's a bad thing?"

"It's not part of the plan."

"The plan? Wow, sounds serious."

"We weren't supposed to fall in love, but he broke the rules and now our friendship is over."

Amelia sat a little straighter. "So, what are you saying—he's available?"

That was a strange question. "I suppose so."

"And you aren't in love with him."

She didn't like the direction this conversation was taking. "I tried. I just can't feel something that I don't."

"You're sure."

Julie blinked. "Of course I'm sure. If I were in love with someone, don't you think I would know it?"

Amelia was quiet for several seconds, mulling something over, her expression serious. "If I tell *you* a secret, do you promise not to tell anyone?"

"Of course."

She looked around and lowered her voice. "This is a little embarrassing, but when I made the decision to come here, I sort of had it in my mind that if Luc was still single, and there was still a spark…"

Julie's heart skipped a beat, then picked up triple time.

"When I thought he was a married man I backed off. But if your marriage is a fake, maybe I should re-think things."

"Maybe you should," Julie agreed.

"That wouldn't bother you? Not even a little? Because now that I know you're not really married, what reason would I have not to go after him myself? It wouldn't technically be cheating."

"No, but—"

"Hell, for all you know, he and I are already fooling around."

She could see what Amelia was doing, and it wasn't going to work. "But you're not."

"How do you know that when he's 'working late' he's not actually with me? I'm at the hospital 24/7 It would be really easy for us to fool around behind your back. Maybe use your condo for a quickie."

"But you wouldn't do that to a friend," Julie said.

"Are you sure? How well do you really know me? Maybe people hate me so much because they've seen Luc and I together. They know we're messing around."

Julie knew Amelia was only trying to make a point, but she felt unsettled nonetheless. "I'm sure someone would have mentioned it."

"You would think so, but all my friends—or should I say ex-friends—knew what Tom was doing and no one said a word to me about it. I didn't find out until after the divorce that he'd had sex with my maid of honor in the men's room at our wedding reception."

Julie gasped. "Did he really?"

"And what about the nurse I saw Luc take into his office the other day after his secretary left? What reason do you think he had to close and lock the door? Maybe you aren't the only friend he's sleeping with."

Julie felt a twinge of something unpleasant. "We are talking hypothetically."

"Are we? If I did see Luc with another woman would you want to know the truth? Would it even matter? If you're not really married—"

"Yes!" Julie said, much louder than she'd intended, causing the people around them to turn and look. She lowered her voice to a whisper. "Yes, I would want to know. And yes, it would matter."

"Why?"

She felt her coffee rising back up her throat.

"You're looking a little pale," Amelia said. "Something eating at you?"

"Is he really seeing someone else?"

"Why does it matter?"

She didn't know why. "It just does."

"Perhaps you're feeling a little jealous?" Amelia said.

Julie's first reaction was to deny it, but whoever the woman was, if there really was another woman, Julie wanted to claw her eyes out.

Oh God, she was jealous. And not just a little. The thought of Luc being intimate with someone besides her made her feel like barfing. "That doesn't mean I'm in love with him."

"Since you became friends, how many serious relationships have either of you been in?" Amelia asked her.

Julie frowned. "Well, I haven't been in any, and if Luc was seeing anyone seriously he never told me. But we're both very focused on our careers. We don't have time for serious relationships."

"Yet you manage to find time for each other."

She was right. Luc had always made time for her and she him. With the exception of the past few days, they'd barely gone twenty-four hours without talking to each other in six years. The day wouldn't feel complete if she didn't hear his voice at least once. And lately, with all the fantastic sex they'd been having...

She thought of him touching another woman the way he touched her, or even just holding another woman's hand, and felt sick inside. Before now she just hadn't let herself think about it. Now she could think of nothing else.

"Oh my God," she said, barely able to catch her breath as reality cracked her hard in the chops. "Oh my God."

She must have started turning blue, because Amelia gave her shoulder a nudge and said, "Breathe, Julie."

She sucked in a deep breath. "Oh my God. I'm in love with Luc."

Amelia was smiling. "Funny how it sneaks up on you."

How had this happened? *When* had it happened? Was she just so used to suppressing her feelings and guarding her heart that she hadn't *allowed* herself to see it?

Now that she had, it was almost overwhelming. She felt happy and excited and scared to death. But in a good way.

"I'm in love with Luc," she said again, the words rolling so naturally off her tongue it was as if they had been there all along, just waiting to be set free. "I. Am in love. With Luc."

In the midst of all those feelings she had another thought, one that sent the air hissing from her balloon of happiness.

"I know what you're thinking," Amelia said, her words startling Julie.

"What am I thinking?"

"You're afraid that it's too late, that you blew it. You're terrified that he's going to reject you."

She'd deny it if she could, but that would be a lie. And hadn't she been lying to herself for long enough? Wasn't it about time that she be honest not just to Luc, but to herself? She'd taken a lot of chances in her life, lived on the edge, but why was she so afraid to take a chance on Luc? And at this point, what did she have to lose?

"I think I need to talk to him," she told Amelia.

"I think you do, too."

Her hands began to shake and her heart went berserk in her chest. "What if it's too late?"

"Then, you can at least say that you tried."

Luc had the courage to put himself out there. To take a chance on her. And for his trouble, all he'd gotten was shot down. Now she needed to do the same for him.

"I have to go," she said. "I have to talk to him."

"Yes you do."

"What time are you leaving tomorrow?"

"As soon as Tommy is discharged. Probably around noon."

"I'll be back to say goodbye." They both stood and Julie hugged her hard. "Thank you so much."

"For what?"

"Making me see what an idiot I am."

"Well, we all act like idiots at one point or another."

If that was the case, Julie was queen of the idiots. She gave Amelia another squeeze, then set off to find Luc, hoping she wasn't too late.

"Are you going to mope around all day?"

Luc looked up from his computer screen, which he hadn't bothered to turn on yet, to find his mother in the doorway of his home office. "I'm not moping. I'm reflecting."

"She'll come around."

He hadn't said a word to his mother about the Julie situation, so either Julie had told her or she'd figured it out on her own.

He'd honestly believed that giving Julie an ultimatum, threatening their friendship, would make her see reason. Five days later he was still waiting.

Talk about a major fail.

Now he'd painted himself into a corner and he wasn't sure how to get back out. If this time apart had proved anything, it was how much he needed her in his life. Even if all she could be to him was a friend. He'd screwed up big-time and now he had to figure out a way to make it right. If that was even a viable option at this point. He had failed Julie in the worst possible way. She needed to know that he was there for her no matter what; instead he'd given up on her. He couldn't imagine a worse betrayal.

"I don't suppose you've seen Houdini."

Luc gestured behind him, to the window valance, where the kitten sat a good eight feet off the ground, happy as could be. Despite being blind, or maybe because of it, he was fearless. In the past few days he'd taken full run of the house, where there were virtually millions of places to disappear. But on the bright side, he was starting to learn his name, and would sometimes come when called. If all else failed, opening a can of cat food usually did the trick.

"Is there anything I can do?" his mother asked, and Luc shook his head. "I just hate to see you both so unhappy."

He swiveled his chair around and looked out the window. It was nearly April and the spring flowers were in full bloom. Yet he'd never felt more depressed and gloomy. "She made her choice."

She sighed. "You're making this so much more complicated than it has to be."

That was easy for her to say.

"She's right, you know."

At the sound of Julie's voice, he swiveled back around. She stood in the doorway behind his mother.

"Would you look at the time," his mother said, wheeling herself out the door. "I'm late for my physical therapy."

"Can we talk?" Julie asked him. She looked almost as bad as he felt. Her voice quivered and he could see that her hands were trembling. What now? Was she going to ask him for a divorce? Put an end to this charade before they caused any more damage?

"I guess that depends what you have to say."

"You can't even imagine how hard this is for me. Letting my guard down. Admitting how wrong I was. I screwed up. I was too scared to admit how I was really feeling. I couldn't even admit it to myself."

"And how are you *really* feeling?"

"I love you. I'm *in love* with you. This week apart has been awful."

He didn't want to appear too eager. After all, he did still have his pride to consider. But he was having a whole lot of trouble keeping his butt in the chair. He needed her in his arms. Needed to smell her hair and taste her lips. He just plain needed her.

Her voice shook when she said, "I know it's a lot to ask, and I probably don't deserve it, but if you could give me just one more chance."

"You're right, it is a lot to ask," he said. And if he didn't love her so much, he may have told her to take a hike. Luckily for them both, he just couldn't seem to live without her. "How do I know that you won't freak out and change your mind?"

"You don't know. And I have no clue how to convince you, if that's even possible. But I had to try."

He rose from his chair and though Julie looked terrified, she stood her ground. He walked over to her, until they were nearly toe to toe, and said, "We could start with a hug, and go from there."

He could see the instant she finally let go. The defenses dropped and she threw her arms around him, a quivering bundle. "I'm so sorry," she said.

He held her tight. This was right where she belonged. With him, forever. He wouldn't be letting her go again. "I'm the one who's sorry. My pride was bruised. I never should have given up on you."

She sighed, laying her cheek against his shirt. "You had to. It was the kick in the pants that I needed."

He cradled her face in his hands. There were tears in her eyes, but they were happy. "I love you, Julie."

"I love you, too," she said, "So much. I can't believe I almost blew it."

He grinned down at her, so relieved and happy it almost didn't seem real. "You didn't. I wouldn't have given up so easily."

"Amelia told me that everyone considers you and I the blueprint for the perfect marriage. The fairy tale come true."

"I guess they were right," he said.

"But we still have one thing left to do," she told him. "To make it official."

"What's that?"

She smiled and kissed him, with so much love in her eyes it almost hurt. "Live happily ever after."

* * * * *

AFFAIR OF PLEASURE

LINDSAY EVANS

To my readers, old and new.
Thank you for sharing your time with me.

Chapter 1

"Nichelle, wait!"

Nichelle Wright turned at the sound of her name, pivoting on the heels of her teal Louboutin stilettos. "What can I help you with, Steve?"

Steve Brooks stood in the middle of the well-lit hallway of Kingston Consulting with his shirtsleeves rolled up and his tie loosened, although it was just past ten in the morning. He shoved his hands in his pockets and relaxed his stance, as if he had all day to waste Nichelle's time.

She tapped the manila folder she carried against her thigh and quirked an eyebrow, wordlessly telling him to hurry it along.

Steve finally started talking. "About the Trestle presentation you did this morning, Nichelle. Can you break something else down for me…?"

Nichelle heard a door click open behind her, far enough away that she knew it was her business partner's office at the end of the hallway. She'd always teased him that for someone who was so friendly and sociable, he was giving mixed signals by taking the office farthest from everyone. Hers was at the opposite end of the hall, in the thick of things.

She glanced over her shoulder. Wolfe Diallo stood in the doorway, getting ready to walk a woman toward the elevators. He was dressed for a day of meetings, his solid six and a half feet clad in a gray three-piece suit. His head looked freshly shaved, and the goatee framing his mouth was crisp and on point, as always. He was a model businessman. Emphasis on *model*. His gorgeous looks made the men between the covers of *Vogue Hommes International* look like toothless hobos.

The woman with him wasn't dressed for business, though. Her voluptuous frame was on display in a tight white dress and red screw-me pumps that gleamed with a suggestive, wet shine. Nichelle's lips twitched.

She caught Wolfe's eye as he walked toward her with the woman by his side. Nichelle tipped her head toward his now closed office door. He paused and said something to the woman, brushed her cheek with his and gave her a brilliant smile. A dismissal. The woman's own smile dimmed, but she still looked up at Wolfe with a mixture of hunger and aloofness. *Come get me but don't think I'm needy.* A true talent.

"Excuse me, Steve." Nichelle returned her full attention to him. "Come to my office a little later if you want to talk more about the project. I'll be around." She met his eyes, daring him to push forward with his obvious delaying tactic. "Okay?"

"Sure." He looked briefly panicked, darting his gaze to the woman with Wolfe.

Nichelle dismissed him and headed down the hallway. As she passed the woman, she nodded, but only got a cold look in return. She felt more than saw the wide doe eyes flickering over her uniform, or what she considered her uniform—white blouse and calf-length black pencil skirt. Her green heels matched her optimistic and peaceful mood.

"Good morning, Wolfe." She walked into the office past him, her shoulder brushing the lapel of his pewter Zegna suit.

The office was cozy and warm, like his den at home, decorated with imported rugs and rust-colored walls. A large painting of Vermont in autumn dominated one wall. On his bookshelf rested a black Bose speaker dock and matching iPod. Next to them sat a vase of irises, Nichelle's favorite flowers that Wolfe's assistant replaced every few days.

"Is it a good morning, or is it great?" He closed the door behind him with a warm chuckle.

The office smelled like the perfume of the woman who'd just left, something musky and warm. Not unpleasant. Nichelle perched her hip on the edge of the wide window in Wolfe's office and glanced down to the street eight stories below.

"For me, it's only a good one," she said. "But it will be even better once we get on the same page about this potential million-dollar contract." She dropped her manila folder and a thumb drive on his desk then went back to her window perch.

Instantly, Wolfe's stance was all business—his smile

more predatory, the velvet eyes hardened to something like steel. He sat behind his desk. "Tell me more."

She started in on her mini presentation. Once she finished giving him the details of her latest project, a client she planned to go after for their management consulting firm, he grinned with all his teeth. Like a shark on the scent of fresh blood.

"Yes," he said. "You know I want it."

"Good." She crossed her legs and glanced down briefly at the long line of her calf, the arch of her feet dipping into the five-inch stilettos. "The thumb drive has everything I've prepared, including the actual proposal. Once you've looked it over—*today* would be lovely—" She flashed him her own toothy smile. "—I'll put in our bid. There are a few others I have in mind, but this is the biggest and the one we need to focus on for now. We're ready to grow and grow big."

"I agree," Wolfe said. "I trust you. That's one of the main reasons I asked you to come work with me."

Nichelle's lips curled in amusement. He hadn't really asked but rather *seduced* her into coming to work with him when he'd decided to leave the family business in favor of striking out on his own. Their families had been friends and neighbors for years, but instead of approaching her like a friend, he made her a business proposition. At first, he asked her to come on as a junior partner, someone to spot trends, grow and shape the management consulting firm in a way that made them money but also positioned them in the most advantageous way possible in the market. But she knew her worth and refused his initial offer.

At Sterling Solutions, the firm he'd hired her away from, her success rate was damned near legendary. Sterling had been on the verge of offering her more—a bigger office, possibly even a full partnership. Somehow Wolfe found out and raised the dollar amount and incentives with his offer. When she refused him again, he laid out the ultimate prize of an equal partnership at Kingston Consulting, plus an indecently large signing bonus.

"I'm just giving you your money's worth," Nichelle said with a pointed smile.

They both knew he'd made back the money he invested in bringing her on within the first quarter and tripled it by the second. So far, three years later, they were both very happy with the arrangement.

"And speaking of which." She dipped a shoulder toward the door. "We might need to fire Steve Brooks."

Wolfe leaned back in his chair and watched her over steepled fingers. "Of course, if you think it's necessary. Care to let me know why?"

She shook her head, almost amused but not quite. "He was trying to stop me from coming into your office and seeing you with your latest…female companion."

"Oh, yeah?"

There was a persistent rumor around the office that Nichelle and Wolfe were more than business partners. Even after three years of seeing nothing more intimate between them than shared laughter and a few platonic touches, nearly everyone at Kingston Consulting was still convinced they were sleeping together.

"I think under the man code, he was trying to protect you from being caught with another woman right under my naïve and unsuspecting nose."

They exchanged crooked smiles at the thought of her being naïve or gullible enough not to know what Wolfe was up to with his myriad and varied lady friends. "He was being deceptive," she said.

"Depends on how you look at it." Wolfe grinned at her from across the desk. "Another CEO would give him a promotion."

She waved a hand in dismissal. They both knew what kind of CEO Wolfe was. "The corporate version of 'bros before hos'?" she murmured.

"That fool is no bro of mine."

"You should probably let him know that."

It was Wolfe's turn to be dismissive. Steve Brooks wasn't important enough to warrant that sort of conversation. He was a damned good software engineer, and that was the reason they both kept him around, despite his persistent attempts to date every woman in the building. The women saw him as mostly harmless, but if Nichelle ever got an actual complaint about Brooks, he was out on his ass without discussion. No matter how good he was at his job.

Wolfe's cell phone buzzed, and he glanced down at it. "Don't forget about dinner at my parents' place on Friday evening." He tapped the phone to dismiss whatever he saw on the screen. "Mama wanted to make sure you're available and don't have to be off someplace saving the world."

"The only thing I'm out there saving on a regular basis is your ass." Nichelle smiled at the thought of his mother, a petite and fashionable fifty-something woman who'd given birth to thirteen energetic kids and somehow still had the time to successfully fulfill her role as chief operations officer at the family-run Diallo Corporation. "You know I'll be there." She pulled out her iPhone and checked the calendar to be sure. "It's already on the schedule."

"Nice to know we rate a slot in your precious schedule."

"Of course." With a gracious smile, she stood up from her improvised window seat. "You always do."

Wolfe came around his desk to walk her to the door. "By the way, I'll have Kathleen in HR draw up Brooks's dismissal letter today."

She paused in the doorway, her head tilted in consideration. "No, don't do that." After all, Steve Brooks had a sister he was helping put through college. He needed the money. "I'll keep an eye on him for now and let you know what happens."

He nodded. "Keep me in the loop."

"Of course." She walked out into the hall and headed to her own office, mind already on her next meeting. "Later alligator." The heels of her stilettos rang sharply against the hardwood floors with every step.

Wolfe very consciously closed his office door instead of watching Nichelle walk away. She was cripplingly beautiful. And those ridiculously sexy shoes she insisted on wearing every day never failed to stir his...interest.

He knew his feelings for her were inappropriate. She was his business partner, the person he trusted more than anyone else on earth. When he was eighteen, he took his father's half-million-dollar antique Bentley without permission. He drove it all over Miami and returned it with, unfortunately, a tiny scratch on the driver's side. His father was furious, demanding the one who stole the car to confess. Wolfe never did. The scar stayed on the car for months before his father eventually grew frustrated and fixed it himself. Nichelle saw Wolfe return the car, though. To this day, she never told a soul. After that, Wolfe trusted her with all his secrets, large and small. She hadn't disappointed him yet.

But in addition to being the keeper of his secrets, Nichelle was also the epitome of walking sex with a genius IQ and a sense of humor that never failed to make him laugh. He'd have to be made of stone not to notice and appreciate everything about her, and he was certainly *not* made of stone.

At his desk, he reopened the text reminder about dinner from his mother. As always, he felt that uncomfortable mix of love and resentment whenever she reached out to him. Each overture from her seemed like an attempt to make amends for that terrible thing she'd done to the family when Wolfe was sixteen years old.

He didn't trust her.

When he'd needed her the most, she'd packed her bags and left the family for another man, a successful painter who'd taken her away to Vanuatu. She was gone for nearly five months, having disappeared into a place Wolfe hadn't even heard of until his father announced a sudden trip there, then brought her back pregnant and far from penitent.

It was a lapse that no one in the family talked about, not even Wolfe's older brother, Kingsley, who must have noticed the same things Wolfe did. After his mother gave birth to her child—a child his father never treated any differently—she settled back into the routine of family life as if her five month defection had never happened.

But for Wolfe, it was the single most defining act of his childhood.

He swiped a finger across the phone screen and

brought up his mother's number, then sent her a text arranging for them to talk later that day. He was checking in on her. He knew it, and she did, too. It irritated him that after sixteen years, he still had the need to call her at least once a week to see where her head was. As if anything he could say would ever change her mind if she decided to leave the family again. Once she wanted something, there was no stopping her from getting it. That was one of the many things, unfortunately, that they had in common.

Wolfe glanced at the closed door of his office and remembered the sleek silhouette of Nichelle standing in the doorway. Her hourglass figure and sinful shoes. How she had sucked on the inside of her bottom lip as she considered the annoyance that was Steve Brooks.

Now *that*, he thought, was something he shouldn't want. But he did.

At the end of a long day, Nichelle was finally getting to the last pieces of mail in the secondary pile her assistant sorted for her every morning. It was mostly junk and solicitations addressed just to her. She fanned them out like a bad hand of poker and tipped them in the recycling, reject or respond pile as necessary. She frowned at an envelope from Sterling Solutions marked "private." There was nothing private she had to discuss with Teague Simonson, her former boss, or anyone else at Sterling. But her assistant, following protocol, hadn't opened the envelope. She tore it with her letter opener.

Nichelle,
It was a pleasure seeing you at the New York sustainability conference last month. I meant what I

*said about having a place for you to come back
to at Sterling. I see the stellar work you've done
with Kingston Solutions and want you to come
back and work that same magic for us. Nothing
less than full partnership and a corner office for
you, of course. Let's talk. I'll run some numbers
by you and see if we can't come to a mutually ben-
eficial arrangement.*

Teague

Nichelle tossed the letter in the recycle pile. She'd
already told Teague, at least half a dozen times, that
she wasn't interested in leaving Kingston. Now his unwanted communications were just obnoxious, no matter their tone. She wasn't going to respond to this latest
one. What was it about certain men that wouldn't let
them take no for an answer?

She sighed and glanced at her computer's clock. It
was nearly six. Wolfe had left the office an hour before
for a late meeting, and most of the staff was already
gone. Time for her to head out. Nichelle grabbed her
purse from its drawer and reached for her cell phone.
Her elbow knocked over the carefully sorted pile of
mail.

"Damn!" The letters slid halfway across her desk,
some falling on the floor. It was definitely time to go
home.

She haphazardly scooped the mail in a pile, determined to deal with it another day. Purse over her shoulder, she quickly left for the parking garage. In her car,
she turned on her favorite classic R&B station and eased
out into rush hour traffic. Seconds later, her phone rang.

Her sister's face showed up on the small screen. "Hey, Madalie."

"What are you up to?"

"Leaving work, which I'm sure you know."

Her sister giggled. "Yeah, I have you in the sights of my high-powered rifle now. I know exactly what you're doing." Madalie was currently indulging her obsession with spy novels and action movies. Everything was a gun or improbable martial arts metaphor.

"I'm at the beach kickin' it with some nice people. You should come."

Nichelle glanced from the slow traffic outside her window to her dashboard clock. "Do you have any idea what time it is?" It would take her at least forty minutes to get to the beach in that traffic.

"Of course. I was the one who called you after work, remember?"

Nichelle rolled her eyes. "Fine." Madalie had been floating her way through life for a few years now, twenty-four years old and still not knowing what she wanted to do for a career. She had her own place, her own money from the dividends of the stocks her father invested in her name. But her lack of direction and re-sulting listlessness worried Nichelle.

"Okay. I'll meet you there as soon as I can. You're at the usual place, right?"

"Of course. You know I don't handle change very well."

Half an hour later found Nichelle hiking across the sand with her high heels in hand. It was just past six thirty in the evening. The sky was hung with thick clouds while sunset burned its bright colors across the water. Her calf-length silk skirt and high-collared blouse weren't exactly made for the beach. The outfit was perfect for her perpetually air-conditioned office, but out here, she was more than a little warm. It didn't make sense for her to go home and change, though. For her sister, she'd endure a little discomfort.

The beach was surprisingly packed. She trudged across the sand, joining a broken line of people making their way to the oceanfront. It was a miracle she'd found parking. There was some sort of party going on. Bass-thumping dub-step music played from speakers set up around a high stage. Men and women, along with some teenagers, danced on the beach. She easily found her sister at the water's edge, her bright blue afro a beacon she followed to where Madalie sat at the edge of a bonfire, one of nearly a dozen or so people sitting in a circle, nodding along to the music and chatting.

"Hey! This party is great, right?" Madalie stood up to pull her into a hug.

"It's something." Nichelle glanced around her. "What's going on? It's a weekday. Shouldn't these people be in school or at work?"

"I think the work day is done." Madalie laughed. "Maybe I should have dragged Wolfe along to make sure you had a good time."

Nichelle ignored that comment. Still laughing, Madalie introduced her to the group gathered around the fire. Most nodded at her in acknowledgment before going back to their mostly silent enjoyment of the music. The smell of marijuana floated from somewhere nearby.

Scattered around on the sand were some blankets and a few folding chairs, abandoned while people danced to the throbbing music pouring out onto the beach. She considered grabbing one of the chairs, not in the mood to get sand and God knew what else on her black Balmain skirt. But at the knowing look from her sister, she dropped down into the sand. She only grumbled a little bit.

"Why did you drag me out here?"

"It's fun," Madalie said with a grin. "I invited Daddy and Willa, too. They're looking for parking now."

"Ah." After a moment's hesitation, Nichelle dropped her shoes at her side and leaned back in the sand. An impromptu family get together. She bumped Madalie's shoulder, and they shared a smile. "This is nice," Nichelle said. She worked so much that she didn't see her father or her two sisters as much as she'd like.

Madalie prowled the art district at all times of the day and night instead of focusing on her life's goals, while the youngest, Willa, was enrolled at the University of Miami, engrossed in her studies and enjoying being away from home. Nichelle barely knew what her father was up to. She didn't know when they had started to live their separate lives. After her mother died twenty years ago, the rest of the family stayed cooped up in the big Key Biscayne house together, none of them strong enough to go out into the world. But somehow, over time, things changed. Nichelle stopped feeling as if she was the only one holding her family together. Her sisters stopped expecting her to play the mother role. Her father started dating again. She'd gotten her life back enough to go off to California for college and then work. And though she didn't realize when exactly the transition happened, she jealously guarded the freedom she had now.

"You want some of this?" A shirtless man stumbled from his shuffling dance around the fire to offer Nichelle a blunt.

She shook her head in refusal. "Thank you, though."

He passed it on to someone else with a happy smile.

"This is what you invited Dad to?"

Madalie groaned and rolled her eyes. "Dad was young once, Nicki. He doesn't have a stick up his butt about stuff like this."

True enough. Their father was firmly of the carpe diem school of life. Grab it now since tomorrow is promised to no one.

"Still, it just seems wrong. If I were into this—" she gestured to the blunt being passed around the fire "—I don't know if I could smoke with him sitting right there."

"You're so uptight. Wolfe is definitely your more fun half." Madalie glanced over Nichelle's shoulder, and her eyes lit up. "Daddy! Willa!" She jumped to her feet and waved frantically at the two figures making their way through the growing crowd. They waved back.

Their father—serious in his Miami Dolphins cap and Wayfarer sunglasses—walked next to Willa, who kicked her way through the sand on bare feet, hands shoved in the pockets of her incredibly short shorts. Their father also wore shorts.

Nichelle greeted their father with a hug. "Hi, Dad." The last time she'd seen him, he was sitting at an outdoor café with a woman young enough to be one of his daughters. Nichelle had driven past the café, barely believing her eyes. But from that brief glimpse, he'd seemed happy.

"I thought you'd be too busy at the office to come

out this evening," he said to Nichelle, then kissed Madalie's forehead.

"Woman cannot live by massive paychecks alone,"
Nichelle said with a teasing smile.

He chuckled and sat next to her in the sand. "My
baby is growing up."

Willa, the image of their long-dead mother with her
stripper's body and angel face, smirked at Nichelle.
"Yeah, I thought you'd be too tied up in the office with
Wolfe to come out and play with us mere mortals."

Madalie snickered. "I wish it was bondage with that
hot man instead of work that kept her in the office all
day and night. It would at least be more interesting."

"And way more fun." Willa hiccupped with laughter.

"Screw you." Nichelle flipped off both her sisters.
She was so tired of them harping on the imagined relationship between her and Wolfe. When it came from
anyone else, she didn't care. But there was something
about the way her sisters teased that always rubbed
her raw.

Their father made a token sound of peacekeeping.
"Girls…"

"Okay, Daddy." The three chorused voices set off a
round of laughter on the beach.

Fire crackled and sparked in the circle of stones, its
light appearing brighter as the sun dimmed and dusk's
softening colors spread across the horizon and over
the ocean.

Nichelle leaned into her father's shoulder to watch
the fire. *This*, she thought with a sigh, *feels perfect*.
After a long day of conferences, meetings and negotiations, it felt good to simply *be*. No stress or expectations.

On the other side of their father, Madalie was asking Willa where she got her shorts. Nichelle hugged her knees to her chest and tilted her head up to the stars.

Chapter 2

"Pass me the rice and peas, Cheryl." Glendon Diallo reached out to his daughter for the white serving platter piled high with the fragrant dish.

The entire Diallo family, along with Nichelle and the rest of the Wrights, sat at the large oval table in the Diallos' dining room. Nineteen people, voices all raised in conversation and laughter. Hyacinth Diallo insisted on having a family gathering every four months that all the Diallos, no matter where they were in the world, had to attend. As next door neighbors and friends for nearly the entire twenty-four years they had shared the same Key Biscayne neighborhood, the Diallos had regularly invited the Wrights to participate in many of their gatherings, subconsciously melding the families over the years.

That melding had become even more deliberate

after Nichelle's mother died. At the time, Nichelle had thought Cin Diallo just felt sorry for them, but now, with the wisdom of adulthood, she realized that was what friends did for each other. Although she helped raise her two sisters after her mother had been killed in a car accident, because of the Diallos, she'd never been alone.

"I hear you and Wolfe are going off to Paris next week," Alice Diallo, one of the youngest at just a few weeks past her twentieth birthday, said with a sigh. "That's going to be so *romantic*." She drew out the last word with a sly smile.

"We're going there for work," Wolfe reminded her as he reached for a platter of ripe plantains. He forked some onto his plate and tilted his head to listen to what his father, seated to his immediate right, was saying.

"But Paris is Paris," Alice said. "When I went there after high school, I totally fell in love with the city and with this gorgeous boy I met there."

"You're always falling in love, Alice. I bet you don't even remember that boy's name."

"Names aren't important," Alice said dismissively. "It's about the feeling."

Good-natured laughter bubbled around the table. She was only twenty but had been in love more times than anyone else at the table. At least according to her. Every man she dated was susceptible to her declarations of love. Once, she'd even fallen in love with a woman. The family refused to talk about it, even though she kept bringing it up and wanting the family to recognize that she was now "queer." Just like all the others, that love affair had blown over after a few weeks.

"It's the city of romance." Alice pointed her fork at Nichelle. "You can't tell me you haven't thought about it."

Nichelle shook her head. "I've been to Paris before, remember? I spent a few days there while I was back-packing through Europe. It's a pretty city, but I didn't see any romance in it, just a lot of people using any ex-cuse to make out in public."

"You're so cynical!" Alice made a dramatic motion with her fork, sending a piece of asparagus flying.

"Hey! Stop wasting food," Willa called out from the other end of the table where the flying vegetable landed.

"I'm practical," Nichelle said to Alice. "There's a difference. When I fell in love, it wasn't in Paris, but I think those feelings are just as legitimate, right?" she teased the young girl.

Wolfe caught her with a stare worthy of his name-sake. "You've been in love?"

Nichelle winced, wanting to kick herself for saying anything about that failed affair. "Yes. Remember the Harvard professor I dated a few years ago?"

"That bourgie douche-bag?"

"Elia!"

Nearly the entire table exploded to scold the fifteen-year-old and youngest Diallo child.

"Don't act." She stared them all down. "You know none of you liked him. Especially not you, Wolfe."

Wolfe bit into a plantain, and Nichelle noticed that the fruit left a sheen of oil on his lower lip. He licked at it, but the glimmer remained, making his mouth look plump and bitable.

"He wasn't very interesting," Wolfe said in his dri-est tone.

"See?" Elia laughed. "And Wolfe usually likes ev-erybody."

"You don't have to say everything you think, darling," her mother gently scolded.

Elia pouted and stabbed her fork into a piece of curry chicken on her plate. But she looked up at her big brother and grinned. Wolfe winked back at her, then smiled innocently at Nichelle when she took note of their exchange.

Mid-meal, the doorbell rang. Since they had dismissed the staff for the day, Glendon Diallo, Wolfe's father, got up to answer the door. He returned a few minutes later with Nala, Nichelle's best friend.

She grinned and hefted a bottle of wine above her head as if she'd just captured it in the wild. "Greetings, family!"

Nala looked as if she'd just stepped from the pages of a Goth magazine in a sheer black shirt flashing her sequined black bra, a black leather skirt and heavy knee-high boots, also black. She wore her hair long and straightened, the inky mass hanging over her shoulders and halfway down her back.

She made her way around the table to greet everyone with a kiss on the cheek, hug or handshake. When she made it to Nichelle's side, she dragged a seat up to squeeze between Nichelle and Madalie.

"Why didn't you just use your key?" Nichelle bumped Nala with her shoulder. Nala had been in the Diallos' lives as long as she'd been in Nichelle's, wholeheartedly welcomed into both families since she didn't have a family of her own. Her keys to both houses were symbols of that welcome.

"I didn't want to be rude," Nala said.

Glendon Diallo sucked his teeth. "How long have you known us?"

Nala laughed. "Good point."

Wolfe's mother slid a plate and utensils in front of her. "We're glad you could make it," she said, squeezing Nala's shoulder.

She thanked Hyacinth with a smile.

"I didn't think you'd be back from Brunei so soon," Nichelle said.

Nala grinned. "Hey, it's free food night. You think I'd miss that?"

Nala and Nichelle met when they were both twelve years old and modeling for the same Miami-based clothing line. It wasn't long before Nala found that she preferred being on the other side of the camera, and Nichelle realized she didn't like any part of the business.

Nala was an orphan, a trust-fund baby whose parents had been killed in a freak shooting in Miami when she was just a toddler. She was raised by lawyers entrusted with her twelve-billion-dollar fortune until she turned twenty-one. Despite all the things she'd been through and the financial fortune that could have turned her into an unbearable person, Nala was a wonderful friend, and Nichelle felt lucky to know her. They were as different as night and day—and just as necessary to each other's lives.

"So tell me, what did I miss?" Nala asked.

"She and Wolfe are running off to Paris together," Kingsley, the oldest, said dryly. Nichelle frowned his way, but he only arched a teasing eyebrow then winked.

Nala giggled and looked at Nichelle. "Finally, huh?"

The dinner was wonderfully long. They spent hours lingering at the table over conversation and laughter and trading stories. As the evening stretched toward midnight, the dining room emptied and people made their way to the large family room or to the terrace overlooking the pool to share cigars and more risqué conversation.

Nichelle snuggled into the hammock at the back of the house, nearly half a bottle of merlot swimming pleasantly through her system. Nala lay on the matching hammock a few feet away, snoring softly.

Light footsteps approached from inside the house. Nichelle turned from her smiling contemplation of her friend to see Wolfe standing in the doorway. The scent of cigar smoke clung to him.

"Hey."

He stood in the light, dress shirt unbuttoned to show the strong line of his throat, and draped perfectly over his wide chest and shoulders. He looked ready to head out on a date.

"You leaving?" she asked softly.

He looked surprised. "Why do you say that?"

She only laughed, saying nothing.

"Yes, I am." His mouth curved in a sinful grin. "A new friend called."

"The one who came by the office?"

"No, another one."

She shot him a disbelieving look, then shrugged. "Just make sure you wrap it up."

"Always." He didn't deny he was heading off on a booty call.

Nichelle shrugged off an unexpected twinge of unease. "Wait." She sat up in the swaying hammock. "Are your parents asleep yet?"

He frowned. "No."

"Then why are you leaving? I'm sure they want to sit

and talk with you some more." Although Wolfe loved his parents, he was often at work, or at play, seeing them maybe once a month tops, and sometimes not for very long. "You should stay," she murmured. "The new booty can wait until tomorrow at least."

She could see his eyebrow tip toward the ceiling, a considering look on his face. He was surprised by her request, she could tell.

"I'll see," he finally said, hands in his pockets.

Nichelle knew what that meant. "Okay." She lay back down. "Have fun tonight, wherever you end up."

He paused in the doorway again, shoulders broad against the light flooding from the sitting room behind him. "Good night."

"Don't let the strange girl bite," she sang out to him softly.

When he left, she heard Nala stirring nearby. Her friend sat up and swung a leg on either side of the hammock.

"Is he really going to leave his parents' house on family dinner night so he can go bang some random chick?" The disbelief was plain in Nala's voice.

"It seems so," Nichelle said. "He is a man, after all. I think it's biologically impossible for him to turn down booty." But even as she said the words, she winced. That wasn't quite true. Wolfe was actually a lot more discriminating than that.

As if reading her mind, Nala snorted with laughter. "If he caught every piece of ass that got thrown his way, he'd never get any damn work done. Hell, he'd never eat."

"At least not food, anyway." Nichelle smiled and

curled up in the hammock. It rocked from the movement of her body.

"Doesn't that piss you off?" Nala asked.

"What?"

"The fact that he's off screwing around when he could be here with you...and his parents?"

"No. Should it?"

Nala sighed. Even in the dark, Nichelle could practically see her rolling her eyes. The assumption that she and Wolfe were, or at least should be, together wasn't limited to people in the office. Nala and just about everyone Nichelle loved rarely missed an opportunity to tease her about him, insinuating that there was a lot more going on between them than she and Wolfe were letting on. But she'd never had any romantic or sexual feelings for him. Yes, he was the most interesting of his eight brothers. But that was all. There was nothing more to her admiration than that. He was gorgeous, but there were gorgeous men all over the place, especially in Miami.

"Go back to sleep, Nala."

Her friend cackled and flopped back down into the hammock. "And *you* should wake up, Nichelle. That man won't wait around forever."

Nichelle snorted, a bad habit she'd picked up from her best friend years ago. "The only one waiting around here is you. For a hookup that's never going to happen."

Only silence greeted her declaration. Apparently, Nala had taken her snarky advice and fallen back asleep. Annoyed, Nichelle stared up at the ceiling of the verandah, the hammock swaying with her weight, her mind drifting. To Wolfe.

Chapter 3

Paris was beautiful, just like Alice had said. The taxi from the airport dropped them off on a breezy and warm day bright with midsummer sunshine and the smell of baking bread from a nearby boulangerie. On the steps of the hotel, Nichelle drew in a deep lungful of scented air and basked in the skin-prickling heat of the sun. Wolfe had to nudge her up the marble steps and through the gold-trimmed doors, where the doorman watched her with an indulgent smile.

"This is nice," she said.

He laughed. "Yes, it is."

Despite her unexpected infatuation with the city, she was more than ready when it came time to unpack and meet Wolfe in his adjoining room for a prewar conference. His narrow windows opened out on to a busy street and a view of the Eiffel Tower. Sunlight poured in like a dream.

Still wearing her travel clothes, she sat across from Wolfe in one of a delicate-looking pair of chairs near the coffee table. Nearly every piece of furniture in the room was lined with gold and perched on spindly legs better suited to effete royalty than a pair of robust Americans. But Wolfe took everything in stride, making himself comfortable in the slight burgundy-and-gold chair that only emphasized his powerful masculinity.

"Let's go over this thing one more time," he said.

She wordlessly handed him the tablet with her proposal and the slight changes she'd made during the taxi ride from the airport. As they talked, Nichelle's gaze slid to the open window. Although she wouldn't admit it just yet, she'd love to go and play outside. Alice's glowing talk about the magic of Paris had affected her more than she realized. Even the sound of traffic flowing in through the fifth-story window, a soothing mix of cars, bicycle bells and voices speaking softly in French, was its own seduction.

She and Wolfe weren't slated to be in Paris long, and the client they were chasing was just as likely to tell them *no* as he was to say *yes*. And it was really just peanuts compared to the Quraishi account, the one she'd given Wolfe the proposal for in Miami.

Jamal al Din Quraishi was the Moroccan head of a multibillion-dollar research and development company that also dabbled in oil. Having him as a client would be a real coup. Nichelle had it from her sources that she wasn't the only one angling for his business. The competition would be high, and gunning for the Quraishi account was going to be a challenge. Luckily, she loved a challenge.

Nichelle stopped in midsentence when she heard her phone chiming from the other room. "One sec."

In her room, she grabbed her cell and frowned at what she read on the screen. "Favreau doesn't want to talk business until after three this afternoon," she said when she got back to his room. She paused to look at the clock. "Four hours from now."

Wolfe tossed his cell on the replica Louis XVI settee across from him with an impatient scowl. "But he did invite us to come to his restaurant for drinks and enjoy his hospitality." Apparently, he'd just gotten the same message.

"I'm not here to socialize with people I'd normally avoid at home." The bright sunlight teased Nichelle through the window, something beautiful and tempting she couldn't have just yet. "I came to close a deal."

Wolfe shrugged. "Well he's happily stringing us along. At this point I'm not even sure if he has any intentions of doing business with us."

"That little weasel better sit down and listen to reason. I am not in the mood." She threw another longing glance toward the open window with its gleam of sunlight.

Wolfe caught her eye and smiled. "You keep looking out that window like you have someplace to be. You want to test out the city of romance theory for yourself?"

Nichelle looked away, not able to hide her smile. It was sometimes disconcerting how transparent she was to him. "Not quite. But if Favreau is going to jerk us around for four hours, we might as well go do something interesting that involves sunshine."

The last time she had been in Paris was for a long trip

in college. She and three friends had only stayed in the city for four days before hopping on a train to Naples. The entire four days had been wet and cool, even though it was summer, the clouds and rain retreating for only a few hours at a time before enveloping the city once more in gloom. She'd been over Paris before they even left. But now, with the sunlight creating its particular enchantment, she could see glimmers of what everyone else talked about when they chattered on about Paris and its ambiance.

"Screw it," Nichelle muttered. "Let's just go out. Okay?"

Wolfe chuckled. "Okay. Just give me about fifteen minutes to change and make a quick phone call."

"Good." She headed to her room.

Like their offices, her hotel room was just like his. No surprises, although it seemed that she was already going to be spending more time in his room than in hers. They tended to take turns monopolizing one of the other's spaces. His room actually had the better view.

Nichelle exchanged her tights and loose blouse for jeans and a thin cotton blouse with a string tied at the throat. She tucked a few things into a small purse and was ready to leave the room within ten minutes when the open laptop caught her eye, a new message on her email screen. Then her cell phone chirped with a message. It was from Favreau.

My apologies. I have meetings for the rest of the afternoon but have the next two hours free. Are you ready to impress me? My offices in 30 minutes.

Damn. Nichelle's fingers tightened around the phone. But she took a breath. She knew the proposal for Favreau backward and forward but dammit, she had been excited about taking advantage of the Parisian sunshine. Phone in hand, she slipped through the door between her room and Wolfe's.

"Favreau just sent an em—" She almost swallowed her tongue.

Wolfe was naked. He stood in the middle of the room covered in nothing but the light pouring through the windows. A pair of briefs dangled from his hand, as if he was giving some thought to pulling them on, but he didn't move a muscle when she walked into the room. If anything, he stood even straighter to give her more to look at.

Oh my God... Nichelle's mouth went dry, and her eyes widened.

His body was angled slightly away from her, a hip and shoulder in her direction, intriguing shadows swimming over his skin. And he was breathtaking. Literally, she could not catch her breath, staring at what she'd never seen before. A man who was beautiful to look at, true. But, having him tucked firmly in the realm of family, she'd never have thought to wonder at what lay beneath his designer suits and expensive jeans. But now she knew.

After the first hot and consuming glance, she dropped her eyes.

His feet were big. The bones strong but delicate-looking at the same time. Narrow ankles, muscled calves. But instead of keeping her eyes low like she should have, she looked up.

Wolfe had solid knees with scars on them from his childhood spent climbing, and sometimes falling out of, trees. There was a mole on his muscled thigh, the blemish like a drop of cocoa on the thickly cut flesh.

She lingered over it, taking her time to visually devour the body she had missed for years.

His thighs were big enough for her to sink her fingers into. Spread wide, they allowed a clear view of his long and heavy sex. Nichelle swallowed and blinked as his body started to respond to her gaze, thickening even more before her eyes, rising toward the slats of muscle in his belly. She yanked her gaze up to his wide chest, pectoral muscles, tiny button nipples that she suddenly imagined flicking with her fingers then soothing the brief hurt with her tongue. His arms bulged with muscle. His shoulders were firm enough to easily take the weight of her legs, her thighs.

Nichelle gripped her phone and apologized stiffly past her throat that was dry as a desert. "Favreau wants us at his office in thirty minutes." Then she very carefully turned and walked back to her room.

Wolfe stood with his briefs clenched in his hand long after Nichelle went back to her side of the door. His whole body was a fist. Tight, hard and aching. He'd been frozen while she looked at him, aware of her cool gaze on his body that suddenly felt too hot. He had hardened helplessly under her intense scrutiny, the blood rushing inexorably south.

He called himself ten types of fool for allowing her to see his physical reaction to her. But that was what he got for not taking advantage of what had been offered to him a few days before they'd left for Paris.

Anise, a woman he'd met while on a business lunch in the Gables, had texted him with a classic booty call invitation. He'd wanted it. He'd wanted *her*. But when, at the family dinner, Nichelle looked at him with disapproval, as if it would have been the worst sin for him to leave his parents' house to sleep with some woman he'd only just met, he reigned himself in. He ended up spending the rest of the night and most of the next day with his parents.

Since then, he'd been too busy with work, getting ready for the Paris trip and working with Nichelle on the Quraishi proposal. He hadn't made time to seek sexual relief from anywhere else, and by the time he'd gotten on the plane for Paris, his body was more than aware that it was suffering through an unintentional dry spell.

He stumbled to the nearest open window and breathed deeply of the cooler air flooding over his bare skin. He had to get it together. They had a meeting in less than half an hour.

Somehow, he got dressed and met up with Nichelle in the hallway outside their shared rooms. Wearing her business clothes like a suit of armor, she acted as if nothing had happened. They made it to the meeting with Favreau on time and worked together to convince the idiot to spend his money with them, then they left for the hotel.

Strangely enough, it wasn't awkward. They talked business in the taxi on the way to the meeting and back. Then, at the hotel, they went their separate ways. There was no more talk of them exploring the city together. Nichelle went for a walk, and Wolfe left for the hotel bar and a double whiskey.

He'd been to Paris before, each time on business. It was just another city for him, with none of the magic that most of the women in his family thought it held. The Eiffel Tower was nice. The brie was pretty good. That was it. Still, he'd been looking forward to sharing the city with Nichelle and learning more about it. But his erection had perked up and ruined any chance of that.

At the bar, he quickly knocked back his first glass of whiskey. The second glass went down even easier than the first, and after the third he was feeling relaxed, easy-going. He reached for his phone and dialed a familiar number. It only rang twice before his best friend picked up. It was still morning, just after nine, in New York.

"Hey," Garrison greeted him. "I thought you were in France this week."

"You thought rightly, my friend." He kept his voice low, aware of the French dislike of audible public conversation. Even though it was barely three in the afternoon, the hotel bar was far from empty. "I'm calling you from a very French hotel right now."

"Everything going well there?"

Wolfe grunted. "Yeah. Well enough. We got the client we came here for at least."

"You don't sound that pleased about it." Faint noises came through the phone, a low voice from nearby.

"The guy is a prick but— Wait, am I interrupting something? If you and Reyna are still getting your honeymoon on—" Wolfe named his best friend's new wife, a woman he'd met a handful of times, the most recent being at their wedding where he was best man.

"Then I wouldn't have answered the phone," Garrison cut him off.

Wolfe smiled, swirling the whiskey in his glass. "I would've been disappointed in you if you had. The grapevine says wives don't take kindly to that sort of thing."

"For once, the grapevine might just be on to something." Garrison paused. "You doing good?" A hint of worry crept through the phone. "You seem a little agitated."

Was he agitated? Wolfe shifted in his chair and tilted his head back to stare at the ornate ceiling with the pale cherubs and half-naked goddesses, the European idea of public art. He swept his tongue across his front teeth, tasting the question he was about to ask. "When did you know you wanted Reyna?"

A huff came through the phone, Garrison's version of a laugh. His friend was restrained to a fault. When they were younger, and hell, he couldn't lie, he did it now, Wolfe often made a game of trying to make Garrison literally laugh out loud. A full guffaw was as rare for his friend as oilfields in Florida.

"What's going on with you? Did you meet a woman over there?"

"Stop deflecting. I'm serious. When did you know you wanted to take her to bed?"

Garrison breathed a sigh into the phone. "The day I met her."

"Really?"

"Of course. You feel the same way about nearly every woman you end up dating." If that's what he wanted to call it. The unsaid words made both men laugh. One more than the other, obviously.

Garrison's laughter trailed off. "If you haven't met anybody over there, what's going on? Did you accidentally drink the water?"

"I'm in France, not Nicaragua, Garrison." Wolfe avoided the more important question.

"You never know what those French people are up to. First it's snails, then before you know it, you'll be

stuck in one of their miniature bathrooms with something explosive like Bonaparte's Revenge."

Wolfe almost choked on his whiskey. "Right."

A waiter, crisp in a white shirt, black slacks and a
long apron, served the high table next to his. The table
full of business people, most of them Canadian by the
sound of it, clinked their glasses in a toast punctuated
with a round of celebratory laughter once the waiter left.

"So what's got you thinking and drinking at three
o'clock in the afternoon?"

Wolfe didn't bother denying he was at a bar. "Does
a man need an excuse to enjoy his favorite whiskey?"

"Not every man needs an excuse, but you do."

He dropped his head back with a slow sigh. "I didn't
used to be this predictable."

Background sounds came from Garrison's end of the
call, the creak of leather, the tap of glass on wood as if
he was having an appropriate drink of his own, probably coffee, at his desk. He didn't say anything, just
waited for Wolfe to break the silence.

Wolfe stroked the whiskey glass with his thumb.
"You know what I've always thought about Nichelle,
right?"

"That she's too important to sleep with. Yes, I remember."

"Well, today I might have had a slight change of
heart."

"She's not that important to you anymore?" That was
Garrison's idea of funny.

"Keep it up, Kevin Hart." He gripped his nearly
empty whiskey glass. "Today, things got a little messy."

"You slept with her?"

"You're just making all the wrong guesses right now."

"I know you want to sleep with her," Garrison said. "I'm simply making the logical leap here. So, if I know you, something happened that made her more appealing than usual, and you're fighting your typical pleasure-seeking impulses."

"Something like that. I want her, you know I do. But now she knows, too."

"What, she saw you staring at her shoes again?" Garrison knew that Wolfe had a thing for women in high heels. Especially *Nichelle* in high heels.

Years before, when Wolfe had the idea to bring Nichelle over to Kingston Consulting, he'd set up an appointment to meet with her. They communicated by phone and email for weeks before he saw her in person, all grown up, for the first time in nearly two years. She stepped into the restaurant where they'd agreed to meet for their business lunch, breath-stealing in black and white, an outfit that made her look like a fifties pinup model but that he later found out she thought of as business attire, some version of a uniform. The dress caught his eye first, but as his eyes went lower, he damned near swallowed his tongue. Her shoes, electric blue stilettos, fit her feet as if they were custom made, creating an elegant silhouette of the already beautiful contours of her feet.

His heart thudded loudly in time to her footsteps as she walked through the restaurant, attracting the stares of nearly everyone she passed. Nichelle looked as if she'd stepped straight out of his fantasies, deep burgundy lips, hourglass figure and shoes he immediately imagined her wearing in bed. *His* bed. He reined in his thoughts before they could go any further and had even managed, he hoped, to get through the meeting with his mind strictly on the business proposition he wanted to make her. Although it was hard, he kept his eyes firmly on her face for the entire two hours.

Yeah, Garrison knew all about that and had laughed at him, another one of his rare belly laughs, when Wolfe told him about the meeting a few days later.

"She definitely caught me looking," Wolfe said. "But this time, she was looking, too."

Garrison hummed a response that was all doubt. "Are you sure you weren't having another one of those dreams again?"

Wolfe dropped his head back against the seat and groaned. "Oh, come on…"

He finished up the call the same time he finished his whiskey, urging Garrison to go back to whatever he had been doing while he tried to do a better job of not lusting after his business partner.

But nighttime came and tore all his resolutions to shreds.

A dream brought him right back to that moment in the room: Nichelle in the doorway with the phone in her hand. Her slender but curvaceous body in jeans and a high-collared white blouse that would have been virginal except for the fact that it was completely see through. In real life, he remembered that she had worn a black bra beneath the blouse and that it was more than the wisp of material it was in the dream. But reality and dream blurred, then the dream became what he wanted.

In the dream, her eyes flickered over him, warming his body, pumping blood rapidly through him, filling him with hard intention. But instead of leaving, she closed the door between their rooms and came closer. Wolfe began to shake. He dropped the underwear from his hand and watched her walk to him. The sinuous dance of her body across the carpeted space between them; the twitch of her hips beneath the thick fabric of the jeans; her slightly parted lips as she stared at his body, then finally, finally at his face.

She may have said something, the dream Nichelle. Or it may have been Wolfe's desire to see those lips part, to hear her call his name. He turned and she touched his chest, tracing the line down the center of his body, down his belly that tightened hard from the light stroke of her fingers. Those fingers skated lower as she met his eyes and held them. His throat was too tight for him to swallow, his lungs incapable of holding or circulating enough air. She touched his intimate flesh.

"Nicki…"

He groaned her name while her hands clasped him, caressed the tip of him with her thumb. A flash of mischief crossed her face.

She sank to her knees in front of him. Her breath stroked him, then her mouth, then her tongue. Her fingernails dug painfully into his thighs, a counterpoint to the humid heaven of her mouth. She hummed her delight around him, and Wolfe exploded with pleasure. He woke up gasping, his belly wet with evidence of his release.

Nichelle was furious at herself. One look at Wolfe's naked body, and she had reacted just like every other empty-headed woman who'd ever seen him, damned near leaping across the room on top of him. Women literally came on to him every day. To get laid, all he had to do was point a finger or nod his head.

And because of this, Wolfe dismissed those women as if they were nothing. He shared a night or three of physical gratification with them, sure. But at the end of it all, they were forgettable, and he could and often did replace them every few weeks. Nichelle didn't want to be like that. Ever.

After the meeting with Favreau, she left to wander the city alone. Instead of going back to change into more suitable walking clothes, she attacked the city in her business blouse and skirt matched with her favorite sunshine-yellow heels.

The heels weren't the most comfortable to walk in, but they forced her to move slowly and take in all the city had to offer. She strolled through the Louvre's courtyard to the Pont des Arts, one of the bridges festooned with locks from people who thought they were in love. The wooden slats of the bridge felt precarious under her high heels, even more so when she looked down and saw the water of the Seine wavering beneath the dark wood.

She wondered if all those couples who'd put their locks on the bridge were still in love and still together. A few feet away, an Asian couple, the woman in a lacy wedding dress, the man in a white tuxedo, posed for a professional photographer. Did they think their love would endure if they took wedding photos framed in the locks of other people's love?

"I bet they won't last a year."

Nichelle nearly jumped out of her skin at the intimate voice near her ear. She turned. It was a Frenchman, or one who looked stereotypically French in close-fitting designer jeans, a T-shirt and a light scarf draped around his neck. His eyes were gray, and his mouth was framed by a sexy, well-trimmed beard.

"I won't take that bet," she said in response to his earlier comment. "They might end up lasting longer than we live."

"True," he said, but hardly looked repentant. "And maybe every fool who latched a lock to this bridge will end up dying happily next to the one they came here with."

"You're awfully cynical for someone who lives in the city of love."

"It's the City of Light, thankfully. The other name is just a dreadful rumor." He flashed her a smile and crowded close to her against the railing. She could smell his cologne, something musky, mixed with his body heat and clean sweat.

Nichelle knew what he was doing. He was handsome, and she was single. She didn't have a lover waiting for her at home and didn't need anyone's permission to enjoy someone of the opposite sex. But even though the strange Frenchman seemed nothing like Wolfe—he wasn't as handsome, and his smell was almost too sweet—Nichelle looked into the teasing flicker of his gray eyes and only thought of the man she'd left behind at the hotel. The man who had stood tall, wrapped in light and kissed by shadow, his virile nakedness stirring a hot ache in the center of her. Nichelle stepped back from the stranger. Her spine connected with the railing of the bridge.

"You're right," she said. "Who needs love?"

His pale eyes sparkled down at her. "Definitely not me." His gaze dropped to her mouth before connecting with her own. "Would you like to have a drink with me?"

She didn't even have to think about it. "I'm sorry, I can't."

He moved back a step, a gentleman. The sparkle in his eyes did not dim in the least. "You've broken my jaded heart today, mademoiselle."

"But I'm sure you'll be better by tomorrow at the latest," she said with a soft laugh.

The stranger brushed her arm with warm fingers. "I hope whoever you're pining for will adore you as much as you deserve." Then he took another step back, still smiling. He winked at her then nodded in parting, deliberately stepping between the photographer and his subjects on the bridge.

Only after he disappeared did his words register. Pining? Hardly. But without prompting, images of Wolfe from the afternoon came back to her in brilliant color. His body, readying itself for sex, the firm muscles under light. His face, frozen in concentration as he stared at her. No, she was definitely *not* pining.

Nichelle left the bridge and the crowds to dip onto a side street. Yes, the city was magical in the sun. What she had missed while in college seemed a bit of a tragedy now. If someone like that flirtatious stranger had tried to pick her up back then, she'd have much better memories of Paris.

Maybe you can make some better memories now. With Wolfe.

The thought froze her on the sidewalk, hissed sudden breath into her lungs. Someone bumped into her, a woman who begged Nichelle's pardon then kept walking and chatting on her cell phone. The sound of her own phone ringing shoved her back into motion. She answered without looking at the display.

"How is Paris treating you?"

She sighed at Nala's voice. "So far the business aspect is going very well."

Her friend immediately pounced on what she *wasn't* saying. "And the personal?"

Nichelle sucked the inside of her bottom lip. "I just saw Wolfe naked."

"Oh! I wasn't expecting that." Nala sounded positively delighted.

"Me, either."

Nala's impatient sigh fluttered through the phone. "So what the hell happened after the naked sighting?"

"Nothing happened. I walked out."

"But…?"

She drew a trembling breath. "He's hot, Nala!"

"Welcome to the world of eyes that see." Nala huffed in amusement and exasperation. "I can't believe you're just now realizing that."

"You know I don't…didn't see him like that." She didn't want to. She'd be damned if she would allow something as petty as sexual attraction to ruin the effortless business relationship she and Wolfe spent over three years building.

"Are you going to do anything about it?" Nala asked.

"No." Nichelle shook her head. "Definitely not."

"Hmm. Okay. Um…" A pregnant silence pressed between them. Nichelle could almost see Nala swelling with curiosity. Despite the gravity of the situation, she smiled.

"Okay. Out with it. I know you're dying to ask something."

A breath of relief came at her over the phone. "Oh, thank God!" Nala giggled. "Is he big? Cut? Interested in you?"

Nichelle strolled down the sidewalk, slipping past two women who walked side by side, smoking cigarettes and talking in rapid Spanish. A bicycle bell trilled from nearby as a biker warned a pedestrian who had wandered into the bike lane. She thought about not answering Nala's questions then decided it wasn't worth the inevitable aggravation.

"Yes. Yes. And I don't think so."

"What do you mean you don't think so? Did he or did he not get hard for you?"

"Well, he's a man. Of course he did, but that doesn't mean anything." Three boys in hip-hop gear boldly looked her over as they walked toward her. She held the phone against her ear, paying them little attention even as they leered in an obvious way, one of them saying something mildly obscene to his friends. Nichelle walked past them.

Nala chortled. "What happens in Paris, stays in Paris."

"Nothing is going to happen between us. You know how I feel about this business partnership."

But it wasn't just about business. She'd known Wolfe since they were children. From practically across the street, she'd watched him grow from an energetic kid to an awkward teenager and now into a gorgeous adult male. In all that time, she hadn't felt a flicker of attraction. Why now, after all these years? If she had a type, it was the over-educated man with an extensive vocabulary, articles published in obscure journals and a track record of romantic stability and fidelity. Not this worldly man who didn't take anything seriously other than his family and work, who had a different woman every other week and didn't seem inclined to settle down at all.

"I know." Nala made a soothing noise. "But don't beat yourself up over this, Nicki. Things happen. Feelings change. It's just another one of those things."

She sighed. "Okay." The dam had already broken. There was no going back. All she had to do was get her unexpected attraction to Wolfe down to a manageable level so she could still effectively do her job. "Thanks for talking me through it."

"What are best friends for?" Nala paused. "But if you change your mind and decide to get down and dirty with Wolfe, you have to tell me everything. Seriously."

"Goodbye, Nala."

She hung up on her friend's laughter.

Chapter 4

When Nichelle and Wolfe returned to Miami, she tried and eventually succeeded in pretending the charged afternoon in the Paris hotel never happened. And it seemed as if Wolfe had, too. He never mentioned it, never asked to talk about it.

On an early Monday morning, Nichelle sat behind her desk with Wolfe distractingly at the back of her mind. She scanned an email from Teague Simonson at Sterling Solutions. He wanted her to come in for a meeting and see if there was anything at Sterling that would "sate her appetite for bigger and better." She hit the delete button. The only thing she wanted from Sterling was for them to leave her alone.

Someone rapped on her door.

"Come in."

Her door opened and Wolfe walked in with Clint,

their general counsel. Wolfe closed the door behind him, his eyes resting easily on her, before heading to his usual seat in her office. Nichelle looked away from him after a single flickering glance.

Nichelle moved from behind her desk to lean against the front of it. She crossed her ankles and her arms. Wolfe sat on the small sofa and kicked his feet up on the small hassock. He sipped his hot chocolate Nichelle's secretary had left for him.

"Tell us the news, Clint," Nichelle said.

The attorney paused in the process of swiping a finger across the face of his tablet. "Nice shoes, Nichelle." He blinked down at her lavender Alexander McQueen pumps, a thoughtful look on his face, before going back to his tablet.

"Thank you, Clint." She smiled at him then glanced at Wolfe. He only sipped from the large mug and gave her a speaking glance, head slightly tilted, body relaxed yet predatory in the Tom Ford suit.

"Tell me something good." She looked at him but directed her words to Clint.

"I don't know about *good*," the lawyer said. "But I can give you some information you can work with."

"I'll take it," she said.

He nodded. "You know the Quraishi proposal is sound. You did an impeccable job, as always."

"But…?"

Clint grimaced, looking as if he'd had a bad attack of indigestion. "You might have to let this potential client go."

Nichelle abruptly straightened. She propped her hands on her hips and planted her feet wide. "Why?

This contract could bring in over five point three million dollars to the firm over the next two years alone."

"I know the numbers, Nichelle." Clint leveled a pleading look at Wolfe. "But I really think we might have to just give up on this one."

Wolfe tipped his head toward Nichelle. "Whatever she decides is what we'll do," he said to Clint.

Over the years, Wolfe had learned to leave the business of client acquisition to her. He was the money and brawn of their operation while she was the seer and fortune builder. It was because of her that the company was as successful as it was now. Everyone knew it. Although it sometimes took other men in the company a little while to know the power structure, and they usually turned to Wolfe for most decisions, she quickly showed them who held the reins.

Clint sighed. "Quraishi is a devout Muslim and family man. You already know that. He won't do business with Kingston because its partners—" he jerked a stubby finger at them "—the two of you, are not a married couple."

"Excuse me?" Nichelle didn't think she'd heard him right.

"Quraishi would think it's improper. You're a heterosexual couple working closely together in business, spending long hours building a company from the ground up. It's very intimate work. He's a traditional guy and won't simply accept that your relationship is platonic. You see how people here at Kingston act. They just think you've been incredibly discreet all these years."

Nichelle didn't give a damn what anybody thought about her and Wolfe's relationship. It was none of their business. She clenched her jaw. "How can we change Quraishi's mind?"

"Aside from getting married to each other, you can't."

"Isn't that a little extreme?" Wolfe's voice rumbled with annoyance, an echo of what Nichelle was feeling.

"This is not the eighteen hundreds!" she snapped. "That doesn't even make sense."

"I think it's stupid, but that's the way he runs his life and his company. There's no morality clause when you work for him, but I hear that if he ever discovers any infidelity or improper sexual dealings among his employees, they are immediately fired." Clint dropped his intense stare to tap out something on the tablet. "You can approach him with your proposal anyway. It's a really good one. But know that once he finds out the two of you are unmarried and working so closely together, you won't get past his secretary."

Nichelle crossed her arms, her nails digging into her elbows through the thin silk blouse. She had done her research on Quraishi and reached a similar conclusion. But she'd been hoping that another perspective would prove her wrong. She wanted the Quraishi account. Badly. It was the key to the future she and Wolfe had discussed when he first brought her to Kingston Consulting. She stalked across the room to sink into the couch at Wolfe's side.

"I want that account, Clint."

The lawyer shrugged and gave her a helpless look. "You could always *pretend* to be married."

"No," Wolfe said immediately, an indecipherable emotion flashing across his face too fast for her to see it. "That's unacceptable. As fun as it would be pretending to be Nichelle's man for a week, absolutely not." His jaw tightened, and a muscle ticked just under the skin. "I'm not going to jump through some ridiculous hoops just for a little money."

A hint of hot chocolate marred the firm curve of his lower lip. The wet smear caught Nichelle's eyes, making her want to stroke it away with her thumb. Or her tongue. She tore her glance away and pulled her mush brain back to the conversation.

"A *little* money?" Nichelle quirked a brow at Wolfe.

"Okay, a lot of money." He flashed her an annoyed look and a smile at once.

Their eyes met and held. A fluttering awareness took wing in Nichelle's belly.

She licked her lips. This was getting a little ridiculous. Damned near every time she looked at Wolfe now, she was ambushed by the feelings that had taken her over in the French hotel room. "Clint, could you give us a few minutes?"

"Take as long as you like. I have another meeting in about an hour." He left and took his tablet with him.

The door barely closed behind him before Nichelle turned to Wolfe. "I want this to happen."

"Easy, tiger." His smile was warm and teasing, but there was a hint of seriousness there. It was obvious he wanted her to really consider what she was going after.

"I have," she said, as if he'd spoken those words out loud.

Nichelle was competitive to a fault. She knew that and most days tried to channel it for good versus evil. This was for good. For both hers and his.

She leaned into him, a hand on his thigh. "Just say yes to this fake marriage, Wolfe. I can make Quraishi come to us. Kingston Consulting needs this. You know we do." She felt the big thigh muscle jump under her palm, and her thoughts derailed.

Damn.

Wolfe didn't speak. Early afternoon light tumbled through the wide windows to fall over his shaved head and the goatee framing the lush and slightly pink firmness of his mouth. In one breathless moment, Nichelle was pulled back to that hotel room in Paris. The Eiffel Tower peeking over his bare shoulder, the low hum of the air conditioner beneath the heavy thud of her pulse as she watched him and realized how easy it would be to cross the room and touch him. Then taste and allow herself to be tasted in turn. She pulled her hand from his thigh.

"Liars get caught," Wolfe said. If his voice was a little shaky, she chose to ignore it.

"We won't be lying," she said. Except for the lack of sex, they practically lived like a married couple anyway.

He gave her a look that forced a rueful laugh from her. She dipped her head to twine her fingers in her lap. "Okay, a little lie. But what's a little lie in business?"

"Are you sure you want to go there?"

She didn't hesitate. "Absolutely."

He pursed his lips, his lashes lowering in thought. "Okay. Then we'll do it. But we have to do it the right way."

What exactly was the right way to lie about being married?

"When do you want to go shopping for a ring?" he asked.

A ring? Her belly tightened oddly at the thought. She shook her head. "No. Let's not take it that far. Some modern couples don't even wear wedding rings."

Wolfe leaned close. The scent of hot chocolate from his lips and traces of his mint-and-mandarin soap overwhelmed her senses. "*My* wife will wear my ring." His voice rumbled with an unfamiliar intensity. He stood up and brushed invisible wrinkles from the front of his tailored slacks. "Tomorrow, we go find rings." He picked up his empty cup and took it with him to the door.

Now that the agreement was made to pretend, second thoughts nipped at Nichelle's conscience. Maybe this wasn't the right thing to do. She straightened on the couch. But if the alternative was to relinquish any opportunity of getting Quraishi's business, she'd rather risk the deception.

"By the way, your shoes are *very* nice today." Wolfe paused at the door, a smile playing on his lips. His gaze dipped to the lavender stilettos before climbing steadily, slowly, up her body. "I just didn't want my appreciation to get lost in the usual round of adoration from everyone else."

The expected "thank you," or even something dismissive, didn't find its way immediately to her lips. His gaze on her was like a hot touch. She shivered in her stilettos, aware that he was looking at her in a way he'd never done before Paris. She felt like a fumbling teenager, uncertain how to respond to the unexpected flirtation. It was flirtation, wasn't it? *Christ! Pull it together, Nichelle.*

"You could never get lost among the masses," she said finally.

Wolfe grinned. "Good to know, especially since I'm about to be the number one man in your life." With another body-skimming look, he left her alone.

What the hell had she just gotten herself into?

* * *

A few days later, Nichelle and Wolfe met at the pier near the Coconut Grove library. He'd had a meeting near Vizcaya and wanted to go home to change before meeting up with Nichelle. She took advantage of the location to have a solitary lunch at one of her favorite spots in Miami.

She stood at the railing looking out over Biscayne Bay and the flotilla of boats anchored in the glimmering blue water. It was strange being out of the office during the week and in the sun. She didn't like to think of herself as a workaholic, but there were far too many days when she was locked in the office from sunrise to sunset without taking advantage of the sunshine, which was one of the best things about living in Miami.

"I hope you're not contemplating jumping off this pier just to escape our fake marriage."

She didn't turn when Wolfe walked up behind her, his footsteps quiet against the wooden planks. She smelled him, fresh from the shower, a different aftershave today, something subtle with the hint of sage. It felt good to anticipate the sight of him, to wait until he was standing next to her, his arms draped over the railing, his scent pressed close to her, his shirt a light brush against her bare arm.

"*You* should be the one with jumping on your mind then." She turned to him finally. "I'm the one who talked you into this, remember?"

He had traded that morning's suit for a short-sleeved gray shirt worn untucked over dark jeans. Sexy. Edible. Other inappropriate words came to mind, but she pushed them firmly away. *Friend. Partner. Platonic.* Those were the words she should be focused on.

He leaned closer to press his arm firmly into hers, a teasing motion. "Once I'm committed to something, I'm all in."

For better or worse, so to speak, that was true. Wolfe was a man of his word who also backed up those words with action. Yet another reason she trusted and loved him. As a friend. Nichelle drank the last swallow of her sparkling water and put the empty bottle in a nearby recycling bin. "You ready?"

They walked the short distance to the jeweler Wolfe suggested. It was a store he'd used for years, apparently. He opened the door for her, a subtly marked storefront that was easy to miss if you walked too fast, and stepped in behind her. As they walked in, the bell above the door jangled. Wolfe was so close that his shirt brushed against her shoulder blades, and his breath stroked the back of her neck. She swallowed.

The store was small and narrow but brightly lit; every piece of jewelry on brilliant display. There was the usual round of diamonds, platinum necklaces, rings and watches. They had only taken a few steps inside when a door at the rear of the shop opened and a slender woman stepped through. She was dressed in a nondescript but obviously expensive skirt suit. Her hair, pulled back from her face in a tight bun, was glossy and woven with strands of gray. She wore little makeup and no jewelry.

"Mr. Diallo!" The woman welcomed Wolfe with a wide smile.

She looked very happy to see him. Nichelle frowned. Just how much did he spend in this place, and how much of a regular was he?

"Martine." He greeted the woman with a firm handshake and one of his warmest smiles. After introducing Nichelle, he turned back to her. "How is your father doing? I was sorry to hear about his heart attack."

The light dimmed slightly in Martine's face. "He's actually doing much better. The doctors expect a full recovery but insist that he stay at home and away from the store for a while."

"I bet he wasn't happy to hear that."

"You know Papa." Then Martine smiled and made a dismissive motion with her hands. Her business sense had kicked in. Enough with the small talk when there were people waiting to spend some money. "But it's good to see you and finally meet the woman you've decided to settle down with." She turned her attention to Nichelle. "You are absolutely gorgeous!"

"Thank you." Nichelle appreciated the woman's kindness. Even if it was motivated by the desire to sell Wolfe more trinkets.

"I picked out a few things after you called," Martine said. She waved them to a small antique table surrounded by four padded chairs. "Let me get them for you."

Nichelle and Wolfe made themselves comfortable at the table in time for Martine to return with four trays of rings. The trays were velvet-lined black rectangles that held some truly breathtaking pieces.

She presented one tray to Wolfe, a selection of simple gold and platinum wedding bands, and the rest, all filled with glittering diamond wedding sets, to Nichelle. Although she'd never been one to be impressed by jewelry, Nichelle had to admit the pieces were beautiful.

A radiant cut canary diamond surrounded by a square of smaller white diamonds immediately caught her eye. But it was too extravagant for a pretense. She didn't have to see the price tag to know that the ring, at least five carats, cost over fifty thousand dollars.

Nichelle pointed to a plain wedding set, a one carat diamond solitaire and a matching platinum band. "That should be fine."

But Wolfe had been watching her. "Try that on." He gestured unerringly to the canary diamond. "I think that would look better on you."

With the gleam of a potential sale in her eyes, Martine gathered up the yellow diamond and matching band. She was about to slip them onto Nichelle's finger when Wolfe reached for them.

"Allow me."

In his hand, the rings looked small. The pale fire of the diamonds flashed prisms of light in his palms. He reached for Nichelle's left hand before she could voice a protest. His skin was warm against hers, and firm. She couldn't stop the tremor in her hand.

"Ready?" His eyes held hers.

Was she? The pretense was her idea, but now, faced with a gorgeous ring and an intent man with his hand on hers, she felt another quiver of trepidation. But then reality set in. This was only going to be for a few days. She took a breath.

"Yes. Yes, I am."

He slid the rings onto her finger.

"A perfect fit." Martine smiled at Nichelle.

Nichelle looked down at her hand. The yellow diamond sat on her finger as if it was made for her. The stone was even more brilliant against her brown skin, the surrounding white diamonds haloing its impressive size.

"It's a pretty rock." She tried to sound unaffected, but even she heard the catch in her voice. The ring was stunning. It seemed criminal to use it only as a prop in a game of pretend.

"We'll take it." Wolfe slowly released her hand.

Nichelle cleared her throat. "Now it's your turn." She curled her hand with the ring on it, fighting the urge to put the fist in her lap. She glanced over the tray of masculine rings. It didn't take her long to find one that vaguely matched hers in style—a wide platinum band with a vein of small yellow diamonds running through its middle.

"Try that one."

It, too, fit perfectly. Nichelle gave Wolfe a teasing smile and echoed his words. "We'll take it."

At the counter, Nichelle insisted on paying for Wolfe's wedding band while he unflinchingly gave Martine his black card for her rings. Despite his insistence that she wear them out of the store, she tucked them in the scarlet box Martine provided and put them in her purse. Having the rings on her finger felt too real, too significant.

They walked out of the store and back out into the sunshine. Nichelle drew a trembling breath. "Let's go get a drink."

They walked the few blocks to Greenstreet Café and found a table outside. Although it was a weekday, it was close to lunchtime with plenty of people watching to be done. Nichelle leaned back in her chair and put her purse in the empty seat to her left, conscious of the seventy-thousand-dollar diamond wedding rings inside it.

When the waitress came to take their order, she immediately asked for a dirty martini. Wolfe got his usual whiskey sour.

"Tell me," he said once the waitress had gone. "What's wrong?"

"Did I say something's wrong?"

"Well, you're not wailing and gnashing your teeth, but don't pretend you haven't frozen up on me on the walk over here."

Nichelle pressed her lips together and drew a deep breath.

"Things have been a little off since France, don't you think?"

"Is this about what happened in Paris?"

They both spoke at the same time, their words tumbling over each other's. The foolishness of it made Nichelle laugh, and Wolfe's deep chuckle soon joined hers. Their mirth only tapered off when the waitress came back with their drinks. Nichelle took a quick sip and sighed at the sharp pleasure of the alcohol on her tongue.

"That was a little ridiculous, wasn't it?"

"Yeah, it's not like I haven't seen a naked man before."

She noticed Wolfe flinch. Then he shrugged. "As long as you don't compare me to some limp Ivy League professor with an inferiority complex, we're good."

Her mouth twisted into a half smile. "You were definitely not limp."

"Jesus…" But Wolfe laughed in a way that made them both a little more relieved and relaxed. "Did that make things awkward? Because that's not what I want."

"Don't worry about it." She didn't want either of them to focus too much on what happened. "I'm the one who walked in without knocking. Serves me right for getting an eyeful of Wolfe untamed."

"Why does that sound so weird when you say it?"

"Maybe because it makes you sound like some sort of rabid dog." She shrugged, still smiling. "I don't really know."

"Normally you know every damn thing." He sipped his drink. "But it's okay. Isn't it?"

"It is," she said. It had to be. "Things don't have to change between us because I know a little bit more about your measurements than I used to."

Wolfe laughed. "So are you impressed? Or should I invest in a gym membership? Or a penis pump?"

A crack of laughter shot from her mouth, but she refused to rise to the bait. "I think you know the answer to all those questions. I'm sure your women, and mirrors, give you plenty of positive feedback on a regular basis."

He chuckled, a pleased and masculine rumble. "So, we're okay then?"

"Yes, we are okay. About everything. Even the fake marriage and that damned diamond." She toyed with her martini glass but didn't lift it to her lips.

Wolfe hummed low in his throat. "So you admit the ring scared you a little."

"It's kind of impossible to ignore."

"I think *you're* already impossible to ignore." Wolfe lifted his glass to his lips with a teasing smile. "The ring is just another accessory to your radiance," he finished.

"Keep talking that way and you'll find yourself with a wife for real."

Wolfe laughed as if that was the funniest thing she'd said all day.

By the time the second round of drinks was almost

gone, they were both relaxed enough to act normally with each other. The ring in Nichelle's purse was just something she would think about at another time. Preferably when she didn't have the distraction of Wolfe near her.

Later that night, she called Nala. It was a long conversation, one of their marathon talks that lasted until nearly sunrise. She told her best friend everything, texted her a picture of the rings, told Nala how it felt, that tingling warmth when Wolfe slid the rings onto her finger, holding her gaze as if the moment meant something. But she didn't fool herself into thinking it was more than just another amusement for him. A fantasy of significance that any of the women who'd fallen into his bed had had before her.

Just before she hung up, Nala put on her serious voice.

"I'll be in Cannes around the time you're in Morocco," she said to Nichelle. "If anything happens, if you need anything, call me and I'll come."

Nichelle hoped she wouldn't have to make that call. But she hung on to the offer like a lifeline.

Chapter 5

In the hush of business class, as the lights in the plane dimmed to allow the passengers on the long flight an easy rest, Nichelle and Wolfe were wide awake and drinking red wine. They sat in adjoining middle seats, chatting quietly while the aircraft winged its way toward Marrakesh.

"I think we should consider investing in a company plane." Wolfe swirled the Chianti in his glass, his eyes half closed while he gazed at Nichelle, who lay fully reclined in her seat but curled toward him. Her wine glass was nearly empty.

"That wouldn't be cost-efficient for us. Pilots want too much money these days." Her words were only a breath above a whisper, giving Wolfe the perfect excuse to lean even closer. She smelled like sleep and Merlot.

"I'd fly the damn plane myself." He licked a drop of

wine from his lower lip, watching the slow rise and fall of her breath beneath the scarf draped over her throat and chest. "Three airports and twenty hours of travel time. That's ridiculous."

Nichelle wore what she called her "plane clothes," delicate-looking flats, leggings and a long blouse that draped down over her butt. A black sweater. All very respectable. Even modest. But he couldn't stop looking at her. At the way she managed to curl up in the seat toward him, the stretch of her thighs under the thin leggings more tempting than any nude stripper who'd given him a lap dance. It was a mystery. It was distracting. He needed to get it together before they landed in Marrakesh.

And he needed to get used to her in ways he never had before. She shifted again in the seat, and the thin sweater fell away from her thighs. He could easily imagine tugging up that fabric to get access to the plump curve of her butt, the perfect size for his hands. She'd moan as he lifted her up to straddle him, her arms falling onto his shoulders while her mouth lowered slowly to his. Wolfe adjusted himself in the seat. *Damn.*

She lifted her hand, her left hand this time, to adjust the scarf she'd draped across her throat for warmth. The diamond rings flashed even in the relative darkness. He caught his breath.

In a way *this* was worse, being distracted by the rings instead of thoughts of making love to her. In all his years of living, he'd never thought much of having a wife. But suddenly he had a woman sitting next to him with his rings on her finger. It wasn't just any woman, thank God, but there was something even more intense because it was Nichelle, *Nicki* to him since that afternoon in Paris. She knew him better than most people. This seemed more dangerous somehow.

She threw out an obscene dollar amount. "That's how much it would cost us to have our own private jet."

He looked at her, amazed. "How did you know that? Tell me you didn't just do that calculation in the past few seconds."

She smirked. "You're not the only one who's considered kicking frequent flyer miles to the curb. But even if the cost wasn't so damn high, I know you love this part of it, too." She made a vague gesture to the cabin full of people. The 747, the stewardesses ready with a drink or an extra pillow or whatever else he wanted, other whispered conversations around them. "You even love the airport. Freak."

Wolfe grunted. He pressed the button to recline his seat to the sleeping position. Sometimes it was scary how well Nichelle knew him. "Go the hell to sleep, woman."

Laughing, she threw a sleep mask at him, left handed, sending the big yellow diamond once again sparkling in the dark.

Nichelle's first impression of Morocco was *heat*. The metal stairs clanked under her ballet flats as she left the airplane with her purse over her shoulder. She was glad she'd taken off her sweater and stuffed it into her rolling suitcase before getting off the plane. At her side, Wolfe made a soft noise, of surprise and pleasure, when the heat hit him.

"I like this place already," he said with a low sigh.

It was the first time for both of them in Morocco.

They followed the path along the tarmac from the

plane to the small airport, passing under the signs in French then Arabic welcoming them to the Marrakech Menara Airport. Other signs in Arabic, French and English pointed them toward arrival and customs. Less than half an hour later, they left the long line with their passports stamped, their carry-on bags rolling along beside them.

"There's our ride." Wolfe nodded toward a man, tall and serious looking, with a sign that read Monsieur and Madame Diallo.

"And so it begins," Nichelle muttered. She felt more than ever the weight of the rings on her finger. Wolfe's ring seemed much more natural on him. She hadn't once seen him adjust his platinum band; he simply seemed to accept the fact that it was there.

Her better-than-average French wasn't at all useful in Miami, so she took particular pleasure in speaking it with the driver. Wolfe was content to lounge in the back of the Mercedes-Benz and let her do most of the talking. He spoke French, too, better than she did, but was busy taking in the sights.

Wolfe rolled the windows down, sighing in sensual appreciation of the hot desert air that poured into the car. He sprawled on the seat, legs spread wide, his left hand—with the all-important wedding band—draped over one muscular thigh. His profile was etched perfectly against the sharp blue of the Moroccan sky. He looked tired. *And sexy*, her traitorous mind supplied.

At the hotel, a vast and gorgeous white building in the Moorish style that Wolfe instantly said he admired, the driver took their bags from the trunk.

"Monsieur Quraishi will call you this evening after you've had a chance to rest," the driver said. "Your rooms in the hotel and any amenities you wish to enjoy have already been taken care of." He passed an envelope to Wolfe, then, with a crisp bow, got into his car and drove away.

Wolfe raised an eyebrow. "It almost feels like he's trying to get *our* business."

He tore open the envelope, his eyes moving quickly as he read the letter inside. He passed it to Nichelle. The letter, in formal and beautiful French, invited them to a party at Quraishi's compound later that evening. He would send a car for them; all they had to do was be dressed and ready promptly at six.

"Our host likes his pleasure before business," Wolfe said.

"That'll give us some time to check out the place." Nichelle tucked the letter in her purse and glanced at Wolfe, noting the tired slump to his shoulders. "And get some rest."

"Good afternoon, *monsieur. Madame.*" A dark-suited young man stepped from the automatic doors of the hotel. "Allow me to show you to the front desk." He took their two small suitcases and made his way briskly back into the hotel and the cool blast of air-conditioning.

"Oh, thank God!" Nichelle sighed when the artificial air poured over her face.

"Come on." Wolfe walked at her side, looking perfectly cool in his pale slacks and long-sleeved shirt rolled up at the elbows. "You've lived in Miami almost all your life. Why are you sweating this heat?"

She gave him a dirty look at the awful pun.

"Bonjour, Madame." Nichelle stepped past him to speak with the smartly dressed woman behind the desk. "We'd like to check in."

After she offered their names, a different uniformed young man took their bags and led them to an elevator and a room on the third floor. He opened the door for them, put their bags inside then quickly disappeared before Wolfe could even reach for his wallet for a tip. The air inside the room was deliciously cool. Nichelle sank into the long burgundy couch, barely noticing the decor. It wasn't stiflingly hot; that was all she cared about.

"This place is incredible," Wolfe said.

Unlike her, he ignored the comfort of the large couch to prowl around the opulent suite of rooms. Which, she could see from the comfort of the plush couch, was beautiful. The rooms were alive with color. The large cabinet, set up with alcohol of all sorts, was painted in lush shades of green and gold that made her want to get up and touch them. But she was a little too exhausted for that. Now that they were out of the heat, the long day of travel abruptly caught up with her. She closed her eyes and curled into the couch.

"You look comfortable." There was something in Wolfe's voice that she was too tired to catch.

She opened one eye to see him looming over her. "It suits my purposes." She closed her eye and snuggled into the cushions that smelled like amber, smoky and sweet.

"I hope so since there's only one bed."

Her eyes fluttered open. "Hmm?"

"You heard me." He flopped down beside her and gave her feet a gentle shove. "You can have it. Go. I'm too tired to act more chivalrous than this."

Wolfe kicked off his shoes and lay back to rest his head on the opposite end of the long and wide sofa, his feet stretching out to touch her hip. But Nichelle was too tired to care. She belatedly shoved him back, or at least the part of his foot she could reach, and curled up tighter on the long couch. Within seconds, she was asleep.

Nichelle woke to the sound of singing. A low, wailing voice. A man. She blinked and sat up, rubbing at her eyes. The sun was still high outside the windows, but its light was a soft gold compared to the brilliant white from when they had just arrived.

"It's the call to prayer," Wolfe said softly.

He lay on the opposite end of the couch, his body still where it touched hers.

The ululating voice drifted through the room, beautiful and heartrending, Arabic words she did not understand. Nichelle breathed quietly in appreciation, keeping still to allow the sounds to wash over her, into her.

When it ended, she opened her eyes to see Wolfe quietly watching her. He looked only a little wrinkled from his nap, the white linen shirt unbuttoned halfway down his chest, showing off beautiful and hard flesh, a glimpse of a flat brown nipple. Nichelle curled her nails into her palm, overcome by a nearly overwhelming desire to touch him. It would be so easy to crawl down to the other end of the couch and finish unbuttoning his shirt, peel the soft linen from his body, bite, kiss and lick every inch of bare flesh.

"It's beautiful, isn't it?" His gaze did not leave hers.

She could only nod, swallowing heavily as the sweet and thick need rolled through her veins. The places where their bodies touched, her hip and his foot through the two layers of cloth, shifted and rubbed. Nichelle pressed her thighs together and clamped down on the inside of her cheek. *Jesus. The next few days are going to be torture.*

"I've wanted to come to Marrakesh since I was a kid," Wolfe said softly.

"Why didn't you?" Nichelle pushed the arousal away, focusing on the conversation happening in the open instead of the one her body was having with his. She tucked her hip deeper into the couch, trying to put some space between their bodies. But the little relief she gained was quickly lost when Wolfe's sock-clad foot followed her skin, tucking into her with a slight and suggestive caress. *Was he doing this to her on purpose?*

But Wolfe was the picture of innocence when he shrugged. "At first, I didn't have time. I wanted to finish school. Then my parents said it was too dangerous. After that, work became more important to me than seeing the world." He sat up on the scrolled arm of the couch, his head resting on his upraised arm. "Getting Kingston Consulting up and running took up most of my time."

The arousal slowly faded away as he spoke. Or at least her awareness of it faded.

"I never thought I'd hear you say work became more important than enjoying life," she murmured.

They were caught in a delicate cocoon together, lulled into a gentle world made simply of their own voices, the lush beauty of the room, the faint smell of Moroccan amber that billowed up from the couch like fine smoke. It felt like blasphemy to speak above a whisper.

"Yeah. I used to call Garrison a workaholic." His best friend spent far too many nights alone in his office working on divorce cases that didn't change the world.

Or at least he had, until he met a woman who dragged him from his tower and into a fully lived life. "Sometimes I think I'm just as bad. I only hide it better."

"I disagree with that," Nichelle said. "You love chasing women too much to work that hard at anything else."

"Now that comment *I* disagree with," he said. "For your information, I haven't done any chasing since the day before the family dinner." His voice was low, rippling with annoyance, most likely at himself.

It took Nichelle a moment to realize what he was talking about. Then she understood what he'd just said. He hadn't been with a woman in over two months? "Are you serious? Why?"

"I haven't had the opportunity?" He made it a question, as if he didn't know why he hadn't slept with any of the, no doubt, many women who'd thrown themselves at him since that night.

"Maybe that means you'll have more focus this week." Not that he'd ever had any trouble giving his complete attention to work.

"Or maybe I'll just have a nice pair of blue balls, like a proper married man," he grumbled.

She chuckled, poking him with her toe. "You don't even know anything about being married."

"Yes, and I'd like to keep it that way. At least for a little while longer."

Then they were both quiet, bathing in the sweet silence of the room left behind by the late afternoon call to prayer. She only heard her own breathing, the faint scratch of his socked feet against the couch as he resettled himself, the whisper of traffic from the street below.

"I'm a little hungry," Wolfe said a little while later.

"Me, too." She'd been drifting back into sleep in the

cool and comfortable silence. She hadn't eaten much on the plane, instead drinking her way through a half bottle of wine plus several carafes of coffee (that still hadn't managed to keep her awake). "There's a restaurant downstairs," she murmured through her sleep. "Let's have some appetizers and proper drinks before we head out tonight."

Wolfe yawned and stretched, his long legs going rigid against her thigh. As he moved, his shirt rode up, exposing the flat plane of his belly, the sprinkling of hair disappearing into his pants. Nichelle licked her lips but, keeping her lashes lowered, did not look away. He was impossibly beautiful. And every time she noticed it, she was shocked she hadn't realized it before.

"Another brilliant idea." He grinned and scratched his flat belly. "I'm going to shower and wake myself up." Wolfe yawned again. "Unless you want to go first."

She shook her head. "You don't take long. I'll wait."

When he disappeared toward the bathroom, she sighed and leaned into the couch and into the warmth he'd abandoned. *This is not going well at all*, she thought. But that didn't stop her body from reveling in the male-scented heat he'd left behind. Her lashes flagged against her cheeks.

"We have about an hour and a half before the limo gets here."

She opened her eyes to Wolfe, fresh and gorgeous in smoke-gray slacks, a white dress shirt and paisley tie. He smelled of his favorite mint soap and a hint of aftershave. She blinked in time to see him grabbing up the matching suit jacket then walking away. His dress shoes, black and handmade Italian leather, tapped the mosaic tile floor. His backside was a firm curve under the gray cotton.

Nichelle bit her lip and closed her eyes again. *Dammit.*

She rolled off the couch and got to her feet. A shower. A cold one. And then she'd be ready.

Half an hour later, she was dressed in a softer version of her usual outfit—a black pencil dress with a high pyramid neckline—when she joined Wolfe in the living room. He shrugged on his suit jacket, tugged on the cuffs of his shirt. She noticed his gaze flicker down to her feet, an eyebrow rising at the scarlet, sky-high and curvy-heeled Walter Steiger pumps. A new purchase.

His mouth opened to say something, then he closed it. He took a breath and looked around him, patted his pockets.

"Ready?"

She grabbed her purse with her cell phone and the hotel key. "Absolutely."

After a quick and light dinner in the hotel restaurant, they agreed to briefly stop by the room to brush their teeth and otherwise freshen up before meeting the limo outside. When they arrived in the lobby, Wolfe put a hand on the edge of the elevator door to allow Nichelle out ahead of him. As she smiled her thanks, she caught the flash of a familiar face from the corner of her eye. She froze.

"What's wrong?" Wolfe released the door and came closer. He touched her arm.

"Isaac Franklin." She spat the name like the bad taste it was.

As if he heard her call his name, Isaac Franklin paused in midstep and glanced over his shoulder at her. The smile he had for the man he'd been walking with froze on his face. For a moment, it seemed as if he would keep going, but he straightened his spine and crossed the opulent lobby to approach her and Wolfe. *Maybe*, Nichelle thought and hoped, *he isn't here for the same reason we are*.

"Diallo. Nichelle. I'd like to say I'm surprised to see you here for the Quraishi account, but I'm not." His words killed her desperate hope before it could have any real life.

Wolfe nodded at the man. They barely knew each other, probably had only been to the same conferences and hotel lobbies where they were competing for the same accounts. Like now.

"It's a small world, and our business is even smaller," Wolfe said.

"True."

Isaac, the man who'd succeeded her at Sterling Solutions, the company she'd left for Wolfe, didn't like her. And he never bothered to hide that dislike, which was something she appreciated over the hypocrisy of his colleagues. It was more than just professional dislike, she knew, but she never let it bother her. She didn't care what he or anyone else at Sterling thought.

"We're late." Nichelle looped her arm through Wolfe's, too thrown to think about how touching him would make her feel. Her diamond caught briefly in the fabric of his jacket. "We'll see you soon, I'm sure."

Isaac nodded. "I'm sure you will."

When she and Wolfe stepped outside the hotel door and into the thick desert heat, the limousine and driver were already waiting. Black suit, white shirt, gleaming shoes. It was a different driver, younger and wearing a slightly flirtatious smile aimed at Nichelle. But he opened the door for them, shut them in the privacy of the dark limousine and rolled up the partition. The lyrics to a Beyoncé song flickered through her mind before she suppressed the images they inspired—her knees, the carpeted floor of the limo, Wolfe's gaping slacks, his mouth parted in a gasp as her own tasted the most intimate part of him—with a brutal bite of the inside of her cheek. The coppery taste of blood burst in her mouth.

"You okay?" Wolfe touched her hand.

"Yes. I'm good." She swallowed the metallic taste in her mouth but didn't bother with a smile. "Do you think we're wasting our time here?"

"Why, just because you know for sure that we have a little competition?"

She shook her head. Isaac was more than competition. He was the shark in their previously calm waters. She cursed softly.

"Relax," Wolfe murmured.

He glanced out the window as the car pulled out from the circular drive of the hotel and onto the main street. Mopeds, motorcycles, cars, horse-drawn carts all competed for the same bit of space on the pavement.

The sky was a bright and vicious blue. Clouds floated in the endless sapphire, barely there, as if they, too, were afraid of the sun's burning heat that gripped Marrakesh, a city that was such an unexpected mix of beauty, noise and spirituality.

"Don't tell me to relax." Nichelle twisted her lips at him, only half joking.

Normally, the sight of her old colleagues would only urge her to do better and be better, leaving no doubt that she would metaphorically drag them through that conference room by the hair and dominate them with a press of her high heels on their collective throats. But seeing Isaac had thrown her.

"Just relax," Wolfe said again. "Tonight is about checking out the competition. We didn't know before that we had any in town, but now we do." He turned from the window and glanced down her body in a slow and thorough gaze that he'd never directed at her before. "And you look very ready to stab the competition in the throat with those weapons you call shoes."

Nichelle hid her surprise. Why was this man reading her mind?

She crossed her legs, and the shoes in question lifted with the stretch of her leg, headed between the sprawl of his thighs. Wolfe only watched her with an amused smile, not trying to protect himself as she teasingly stretched out her deadly heel toward his crotch. He trusted her, the bastard. With a roll of her eyes, she dropped the threatening leg.

Wolfe laughed, then leaned forward briefly to tap her silk-covered knee. "You can kill me later."

He turned his attention back to the scene passing the window, a smile lingering around his mouth. He had no problem relaxing, his body swaying gently against the leather seats from the movement of the car. Nichelle couldn't help but notice that the pale material of his suit was the perfect foil for his cedar skin. Her fingers itched to touch him. She sat on them and tried harder not to stare.

Only when the driver opened the door nearly half an hour later at a mansion miles from the city center did she realize she hadn't thought about the "competition" once after Wolfe told her to relax. But he probably hadn't meant to distract her from her foolish thoughts quite *that* way.

The mansion was truly, truly opulent. All gorgeous curves and mosaics, straight out of the dreams of *One Hundred and One Arabian Nights*. It was a tall, three-story structure, more desert palace than everyday mansion, with ribbons of lights bordering the drive-way. There were three other limousines farther up in the drive, empty and with the drivers standing nearby smoking cigarettes and speaking quietly to each other in Arabic.

"Bonsoir, madame. Monsieur."

Wolfe got out first and stepped back, offering his hand to help Nichelle out of the car. She shivered when his big hand closed around hers, strong and warm. Okay. This attraction of hers was stupid and had to stop. How many times had he held her hand? How many times had he helped her out of cars and she hadn't reacted this way? She suddenly hated Paris with a burning passion.

Nichelle thanked him for his chivalry anyway.

A uniformed man approached them. "This way."

Wolfe offered his arm to Nichelle, and she curved her own through it after a brief hesitation. She squared her shoulders, ready to face whatever the night would throw at them. They followed their escort through a long foyer toward soft conversation, the music of sitars and haunting Moroccan drums.

The party was in full swing. The man ushered them through high doors, into the thick of the party, a room scented with rose water, the sound of at least five lan-guages rising and falling in conversation and weaving with the music that wasn't loud enough to be overwhelming. Their escort took them directly to a robed man holding court before an international group of business people.

He was short—shorter than Wolfe at any rate—and handsome with his sand-colored skin, closely clipped beard with flecks of gray, and flowing white robes.

"*Monsieur* Quraishi. Your guests."

The man, Monsieur Quraishi, excused himself from the circle of attentive men and women with a quick nod. "*Monsieur* and *Madame* Diallo. Welcome." His voice was a deep, booming bass, the perfect accompaniment to his gentle and paternal smile. "At last I can put a face to the memos and emails." As if he hadn't thoroughly researched them through every means available, social media included. "Your wife is even more beautiful in person." Quraishi's look was appreciative but respectful, his gaze lingering briefly on Nichelle's shoes. She sensed Wolfe's amusement.

"Even though I claim no responsibility for that fact," Wolfe said with a glance of admiration at Nichelle. "I am glad to reap the benefits."

If she didn't know any better, she swore he was flirting with her. He was either being a shameless opportunist or a very good actor.

"I've trained you well, Mr. Diallo," she teased him back.

Nichelle was very aware of the ring on her left hand, even though it was the right hand that Jamal al Din Quraishi lifted to kiss. He greeted Wolfe with a firm handshake and an appraising look that his genial smile could not mask.

"It's rare to meet a couple who work so well together," Quraishi said.

"The secret, if you call it that, is we keep our personal lives away from the office," Wolfe said, all smiling teeth and handsome sincerity. "Because of that, not many people even know we're married."

Nichelle forced herself not to frown his way. If that was the story they were going with, why did he even suggest they buy rings? As if Wolfe sensed her thoughts, he lightly touched her hand, a calming stroke of her ring finger. She did quiet her thoughts, but made a mental note to ask him about it later.

"Very smart." Quraishi squeezed Wolfe's shoulder with a conspiratorial wink. "Come, let me introduce you two to some of the competition and to some colleagues of mine."

Nichelle and Wolfe exchanged a look as they walked ahead of Quraishi. *Some* of the competition? It wasn't just Sterling Solutions they had to worry about?

It turned out that there were two other firms in the ring. Quraishi introduced Nichelle and Wolfe to the group of men he'd been talking with, including the head of a Canadian firm whose work they were already familiar with. Nichelle immediately dismissed them as any real competition, but shook hands with a respectful smile. It wasn't long before the other men and women wandered off with the excuse of finding drinks, leaving her and Wolfe with Quraishi.

"Thank you for your excellent hospitality," Wolfe said to him. "The accommodations are exceptional."

"Yes, you're already taking excellent care of us," Nichelle said with a smile. "We were pleasantly surprised."

"So the desert hospitality is not as harsh as you envisioned?" The sharp-toothed smile challenged her, but there was humor there, as well.

Nichelle amped up her smile and added a soft laugh for good measure. "We had no expectations, *monsieur*. But I haven't been so well cared for in years." She could feel herself floundering and willed her tongue not to stumble. "Your country is exceptional."

At her side, she could feel Wolfe's silent laughter. He was the politician of the partnership. Better at smoothing ruffled feathers and making people feel at ease. She almost sighed in relief when he came to her rescue.

"The hotel is quite luxurious, even by our standards," Wolfe said. "My wife is very pleased with our first visit to your country."

My wife. Nichelle shivered at the intimacy the words conveyed.

Quraishi reined in his smile, made it warmer and less challenging. "In that case, thank you. Your comfort is my pleasure. Anything you want here is yours." He made a wide gesture to the ballroom and the mansion around them.

"Yes, thank you." Nichelle glanced around again.

Just then, she saw Isaac and his companion from the hotel, a man she'd never seen before. They made a beeline for Quraishi.

Wolfe dipped his head, mouth brushing against Nichelle's ear. "I think that's our cue to mingle," he murmured low enough for only her to hear.

"Of course, darling." She nodded to their host. "Thank you again for your hospitality, *Monsieur* Quraishi. We look forward to talking with you more later on this evening."

Wolfe guided her to the bar, where they ordered

glasses of orange juice mixed with sparkling water. "So how do you want to handle this?" he asked once they had their drinks. They stood with their backs to the wall, appraising the room.

"Let's mingle," Nichelle said. "See what we can find out about the so-called competition."

"Sounds like a plan, General." He touched his glass briefly to hers, his firm mouth curved into an intimate smile at odds with his words. "Good hunting."

When they separated, at least a dozen pairs of feminine eyes followed Wolfe as he made his way toward one of the men they'd been introduced to earlier, the Frenchman. His strong and graceful stride, the swagger in his hips, drew an almost indecent amount of sexual attention, Nichelle's included. Before Paris, she'd never given any, or at least not much, thought to how women always flocked to him. But now the amount of interest he attracted made her grit her teeth. If they were really married, she wasn't sure she'd be able to handle it.

Nichelle took a breath and made her way into the fray.

After nearly an hour of mingling, Nichelle's attention began to stray. It took more to keep up the social face, but she smiled and asked questions, shared information, made small talk with the best of them.

"So your firm is based in Miami." A gorgeous man with lambent brown eyes and a subtle Arabic accent nodded in her direction. "It must be difficult to keep your attention focused on work when there is so much beauty to distract you." His eyes dipped over her body, more than implying she was part of that irresistible landscape he mentioned.

"Pardon me, ladies. Gentlemen." Wolfe appeared out

of the crowd to touch Nichelle's shoulder. He aimed a narrow-eyed stare at the man with her. "I'd like to claim Madame Nichelle for this dance." His jacket was unbuttoned, and a crooked smile shaped his mouth. She wanted to stroke the firm line of his lower lip in welcome.

He tugged her to his side. "Is that okay with you?"

She grinned at his mischievous smile. "Of course. You can sweep me away anytime."

He led her to the dance floor.

"Are you doing all right? You looked like it was time for a break. Especially from your new admirer." Wolfe growled in mock jealousy, and she rolled her eyes.

One hand pressed into the small of her back, and the other claimed her hand in a modified waltz to the sitar music.

"Not from him so much, but yeah." She blew out a breath, relieved that he knew her so well but also annoyed that she had allowed her exhaustion to show. Although she loved her work and the business of making people bow to her will, there were some days that she only had so much to give before she needed to replenish her internal reserves. And today, playing married, being tense in a room full of strangers and potential enemies, had her mind working overtime.

She was strategizing and planning, modifying her approach to the presentation she and Wolfe were slated to give the next day. She was nearly exhausted. But with Wolfe's arms around her, she felt the beginnings of a burst of energy. She tossed her head back to look at him.

"They had me on the ropes," she said.

"Never say that. Whatever happened to 'float like a butterfly and sting like a bee'?"

"This Ali is tired."

Wolfe drew her closer, turned her in the steps of the dance. "We're almost done."

But the tiredness was rapidly draining away. Electricity crackled at the contact points between their flesh. She was slightly breathless, but had the growing feeling she could go for hours. She slipped her arms around his neck and rested her head on his chest.

"I'm feeling better by the minute, husband."

His hands tightened briefly around her waist, and soft breath that felt like a quiet gasp huffed at her temple. A humming sound rumbled in his chest.

Despite her better judgment, she'd switched from orange juice to vodka tonics. Wolfe's presence and her irrational jealousy of the women following him around were leading her toward a tiny internal meltdown. Even with that, she couldn't deny the comfort and peace of his arms. That, at least, hadn't changed. The majority of the crowd—which was mostly Muslim, she assumed—wasn't drinking. Most of the Westerners made unending trips to the open bar, although she'd limited herself to two drinks over the past hour. In Wolfe's arms, she caught the slightly sweet scent on his breath. Whiskey. He had switched to alcohol, too.

The music pulsed, and she allowed it to take her away. She melted into Wolfe's strong arms. His legs brushed against hers, and butterfly wings of awareness fluttered in her stomach.

"Good," Wolfe murmured into her hair. "I can't do this without my better half."

If they'd both been completely sober, they probably wouldn't joke this freely about their "marriage." But in that moment, it felt like a harmless ruse, something to take comfort in rather than run away from.

"You're right about that," she replied.

Wolfe laughed, spun her into a twirl then drew her back into his arms. He was even more relaxed than usual. Seeing him like this made her realize just how tense he had been. It felt good. Too good.

"See any women here you want to take back to the room and introduce to your little friend?"

He gave her a teasing glance. "Little?"

She laughed. "Relative to the size of the rest of you then."

He chuckled, slipping both arms around her waist and maneuvering her into a more modern dance, hips moving to the sensual beat of the drums. She'd forgotten how well he could move.

"Anyway, I only have eyes for one woman tonight," he murmured.

Her heart thumped in her chest. "Liar."

"Never to you." The faint scent of his exertion brushed her nose. Sweat. His cologne. Whiskey on his breath. He jerked his head toward a voluptuous woman standing almost in the center of a group of nearly salivating men. "That's the woman over there. She's too beautiful to ignore, don't you think?"

She pinched the taut skin at the bottom of his jaw.

"Ouch!" He laughed and gathered her in his arms again. "I'm just joking. I'm being very careful who I pay attention to this evening." His voice was low and intimate, soft as he spoke into her throat in English. "I feel as if Quraishi is watching us."

"Of course he is." She couldn't stop the ache of disappointment that it was the job, his diligence about keeping up the appearances of their pretense, that made him pay this much attention to her.

Something must have leaked through her voice because he held her closer. "Not to mention you are the most beautiful woman in the room. Where else would I be but by your side?"

She shook her head, quietly laughing at herself and at him. "Dial it down a notch, Casanova. I don't think I'm that needy tonight." But wasn't she? Nichelle moved closer to him, wound her arms around his neck and linked her fingers. She briefly felt the contours of the wedding rings beneath her fingertips before her hands settled at the back of his neck. His skin was warm seduction. His breath touched her mouth.

They moved slowly against each other, her hips following his hips, rocking to the sensual music, a slow winding that poured the honey of desire steadily into her veins until she was overcome by sweetness. She wanted to kiss him.

"You keep looking at me like that, and I'm going to forget all about this pretense." His eyes flickered down to her mouth, and she licked her lips. He hungrily followed the motion with his gaze, and she drew a sharp breath at the jolt of heat in her belly.

Oh no, no, no.

She drew another sharp breath. "I think..." Nichelle licked her lips and tried again. "I think I'm going to get some fresh air." Then she carefully drew back from him, her aching and needy body, her arms, her fingers, her tangled thoughts. She turned and left. Nichelle fumbled her way through the crowd that seemed intent on keeping her in the small room and shoving her back toward Wolfe. But maybe all of that was in her mind. Maybe.

She found her way out to a balcony overlooking the courtyard. A mazelike garden made from fruit-heavy orange trees, purple and white bougainvillea, a large tiled fountain in its center. The night was scented and warm, its darkness heavy around her shoulders, broken only by the gentle illumination from the pair of floor lamps on each side of the wide balcony.

Nichelle drew deep breaths until her thoughts calmed. But her brain still fuzzed at the edges from the alcohol she'd had earlier. She wasn't a drinker, never had a high tolerance for alcohol. In fact, she only normally needed one drink. Drink number two was begging for trouble. And now, she found herself firmly in trouble. And in lust.

She twisted the rings on her finger.

"Are you well?"

The question, asked softly in French, made her jerk in surprise. She turned to face the source of the inquiry, although she could tell by the voice who it was.

"*Monsieur* Quraishi." She greeted him with a deliberately unconcerned smile. "Yes, I am doing fine. Thank you for asking." She curled her hands around the stone of the balcony, taking comfort in the firm and slick marble under her palms. "It's beautiful out here. I wanted to share it with my husband. He loves the architecture of the city."

Her host moved to her side with a whisper of his robes. He searched her face as if he was looking for something in particular, his deep-set eyes steady and astute. "Yes, Moorish design is some of the best in the world. There is nothing else like it on earth. It is beauty personified." His bearded mouth twitched, daring her to disagree.

But Nichelle wasn't anyone's yes-man. "Wolfe might agree with you on that."

"You do not?"

She weighed her answer carefully, hoping her intellect would override the alcohol that had nearly made her throw herself at Wolfe on the dance floor. "I do find it beautiful, yes. There is nothing else like it."

He chuckled. "Truthful while being diplomatic. I like that."

On the inside, Nichelle flinched. The guilt at their deception twisted unpleasantly in her chest. Maybe this hadn't been one of her best ideas.

Footsteps tapped toward them. "*Monsieur* Quraishi."

The man who'd escorted her and Wolfe into the party appeared around the corner. Isaac Franklin closely followed him.

"Yes?"

"A word, sir?"

Quraishi dipped his head toward Nichelle. "If you'd excuse me, *Madame.*"

"Of course."

As he walked away, she noticed Isaac watching her with hawkish eyes. Suspicion and a barely leashed anger burned in his gaze. She kept her expression neutral and did not look away from him. Eventually, Quraishi's presence forced him to turn away.

When she was once again alone, she cursed beneath her breath. The balcony was hardly the sanctuary she'd thought it would be. But at least she'd stopped thinking about Wolfe, about stripping that mouthwatering suit from his body and climbing into his lap to suckle on his tongue as if she was starved for a taste of him.

Nichelle blew out a breath and straightened her spine.

This was a challenge, both her attraction for Wolfe and the unexpected complication of Isaac Franklin. She'd never backed away from a challenge in her life and wasn't about to start now.

Chapter 6

A hot knot of arousal burned in Wolfe's belly as he watched Nichelle walk away. For the more informal party, she'd worn something softer, a black dress that skimmed her curves, the neckline as high as most of her blouses and the hemline inches below her knees. But the silk emphasized the perfect hourglass of her figure, and each step in those very high red heels twitched the enticing curves of her bottom. He longed to watch her walk away just like that toward his bedroom. He licked his lips.

"Your wife is a lucky woman. My husband hasn't looked at me like that in years."

A woman stood near him—the one he had jokingly pointed out to Nichelle a few minutes before. She *was* beautiful. But not like Nichelle.

"Then he's a fool," he said about the woman's unappreciative husband.

She laughed. "Or maybe I am." She looked him over with a familiar, predatory gleam, taking in everything about him. Maybe she was the one finished with her husband and not the other way around.

"Can I get you another whiskey?" she asked.

She must have watched him closely enough to know what he was drinking. He'd cut himself off nearly half an hour before, but he suddenly felt the need for another drink. He wasn't getting what he wanted tonight, Nichelle in his bed, sighing his name as he licked and stroked her body to completion. Another drink was close enough.

"Of course," he said to the beautiful woman. "Lead the way."

At the bar, she asked the bartender for another whiskey on the rocks, light on the rocks. Without asking, the bartender gave the drink to Wolfe while the woman, Saleema, she told him, asked for orange juice, no ice. She thanked the bartender and slipped a two-hundred dirham note across the gleaming surface of the bar.

Saleema said something that Wolfe assumed was "thank you" in Arabic, then turned her attention back to him. They wandered through the crowded room, stopping occasionally to speak with other guests, before she led him to one of the low couches at the back of the room. Like Nichelle earlier, he was done socializing. But this, socializing at Quraishi's party, was business, and it didn't matter what he actually wanted.

In the middle of conversation about something forgettable, the man he'd seen earlier with Isaac Franklin invited himself to sit with them.

"Orlando Green," he said with a smile that was more of a snarl.

Wolfe shook his hand, resisting the urge to wipe his palm on his slacks afterward. Although the man was well put together—he'd worn a suit to the party like most of the businessmen there—there was something a little oily about him.

"So what brings you here, Diallo?"

"Probably the same thing that brought *you* here," Wolfe countered.

Green's face grew tight. But he forced a smile past a tightened jaw.

"There's no need to talk business tonight." Saleema put a hand on Wolfe's knee, then on Green's, bending over so the high collar of her dress dipped to show the tops of her breasts. Wolfe stiffened, although he noticed the other man loosening his jaw to give her a real smile.

"You're right, Saleema," Green said.

So they'd already been introduced. Interesting. Or not.

Wolfe took a sip of his drink for want of something to do. The whiskey burned, a hot kiss all the way down his chest. With the heat spreading through him, he leaned back in the couch and widened his thighs, incidentally shaking Saleema's hand from his knee.

He put on one of his charming smiles and asked her something he didn't really care to know the answer to. Saleema opened her mouth to answer just as Green looked past Wolfe to something that made his eyes widen in appreciation.

It was Nichelle.

She stood a few feet away, a hand on her hip, eyes locked on the knee Saleema had just been stroking. She lifted her eyes to his, then to the woman at his side. There was something dangerous in that look of hers, both a command and a threat. It wasn't an expression he'd seen on her face before.

Something low in him growled at it, recognized the look for what it was. When Nichelle turned and walked away from him, heading toward the exit, Wolfe did the only thing that made sense. He followed. He mumbled something to Saleema and Green, abandoned his too-strong whiskey on the nearby coffee table and walked quickly after Nichelle, keeping his eyes on the firm one-two switch of her backside. He didn't want to lose sight of her this time.

She took them down a wide hallway, a path that she seemed familiar with, although she'd never been to the mansion before. He didn't know where she was going, and he doubted that she knew, either. But her steps were certain, and he was only certain that he wanted her. He ached with the want, barely able to walk properly. They moved through a high corridor, past servants slipping silently in and out of rooms, down a wide staircase with a banister that was cool under his hand, the many tiles making up its design a small road map to wherever she led them.

He heard her high heels echoing from below. The smell of chlorine drifted up to meet him as he descended the stairs. An indoor pool. There were no windows, only the single set of stairs they'd come down together. Blue water rippled and reflected on the tiled ceiling etched with a blue-and-white starburst design.

Such beauty would make him weep if he wasn't already looking at the most beautiful woman he'd ever seen in his life. Distantly, he was aware he was waxing more poetic than usual. His mind wasn't quite all there, and feelings and impulses he would normally have under proper control were bursting all over the place.

There was no one else in the enclosed pool chamber except for them. No music. No distractions. Only the faint hum of the pool's filter, soft sounds of the water lapping against tiled walls. Wolfe followed the echoing rap of Nichelle's footsteps until she was only inches away.

"Why did you leave?" His voice came out with a growl.

She crossed her arms under her breasts. Combative. Confrontational. "You shouldn't have let that woman touch you."

"Do you think that's something you should concern yourself with?"

"Hell, yes!" Her shout echoed in the tiled room. "I'm supposed to be your wife, remember?"

"In name only, sweetheart." *Sweetheart?* When the hell did he ever talk to Nichelle like that? But the strong liquor was scorching a trail in him still, and he barely stopped himself from dragging Nichelle against his body so she could feel how he burned.

"Wolfe, you're acting like a whore."

His spine jerked tight at the insult. "Why? Because some woman I don't know wants to put her hands on me?"

"You're right." She turned away to pace the very edge of the pool. "You're just acting like *yourself.*"

He drew in a sharp breath, a gasp from the pain of hurt feelings. Was that how she saw him? "Nichelle, don't say anything else to me that you'll regret."

"Regret? Hardly."

She spun to look at him, tall and regal in the bright

light bouncing from the white walls. The wavering reflection of the water rippled on her face, her bare arms.
Her mouth was red and moist in the undulating light,
her curved body a wicked temptation. He flushed hot.
He wanted to touch her. But beneath the desire, an unfamiliar emotion tore at him.

"I wasn't doing anything with her," he said.

He realized then that the emotion was regret. He felt
like an idiot for allowing Saleema to touch him and for
letting Nichelle see it.

"You didn't stop her," Nichelle said.

She turned and walked away from him again, heels
stabbing the tiles. She didn't raise her voice, but she
fairly vibrated with anger and frustration. "You could've
jeopardized everything by flirting with her. What if
anyone important had seen the way you were damn
near begging that slut to put her hand in your pants?"

"That's not what was happening by any damn stretch
of the imagination. Don't resort to unnecessary exag-
geration."

She turned back to face him, raising an eyebrow in
disbelief and anger. "Fu—"

He tugged her into his arms and kissed her. She stiffened against him. Wolfe swallowed her gasp of surprise.
Their lips pressed together, a dry connection. A *forced*
connection. Something that he had initiated against her
will. Wolfe drew in a ragged breath and began to pull
away, feeling awful, as if he'd crossed some line that
could never be uncrossed. But she grabbed his arms and
kept him close, melted into him. Her lips parted, and
her tongue flickered out to stroke his mouth.

His mind spun out.

The slick heat of her tongue was his undoing. He

cupped the back of her head, angling for more of the sweet taste of her. His heart thudded hard in his chest with the realization that, *yes,* she wanted him, too. He pulled her closer, shifting his chest to rub the hardened peaks of her breasts he could feel through the layers of cloth. A shock of sound left her throat: need and surprise. Wolfe gripped her hips and pulled her tight against him.

He ached with a need he hadn't even known he was capable of feeling. His entire body was hard with it, muscles, bones and sex all at fierce attention to the things she was making him feel. Her fingers scraped the back of his head, nails raking the light stubble. Wolfe circled his hips into hers, telling her wordlessly of his need. Nichelle gasped again and drew back, stumbling away from him. Her eyes flickered down to the thickness in his pants, then away. Wolfe swallowed, pressed his lips together to stop himself from telling her what he wanted.

I want to make love to you. The words hovered just a breath away.

The need was rampant in him. Like that time in the hotel in Paris, he wasn't ashamed for her to know he wanted her. She was so damned beautiful. If he'd known there had been even the most remote chance of having her, they would have been screwing in his office, in that uncomfortable couch in her office she loved so much, everywhere she would let him. Wolfe groaned, shocked at the thoughts that spilled all too easily through his mind.

He opened his mouth to apologize.

"You don't mean it," she said.

The lipstick was only slightly smudged on her swollen mouth. Her breath came quickly, but her eyes sparkled with challenge. And she was more than a little drunk, just like he was. Wolfe shook his head.

"You don't know what I was going to say. You can't predict me like a company's stock prices."

But that wasn't true. She knew him. More than most, she knew him. Maybe she even knew the level of his desperate want. If she allowed him to, he would press her against the cool wall of their underground hideaway and sink to his knees in worship of her. He licked his lips at the thought of pleasing her that way.

"Nicki…"

"Don't! Don't call me that." She backed away from him again, controlling her breathing with visible effort. "You don't get to turn me into one of your whores tonight, Wolfe. That's not what this arrangement is about."

Her words were like a punch to the gut. "You could never be…that. Not to me or anyone." He cursed savagely and turned away.

"This is stupid," she hissed.

He breathed deeply, his hand on the banister. "It is. I think I need to sleep off whatever I was drinking and talk with you tomorrow."

He couldn't look at her without feeling the endless depth of his want. An abyss of aching feeling and reckless desire. It had come out of nowhere. One moment, he was prepared to endure the flicker of attraction he felt for her. And the next, his body flared to life, like a gasoline-soaked wick, and all he could think of was Nichelle, Nicki, her body ready to receive him, the two of them making love like sex-starved animals on the cool tiles.

Yes, he was drunk. But that was no excuse.

He looked at her over his shoulder. "Let's have breakfast tomorrow and talk, okay?"

She sighed, a steadying sound. "Okay."

He took a step toward the upper level. "I'll tell Quraishi that we're ready to go?" He framed it as a question.

"Yes." Her controlled breathing was audible in the cavernous room. "I'm ready."

Wolfe turned his back to her and quickly climbed the stairs as if the very hounds of hell were chasing him. But he couldn't outrun himself.

Chapter 7

Nichelle lay on top of the sheets staring at the ceiling. She could sense Wolfe's presence, as awake as she was, on the other side of the bedroom door. She felt a million kinds of foolish. How could she have allowed irrational jealousy to make her chastise Wolfe for doing what he'd always done?

But she remembered the flare, no the *explosion*, of anger in her chest when the woman put her hand on Wolfe's knee. And how he sat there and allowed it, as if she had an invitation to touch him in a way that Nichelle had never gotten to.

She turned over in the bed and groaned silently with embarrassment. This was not how she'd planned to spend the time in Morocco, burning with alternating waves of regret and lust for the man she hadn't even known she wanted until Paris. If she didn't know any better, she'd have sworn that he put something in her drink.

But she was never one to blame someone else for her own actions. She wanted him. It wasn't the best idea. She knew that. Getting sexually involved would only hurt them both, and possibly their partnership, in the long run. He treated women like tissues, and she didn't want to be the next one. But the ache for him had been so swift, so unexpected, that it took her by surprise and she could only stand, gasping, in the wake of it and hope not to wake up emotionally bruised and bloodied in the end.

Nichelle squeezed her eyes shut and rolled over, trying again for sleep.

She and Wolfe needed to talk about what was between them. But more importantly, they needed to convince Quraishi that Kingston was the best firm for the job.

Tomorrow was going to be a hell of a day.

The next morning, she woke up long before sunrise to the sound of rattling dishes and a door closing. She left the bedroom, belting a robe around her waist, to see Wolfe already awake in the sitting room of the suite, a room service tray for two and papers in front of him at the dining table.

"You're just in time," he said, voice rough with sleep. "Room service just left."

He was bare-chested, black pajama bottoms on, his face serious. She stared at his chest then looked away, flutters of arousal making her throat dry.

Would it kill him to put on a shirt? Nichelle lingered between the bedroom door and the table where Wolfe sat, acknowledgment of what happened between them last night on the tip of her tongue.

"Are we okay?" she asked.

Wolfe dipped his head. "Yes, we are." But his face was blank.

Nichelle ran her tongue along the inside of her lip, joining him for the small breakfast of mint tea, yogurt and Moroccan crepes. He poured tea for them both, the scented steam rising from the stream of sweetened mixture, his attention completely focused on the task. With a flicker of his lush lashes, his eyes met hers.

She gasped at the wealth of feeling she saw there— desire, frustration, resolve. He cleared his throat, and his expression went blank again.

"All right," she said. "Then let's get to work."

He nodded again and passed her the jar of honey.

Later, they were effortlessly in sync when Nichelle stood in front of the room full of mostly men and did her best to convince Jamal al Din Quraishi that Kingston Consulting was the best firm to help him create a successful long-term business strategy for his company.

She presented the raw data and the statistics while Wolfe backed her up by answering any questions related to logistics that Quraishi or any of his associates had. It was a perfect meeting, so perfect that Nichelle wondered just what she had been worried about before. Isaac Franklin was good, but while she had been at Sterling Solutions, he was never good enough to outperform her.

"That was brilliantly done." Yasmina, one of Quraishi's representatives, reached out to shake Nichelle's hand at the end of the meeting. "Thank you." She was sternly beautiful, her thick black hair pulled back from her strong-jawed face in a high, crowning bun. Her severely cut black skirt-suit hinted at a lush figure.

"It was our pleasure. Please don't hesitate to ask questions if there is anything we can clarify for you." Nichelle teasingly nodded her head in Wolfe's direction. "He can answer any queries that pop up."

"I already know the drill," Wolfe said. "I don't just stand around and look pretty."

Yasmina gave him a quick glance, an appreciative one, but she kept herself at a respectful distance. She gave Nichelle a subtle look, as if congratulating her on snagging such a fine specimen. Nichelle blinked, never having been the recipient of that kind of look before, congratulatory rather than avaricious.

"We'll be in touch with you within twenty-four hours about our decision," Yasmina said. "In the meantime, feel free to enjoy our hospitality for as long as you like."

Nichelle glanced at Wolfe.

"Thank you," he said. "You and Monsieur Quraishi have been very generous. We have a few things brewing in Miami so we'll be leaving soon."

Yasmina nodded. "Your wife tells me you are a fan of Moorish architecture, the desert and our way of life."

Nichelle knew Wolfe was looking at her. He probably wondered when she'd found time to talk to Yasmina alone and to talk about him in particular.

"Yes." He flashed one of his knee-weakening smiles. "I do enjoy your country."

Yasmina stared at him for a moment, seemingly stunned by his sheer beauty. Nichelle knew how she felt. Yasmina cleared her throat. "Please allow our guides to take you out into the desert and show you more of it. You will be bored sitting in an air-conditioned room for the rest of the day. Although I'm sure, if forced, you can find some ways of entertaining yourselves."

Though Yasmina's voice wasn't the least bit suggestive—she could have been talking about knitting and Parcheesi for all Nichelle knew—Nichelle blushed. It would be all too easy to fall into bed with Wolfe and spend the next few hours rolling around in the sheets with him and screaming his name until she was hoarse.

Nichelle nodded but did not meet Wolfe's eyes. "Thank you for that," she said. "We may take you up on the offer." Nichelle glanced at Wolfe, an inquiry in her gaze. "Yes?"

He nodded, almost looking bored. "Yes."

Yasmina nodded, everything decided.

"That went well." Wolfe stated the obvious when they were back in the limo and heading for the hotel. He shrugged out of his jacket and dropped his head back against the leather seat. "You were amazing in there." He winked at her before going back to his impression of a bored corporate tycoon. "But I don't want to talk about it until he gives us his answer."

"And Yasmina said they'll let us know by tomorrow." *It seemed like too much time to wait.*

"Yes." He'd also been surprised when the efficient woman promised them results sooner than anticipated. "So...the desert." Wolfe's eyes were closed, hands balanced on his thighs spread wide in the smoke-colored slacks. He was fighting a grin of excitement. Nichelle was fighting the urge to crawl into his lap and kiss the smile from his face, nibble on his bottom lip and lick the inside of his mouth until he made the same hungry noises from last night.

She shifted in her seat. "I think you'd like the desert."

And it would be a relief to escape the stifling intimacy of the hotel and the city. Maybe a desert ride was what they needed to put things in perspective.

He made a sound of agreement and reached for his phone to make the arrangements. Silk whispered against leather as she stretched out full length in the seat across from him and gladly allowed him to take charge of the excursion. She was drained from the performance but knew she wouldn't completely relax until they got word of Quraishi's decision. The next few hours were going to feel like forever.

Two hours later, after a meal and change of clothes, they strode down the front steps of the hotel again and back into the day's heat. Nichelle fumbled to a stop. Walking just ahead of them and dressed in casual clothes were Isaac Franklin and Orlando Green. Nichelle had a feeling that this wasn't just coincidence. What the hell was Quraishi playing at?

"I think we're going to have a little company." Wolfe's breath brushed her ear as he murmured the words.

She shivered from the contact and roughly corralled her attention before it could wander. "Unfortunately, I think you're right."

He straightened at her side, a hand tucked into the small of her back guiding her toward the Mercedes-Benz SUV idling at the curb. A driver, in the familiar black and white, stood holding the door open.

"*Monsieurs* and *madame*." The driver greeted them all with a formal bow, his hand still on the edge of the open door. He took Wolfe's bag and put it in the trunk.

Isaac looked at Nichelle with familiar and barely concealed dislike. "Ladies first," he said.

She shook her head with a cool smile. "Age before beauty." Then she tipped her gaze to Wolfe, giving herself time to get acclimated to this new situation. "That means you're last."

Wolfe gave a shout of laughter. "If I didn't know better, I'd swear you were trying to butter me up for something later."

"*Do* you know better?"

While the banter flowed light and easy between them, the two men got into the car ahead of them, having no choice but to climb into the two rear seats of the boxy but luxurious truck while Nichelle and Wolfe claimed the seats in the middle row behind the driver.

The truck smelled like new leather. If luxury had a smell, this was it—leather and wood mixed with the particular chemical tang of the air-conditioning. The truck pulled away from the curb with a throaty purr moments before mellow jazz began to play from the harman/kardon speakers.

In the seats behind her, Nichelle heard the shift of bodies against leather, and a low rumbling question she didn't catch. She sighed, not wanting to talk to either of the two men behind her. She scraped her nails through her short curls and leaned back in the seat. Beside her, Wolfe caught her eyes and smiled. In his gaze she saw the faint reminder of their night, the kiss, the restless evening they'd shared separately.

"Relax," he murmured.

He offered his hand, glancing down at her legs. She sighed, silently this time, not having the strength of will to stand up to the temptation he offered, even in the midst of their awkwardness. She did what he silently asked, what she always wanted from him, which was to slip off her red-and-black Jordan high-tops and her socks and drape her feet in his lap while she lay with her back pressed to the locked door. With the fine attention to detail that he did everything he thought important, he began to massage her feet.

His sinful hands stroked every inch of her feet, up to her ankles and her calves, while she breathed deeply and just barely stopped the most obscene noises from leaving her lips.

"Oh, God... I love you," she breathed deeply and closed her eyes. Wolfe's hands paused on her feet. His gaze touched her face; she felt it as surely as if he'd put his hand there. There was so much she wanted to say to him, maybe even *needed* to say. But she was very aware of the eavesdropping ears of the men behind them.

Outside the window of the SUV, the surroundings slowly changed from hotels and spas and nightclubs to languid stretches of desert as they left the clutter of the city behind.

The AC pumped cool air over Nichelle's face, nearly lulling her into sleep as she watched Wolfe with her feet in his lap. He looked so content that suddenly nothing mattered. Not the awkwardness that had been between them the night before. Not the kiss that sparked many dreams, and certainly not the bright diamonds that sparkled from her left hand.

She'd wanted to take off the rings once the meeting was over, but Wolfe waved a hand in dismissal of her discomfort. "The show doesn't end until we get back to Miami," he'd said.

She knew he was right, but that didn't make the rings any more comfortable to wear. Although, if she was being really honest, part of the discomfort lay in how *right* the wedding band felt on her finger. If she wasn't looking at it and obsessing about thoughts of a nude Wolfe, it would be completely natural to have it there, a beam of light between her and him, on her hand.

Over an hour later, the SUV pulled into the sandy drive of a house that seemed to appear out of nowhere in the flat, beige landscape. The house was white, a simple and squat rectangle with an attached verandah. In the yard, two hammocks hung parallel to each other under a large fig tree. One hammock was occupied while the other swayed, empty.

Just then, a man in gorgeous cobalt blue robes opened the door of the SUV and welcomed the four of them out into the desert heat. A dry wind blew against Nichelle's face and her bare throat. She adjusted the sunglasses over her eyes, glad she'd packed her darkest and most effective pair. The sun was a bright and oppressive presence in the sky.

The man in blue smiled widely at them. He was tall, and Nichelle had noticed that most of the men in Marrakesh were not. His height was a graceful counterpoint to his body moving like water beneath the calf-length robes. Incongruous acid-washed jeans and black flip-flops completed the rest of his outfit.

"Greetings!" he called out. "I am Mahmoud."

Another man, similarly dressed but in pale blue-and-white-striped robes, came up behind him. He bowed and introduced himself, first in French, then in Arabic, as Kareef.

"Mahmoud and I will be taking care of you this evening and through the night," Kareef said. "We will try not to lose you in the desert and earn Monsieur Quraishi's displeasure."

Although he was joking, there was something in the look his partner threw him, a warning and tight-lipped smile. But Kareef ignored Mahmoud.

"Come." Kareef gestured toward the house.

On the verandah, he gave Nichelle and Wolfe packs filled with bottles of water and face towels. Mahmoud wrapped a flowing piece of cloth around Nichelle's head and face while Wolfe watched, paying close enough attention that he was able to securely wrap his own when the time came.

The camels were already saddled and waiting in a patch of sand nearby, crouched on their stomachs, almost like cats, their backs burdened with large padded saddles and their heads and mouths harnessed with leading ropes. Even on their bellies, the beasts looked tall.

Nichelle narrowed her eyes at the camel closest to her. Its big eyes blinked back, placid as a cow's.

"Don't be afraid." Wolfe touched her back and she shivered, despite her earlier determination to shrug off his effect on her and act as if Paris had never happened. Or last night.

She looked at him as if he were crazy. But too late, she caught the glimmer of a tease in his eyes. He knew that he had essentially just challenged her to climb on top of this moving mountain and show no fear. She clenched her jaw. "Right."

"Madame." Mahmoud waved her toward the beast she had just been eyeballing. "Your chariot awaits." His French was fluid, flavored with something else that made it even more beautiful.

Kareef called out something to him in Arabic and he shouted back, not turning away from Nichelle. He guided her toward the camel. She held her breath, expecting a stench from the beast. But an accidental breath had her sighing in surprise. All she could smell was the dry desert air, faint sweat from the men and, very, very lightly, Wolfe's particular, masculine scent.

"Climb on and lean back. Relax and keep your thighs tight around her while she stands up." He nodded at the camel who almost looked...friendly.

Aware of Wolfe and his laughing gaze, she swung her leg over the large animal and held on to the front of the saddle.

"Hold on!" he called out to the camel, and the beast rose to her full height. Nichelle rocked in the high saddle, gripping it tightly from the expected but no less startling movement, the sensation of the ground receding even farther away.

Oh God!

The guide held the reins in his hand, watching to see if she was okay with the current state of affairs. When she nodded, he passed the reins to her.

"Hold these and wait."

Nichelle nodded again.

She controlled herself enough to see Wolfe taking a more graceful seat, swinging his leg in a movement that stretched his slacks taut against his backside. With a confident nod to their guide, his beautiful body rose into the air atop the camel as the animal stood up. Why did he have to be so damned gorgeous?

After seeing to Isaac and Green, the two guides mounted their camels with a minimum of fuss and led the foursome under the bright sun into the desert. Nichelle knew it was Wolfe's dream to be here in the heat with nothing around them, no cars, no city, no burdens. He had often shared with her while they sat in the aftermath of one project or another in the office, his tie loosened and her shoes kicked aside, that sometimes he just wanted to jump on a horse and ride. Keep going until the horse got tired and just see where they ended up. It wasn't about escape for him, but an exploration and love of the unfamiliar.

He sat atop the camel next to her, chatting amicably with their guides, his body swaying with the movement of the beast, as if this ride and this desert were the most familiar things in the world. Isaac and Green rode together at the very back.

"Yasmina tells me you are here on business," Mahmoud said to Nichelle, his brilliant blue robes blowing in the strong wind. "You are a woman of glass towers like her?" He seemed genuinely interested.

"Not like her." Then Nichelle shrugged. "Well, maybe. She is wonderful, whatever she is. I only met her a few days ago."

"Yes, she is wonderful." Something moved behind his eyes, more than admiration for the absent business-woman perhaps? Nichelle wondered how they knew each other.

When she asked, Mahmoud seemed happy to share. "My father worked with hers when I was a child. I saw her grow up."

Ah. Nichelle nodded. Mahmoud didn't seem much older than his midtwenties, handsome and relaxed under the desert sun, the turbaned blue cloth protecting his head, white teeth flashing as he spoke.

"I didn't realize she was so young."

"Yes. She has come very far from her station." He

looked proud. "One day, she will own that glass tower she works in."

Nichelle didn't doubt him. In just the few times she'd had the chance to speak with Yasmina, the woman seemed determined and strong-willed, allowing nothing, not even the perceived role of Muslim women, to get in the way of what she wanted. Her drive was inspiring. Nichelle said as much to Mahmoud.

"Yes, she has her eyes on the stars, that one."

But what about the diamonds scattered at her feet? It wasn't difficult to see that he was in love with her. Or at least something very much like love. He seemed to want the best for her. The longing in his voice was unmistakable.

"You love her?" she asked in English.

He was quiet for a moment, and she thought he didn't understand. Then he shook his head. "It is not my place to love one such as her," he replied in the same language. "I would only weigh her down and prevent her from reaching the glimmer above that she's always wanted."

Nichelle could identify with wanting everything. Sun, moon and stars. Even if she had a lover whom she wanted as much as he wanted her. But, if she had to choose, could she give up the glimmering heavens of corporate success for a chance at love? She didn't know. She'd never been in the position to choose. Her gaze flickered to Wolfe. As if he sensed her regard, he looked back over his shoulder. He hitched a brow, silently asking if anything was wrong. She gave him back a tiny shake of her head. *All clear.*

Mahmoud didn't miss a thing. He chuckled. "I see."

They rode on, Mahmoud and Kareef telling them

different facts about the desert, plant life, stories of Westerners getting lost under the burning sun and not found until their bones had bleached white in the hot sands. Wolfe laughed and encouraged them to tell more stories, the more gruesome and ridiculous the better, until Mahmoud and Kareef were trying to outdo each other with the most outrageous stories, the six of them laughing until the two-hour ride was finished for the afternoon. They stopped under a cluster of tall palm trees to drink water, tend to personal business and take a brief shelter from the sun.

Nichelle clambered down from her seated camel and found a big rock near the pond that rippled under the palm trees. An honest-to-God oasis. Sweat dripped down her back and between her breasts. Her thin jeans clung to her skin, damp in places. The turban she wore caught the sweat on her forehead, preventing the sting to her eyes. But she still squinted behind her sunglasses, actually enjoying the novelty of the experience. Who'd have thought it, this Miami girl surrounded by sand and no ocean in sight? She mopped her throat and chest with her handkerchief.

Wolfe looked cool and relaxed, laughing with the two guides. Yes, he was definitely enjoying himself. She looked up when she felt another presence. Isaac Franklin. His friend was sticking close to Mahmoud and Kareef, who had drifted, like most people, into Wolfe's irresistible orbit.

"So, who do you think will get this contract?" Isaac asked.

She immediately tensed at his fake good humor. They both had the mentality of sharks in bloody water, and she despised him for acting otherwise, especially out here where it didn't matter.

"That's not something I want to think about right now." She didn't bother to smile.

Isaac nodded as if she had just uttered the sagest of recommendations. Nichelle knew she had her bitch face on, but didn't feel inclined to change it. It was annoying enough that she and Wolfe had been herded together with Isaac and his colleague for this desert tour. She'd wanted it just to be her and Wolfe, for him to enjoy the journey without the annoyance of Isaac's presence to derail his good mood. Though to be fair, she was the one getting irritated. Wolfe seemed perfectly fine. A few feet away, he laughed with the guides, his head flung back, white teeth a brilliant contrast in his darkening face. She smiled from just the sound of his laughter.

Isaac didn't miss the direction of her gaze. "So you and Diallo, huh?"

"That's none of your business."

Yes, she was perpetrating a fraud for their would-be client. But she'd be damned if she'd discuss anything to do with her personal life with Isaac.

But he wouldn't drop it. "Everybody at Sterling thought that was why you left us in the first place. From what I hear around town, that's some first class pipe you left us for."

Nichelle drew a deep breath. No, she was not talking about Wolfe's sex game with anyone, least of all Isaac Franklin. She stood up and wiped off the bottom of her jeans.

"Go screw yourself." She turned and walked away.

The desert excursion was a challenge of some type. That was becoming more obvious with each passing moment she spent with Isaac. Quraishi hadn't just taken four people out in the desert on camels, all expenses paid, simply out of the kindness of his heart.

But Nichelle had to admit she was a little too frazzled to play whatever game was afoot. Her head wasn't quite there. She glanced again at the reason why and kept walking until she was just about on the water's edge, opposite where Isaac stood glaring at her. She wet her handkerchief and pressed it to her face, sighing at the relief from the heat.

After only a half hour at the oasis where they refreshed themselves, adjusted wilting turbans and drank water, their group prepared to move on.

Wolfe wandered over to Nichelle. "I wonder how much pee ends up in the water." He jerked his head toward the small pond where she had dipped her rag and wiped her face at least half a dozen times since they'd stopped. She noticed Orlando Green zipping himself up as he moved from behind a tree.

Nichelle glared at Wolfe. "I wish you'd kept that thought to yourself."

He chuckled and strolled over to his camel who rolled her big and moist eyes over to him as soon as he came within a few feet of her. Even the camel was head over heels in love with him. Wolfe playfully scratched her head and murmured soft nonsense in her ear that Nichelle was too far away to hear. Figured.

Then they were off again, riding beneath the desert sun with the sound of Mahmoud's melodic singing, Kareef clapping and providing accompanying laughter. The sunset, when they found it, was spectacular. They rode over the powdery sand, the edges of their turbans pulled down over their mouths and noses to block the sand being tossed around in the wind.

Nichelle's camel rocked beneath her while the sky turned to amber, then gold, catching fire above them as their small caravan rode toward a mysterious destination. She had done her job with the presentation. Wolfe was happy. They would go back to Miami soon enough. Even with the presence of Isaac and his sycophantic friend, the desert ride was an amazing experience she would not soon forget.

As the last of the light disappeared from the sky, they crested a mountain of sand. Nichelle exhaled in wonder. Below them sat a pair of large tents, white and stretched out beneath the darkening sky. A fire already burned a few dozen feet away from the tents, crackling and showering sparks into the air.

They had arrived at their home for the night.

Chapter 8

Wolfe sat around the fire with Nichelle, Franklin, Green and their guides, sipping from his small glass of mint tea. His thighs ached dimly from the ride, but overall he felt both energized and relaxed, completely at peace. His wants were few.

In the surprising coolness of the desert, the fire's warmth tempted him closer. But Nichelle's heat drew him even more. In her jeans and white blouse, she looked very much the modern woman, but with the winds howling through the sand and the camels only a few feet away, it was easy to imagine he was with her in another time and free of the responsibilities that had brought them to Morocco in the first place.

"It is a good night, yes?" Mahmoud nodded to everyone around the fire.

Wolfe nodded back. The trip hadn't gone quite as

expected, but he had enjoyed himself very much. Only one thing would make his desert adventure sweeter. He glanced at Nichelle. Her mouth was curved into a smile and her eyes sparkled with warmth. She looked happy.

"A good night calls for a good song," Kareef said. Then he launched into the opening words of Pharrell Williams's "*Happy.*"

After exchanging a look and "why not?" shrugs, Wolfe and Nichelle started singing along. Franklin and Green looked at them as if they were crazy. The two men's uptight frowns only made Wolfe sing louder, while Nichelle's bright gaze warmed him like the midday sun.

The sing-along, scattered with talk of world politics, lasted until their Berber host brought dinner. They ate the small meal of chicken tagine over sweet couscous, talked and laughed around the fire until, one by one, the other men excused themselves for more restful evening pursuits. Franklin and Green went off to their beds in the tent while Mahmoud and Kareef wandered off to smoke, their deep voices in Arabic filling the night with another kind of music.

Wolfe sank lower onto his pallet in front of the fire until he was lying on his back and facing away from the tents. The makeshift bed inside the tent was more comfortable, but in the darkness of the desert, the stars were shimmering and bright. It seemed a shame to sleep indoors when this was happening in the heavens above him.

"Stay out here with me," he said to Nichelle.

He turned his head to watch her, similarly slumped in her pallet but much more gracefully, her long, jean-clad legs stretched toward the fire while a pillow she'd brought outside supported her neck.

She smiled at him, lazy and sweet. "Do you see me going anywhere?"

Once we get to Miami, yes.

But he said nothing. The profile of her face was awash in light from the fire, teasing out the fullness of her lips, her sharp cheekbones, the line of her neck. He couldn't think of any place he'd rather be, or anyone else he'd rather share the beauty of the desert with.

"I want to kiss you," he said.

She didn't move. He could've pretended she hadn't heard him. Except he noticed the flicker of her eyelashes, the shudder that rippled through her long body.

"Wolfe," she finally said, her voice softer than the breeze that fluttered the loose turban on his head. "This is the worst idea we've ever had."

He released a breath of relief, a breath he hadn't even realized he'd been holding. She wanted this, too. And she felt it, whatever "this" was. The pallet was soft under his back, the sand beneath even softer, and it moved when he shifted.

Nichelle stood up and grabbed the edge of her pallet. His stomach dropped in disappointment. She was going inside. But instead of heading toward the tent, she dragged her pallet closer to his until they touched. She lay down beside him, bringing her scent of honey and sage and sweat from their long day's ride.

"This is a bad idea." She touched his chest through his linen shirt and jacket, burning him. "Only here," she said. "This can't happen again when we get home."

He wanted to say *No. I want this all the time. We'd be so good together.* But the more desperate part of him simply wanted whatever she had to give him now. Anything that she would share. Her pallet, her breath, her lips. She hovered close to him, her breath puffing against his mouth, her hand making gentle circles over his chest.

"Wolfe…"

She kissed him.

A light touch on his mouth, a tentative press of warm flesh that made him gasp at the instant heat low in his belly. She hummed in approval and smiled against his lips. But he was beyond amusement. His flesh was on fire with a slow, pulsing need. That need built steadily between them as their mouths came together more firmly, no longer timid, both of them perfectly sober, perfectly clear-eyed and wanting. He settled a hand on her hip and carefully drew her close to him, allowed her to feel how much he wanted her.

He groaned. "You taste so good…"

Then he was done talking. Nichelle was soft and feminine and her mouth was a drugging, wet heat. Sweet mother of all that was good, he'd never felt anything like this in his entire life. With a touch of her tongue to his, he wanted to flip her over on her back and roughly take her and make her his. But he also wanted to treasure her, make sure that no one ever hurt her again, least of all him.

Her fingernails dug into his chest through his shirt, plucked apart the buttons to expose his bare skin. Arousal bucked harder in his belly. He licked the damp interior of her mouth, and she sucked on his tongue, a hot and suggestive suction that had him thick and firm in his pants.

He growled and pressed closer to her, then rolled

over until he was balanced carefully over her but cradled between her thighs. Her belly was soft under his hands, her nipples firm. Nichelle's breath hitched. She bit his lip, her hands drifting down to his sides, shoving up his shirt to get more of his overheated skin. He circled his hips into hers and they shivered together. His pulse was out of control, a mad riot under his skin. Wolfe panted into the soft curve of her neck, bit her. Nichelle whimpered his name. Her hand slipped under his shirt, an inciting warmth along his back, stroking the muscles hard and rippling from the control he was exerting over himself.

It would be easy to take this to its logical conclusion. To slip the jeans down her thighs, tug down his zipper, join with her in a way he had done before with countless women. But this was Nichelle. His Nicki. She was so many things to him that the act which should have been simple—muscle memory wrapped up with the unfamiliar emotions that made him grasp her body even more tightly to him—was not.

He wanted her. Wasn't it that straightforward? They were both adults. No one in Marrakesh really knew them. As far as these people were concerned, they were a married couple and didn't need anyone's permission to have sex under the stars. His thoughts skittered away with the slow stroke of her thumb over his nipple. He shuddered and jerked down into her.

"Nicki..."

Nichelle looked up at him, mouth open in a wet and hungry smile. "Yes, Wolfe?"

She lightly pinched his nipple, watching his reaction from under half-closed lids. Arousal drew Wolfe down to kiss her again. Her mouth was soft between his teeth.

She whimpered and the sound went straight down his middle, made him want to please her and show her he was there for her, no matter what she needed or how long she needed it.

He stroked her hip through the jeans, fingers hovering above her belt buckle. She arched up into him. Their tongues tangled and meshed, a slow and wet sound that dragged him deeper into the morass of lust and want. Her zipper slid down. Gasping, she wrenched her mouth from his when he touched her outside the delicate fabric of her panties. Wolfe stopped.

She whimpered again. "Keep going. Please."

That was all the permission he needed. Wolfe slid his hands into the underwear, parted her damp folds and found the source of her desire's heat. Nichelle breathed his name, a hot gust of breath against his neck. She fumbled against his bare skin, fingers clumsy in her lust, scraping and squeezing his nipples while she whimpered and twisted against him. Wolfe panted into her mouth.

She was hot and wet around his fingers, nails digging into his side while she rolled her hips, begging wordlessly for more of his touch. Her breath sped up. The motion of her hips on the pallet grew more desperate. Wolfe ached to fill her. But he ached even more to satisfy her.

"Oh my God. Oh G—!"

She sank her teeth into his neck to muffle her scream. He bucked with the sharpness of the pain but didn't stop touching her. She jerked her hips, and he encouraged her abandon with the curl and thrust of his fingers. Nichelle stiffened abruptly then shuddered against him, panting.

"You…" She licked her lips and tried again. "That

was so unfair." Her voice was broken as if she'd been screaming for hours.

Wolfe bent to kiss her again. But the noise of people coming closer pulled him from his stupor. He quickly searched the darkness to find Mahmoud and Kareef. They had finished their cigarettes and were coming back to the fire. Wolfe pulled his fingers from Nichelle's body, zipped her pants and pulled down her blouse.

Against him, she was lust-drunk, mouth swollen and soft. Her lashes fluttered down to hide her eyes, and she bit her lip. She looked vulnerable and delicate, the soft underside of her woman-in-charge attitude revealed. He didn't want anyone else to see her this way.

Wolfe grabbed a blanket from beneath his pallet and pulled it over her. She blinked in surprise. Then her eyes flickered toward the sound of the two approaching men. He dipped his mouth close to her ear, told her how much he wanted her and made a promise he intended to keep. Then he pulled away and put some necessary space between them. Nichelle rolled over onto her side, curling under the blanket and pulling it up to her ears.

The men came close, with a flurry of Arabic. But within moments they seemed to grasp the situation and vanish toward the tents.

"That was a little embarrassing," Nichelle said softly.

The light from the fire played over the planes of her face, revealing the subtle tremor to her mouth, its damp curve.

"Only a little." He made sure that the men hadn't seen anything. Just a married couple lying close together by the fire. She was fully covered up, and his aroused body pressed down into the pallet, away from unwanted eyes.

Wolfe touched her shoulder. "We should probably get some sleep," he whispered.

She nodded in the flickering light and rolled into him, bringing back her warmth and the salty intimacy of her scent. "This is just for tonight," Nichelle said. "It's cold and I don't want to go back to the tent."

Inside the tent was everything they'd come here to do. Business. Just like their pretend marriage was business—but Wolfe echoed her sentiment. For him, going back inside the tent meant a loss of their privacy. A privacy that the two Moroccan men had given them under the stars.

"Get some rest." This time she was the one who tried to soothe the situation. "I promise not to molest you while you sleep."

Wolfe smiled. "Don't make promises I don't want you to keep."

Chapter 9

The next morning, Nichelle woke to the insistent vibration of her hybrid satellite-mobile phone. Although they were ostensibly on a mini vacation, she kept her phone with her, ready to hear whatever Quraishi's decision was. She slid her arm under the blanket to reach for the phone, incidentally touching a warmth that did not belong to her. Wolfe.

She grabbed the phone, but her eyes tripped over the beauty of him stretched out on the pallet beside her, breathtaking in the rising sun. Her hand fluttered to her heart with the return of last night's memories. She tore her eyes away from Wolfe to answer and pay attention to the call.

"Nichelle Wright speaking."

"Madame." It was Yasmina. "A decision has been reached." Her voice gave no indication which of the

firms had been chosen. There was the general warmth, a pleasant camaraderie, but that was all.

Nichelle tamped down the feeling of impatience. "Yes?"

"We would like for you to come back to your hotel," Yasmina said. "I will meet you there at ten this morning."

"Very well." Nichelle peeled the rest of the blankets from her and ran her fingernails through her short hair. "See you then." She disconnected the call. "Wolfe."

"I'm awake." The words rumbled from him, low and sexy. His eyes stayed closed, though he moved his legs against hers, a smile on his lips. "What did they say?"

"We're meeting with them for a decision in a few hours. No hint about what it is."

He sighed and opened his eyes. "More games."

He shook his head, feet brushing hers again in a final stroke of intimacy as he turned away from her to stretch and yawn. She watched the arch of his neck, the muscles that rippled beneath his unbuttoned shirt. The memory of how the shirt came to be unbuttoned teased her: her hand against his chest, his thudding heartbeat under her palm, which echoed the frantic pulse between her legs.

He had felt so good last night, touching her in ways that made her whimper with surrender and need. If Mahmoud and Kareef hadn't returned, she wasn't sure she would've been able to stop herself from throwing away every ounce of decency just to have Wolfe under the stars. He had been the voice of reason, whispering his desire for her, but pulling away.

"I want you," she remembered him whispering. "But not here. I want to..." And he'd whispered filthy and raw things in her ear while he pulled away from her, inflaming her while depriving her of his aroused body and the means to sate it. "The next time I have you like this—" he'd briefly pressed his hardness between her thighs, curled into her, fingers tight on her hips "—I won't leave until we're both satisfied."

Nichelle trembled with the memory of those heated words. Much like she had trembled last night, wishing the two guides to hell for interrupting them but knowing deep down—very, *very* deep down—that the interruption was for the best.

It was one thing to lust after her business partner. It was quite another to actually make love with him and to share the physical satisfaction they both obviously craved. Even if it was the best sex of her life, once they broached that final intimacy, there would be no going back.

But what if the thing you can't undo is better than what you had?

She ignored the whiny voice in her head and drew back even more from the tempting man only a few inches away. She dusted the sand from her shoes and pulled them on, then started to gather up the pieces of her pallet. It took Wolfe a moment, but soon he was doing the same, getting himself ready for the trip back into Marrakesh.

Now that she wasn't completely absorbed in Wolfe and the promises of his hard and tempting body, Nichelle realized that the camp was already bustling with activity. A few yards away, a young boy was tending to the camels. The older man who had brought them dinner—and she assumed he was the one who'd set up the two large tents—stood nearby with his pale robes billowing in the breeze. He held a cell phone to his ear.

Mahmoud and Kareef came from their tent fully dressed and smiling.

"Good morning."

It was as if they had been waiting for Wolfe and Nichelle to wake before approaching the already ashen fire.

"Did you sleep well?" There was no hint of a smirk, no double meaning in his voice, for which Nichelle was extremely grateful.

"Yes, we did. Thank you." Wolfe answered for both of them.

"Don't worry about those pallets." Mahmoud handed them bottles of water. "A Jeep will be here for you in a few minutes to take you back to the hotel. It's faster than the camels."

"Why the rush?" Nichelle asked, although she assumed that getting back to their hotel via camel by ten was just not going to happen.

Mahmoud shrugged. "I do not know the minds of the rich. There is a meeting, they say. It is soon."

"Yes." Wolfe glanced at his watch. "Is there a place where we can wash up?"

"Inside the tents you will find everything you need, and an area behind it to tend to everything else."

Nichelle thanked Mahmoud and made her way toward the tent. When the car came for them, she felt gritty from the sand, but prepared. The night in the desert had loosened her up in ways she hadn't anticipated. She was still nervous about Quraishi's decision, but she didn't worry about it as much as she would have before. Instead, she was thinking about Wolfe. About being with him in *every* way. She ached with curiosity and with need. But she also knew that she'd have to leave both those things unsatisfied. For now.

She and Wolfe slid into the back of the SUV this time and allowed Isaac and Green to sit behind the driver. The SUV powered over the sand, roaring and rocking over ridges of high, powdery gold until they finally found solid road. Nine thirty caught them at the hotel, quickly separating from her former colleagues to head in for quick showers and more businesslike attire.

"You look beautiful," Wolfe said.

She paused in front of the full-length mirror in the sitting room of their suite, smoothing the black tie that matched the sleek faux masculine lines of her blouse and pencil skirt.

"Thank you."

Before, those words would have meant next to nothing. But now, after the night of shared kisses and sated desire, they held a universe of meaning. They meant, *I remember last night.* They meant, *I still want you.*

Nichelle tugged her gaze from Wolfe's. She shook herself and grabbed the hotel key and her small shoulder bag.

Wolfe stepped ahead of her to open the door.

The meeting was in a small conference room a few floors below them. The room was bare except for a long table and three manila folders in front of three chairs. No fruit. No coffee. They apparently didn't intend for it to be a long meeting.

Yasmina was already there when they walked in. She was talking with Mahmoud, who was dressed in a dark suit instead of the robes he had worn in the desert. Nichelle briefly met his eyes and smiled. He acknowledged her greeting, then quickly left the room. There was something going on here. She tilted an eyebrow in inquiry at Wolfe, but he gave only the smallest shrug. He didn't know what was going on, either. But the look on his face said he would soon find out.

Yasmina shook Nichelle's hand, then Wolfe's. "Good morning," she said. "I know you have other things to do so I will make this quick." Yasmina picked up a folder from the table and put it in Wolfe's hand. Before she could say anything else, the door to the conference room opened. Isaac and Orlando Green walked in. Yasmina excused herself to welcome them just as warmly as she had Nichelle and Wolfe. She gave them a manila folder of their own.

"Let me know if you have any questions," she said.

Wolfe handed the folder to Nichelle without opening it. "This is yours, whatever the answer."

She flipped the folder open with a casual hand, betraying none of the anxiety she felt. What she saw written inside made her draw a quick breath.

"Okay." Nichelle nodded once and gave the folder back to Wolfe. The brief flicker of a smile touched the corner of his mouth when he read the few lines written on the crisp sheet of white paper bearing Quraishi's letterhead and signature.

"Okay," Wolfe echoed.

Across the room, Isaac and Green were glaring at the contents of their folder, obviously not liking what they saw. Reps from the other firm in the running for the Quraishi account took their folder and glanced briefly at it before speaking with Yasmina then leaving.

"Thank you." Wolfe shook Yasmina's hand.

"I'll be in touch," she said, then lifted her head so the other men in the room could hear her. "Please have some breakfast in the restaurant downstairs with Monsieur Quraishi's compliments. If you need to follow up, please don't hesitate to contact me."

She smiled again at Nichelle and left the room.

Oh my God! Nichelle stood with her legs braced wide, hands crossed over her chest. They'd actually done it. Her knees shook, and her entire body went limp with relief.

"We did it," she said to Wolfe, barely whispering the words. They shared a look of satisfaction. Nichelle turned away from Wolfe's smile when footsteps sounded behind her.

"You don't play fair, Nichelle." Isaac stood far too close to her, his face a tight mask of anger.

"Fair?"

"You did *something.*" A vein ticked in his forehead. "You cheated your way into this deal. I don't know how you did it, but I'm going to find out."

"No cheating happened, Isaac." She bared her teeth at him. "You always think there's some great conspiracy at work when it's just your own incompetence that cost you the prize. Grow up and get better." She tapped the folder against her thigh. "Now, if you'll excuse us, Wolfe and I have packing to do." No sooner had she turned away from Isaac and Green than Wolfe was guiding her toward the door and down the lushly carpeted hallway.

She felt like singing.

"Franklin seems to be taking this a little too personally." Wolfe's tone seemed deliberately casual. As if he was trying to ask her something that he didn't quite want to know the answer to. "Why is that?"

"He's a sore loser about everything." She shrugged.

Sudden tension radiated from Wolfe. His footsteps slowed. "Did you two used to be lovers?"

"No. But he wanted us to be." She started to say something about not ever mixing business with pleasure, but the memory of last night wouldn't let the hypocrisy past her lips.

"And here I was thinking he was just another stupid desk jockey." Wolfe looked relieved. "But he's smart enough to pursue you."

"I'm not sure if smart is the right word," she murmured wryly, remembering all the ridiculous things Isaac had done to get her attention while they worked together. Calling her father for permission to date her. Threatening to tattoo her name on his bicep. Asking her out on dates, multiple times, when she'd plainly told him she wasn't interested. He had been persistent. Then belligerent, when she firmly denied him in no uncertain terms. Somehow, he'd convinced himself she was just holding out for bigger corporate fish and would only sleep with someone higher up in the company than him. Isaac Franklin was the very definition of a sore loser.

Wolfe stopped walking. "Office hookups can be tricky." His eyes dipped to Nichelle's mouth then lower. He wasn't talking about Isaac at all.

"Yes, they can be." She licked her lips as her heart began to beat faster. There was a question in his eyes, a demand, and she longed to answer it. Nichelle stepped back until her butt hit the wall. Wolfe followed.

His breath brushed her cheek. "Why don't we—?"

"*Monsieur* and *Madame* Diallo!"

Wolfe broke off at their new client's voice. He stepped back, smoothing his tie. Monsieur Quraishi waited for them by the elevator, looking well-rested and dapper in a pale blue suit. "I wish I could have been there for the reveal, but my daughter had a concert nearby that just finished." He clapped Wolfe on the back and shook Nichelle's hand. "Do you have time for a celebratory lunch?"

"Of course," Wolfe said, although Nichelle wasn't hungry. At least not for food.

"We'd love to," she added for good measure, giving their new client a real smile even though, for one heart-stopping moment, she wanted to throw the account back in Quraishi's lap just so she could hear what Wolfe had to say.

Wolfe tugged down his cuffs and put his game face back on. "Let's go." His grimace could have passed for a smile under a certain light.

"Excellent." Quraishi waved them toward the entrance. "My driver is waiting outside."

He took them to a small restaurant near the Jamaa el Fna market. The chauffeur let them out near the depot for the horse-drawn carriages at the entrance to the square, and they braved the heat, winding through the madness of the square toward the restaurant.

"It is chaos here," Quraishi said. "But I would not trade it for anything."

A member of his security team, hardly unobtrusive in his dark suit and with the clear surveillance earpiece coiled against his neck, drifted behind them. Beggars emerged from the crowd to hold out their hands, to murmur pleas in Arabic and French. Wolfe, without hesitating, pulled loose bills from his pants pocket, passing out dirham notes to anyone who approached him. When one of the security team moved to push the beggars back, Quraishi waved him away.

He gently shook his head at a woman who came close, her head and face covered in a dirty hijab. "If you give to one," he said, "all fall forward with their hands held out."

As if to perfectly illustrate his point, another beggar materialized from the crowd, this time with a child on her hip. "*Monsieurs*," she murmured. "*Madame, s'il vous plaît.*"

Wolfe gave money to her, too.

By the time they had completed the short walk to the restaurant, over a dozen beggars had approached them, with more on the way.

"You are a kind man," Quraishi said. "I'm very pleased with my decision to employ your firm."

"But kindness doesn't equal effectiveness," Nichelle felt it her duty to say.

Their new client's eyes twinkled. "True. But it does make the working relationship, and the marriage, more pleasant."

At the restaurant, they sat upstairs on its terrace overlooking the square. The host seated them at a table under a wide, fluttering canopy, sun-washed white and reminiscent of the tent they had almost slept in while in the desert. Pedestal fans moved the air around them, keeping the terrace cool.

A sudden breeze floated up and brushed the back of Nichelle's neck. The same breeze flapped the tablecloth and caught the end of Wolfe's tie secured by a platinum tie clip. She gave in to the impulse to stroke the paisley silk. It slid cool and soft between her fingers and over his solid chest. They exchanged a smile. Nichelle turned away from Wolfe in time to catch a grin on Quraishi's usually reserved face.

"It is good that you two work and love so well together."

Nichelle's face heated, but she refused to act like
some blushing, infatuated girl. "He is both easy to work
with and to love." She deliberately did not look at Wolfe,
but she sensed his amusement.

"She is neither of those things," Wolfe said. "But I
enjoy a challenge." He grinned.

"Marriage should keep you on your toes, yes?"
Quraishi said. "Complacency is the way to lose everything important in a relationship."

"We're not at that stage yet," Nichelle murmured.
"My Wolfe is a constant source of surprises. Aren't
you, darling?"

"Anything to keep you by my side," Wolfe said. His
tongue, pink and damp, flicked out to touch the corner
of his mouth.

Arousal flooded Nichelle in an instant. She swallowed and looked down at the napkin in her lap, fighting a blush. Quraishi chuckled with delight.

"By the way, before we go any further, please forgive
my machinations regarding the desert trip, but I wanted
to see how well you do under pressure. It helped me to
finalize my decision."

The corner of Wolfe's mouth tilted up. *Is that what
having Franklin and Green with them was about?*

Nichelle pressed her lips together. "As long as you
got what you needed out of it," she said. "I know we
did."

Quraishi chuckled. "I like your wife very much, Mr.
Diallo. I think we'll all work very well together."

When the waiter came, Quraishi ordered nearly half
the menu for their table, advising Nichelle and Wolfe

what to try, telling them what were his favorites, and his wife's, as well. The terrace level of the restaurant filled up as they talked and ate, the noise of other diners rising around them while their own conversation dwelled on nothing in particular. Despite the pleasantness of the meal, Nichelle wondered why they were having lunch together at all. Why the celebration? Why the interest in her and Wolfe? Not that they weren't an amazing team. But still.

She noticed in her periphery when a group of Western women appeared on the terrace near them. The women were English and pretty, their familiar language oddly soothing after being enclosed within a French and Arabic speaking milieu for most of their trip.

Quraishi was explaining why she and Wolfe should travel to Essaouira, a nearby seaside town with a rich history and artisans who excelled in cabinet making, when a low voice in English interrupted them. It was one of the foreign women. This one was exceptionally pretty, with honey-colored skin and a tumble of curls down to the small of her back. A white dress made the most of her naturally dark skin.

"Pardon me for interrupting," she said to Wolfe. "But my friend over there—" she pointed to the table where four other women watched her with expectant smiles "—was wondering if you would be interested in going out with us tonight." A woman from her table waved at them.

The women were gorgeous and flirty, just the type that Wolfe would love in Miami. Nichelle knew he didn't take up every offer thrown his way, but when it came to carpe diem, he was a master. And the women, an international collection of beauties with their skin shades ranging from palest cream to oak, seemed like a temptation difficult for any heterosexual man to resist. Even if he was pretending to be married.

Quraishi looked amused as he sat back in his chair and watched Nichelle's face. He wasn't looking at Wolfe at all. Not even a glance. She schooled her expression into bland lines and turned her attention to her pretend husband.

Wolfe offered a smile to the woman, the smile that probably had her melting in her summer sandals. Nichelle had seen that smile, and the pleasant devastation it often left in its wake.

"That's very flattering," he said. "Thank you. But I'll be with my wife most of the day." He tilted his head toward Nichelle, but did not reach for her in what she was sure would have seemed like fake affection.

The Englishwoman clapped a hand to her mouth. "Oh, I'm so sorry!" she said to Nichelle. "I didn't know he was yours."

"No apologies necessary," Nichelle said in what she hoped was a gracious tone, even though inside she was seething. "This happens to us everywhere we go."

The woman stood back with a cocked hip, eyes flickering to Wolfe, although she was speaking with Nichelle. "It must be frustrating for you."

Is that what you're going with, bitch? "Not really." Nichelle stretched her lips at the woman. "He was gorgeous when I slipped the ring on his finger, and he's one of those lucky people who will be pretty until the grave. Women tend to notice that sort of thing." She dipped her head to the ring in question and smiled at Wolfe, who watched her with a careful expression.

The woman apologized again. "I'll tell my friends

he's off the market!" Then she left them to rejoin her own table.

Wolfe spread his napkin across his lap. "That went well."

Nichelle made a noise of irritation. "They didn't miss that damn ring on your finger. They all stared at you close enough to memorize the size of your inseam."

Quraishi choked on a laugh.

Nichelle abruptly realized what she'd just said, and in front of whom. "My apologies," she said.

"None necessary." Quraishi shook his head, still chuckling. "It was interesting seeing what a modern woman like you would do when challenged for her mate."

At the word *mate*, she looked at Wolfe again, who was noncommittally drinking from his glass of mint tea.

In for a penny, in for a pound. Nichelle shrugged. "It really does happen all the time, though. Sometimes it's fine, because there is a certain amount of flattery involved. Women want this beautiful man I call my own." Their eyes met and Wolfe slowly lowered the glass, not breaking their gaze. "But sometimes, it can get a little irritating when rude women press the issue after it becomes obvious who I am."

As she spoke, she realized she was telling the truth. For years she'd watched women flirt openly with Wolfe, even slipping him their numbers when they thought she wasn't looking. It had all been blatantly disrespectful. She never blamed Wolfe for it. At least not always.

In the past, she *had* been upset when he returned the attentions of the rude ones who boldly came up to him when they were together. These women didn't care that he was a married or taken man. They were simply intent on getting what they wanted. If Nichelle saw two people dining privately together, she assumed they were a couple, even if their body language was distant. She would never proposition a man while another woman sat only a few feet away. With or without a wedding ring.

On the occasions she'd been bothered by those women and Wolfe's response to them, she lacked the emotional awareness to know *why* she had been irritated. But now she knew. She wanted him for herself. She might even...

Nichelle choked on a gasp. She swallowed. "You know, I'm actually not in the mood for lunch at all." She put her napkin on the table and stood. "If you'll excuse me, gentlemen."

Both men got to their feet, talking at once.

"We can leave now, *Madame* Diallo. It is no problem."

"Let me get a cab and we can go back," Wolfe said.

"No, please stay and enjoy your lunch." She pushed her chair aside to escape the sudden prison of the table. "I saw plenty of cabs near the square. I'm sure I can grab one to take me back to the hotel."

"Nichelle—"

"No." She stared at Wolfe. "Stay. I insist."

Then she fixed her face for her new client and offered her hand to shake. "I'll be in touch with you soon."

Then she was walking through the restaurant, past the women who all watched her with amused curiosity, and out into the sun. She drew a deep breath, cursing herself for allowing her emotions to push her out of the restaurant and make her look like a fool in front of Quraishi. But what was done was done. Nichelle straightened her spine and waded through the thick crowd in the square. It didn't take her long to find a cab back to the hotel.

Once in the cool confines of the suite, she called Nala. "I think I'm totally screwed here," she said in greeting when Nala answered the phone.

"Do you mean that literally?" Her friend sounded tired despite the teasing tone of her voice. "Because if so, this is not the time to call me. We can celebrate you and Wolfe finally sleeping together when I see you again."

Nichelle frowned. Their connection was incredibly clear. "Where are you?"

"A riad not far from the main square. When you told me you were having trouble keeping yourself together around Wolfe, I hopped on a plane. Cannes is only a three hour flight from here."

"Oh, thank you..." Nichelle sank into the bed with relief, glad for her best friend's impulsive nature and the love that she showered her with so completely. And of course, her ridiculous bank account that allowed her to jump on a plane from France with just a few hours' notice. She gave Nala the name of her hotel.

"Come pick me up. I feel like having the biggest drink in Africa right now."

Through the phone, she heard the hush of fabric on fabric, as if Nala was in bed and getting up. "Give me a half hour."

"Take your time." She instantly felt a twinge of guilt, knowing that Nala was more than likely still exhausted from her flight.

But an hour later, Nala texted to say she was downstairs and ready to buy all the drinks.

* * *

Wolfe watched Nichelle leave the restaurant, aware of Quraishi's thoughtful stare. He seated himself back at the table and rearranged the napkin carefully across his lap. Everything in him screamed to follow her and find out what was wrong. But the look she left him with as she said "stay" froze him in his seat.

Quraishi looked concerned. "Why are you letting her go?"

Good question. "She wants to be alone."

"Or does she want her husband to follow her and show her that these women, no matter how tempting—" He waved a hand toward the chattering Englishwomen. "—are nothing compared to her?"

"She knows that already." At least he hoped she did.

"But she may need to hear you say it."

Wolfe's hand hovered near his tie, twitchy with the urge to yank it off in frustration. They weren't married, dammit! And this situation was nothing new. Women came on to him all the time. Was she just putting on an act for Quraishi? Had she simply wanted to be alone instead of pretending through another endless public appearance?

"I'll give her the time she needs," he said.

Her face had been coolly stoic the entire time the Englishwoman talked to them. Nichelle didn't seem upset at all, simply bored. Even when she made the comment about certain "rude women." She'd simply been acting the jealous wife for Quraishi. Right? Wolfe picked up his now cold glass of mint tea and sipped.

"My wife is fine," he said finally.

But that didn't stop his mind from lingering on her during the meal. The business part of his brain was fully

conscious of the things Quraishi outlined about their
pending contract. But the other part of him remembered
her face when the woman first approached their table.
The flicker of annoyance that she had not bothered to
hide. And he remembered the night they spent in the
desert together. Waking up next to her. Her scent filling the waking morning and making him hard with
need while an unfamiliar softness unfurled inside him,
making him want to bring her closer to him on the pallet for nothing more than kisses and intimate whispers.

Quraishi tolerated his divided attention for another
hour before asking for the check, his look both amused
and understanding. When the car stopped in front of the
hotel, Quraishi patted his shoulder. "Go to your wife.
Show her there are no others. Tell her. Make her believe
it since it's obvious you already do."

Wolfe thanked Quraishi for his hospitality once again
and slipped from the car. On his way up to the room,
he thought about what to say to Nichelle and how. But
when he got to the suite, she wasn't there. He called her
phone and, after it rang only once, got her voice mail.
Worried, he sent a text. Seconds later, she replied with
a brief message. She was out and would see him later.

Wolfe clamped down on his anger. What the hell
was going on? Whatever it was, he couldn't stay in the
room. He changed into his swim trunks and left for the
pool. He exhausted his body with laps, his chest heaving, stomach and shoulder muscles aching with effort.
But no matter how much he pushed himself, he couldn't
stop thinking about her.

It was late when he went back to the room. She still
wasn't there. So he packed his suitcase, getting ready
for their flight back to Miami the next morning. He

fell asleep waiting for her. One moment, he was sitting on the couch with his suitcase at his feet, and the next, he was opening his eyes at the sound of the door clicking open.

It was dark. Definitely past midnight. The smell of clove cigarettes came into the room with Nichelle, scents of a bar, something faintly alcoholic.

"Where have you been?" He choked out the question, not bothering to hide his anger and worry.

She froze in front of the door in surprise. The lamplight from the terrace highlighted her as she stood, looking slightly guilty. She wore the same clothes from earlier that day, but the collar of her high-necked blouse was unbuttoned. She carried her shoes in her hands. Then she seemed to shake herself and realize who he was, who *she* was. She visibly gathered her shield of coldness around her.

"In case your convenient memory has forgotten, I'm *not* actually your wife."

With a pointed glance in his direction, she slid past him for the bedroom then shut the door softly behind her. It wasn't until he heard the hiss of the shower that he realized she hadn't been wearing his rings.

Chapter 10

They went back to Miami and to business as usual. The firm settled into having Quraishi as a client. Nichelle and Wolfe stopped traveling as much. Days of sameness passed. If things between them weren't quite the same as before the Morocco trip, Wolfe blamed it on their differing schedules, on the additional work they had to do now that they were officially a million-dollar-earning firm.

He never stopped yearning for how things had been between them before, the ease they had had with each other, the feeling like it was the two of them against the world. But he also wanted something new.

Wolfe often woke from dreams of having her in his arms again, of filling her body with his love until they were both drunk with it, their voices rising in shared pleasure. But Nichelle seemed the same as ever. If it wasn't for the fact that he didn't see her as much as he used to, he could fool himself into thinking she was completely unmoved by what happened between them in Morocco.

As it was, she never lingered in the same room with him for long. She didn't put her feet in his lap anymore to demand a foot rub. She rarely came to his office.

As for Wolfe, he hadn't had a woman in weeks. Maybe that was his problem. He just needed to get laid. And because he was a problem solver, he immediately decided to do something about it, setting up a Friday evening date with a woman he'd met during a business lunch on Key Biscayne. Chantal.

Something about her had been interesting. It may have been that her cool, tall beauty, severe in a certain light, captivating in others, reminded him of Nichelle. How she seemed as cool as Greenland, but was a steamy and alluring woman of surprising lushness and warmth. Iceland, the woman. Or maybe he just wanted to make Chantal seem interesting. Either way, it was a date. And he needed the distraction.

A sharp and distinctive rap on his office door interrupted his thoughts.

"Come in, Philip."

His assistant came in with a vase of irises. "It's time for these to be replaced," Philip said, going immediately to the bookshelf where a handful of iris blossoms, just a little wilted around the edges, sat in an identical square vase. Wolfe started to tell Philip to cancel the fresh flowers, a standing order he had at the florist every week since he'd found out they were Nichelle's favorite.

With the sweet scent of the irises in his office, it was as if Nichelle was always there with him. A dangerous impulse, but one that he'd indulged in. The purple flowers lent an air of softness to the otherwise masculine space, he'd told her when she asked him why he kept the irises.

"Thanks, Philip." He let his assistant carry on without cancelling the flowers. Next week he'd do it.

"Of course, sir."

Philip took the old vase with him when he left. Wolfe immediately noticed the difference in the office, the hot and sugary smell of the fresh flowers that made him think even more about Nichelle.

He glowered at the vase, breaking his gaze only when his cell phone rang. It was his mother.

"Baby, am I interrupting anything?"

"Never, Mama."

His mother laughed softly through the phone. "I doubt you'd tell me if I was."

True. "I always have time for you."

"I'm glad you say that. How about lunch this afternoon?"

Just like he often called to check in on his mother, she checked in with him, too. It was something he didn't think she did with any of his siblings, even though he was sure he wasn't the only one who had figured out the family secret of her infidelity.

He mentally reviewed his calendar for the day. There was a project update meeting scheduled for one o'clock, but it wasn't anything he couldn't push back.

"Of course," he said. "Where do you have in mind?"

"I was thinking we could try out that new place with the fish."

"Oceana." He knew immediately which place she

was talking about. "The underwater restaurant that feels like you're eating in an aquarium?"

She chuckled. "Exactly."

As usual, she seemed to get a kick out of how alike they were. She and Wolfe had similar tastes in nearly everything—food, entertainment, wines. Even their temperament, a leaning toward pleasure simply for pleasure's sake, was eerily the same. It terrified him.

He opened his email and sent a quick note to the meeting participants to meet a half hour later. "Should I pick you up, or do you want to meet me there?"

"I'll meet you there, darling. I don't want to keep you away from work any longer than necessary."

"I'm the boss, remember? I can do what I like."

"Don't let Nichelle hear you say that," his mother teased. "I don't want her to blame me for your cavalier attitude toward your office responsibilities."

"Let me worry about Nichelle, Mama."

"As if you don't already?" she said with a laugh.

They met a few minutes past twelve. The elevator doors that took Wolfe twenty feet below sea level opened into a massive aquarium. The restaurant patrons were literally under glass and under the ocean, dining with sea life swimming languorously over and around them. A beautiful view. All the tables were situated along the transparent wall, leaving a long walkway leading back to the restrooms on one end and the elevator at the other.

The floor underneath his Italian loafers was hardwood and a deep brown, and the sound of his footsteps was absorbed by the low-grade noise of the already heavy lunch crowd.

His mother sat at a table near the middle of the restaurant. She had a glass of red wine, ignoring it in favor of looking around Oceana with a rapt expression.

"Mama." He leaned down to kiss her cheek.

"Darling." Her fingers lingered on his jaw before she withdrew it with a smile. "I hope you don't mind that I started without you." She indicated her wine. "It didn't take me as long as I thought to get seated."

"Good." Since Oceana had been written up in the *Miami Herald* and a few other places, he'd called ahead to ensure a reservation. It was very popular for a new spot that wasn't endorsed by a celebrity or porn star. "I wouldn't want you to wait for me," he said.

A waitress appeared at their table and handed him two sleek menus. "Welcome to Oceana, sir. Madam. May I get you something to drink?"

He ordered sparkling water, glanced quickly at the menu and ordered the fish of the day. His mother asked for the same.

"So what's happening in your life these days, my Wolfe? I never can get a moment alone with you when you come home for family dinner."

"That's the struggle of having thirteen children and not as many pairs of ears." He smiled, leaning back in his chair.

She looked beautiful. Two years away from sixty, but with a deep and dewy mahogany skin that made her look no older than forty. She wore her long, silver hair in a loose bun. Subtle makeup highlighted her mischievous eyes and mobile mouth, the soft curve of her chin.

She wore an indigo dress and black low-heeled shoes,

with touches of gold jewelry at her wrists and throat. Her wedding rings winked in the soft, undersea light.

"No struggle, love. Only a pleasure." The words she spoke were the truth, Wolfe knew, but she hadn't always felt that way. Hence the reason she had left her family for another man.

"I'm glad, Mama."

They had never talked openly about her betrayal, only circled the obvious empty space of words between them, what had happened the morning Wolfe, at twenty years old, had come to her with the small wooden box he found in her office after a long and thorough search. The box held a lipstick-stained silk tie, a small book of Neruda's love poetry and a photograph of her seated in a man's lap and looking defiantly happy.

His mother's face had caved in on itself when he gave her the box, the happy spark in her eyes abruptly extinguished. Later that night, he woke to the smell of smoke and looked downstairs from his bedroom window to see her burning the contents of the box in a copper bowl. She held the empty box in her hand, staring off into space while tears tracked down her cheeks.

"Here you are, sir." The waitress reappeared carrying an empty glass with a slice of lime perched on its edge, along with a bottle of Perrier. "Can I get you anything else while your meal is being prepared?"

Wolfe's mother met his gaze, a brow raised, a tiny smile at the corner of her mouth. "Yes, darling. Are you content? Or would you like something else?"

"I'm good for now." He nodded at the waitress. "Thank you."

She disappeared from the table, leaving him and his mother once again alone with their shared secret.

"So, my darling—" His mother leaned forward with the glass of red wine balanced between delicate fingers. "—is there anything in particular you want to talk about today?"

Wolfe left lunch with his mother feeling almost as on edge as when he'd sat down at the table with her. They'd talked about relationships, forming unhealthy attachments, following that particular seductive path to pleasure. Like his mother, Wolfe was a hedonist. Pleasure was his reason to live. Once something stopped feeling good, he was finished with it. And when there was something within reach that he imagined would both sate and excite him, he wanted it with a desperation that bordered on pain. Nichelle was like that for him.

He had circled around his desire for Nichelle during the conversation with his mother. And she had told him, in her own way, to take what he wanted. He wasn't sure he was ready for the consequences of that.

So, after work, he reached out for the safer option. Chantal, the woman who wanted him.

He took her to a restaurant Nichelle would never enjoy. "I'm glad you were able to meet me on such short notice," he said.

She laughed at him. "Even if you'd reached out to me an hour before, I would come. I'm very glad you called."

Wolfe watched her through the flickering candlelight on their table. She wore a pretty white dress and was beautiful, but she did not look as much like Nichelle as he first thought. There was something almost brittle about her, a desperation that seemed to have nothing to do with him and everything to do with whatever she was going through in her life. And she wasn't funny.

Nichelle had a way of laughing at the world, herself in-cluded, that he'd always found irresistible. That amuse-ment had been there as a child but grew even more pointed, more effective, after she came back from col-lege.

"You're very beautiful," he said to Chantal. Compli-ments were his usual way of putting himself back in the game when his attention wandered.

"Thank you. You are too. Beautiful that is." She blushed, and her skin, paler than Nichelle's, reddened. "I thought that when I first saw you."

"Thank you."

But that was really all the conversation they had for each other. The waitress came and left, dropping off drinks and food and pleasant enough service. It was a gourmet place, one that served small portions on pretty plates and where you left feeling as if you'd just eaten air. He toyed with his glass of whiskey and watched Chantal, carefully keeping a smile on his face.

He was usually better than this. Talking to women until their lingering unease, if there was any at all, dis-appeared. But despite Chantal's beauty, he wanted the date to be over. Wanted to be doing something effort-less but filled to the brim with pleasure. He wanted to talk with Nichelle.

Wolfe took a long sip of his whiskey. The drink burned going down and made him think, again, of Nichelle. He wished that it was his business partner, his pretend wife, who sat on the other side of the table with a wicked eyebrow raised, daring him to be himself while heat and expectation shimmered between them like dust after a light spring rain.

The meal came, then a second round of drinks. He

found out that Chantal was an only child. That she enjoyed white water rafting, even though she couldn't
swim, that her ideal vacation involved spa treatments
and couples massages. Was she fishing for a relationship out of this date?

By the time they'd eaten the food and exhausted
their meager small talk, Wolfe was ready to leave. But
he stayed longer, drank more whiskey until the date
seemed almost like a good idea.

"I like you," Chantal said, eyeing him over her third
glass of champagne.

Wolfe shook his head. "You don't know me."

"But I want to."

He shook his head again, thinking about the best
way to get out of Brickell and back home in his slightly
drunken state. A cab. He needed to call a cab. Well, two.
One for Chantal and one for himself.

"You seem so perfect," Chantal was saying. She
tapped a pink-tipped fingernail against her champagne
flute. "The perfect gentleman."

Wolfe grinned, feeling his teeth flash, sharklike.
"You definitely don't know me."

He always treated the women he dated well. But if
he wanted to sleep with them, wanted more than a date,
then a little of the beast came out. He'd be growling desire into her ear by the main course, or at least flirting
in a way that made her know he was thinking of taking
her to bed. But he felt none of that with Chantal, so it
was easy to stay the perfect, sexless gentleman.

After dinner, he called a cab, waited with her and
watched her ride away in the yellow car, waving at him
and smiling shyly.

Once she disappeared from sight, he got into the second cab and gave the driver an address. He was done being a perfect gentleman for the night. All evening, a pretty image had dangled in front of his eyes, making him realize what he really wanted.

It had been easy to pretend with Chantal that it was her making the blood heat in his veins, the charm surface so effortlessly while they shared their meal. But once she was gone and the date was over, he was free to be himself again. And he was free to want what he wanted. *Whom* he wanted.

He knocked on the door to the small house in Wynwood, put his hands in his pockets and waited, imagining that she was waking up in something pretty and sheer, sliding on the robe to open the door and welcome him.

"What are you doing here?"

Nichelle stood in her doorway in thin pajama pants and a T-shirt, a mirror of what Wolfe usually wore to bed. Nothing like the negligée he'd pictured. He had to laugh at himself.

"I want to talk," he said.

She made a show of looking at the skin on her wrist where she normally wore a watch. It was well past ten o'clock. "I doubt that very much." But she opened the door and let him in anyway.

Wolfe walked in, hands curled loosely in his pockets, part of him still trying to process what he was doing at Nichelle's house so late at night.

"Why have you been avoiding me?"

He followed her into the darkened living room. A sliver of light from an open doorway, her bedroom, caught his eye. Nothing else was visible in the golden light, but the fact that it was her bedroom made him painfully hard just thinking of it. Of her.

"I wasn't avoiding you," she said. "You know more than anyone how busy things have been since we took on Quraishi as a client."

She snapped on a light and stood in the middle of her pretty but efficiently designed sitting room with arms crossed.

"Tell me, really, Wolfe. Why are you here?"

She watched him with a narrowed gaze as he approached, coming even closer than he'd intended, crowding into her personal space, breathing deep to find the scent of sleep or of her bedroom nestled into the curves of her body.

"Didn't you have a date tonight?" Nichelle asked.

So she *did* know what he was doing. Not that he'd hidden his evening activities from her or from anyone. Hiding was not his style.

"Yes, I did have a date," he said. "She went home."

"And you came here." If possible, she looked even more irritated. "Why don't *you* go home?"

"Because I want to talk with you. Is there anything wrong with that?"

He stepped even closer to her. She wrinkled her nose.

"Are you drunk?"

"Buzzed. Feeling good."

An unamused smile lifted the corner of her mouth. "Don't you see the billboards? Buzzed driving is still drunk driving." She quoted the slogan with a sneer. "You could've gotten yourself arrested coming over here."

"I took a cab."

She stared at him in disbelief. The implication of his

actions occurred to him the moment her face hardened. "Get the hell out of here, Wolfe. Now."

"Stop, Nichelle." He raised his hands in surrender. "It's not like that."

"No? Then tell me that you didn't send the girl home and bring your ass over here to get some because she didn't want to put out."

"Of course she wanted to put out," he murmured with a smile. "They always do. But I want…"

"Want what?"

"I want my wife."

She drew in a sharp breath and stepped back. "No. No. You don't get to do this here. The pretense is over. Dammit—"

He kissed the next words from her mouth. Then he drifted his hands down the taut line of her back. "Nicki…" He breathed his need against her closed lips, hands on her waist, on her hips. He felt her resistance, her own hands dangling at her sides. But within the span of a heartbeat those same hands were fisting into his shirt.

"I hate you for this." And she kissed him back.

It was nothing like Morocco. Before, everything seemed like a prelude. A waiting period. Knowing that nothing would come of their touches, but wanting them anyway, savoring them. But with the release of her breath into his, the warm wet of her tongue licking his mouth, his teeth, the waiting was over.

Tonight was about taking the desire they'd shyly unfurled to each other to another level. Hunger and lust and frustration lashed between them. Wolfe was instantly sober, effortlessly throwing off that flimsy curtain of drunkenness that had given him the excuse to come to the house where the woman he wanted lived, to knock on her door and ask her things he hadn't had the courage to before.

"I want you." He breathed the words against her mouth.

She moaned and shoved into him, bit his lips. He flinched *into* her from the pain. Her hands yanked at his shirt and scattered buttons across the living room floor. He vaguely heard them bounce across the tiles, focused more on their desperate breathing, panting lust and hands on flesh, flesh against cloth, the wet sounds of their kissing.

He pressed his aching hardness into the sweet seat of her. "I want to—"

"Then do it."

Without waiting for him to do what he wanted, she shoved the shirt from his shoulders, grasping desperately at him with cool hands. She yanked his belt and fly open, slid her hand into his underwear and gripped him.

"God!"

They made it as far as the couch, Wolfe on his back, Nichelle on top, her pants discarded on the floor next to everything he'd had on.

Nichelle gasped as he mouthed his way down her throat. "I swear to God if you say tomorrow that you don't remember any of this..."

She fumbled a condom from his wallet—because his brain was too fried to remember even the simplest things—sheathed him in latex, and climbed onto him. Her wet heat sucked him in, and everything he was collapsed with the feel of her body around him. Firm clutch, tight heat, her thighs pressed to his hips. He swallowed past a rough gasp as she moved on top of him, controlling the pace.

"Wolfe." She was still. She squeezed him inside, paused to pull off her shirt.

He groaned at the sight of her small breasts and reached up to touch them. She shivered when he thumbed the firm buds of her nipples, her muscled belly rippling with reaction. Yes, he wanted this. He needed this.

She moved on top of him, a slowly rolling tide. But he wanted more. He wanted the instant explosion of it. And normally he'd be more than happy to have her control the situation, but he'd been waiting years for this moment to come. Years. And if he watched her any longer, her beautiful breasts bouncing with every movement of her on him, her wet mouth, the panting breaths that left her even more beautiful, he would lose it. He would explode, and it would all be over before it even got started.

Wolfe sat up on the couch, taking her with him. She gasped at the shifting angle, then held on to him during the stumbling, kissing and tangled fingers that comprised their journey from the living room to the bedroom. Her bed had only one side turned down, a book on the bedside table, a single lamp burning. He bore her down into the sheets without losing the hot clutch of her around him.

"I've dreamed of this for so damn long." He sank into her, even more deeply. She whimpered, her nails dragging down his back, digging into him, urging him on. "You feel so good."

Wolfe quickly lost track of what he was saying but knew that whatever it was, she liked it, her nails scoring his shoulders and flanks as they moved together on the bed. He was close already, so perilously close, but he wanted her to come first. He wanted to watch her lose control. He climbed to his knees, lifted her hips, drove into her.

She wailed. Her whole body shivered. The line of her arched neck was wet with sweat. Tears of need leaked from her closed eyes and spilled down the sides of her face and onto his tongue. She was so beautiful. He loved her harder, filling her with his heat, every inch of his pleasure. His body quivered from the feel of her, hot and humid around him, pulling him deeper, squeezing him. Pulling him closer and closer to explosion.

She cried out his name. A plea. The scent of sweat and their sex rose up around him. Wolfe pressed his thumb on the hot little button while his hips snapped into hers. She fell apart around him, screaming, shuddering into him.

The hot clasp of her destroyed the rest of his self-control. One moment, he was watching the frantic breath and heaving breasts. Her teeth anchored in her swollen lips, the agony of lust on her face. And the next he was growling out his own orgasm, jerking viciously as his body emptied into her.

His eyes rolled back in his head, and he slumped heavily over her, frozen in that instant of indescribable bliss. Spent. Under him, she panted softly, blinking sweat from her eyes. She was so damned beautiful, he almost didn't deserve her.

Wolfe pressed a kiss under her ear, down the damp line of her throat. She murmured something he lost in the still pounding rush of blood through his body. But he gathered her tenderly through all that, settled her into the bed. And kissed her again. She sighed into his mouth and her arms draped down his neck, still trembling.

His body was spent for the night. But he wanted to please her more, to give her even a fraction of the spine-melting pleasure she'd gifted to him.

How could he have gotten this lucky to have her? He kissed down her body, pausing at each rise of flesh to lick and suck, stroke and hum his enjoyment. She moaned softly. Then gasped when he settled between her thighs. She was tender there, slightly swollen from where he had loved her. He kissed the delicate flesh. She sighed, fingers sliding over his head, alighting on his neck, his shoulders.

She smelled like perfection, like sex and fulfillment. A combination to him that usually signaled the end of the evening. But now his mouth watered for a taste of what he'd only touched before. He licked her. She gasped, trembled, her thighs pressing wide open.

He smiled against her flesh at the greediness of her action. Much of her personality translated to how she was in bed, nakedly wanting, desiring and going after what she wanted. Her nails dug into his shoulders, into the back of his neck to push him deeper into her damp center. She wanted him and wasn't afraid to let him know.

He burrowed into the tight, seafoam-scented wet of her, and she gave him the slick of her arousal, her stuttering moans, the wild flex of her thighs around his head. The mattress heaved with the rough toss of her body. She writhed under him as he loved her with his mouth, teased her wetness, the firm pearl of her clitoris, skimmed with his curled fingers the space inside of her that made her shout out his name.

"Wolfe!" Her sharp demand cut his teasing off at the knees.

He stopped playing and latched his lips to the firm bud, slid his fingers deep, lashed her with his tongue, hummed into her hot flesh.

"God. Yes! Please. Yes. More..."

She moaned as if in pain, her hips circling in the bed, curling up into his face, the circles growing tighter and more frantic the more he thrust his fingers, fluttered his tongue. She cried out again, his name a screaming wail. But he still didn't stop.

Her nails dug into his shoulders again, deeper. Another tremor quaked through her, thighs vibrating. Then another and another. Wailing cries and pleas. She pressed the heels of her hands into her eyes as she cried out still, her hips bucking and wild beneath the steely grip of his hands.

"More," she moaned.

And he gave it to her. Fingers, his tongue, until his body was firm again, and he pulled her up in the bed, bent her over the pillows and took her until she screamed in satisfaction again and again. He exploded with her, an electric current. They collapsed together into the sheets, gasping, damp flesh sliding together.

He gathered her into his arms and rolled to one side of the massive bed. A sound of contentment purred from her, then she became a limp weight on top of him. Asleep. His own eyes drooped, his lust satisfied, his woman put to sleep, but he glanced down at himself sleepily, pulled off the condom and slid from beneath her to go to the bathroom. She made a soft noise but didn't move.

When he got back to the bed, she was right where he left her. He curled protectively around her soft and scented weight and draped a hand over her hip. He fell asleep to the thought that he could very well get used to this, falling asleep next to his very own wife.

Nichelle opened her eyes to the pale light of dawn. She stretched in her bed, sighing into the feeling of satisfaction and contentment. The hard warmth at her back felt completely natural, something she'd wanted for so long that it didn't register as strange until a deep voice groaned in sleepy protest and firm hands settled on her hips to pull her closer.

She blinked and slowly turned to face the man in her bed. It hadn't been a dream. He was as beautiful as she'd always known he would be, stretched out on her pale linens, his lashes resting on his high cheekbones, mouth slack in sleep. He breathed deeply and easily as he slept, in contrast to the way her own breath sped up, her pulse knocking frantically in her neck.

Oh my God...

She slid from the bed, her knees trembling as she stared down at the beautiful man spread out on her sheets.

What the...?

She stumbled to the bathroom and snapped on the light. In the mirror, she saw she was a wreck, mouth still swollen, her neck and chest dotted with love bites, her eyes drowsy with satisfaction. Probably looked just like any other woman Wolfe had been with.

She didn't want to be one of them. Screwed today,

tossed out tomorrow. And she didn't want to ruin what she and Wolfe had at the firm. But now, they could no longer go back to what they had been. It was impossible. The thought made her slump against the sink, her arms trembling from holding up her weight.

She needed to leave.

Nichelle shook herself into motion, quickly got dressed in what was sitting on top of the laundry hamper—sweat pants and a tank top—and left the bathroom then the house. In the car, she grabbed her phone and redialed the last number she'd called the night before.

Barely half an hour later, she walked into Novlette's café, one of her favorite coffee and brunch places. She grabbed a salted caramel latte and almond croissant at the front counter before heading out to the terrace to search for Nala. Nichelle found her at one of the little French café-style tables, her hands clasped around a coffee cup, head down.

Nichelle shoved the croissant toward her friend, then sat in the empty seat across from her in silence while the sun struggled for the horizon.

"Thanks for meeting me," she croaked. "I just had to talk to you." Nichelle swallowed around the thick lump in her throat.

"I can't believe you dragged me out at ass crack of morning and expect actual coherent conversation." Nala held her cup of coffee under her nose, sniffed the rising steam but did not drink. She barely glanced at the pastry Nichelle brought her.

Her hair was scraped back from her face with a steel headband, a black cat suit hugged her body and a red cropped top drooped from one shoulder.

"You've dragged me out of my house for worse," Nichelle muttered.

They'd remained friends through much drama, including the time in high school when the girl Nala was dating also tried to get under Nichelle's boyfriend at the time. One school fight and countless ride-or-die sidekick missions later, neither woman was going anywhere.

Nala chuckled, beginning to wake up over her coffee. "Oh my God, remember that time when—"

"Nichelle, how nice to see you."

A man unexpectedly appeared over Nala's shoulder.

"Good morning, Isaac." She greeted him with her most civil smile. What the hell was he doing on the East Coast?

Nala turned around, gave him the once over, then dismissed him in favor of sniffing more of her coffee. Nichelle sipped hers. Maybe she wasn't awake enough for this, either.

Isaac looked disgustingly well-rested, ready for the day in boat shoes, pressed khakis and a white dress shirt rolled up to the elbows. He carried a cardboard to-go tray with three large coffees.

"I see you're not wearing your pretty sparkler these days." He nodded toward her ring finger. When she realized she was rubbing the bare spot on her finger with her thumb, she stopped the motion. It had taken her days to get used to its absence. And now with just a few words, Isaac made her aware again of how naked her finger felt without that reminder of Wolfe wrapped around it.

"I see that your eyes are working." She tipped her head over her shoulder to see a car idling near them in the parking lot. Then she turned back to pointedly look at him. "It was interesting running into you, Isaac. Please don't make a habit of it." Then she turned back to Nala. "I could go for a walk," she said to her friend. "How about you?"

"Screw that. I just sat down. We can go for a walk when there's more sun and I'm in a better mood."

When Isaac didn't leave, Nala showed him a finger that also didn't have a ring on it. "My sparkler is at the jeweler's," she said with a smirk.

He said something under his breath about immature women and strode away toward the car waiting for him.

"Was he an ass, or is it me?"

"I think it's a tie," Nichelle muttered.

Nala laughed and choked on her coffee. "Bitch."

The sun gradually rolled higher in the sky above them, spreading its warm light over the terrace where they sat. With the rising sun came Nala's coherence and better mood. She poked at the croissant in front of her.

"So, from this random outfit, am I to assume you just rolled out of a bed not your own?"

"It was my bed, but I left Wolfe in it."

Nala's mouth dropped open. "So you finally got some of that?"

"You make it sound like I've been waiting forever to screw my business partner."

"Weren't you?"

She flushed, aware there was some truth to the question, the desire she'd harbored for longer than she'd even been aware of. "Shut up." She sipped her lukewarm coffee and wrinkled her nose at the taste. "I wasn't planning for it to happen. He came to my house after a date."

"A date?" Nala choked on her laughter, shaking her head as if the idea of him leaving another woman to climb into Nichelle's bed was awful but also awfully hilarious. "Are you serious?"

"That's pretty much what I said when he walked in my door."

"And you let him through your door…?"

She blushed again. But it was true. As if she could ever turn him away. "I did. But it was incredibly stupid. He can get sex from just about any woman on the planet. Why the hell did I allow him in my house last night?"

"Because you wanted to. It's been a long time, Nicki." Nala held up eight fingers, ticking them off one by one as she listed all the months since Nichelle had had a man in her bed.

"I wasn't starved for it."

"So you say, but if not, why jump on Wolfe?"

"Because…" But she didn't have a reason beyond her desperate and sudden yearning for him.

Every woman wanted Wolfe. But what good did that do them? He loved women, but they tumbled so cheerfully and easily into his bed that he took them for granted. All of them. He easily moved on to the next one because there would always be a next.

And last night, she felt as if she'd been easy for him. The week in Marrakesh had teased them both with the possibility of how intimacy would be between them. In some ways, she could have even justified sleeping with him there. But here, in Miami, for Wolfe, making love with her had been convenient, a novelty that would wear off with the coming of the morning sun.

Nichelle cursed. "I feel like such an idiot."

Nala waved a dismissive hand. "Stop beating yourself up. It was only sex. And sex that you both wanted.

It wasn't like you raped him or destroyed the whole world with the force of your orgasm."

"Orgasms," Nichelle corrected. She shoved her coffee cup against her mouth to stop herself from saying anything else. But that didn't stop her thoughts from stuttering back to hours before, her body arched in the bed under the force of Wolfe's merciless tongue and fingers, while she cried out for him to stop, but *not* stop, what he was doing.

Nala chortled. "And you have regrets about this one? Damn, you should have regretted that boring University of Miami professor with the tiny penis. Now that was a waste of your three minutes."

Her comment teased a smile out of Nichelle. She agreed with Nala. The decision to let the professor go had been an easy one. Wolfe and his magical mouth and hands, not so much. But she had to let him go before he dropped her like he had so many of the others before her.

"I can't let him hurt me, Nala. I just can't."

"Who's to say that he will? You're assuming an awful lot, friend."

"I'm not assuming. I'm inferring based on the behavior I've observed over the years." Nichelle toyed with the handle of her cup. "I can't do this with him. It's not going to end well, and I won't allow him to treat me like the others who ended up falling for him."

Nala plucked apart her almond croissant, finger-painted the nutty filling across the plate and licked her thumb. "I never realized before what a pessimist you are, Nichelle. You're throwing away something sweet.

But I'll be here for you when you regret it and need a shoulder to cry on."

"That won't happen," Nichelle said.

But even to her, the words sounded empty and false.

Chapter 11

Wolfe woke up alone in Nichelle's bed.

He opened his eyes and blinked around the unfamiliar room. No, not unfamiliar. He'd seen this bedroom before, but had never been in the bed and certainly not naked. He sat up and called out Nichelle's name.

But the house was quiet. He glanced by reflex to the bedside table, expecting...something. But there was no note, certainly no breakfast and no other sound in the house except the softly humming air conditioner. The bedroom door was closed. He'd never woken up alone in someone else's bed before. He'd thought he and Nichelle would—

He scrubbed a hand over his face. He wasn't sure what he thought.

Wolfe took a breath and jumped from the bed. He couldn't stand being there anymore. He got dressed and left the house, locking the front door behind him. Sex with Nichelle was supposed to be about pleasure and enjoying the uncomplicated joy of their bodies. This part wasn't fun, though—waking up alone under the weight of his crushed expectations and wondering why she'd left. This role reversal was a bitch.

The day after Nichelle left him in her bed, Wolfe was still feeling hollowed out by the aftermath of his night with her. But this time, he blamed himself. He had wanted her, and so he took, without regard for the potential consequences of his actions. The bittersweet memory of her, warm and clutching around him, haunted him from his sprawl on the back terrace of his Coconut Grove house. The rising sun threw its faint light across the backyard and through the rippling waters of the pool.

The night with her had exceeded every fantasy. She'd touched him and welcomed him into her body in ways that both shocked and pleased him. Her soft mouth and hands, the sweetness of her most intimate flesh pulling him toward bliss. And then to see even more of her cool facade melt away in the wake of their passion had been humbling. And sexy as hell.

Wolfe dropped his head back and hissed, hands tightening on his thighs, his body hard already from the memory of having her and wanting her again. His drunkenness had been no excuse. He didn't want any excuses made for taking what he had desired for so long. But he knew things were different now. Every good thing between them had been destroyed.

His phone vibrated on the table in front of him, tapping a harsh rhythm against the glass top. He didn't look at it. A few seconds later, it rang again. He turned it over just as a text from his mother came through.

I'm coming in. Get dressed if you're indecent.

Wolfe looked down at himself. Bare chest, cotton pajama bottoms. Decent enough. When she let herself into the house barely two minutes later, he already had the kettle on and was reaching into his cupboard for her favorite tea, a Japanese concoction that cost a small fortune.

"Good morning, darling." She brought the smell of pumpkin-spice coffee with her. When she saw him, she paused in the doorway. "You look like hell."

"Is that why you came over here so early, to shower me with compliments?"

She sailed into the open-plan dining room and kitchen, looking much too lively for six o'clock in the morning, and carrying a large cup of coffee held out like a peace offering. Her yellow dress was a burst of sunshine in the dawn-shrouded room. She frowned and touched his cheek, fingers rasping through his overnight whiskers.

"You look like you've overindulged," she said.

Still feeling raw and not exactly ready to be civil to another human, Wolfe carefully stepped away from her touch. "I *don't* have a hangover."

"I didn't say anything about a hangover. You, my son, look like regret."

She put the coffee on the bar and uncapped it to release the aromatic trail of steam. The smell of pumpkin spice became even stronger, perking up Wolfe's taste buds. She must have stopped by one of the few places in all of Miami that served pumpkin-spice coffee, his secret pleasure, all year long. He reached for the cup.

"Sometimes you want something very badly," his mother murmured, almost meditatively. "When you take it, it's good. So good that you wonder why you'd never taken it before, and you want to keep having it. But you can't. That's the regret I see in you."

Wolfe stopped at the bar with his hands braced on either side of the open coffee cup. He put them into fists and closed his eyes, sickened suddenly by the coffee smell.

"I'm not like you," he said. But because his words sounded weak and unconvincing, he said them louder, slamming his fist against the granite counter. "I'm *not* like you!"

In the kitchen, the kettle screamed. They both ignored it.

His mother arranged herself on a bar stool, draping the hem of her dress carefully over her legs. "What happened to you, darling?"

Was she even listening to him? "Shi—!"

"Do not curse in front of your mother, Wolfe Forsythe Diallo." She didn't even have to raise her voice.

He clamped his mouth shut but could not look at her. The tangled emotions, the frustration, bubbled in him like acid. The kettle's hysterical scream wasn't helping matters. In the kitchen, he snapped off the flame and moved the kettle to a cold burner. The sudden silence between them was even louder.

"When you left us sixteen years ago, I thought my life as I knew it was over." Wolfe stepped back from the stove and into the dining area, hands on his hips so he wouldn't be tempted to hit something again. "I thought that was the worst of it, you know. You leaving and taking every ounce of joy in our house with you."

He took a harsh breath, and the feelings from that long ago cool Miami afternoon rushed back to punch him in the chest. "But I was wrong about that day. The worst of it was when I realized I was like you." He gritted his teeth to stop the shout of anger and disappointment rising up in his throat. "Like you, I crushed one of the best things I'd ever had just because I couldn't keep it in my pants." He finally turned to face his mother. "I slept with Nichelle."

Her reaction wasn't quite what he'd thought it would be. "It's about damn time," she said.

"No, I don't think you heard me. I just ruined one of the best relationships I've ever had. She told me to back off, but I just wouldn't leave well enough alone."

"You've been dancing around each other for years now." His mother rapped her fingers against the bar's granite surface for emphasis. "Everyone can see you're perfect for each other. Even Kingsley, your own brother, has been baiting you so you'd step in and challenge him for her."

As if that would even be a challenge. Wolfe ignored the thought. "No. It's not like that." He ground his teeth together, frustrated again by his inability to think clearly where Nichelle was concerned. "She is everything to me."

The words surprised him. He gasped softly as the truth of them tumbled over him. "But I'd rather have her as a business partner, the way things were, than how they are now. I honestly think that she hates me. She left me alone in her bed, for Christ's sake."

"Listen." She held up a hand to stall him. "Before you slept with her, did you tell her how you feel?"

He grunted, a dismissive sound. "That would have

had her running for the hills for sure." Wolfe didn't want their relationship to linger on in its platonic limbo, but he didn't want to lose her, either.

"You don't know that she would run," his mother said.

He turned his back to her, head dropping low, footsteps taking him toward the open doors of the terrace. "Mother..."

"Wolfe. I didn't raise a coward. I didn't raise a carbon copy of myself, either. Because you were so busy avoiding being me, you've always taken the path to easy happiness. But without risks, my darling boy, there can be no blissful forever."

His mother pressed her lips together, hopped from the bar stool and paced to the kitchen to make her tea. She created a slow ceremony of scooping the right amount of tea leaves into the round infuser and pouring the hot water and agave into the clear teacup, then a slice of ginger. She was stalling. Which seemed so absolutely wrong because his mother *never* paused, *never* stalled. Instead she always rushed headlong into whatever decision she made, damn the consequences.

Finally, after the tea was made to her satisfaction, or she had delayed as much as she could get away with, she met his gaze.

"The weeks up until I left your father, I was in the middle of the worst postpartum depression I'd ever been through."

He flinched in surprise. *Depression?* The strongest woman he'd ever known?

"I was crying all the time," his mother continued. "Home began to feel like a prison. All those needy children plus the newborn twins made me want to do something drastic, something…awful."

Wolfe's stomach tightened. He swallowed the sudden lump in his throat. He'd read some terrible things about women dealing with postpartum depression, how they'd killed themselves or their children. Sometimes both.

His mother lifted the tea to her mouth, held the steaming cup under her nose. She stood in his kitchen, surrounded by stainless steel, a softness that he'd never seen from her before emerging as if by painful alchemy. It was an unfamiliar tableau.

"Royce, the man I left my family for, appeared at a time when I needed the distraction. I never loved him, but he saved me from myself. Sometimes I like to think he saved my family, too." She paused and sipped the hot tea, flinching from where it must have burned her lips, but she took another sip. "With him in Vanuatu, I let everything go. That distance gave me the clarity and strength I needed. When your father came to get me, it was because I called him. I was ready to come home and be with my children and husband again. I don't call myself a saint. I enjoyed Royce's body…" Wolfe flinched again. He wasn't ready to hear any of that about his mother. "And I enjoyed the sunshine and sea water on my skin. But that was the reason I left. To wash away the scum of depression that had formed over my life. I had three sets of twins, teenagers, newborns. Even with your father being there and being wonderful, it was still too much."

"I don't know why you two had so many damn kids in the first place." Wolfe tried to make light of it, although his hands were cold from the shock of her confession.

"That's what we both wanted and agreed to. Honestly, your father and I didn't know what we were setting ourselves up for." A twisted version of a smile tugged at her mouth. She was slowly becoming herself again.

"So what you're saying to me, then, is that I've been wrong about what happened for all these years?"

"You were a child, Wolfe. I didn't expect you to understand adult things." Her mouth tilted up. "Nor did I owe you any explanations. My husband understood."

"But... I spent so many years hating you."

"And yourself, too, apparently."

Heat flooded the back of Wolfe's neck. He scratched at his nape, unable to meet her gaze. "I don't hate myself."

"But you're not giving yourself what you need, either." His mother gave him a pitying look. "Making love to Nichelle was not an act of selfishness. From now on, what *you* do will determine the ultimate meaning of Friday night. Don't treat her like she's nothing. Let her know that what you experienced together can be worth more than the deal you two just closed on. Emotionally, that is."

Wolfe shook his head. "How do you know that?"

"Because I know my son." She passed him on the way out to the terrace. "Now grab your coffee and come sit out here with me. Let's not waste this beautiful sunrise."

Because he was a good son, he did what she told him, the words of their conversation ringing in his ears. Slowly, he relaxed, his tight shoulders loosening, the pressure in his chest nearly gone. Wolfe sat across the table from her and put his bare feet up next to hers in the same empty chair. He lifted his cup.

"Thanks for bringing the coffee."

She smiled around the lip of the teacup, her eyes warm and golden brown in the thickening light. "Anytime."

Monday morning, Wolfe walked into the office just after eight o'clock, eager to talk with Nichelle. He rounded a corner in time to see her back disappearing down the hallway. He buttoned his suit jacket, took a breath and walked quickly after her.

"Good morning, Nichelle."

She stopped. Her gaze dropped to his tie, the green silk paisley she'd bought him years ago for their first business trip together, and she smiled, a barely there tug at the corners of her mouth. Although she stood just a few feet from him, she felt as distant as the moon.

"Hi." Nichelle reached out to touch the tie, then caught herself, dropping her hand back to her side. She cleared her throat. "I was expecting you earlier. The strategy meeting is just about to start."

Wolfe glanced at his watch, annoyed that he wouldn't get to talk with her. "Who the hell scheduled a meeting so damn early in the morning?"

"You did," she said serenely. "I've got to grab some papers from my office. Meet you in the conference room."

Then she was walking away again. Back straight under a pale yellow blouse tucked into a black skirt. Her shoes were also yellow today. Their red soles flashed at him with each step, signaling both danger and desire. He wanted to follow but knew it was a bad idea.

How often had women come up to him after a memorable night asking why he'd left or hadn't called for a second date? The flipped script was grating on his nerves *and* his pride, only made worse by the fact that it was Nichelle doing it. But if she knew that the night had been about more than satisfying a temporary itch, would she turn to him in welcome? Or would she walk away even faster? Maybe his mother *had* raised a coward.

Damn.

Wolfe looked at his watch again. He didn't have time to moon over Nichelle like some punany-struck teenager. There were notes he had to look over for the forgotten meeting. He strode quickly toward his office.

Despite the disaster of his forgetfulness, the strategy meeting went off without a hitch. The room of Kingston executives even came up with workable solutions to the potential problems Nichelle saw on the horizon.

He left the meeting split in two. His mind was on the strategies he needed to begin implementing on his end. Everything else was fiercely focused on Nichelle and the way the yellow blouse looked over her summer-ripe skin. How, during the meeting, she had stroked a pen against her lips in thought, tapping the shiny black pen against the plump red of her mouth in a steady rhythm that echoed in his groin. He could swear his flesh was still imprinted with the shape of her kisses, lust bites on his throat and chest, her teeth marks on his belly.

Wolfe had to pull himself together before he was able to stand up from the conference table. He immediately went to find Nichelle. He rapped on her office door once before pushing it open.

"Hey."

She sat at her desk, fingers poised on her computer keyboard.

"Hey." She smiled back at him, but had that same distant look, her eyes a dark ocean he had no chance of sailing safely through. "What's going on?" she asked.

"About Friday night…" Wolfe closed her office door behind him. He didn't miss the slight tightening of her shoulders at his approach. He stopped, shoved his hands in his pockets and gave her the space she so obviously wanted.

"We're okay," she said, dismissive and calm. "You needed a little something, and I was there. No big deal."

No big deal? The pleasure he'd shared with her far eclipsed any he'd had with any other woman. It had only been one night, but he wanted more. He wanted *her.*

Nichelle took a deep breath and put down her pen. She clasped her hands together on the desk. "This doesn't need to go any further, Wolfe. Really."

"And that's all you want to say about this?" *It can't be.* The thought pulsed in him, hard and painful. After the things they'd shared in Morocco and the way she responded with him in bed, this couldn't be the end.

"Yes, it is."

She tapped the keyboard, obviously ready to get back to work. Dismissing him. But a flicker of something unfamiliar in her eyes caught him. She was…afraid. Then the fear was gone, and it was just Nichelle staring at him with an upraised brow. Whatever she was feeling, she didn't want him to see it. He had to respect that.

"Okay." He nodded. "I have a lunch meeting in Fort Lauderdale. I'm heading that way now."

"Sounds good. See you when you get back." She turned back to her computer.

Wolfe's lips tightened. But he let himself out and closed her door very deliberately behind him. This was going to be a long, damned day.

Nichelle kept her eyes on the computer for a full thirty seconds after Wolfe walked out of her office, only blinking, unseeing, at the screen. Regret, a spiked and hard thing, rolled through her chest. She clenched her teeth to prevent the words that would call Wolfe back to her. He'd looked so hurt. Maybe there was a way they could—

The telephone rang, derailing her train of thought. Was it Wolfe calling?

But it was her assistant's voice that came over the line. "There's an Isaac Franklin on the phone for you, Ms. Wright."

What would he want to talk to her about? She pursed her lips, considering. "Put him through, please."

"I know what you did to get the Quraishi account." Isaac didn't bother with any pleasantries.

Nichelle hissed an indrawn breath, then forced herself to stay calm. Isaac was a bully and not very smart. What he thought might be dirt on her and Wolfe might actually be nothing. "What do you mean? That I had the best proposal, better resources, and was more prepared to do my job than you?" She leaned back at her desk, consciously relaxing her body.

"The two of you were pretending to be married to impress Quraishi. You took advantage of his conservative stance to push your proposal through."

"What he may or may not think about my personal life with Wolfe has no bearing on the job we'll do for him as his business management consultants." She gave him the party line, hoping he'd give up and get off her phone.

"If Quraishi knew you two played him, he would snatch that account from Kingston Consulting so damn fast you'd get whiplash."

Nichelle tapped her fingers against the desk, already mentally doing damage control. "What's the point of this call, Isaac? What do you want?"

"You know what I want."

"To grow a few more inches?" She was deliberately nasty, adding a sneer in her voice. She wished he was standing in front of her so she could stare witheringly at his crotch for maximum effect.

"You're going to tell Quraishi everything," Isaac said. "*Or* you drop Diallo and come back to work for us. If you come back to Sterling, I won't say a word to Quraishi."

And by leaving Kingston, she was as good as telling Quraishi she'd lied anyway. What wife would abandon her husband and his business to work for a mediocre competitor? Not a very smart one. "Why the hell would I do any of that?"

"If you care anything for Diallo and his company, why wouldn't you?" Then he hung up.

Nichelle glared at the silent telephone as anger knocked an erratic pulse in her throat, and she pressed her teeth viciously together. She wanted to find Isaac wherever he was in Miami and gut him like the useless bottom-feeder he was. She buzzed her assistant instead.

"Isaac Franklin doesn't get through to me again."

"Yes, ma'am. Understood."

Nichelle disconnected the call, only to have her cell phone chime a second later. It was a text from Nala inviting her out to lunch. She texted back: I can't. Something came up at work. Dinner tonight?

A minute later Nala wrote back: Fine. But you're buying. Romeo's Café.

A brief smile quirked Nichelle's mouth. Her friend *would* pick one of the most expensive restaurants in Miami in retaliation for Nichelle not being available when she wanted. She texted: Fine. But you're picking me up.

Nala: You're on.

She put the phone down, already thinking again of Isaac and the threats he made. She had to find a way to fix this. No matter what was going on between her and Wolfe, she wouldn't allow someone else to hurt him. But her usually quick mental reflexes couldn't find a solution to the conundrum Isaac had left her with. She could only sit in the chair, frozen, remembering Wolfe's face only minutes before when she'd basically told him to leave her alone. That had hurt his feelings, but Isaac Franklin had the power to cripple his business.

Nichelle's hand clenched into a fist.

Wolfe maneuvered his sleek burgundy Mercedes-Benz through downtown Fort Lauderdale while 2 Chainz growled from the car's speakers. His meeting had gone well, another guaranteed win for Kingston Consulting, but dissatisfaction writhed under his skin. He couldn't get Nichelle out of his mind. Not the way she dismissed him that morning, not the way she had felt moving beneath him as they'd made love only days before.

The music in the car faded to nothing when his phone started to ring. A photo of Nichelle appeared on the screen of his cell, a picture he'd taken of her at a family dinner. Velvet eyes smiling, her mouth bare of lipstick, a peacock-blue dress making her skin look like black gold. She was so breathtakingly beautiful.

A car horn honked sharply behind him, jerking his attention back to the road and the green light he was currently wasting. He set the car back in motion the same time the phone stopped ringing.

He lifted his thumb to hit the redial button when the phone rang again.

"Good, I'm glad you called back."

"Are you sure you're talking to the right person?"

The masculine voice at the other end of the line made him glance at the caller ID he'd ignored before. An unknown local number. But his brain caught up and he recognized the voice.

"Isaac Franklin."

"Got it in one."

"I didn't know we were playing guessing games."

Franklin laughed, but there was no humor in it. "I just talked to your wife."

"I don't have a wife," Wolfe said before he could stop himself.

"That's not what Quraishi thinks."

Wolfe sucked in a silent breath. "What he may or may not think is none of your business. In case you already forgot, he's not your client. He's ours."

"In case *you* forgot, you told him a lie to get the contract. He wouldn't take very kindly to knowing that."

"Get the hell off my line, Franklin." He hung up.

Wolfe was getting off on the exit toward Coral Gables, passing the airport with planes taking off low overhead, when his phone rang again, from another line he had forwarded to his cell. The phone number plainly said it was from California. It had to be Franklin again. Despite the unease in his gut, he answered the call.

"Whatever you have to say, make it quick," he growled into the phone.

"You may not know Nichelle as well as you think, Diallo." Franklin sounded smug. "I know what you two got up to in Morocco." Had he watched them from the tent while they'd pressed together under the desert stars? No. Franklin wasn't talking about that.

"She's beautiful, isn't she?" Franklin continued. "That heart-shaped mole on her hip is like a stamp of perfection. They don't make them like that anymore."

A cold shiver raked through Wolfe. He'd never seen the mole until the night he and Nichelle made love. It was an inky beauty mark near the seat of her sex that he'd licked and bit until she gasped his name, begged him to move his mouth lower. Bile rose in his throat at the thought of Franklin touching it.

"You've never been that lucky in your life," Wolfe rumbled. He slammed on the brakes when he almost rear-ended the car in front of him.

"I *have* been that lucky," Franklin said. "And could have been again if a man higher up on the food chain hadn't come along for her to sink her claws into."

Wolfe remembered their night together, her nails raking his shoulders and back, the sharp tips digging into his skin, bringing him unbearable pleasure mixed with pain. The images rampaging through his head struck him dumb, made him grip and release his hand around the steering wheel.

"You need to realize that she's all for herself. She's going to leave you and Kingston Consulting and take the Quraishi contract with her. Watch her carefully and see. I didn't pay attention to my own advice, and she damn near crushed me."

"She never slept with you," Wolfe finally hissed.

"Is that what she told you?"

The indistinct sounds of conversation came through the phone, a jarring noise given the absolute quiet of moments before. Franklin was on the move.

"Good luck with that viper, Diallo. I'm just telling you the score before you become another one of her victims. It's not a good look on any man."

Wolfe hung up, clenching his jaw so hard it hurt. He looked around, saw that he had driven on autopilot back to the office and he sat in the parking lot, listening to the music that had pulsed back on once the call ended. Anger churned in his belly. He silenced the speakers.

Franklin was a liar. There was nothing he could tell Wolfe about Nichelle that he would believe. Certainly no ridiculous story about her stooping low enough to sleep with a colleague to advance her career. But the echoing silence in the car was haunting. A chill washed over him. He needed to talk with her. Now.

But when he got back into the building, Nichelle wasn't there. Wolfe hesitated in the open door of her office, the specter of their Friday night encounter haunting him even more than what Franklin said. She'd left him alone in her bed, for God's sake!

It looked as if she had packed up for the day, the computer shut down, her purse gone. He sat down behind her desk and leaned back in her chair, fitting his body to the same contours she did nearly every day.

Okay, this is getting creepy.

Wolfe started to get up when an envelope, propped

on the footrest under the desk, drew his attention. He plucked it from its perch—and drew a surprised breath. The envelope was from Sterling Solutions and stamped "private." There was nothing inside it. What the hell did this mean? He thought back to Franklin's phone call.

"No." *No way.*

He dropped the empty envelope on Nichelle's desk as if it were on fire and turned, nearly stumbling on a floor lamp, to make his way to his own office. A reminder on his phone beeped.

Family dinner tonight.

He'd forgotten all about it, which was the purpose of reminders, he thought with a wry twist of his mouth. With effort, he pushed the Sterling envelope from his mind and called his mother as soon as he got back to his desk.

"Dinner is still on for tonight?"

"Of course. When do I cancel something this important at the last minute?" The answer was never. She treasured the family dinners perhaps more than anyone, proof and celebration that she still had a family despite everything that had happened years before. "Bring a bottle or two of your favorite red wine. Your father asked for steak tonight, but our last party sucked up the last of our good wine."

"Yes, ma'am."

"You're such a good son." She laughed. "See you tonight."

Hours later, freshly showered and shaved, he rang his parents' doorbell. Nala opened the door. He automatically looked behind her, searching for Nichelle.

"Why are you ringing your own doorbell?"

"Mama will be the first to tell you that this doorbell

is definitely not mine." He greeted her with a brief kiss to the cheek, then walked past her with a carton of wine under his arm. The bottles clinked in the box as he put them down to give her a proper hug. "Besides, the times I walked in on something I didn't want to see as a kid made the practice of ringing a doorbell and knocking once or twice the rule rather than the exception."

Jealousy flashed briefly across Nala's face. Even before her parents died and left her alone, they'd never been as close or as passionate as his own. He squeezed her waist in sympathy.

"You on your own tonight?"

"Nope." Nala gave him a knowing look, the jealousy gone from her face as if it had never been. "Nicki is upstairs. Chatting with your father, I think."

She's here. Okay. He took a deep breath. "Cool."

The house was already lively with conversation and music, Toots and the Maytals playing from the stereo, two sets of twins smack talking over a game of spades in the sitting room. Sounds of a playful disagreement drifted down at him from upstairs.

He found his mother in the kitchen, laughing with his sister Alice and maneuvering a large casserole dish, steaming with the scents of broccoli and cheese, to the large center island.

"Wolfe." She shucked off the potholders to hug him and kiss his cheek. The mingled scents of cooking food—steak, garlic sautéed vegetables, rosemary potatoes—made his mouth water.

"Hey, Mama." He gave her a long and tight hug, then pulled back to smile into her eyes. "Where's Daddy?"

"In the den. Jaxon is trying to convince him to buy some new gadget or other."

"So he can inherit it after Daddy gets frustrated with trying to learn the new tech?"

"Exactly."

Wolfe laughed. "Some things never change."

He greeted everyone else he found lingering in the kitchen, before wandering off to find his father. In the den, his father sat at his desk, the computer on, and Jaxon, half of the youngest set of three twins, perched on the edge talking about terabytes and hardware upgrades.

Wolfe stopped when he noticed Nichelle on the other side of the desk, her arms loosely crossed over her stomach while she nodded in response to something his older brother, Kingsley, was saying. She was wearing a houndstooth check dress tonight, the black-and-white fabric hugging her body from collar to knees. Wolfe's gaze drifted to her hands, over her bare wedding ring finger where he'd grown used to seeing that flare of yellow fire.

Nichelle glanced at him then, a flash of her long-lashed gaze lingering on him before turning back to his brother. He shook off his stupor and went over to his father, squeezed his shoulder. "Daddy."

"My boy!"

His father shoved away from the desk, and from Jaxon's look of annoyance at being interrupted, to embrace Wolfe in a giant, breath-stealing hug.

Maybe I need to visit home more often, Wolfe thought. "Is this one trying to get you to spend more money on crap that's going to be obsolete in six months?"

His father chuckled, a deep rumble in his wide chest. "Something like that."

"Keep your opinions to yourself, Wolfe," Jaxon said. "You don't know a damn thing about tech." His brother, a nineteen-year-old who knew everything, was only half teasing.

"I know enough to realize when spending money is a waste."

"Aren't you a millionaire or something? Why are you here counting somebody else's pennies? Look out for your own business." He jerked his chin toward Nichelle, who laughed while Kingsley stepped closer to touch her shoulder much too intimately.

Wolfe told his brother what he could do with his opinion.

"You first." Jaxon grinned.

"None of that talk around here, boys. If your mother caught you, she'd give me hell for it." His father sat again at the desk and waved toward his youngest son. "If you think this thing isn't a waste, show us what you're about."

Jaxon grinned at the challenge and hunkered even closer to the large computer screen, gripping the mouse. "Okay, take a look at this..."

Wolfe stopped paying attention to his brother. Instead, he listened to the conversation Nichelle was having with Kingsley, a conversation that seemed intimate despite the very public atmosphere of the den.

Nichelle's voice was low and interested as she talked with his brother. Kingsley said something to her about the new account with Quraishi Industries, about her possibly moving on to another firm. She shrugged, but didn't say anything about staying.

"Business is always changing," she said. "For better or worse. The people you align with today might be your enemy tomorrow or vice versa."

"That's true," he said. "But what about doing something more for yourself? Building your own firm, branching out and taking the initiative, grabbing another challenging project?"

"Why? Are you trying to make me an offer I can't refuse?"

Kingsley laughed, the dimples flashing in his cheeks. "I don't think I have that much money at my disposal. At least not yet. But I'm really envious of what my brother did with your help. I don't think he could have come this far without you."

"Envy is a fine enough emotion," she said, her mouth red and moist in the soft lamplight. "But your brother worked hard for what he has, separate from me, and you would have to, as well."

"Damn, I know that but—"

Wolfe had had enough. "Hey." He drifted over to them, brushed a hand over Nichelle's shoulder. "Can we talk for a minute?"

Did he imagine it, or had she closed her eyes just the tiniest bit at his touch?

Kingsley bristled. "We're discussing something important here." He gave Wolfe a narrow-eyed stare. His brother had grown up alongside Wolfe to notice how beautiful Nichelle was, even though Wolfe had been telling Kingsley for years to search elsewhere for his next woman. He had only laughed at Wolfe, asking with an infuriating look if Nichelle was already taken. "You can get her anytime you want," Kingsley said. "Piss off."

With a touch of reluctance that Wolfe noticed,

Nichelle turned away from his brother. "I'll be right back, Kingsley."

With Nichelle in front of him, Wolfe suddenly didn't know what to do. Her eyes were soft tonight, the off-the-shoulder dress tempting his hands to explore the body on delectable display. He curled fingers around her arm just above the elbow and lost his breath. Her skin felt soft, so soft. He was aware of Kingsley's stare, but he didn't care.

Because he wasn't quite thinking with the head on his shoulders, Wolfe led her upstairs to his old room. He closed the door behind them.

"What's on your mind?" she asked as the lock clicked into place.

Nichelle crossed her arms and took a step back, hyper-aware of their isolation from the rest of the family. It was only her and Wolfe in his childhood room, the smell of furniture polish and old books thick around them. His *bedroom*.

"I talked to Franklin today."

She blinked in surprise. That wasn't what she'd expected him to say. Earlier that day, she'd finally made a decision about what to do with Isaac and his threats, an entire damned day devoted to that foolishness when she had more important things to do with her time. The solution she found was a workable one. It kept Quraishi and Wolfe still working together and did not leave her at Isaac's mercy as he obviously hoped.

"What was that conversation about?" Nichelle crossed her arms. "Or should I even ask?"

"It looks like you already know."

She turned away from him to sit on the wide mahogany trunk under the window, pressing her palms down into the wood on either side of her hips. "I don't like to make assumptions."

"He said you were leaving me."

She flinched. That had been part of her solution. Not an ideal one, but the only one she had been able to come up with in such a short amount of time. She'd figured Isaac would strike, but not this soon.

"Yes." She pursed her lips, wondering if she would have the courage to leave when it was time. "I am."

"What the hell?" He looked shocked. Then his face blanked, emotional walls slamming down. "How could you do this?"

"I've made the decision, and this seems to be the best thing to do. I leave Kingston Consulting, no foul."

"And take Quraishi's business with you?" His eyes narrowed, the blank look on his face leeching away to leave coldness in its place. "Are you going to sleep with him, too?"

She shot to her feet. "What did you just say to me?"

"Franklin said—" He stopped, hopefully reconsidering what he was going to say.

"No, tell me exactly what he said and what you thought I would do." She stalked to him, her high heels cracking against the hardwood floors before being muffled by the carpet near his bed. "Tell me exactly what you think I'm capable of. Tell me you don't trust me anymore."

He didn't back away from her, but his face became impossibly even colder than before. His eyes were like flint with none of the amused glimmer she was used to, even in the midst of their most ridiculous arguments.

He opened his mouth and dropped the words in the

room. Vile words. She'd said that and worse of other people, men and women, but not people she knew better of. And she would damned sure not repeat them if they weren't true.

She ignored the twisting pain in her stomach, the pressure in her chest as if someone had just shoved her to the ground and stomped on her. "And you never once questioned anything he said about me?"

"You're leaving," he said by way of an answer.

She pressed her lips together. A cry wanted to wrench free from her throat. Nichelle swallowed until the sound slid back down into her stomach and away. "You're a dick."

She fought back against him the only way she knew how. By pulling away. Wolfe wasn't like everyone else. She couldn't hurt him without hurting herself. But even this—shoving all emotion aside and emptying her face of all expression, drawing her spine tight and preparing to walk out of the room and out of his life—cracked her wide open. The back of her eyes stung. Her limbs were heavy with disappointment. With sadness.

She turned toward the door.

"Don't do that," he said, his voice deep and threatening. "Don't walk away from me."

"You don't get to make demands of me, Wolfe." She did him one better, growling low in her throat. "Not after what you just said to me. If you believe I'm the kind of parasite Isaac described, then you shouldn't want anything to do with me." She took a steadying breath and moved toward the door again. "I think we're done."

"No." He grabbed her elbow but she yanked away, gasping at the slight pain.

"Don't touch me!"

He hissed. "That's not what you said to me the other night." And there it was for the first time, his feelings in the open about what they had shared. But this was not the place, and this was not the way to do it.

"You don't get to do this to me, Wolfe. You came to *my* house with your wants."

"Tell me you didn't want me to." It was a dare.

But she couldn't say it because it wasn't true. She had wanted him so badly that it burned. Her every breath had been painful with the need of him, nothing right until she had her hands and mouth on him, their bodies twined and twisted together, heaving in the bed toward satisfaction. Wolfe stepped close, obliterating the few feet of space she had placed between them.

Clean. He smelled clean, a hint of mint toothpaste on his breath, his sandalwood aftershave.

"Tell me you don't want me now."

His confidence rubbed her raw. "I don't want you now." She threw the words defiantly at him. "And how can you even pretend to want me when you see me as nothing more than a manipulative bitch with no sense of loyalty?"

"No!" He dipped his head and kissed her.

She gasped as his open mouth touched hers, his tongue a rough inquiry, wet and instantly knee-weakening. Nichelle fisted her hands in his shirt to push him away, but ended up pulling him to her instead. Her mouth opened, releasing a gasping breath when their tongues met. They kissed as if they were starved for each other, wet and noisy and sloppy. Needful.

The sting of sudden arousal burned between her legs, and she clutched at his shoulders, moaned into the unrelenting heat of his mouth. His hands gripped her hips. Then the wall was at her back, the hard press of him at her front. She whimpered with want. The fury of earlier sloughed off to revel in the "at last" of him against her body.

Nichelle sucked on Wolfe's tongue and raked her nails under his shirt, shoving it out of the way to press her hands into the dense muscle of his stomach, his pecs. She pinched his nipples, roughly. He gasped in her mouth, pushed her harder into the wall, his hands shoving up her dress. She heard it tearing, the twenty-five-hundred-dollar Carolina Herrera sheath destroyed in the frantic heat of their lust. He ripped aside her underwear. She fumbled for his zipper, for the hard heat of him.

They came together with a thick gasp, his hands digging into her hips. Her legs locked around his waist as he slid into her again, a deep and rough claiming. She tightened her legs around him and twisted her hips, wanting more from him, more than what they had become.

He was hot and sweet and firm inside her. Her center gripped him and squeezed while her thoughts scattered beyond retrieval. His breath puffed hot against her ear. He groaned her name, like pain. Sweat shuddered to the surface of her skin, heat under her clothes while she panted and twisted, her fingernails tight in the back of his neck.

"Don't leave me!" he groaned into her neck, panting as they slammed together, fury and fear, dread and desire driving them together toward a shuddering conclusion. Her legs locked tighter around his waist. Their breaths came faster. The wall knocked with the force of his thrusts.

But—she gasped and gripped him tighter—what if someone heard them? The bed. They should move to the perfectly good bed across the room. But he shifted his grip to her buttocks, tilted the angle of his hips and slammed into her just perfectly. A screaming cry left her lips.

And she forgot all about the bed.

Her hand scrambled back, found a shelf hooked to the wall and held on as he dove up into her, slamming the delight into her again and again. They rocked against the wall, fierce and sweaty. The scent of sweat and sex, desperation and anger and heat rose up like steam. Pleasure scraped her raw, twisting in her middle, gripping her so hard that she gasped his name, raked her nails down his sides. He hissed but did not stop the relentless work of his hips.

He clutched the back of her neck, forcing her head back. He showed his teeth, his canines bared, sweat dripping down his face.

"Don't. Leave. Me." He punctuated each word with a pump of his hips. "Please. Stay. Don't—" The words fell away into scattered curses. His eyes squeezed shut as his orgasm felled him. She felt the heated spurt of him between her thighs, and was then racing to catch up with him. A breathless moment later, she was shuddering, too, and crying out into the soaked collar of his shirt.

They trembled against each other, falling as one from the height they'd achieved together.

"Wolfe…" His name shuddered from her lips when her feet touched the ground.

Nichelle staggered on her high heels, panting and holding on to the wall with trembling fingers. She was slippery and hot under her clothes, between her legs. What had she done? She stared at Wolfe. He stumbled back from her, looking as shocked and breathless as she felt. He shoved himself back into his pants, looking anywhere but at her.

Nichelle yanked down her dress, feeling every bit the fool, even more than last time. His trust was just as important to her as his love. The fact that he didn't trust her anymore and could take the word of some nobody over what they'd shared for most of their lives made her sick to her stomach. She searched for the right words. "I'll leave the partnership dissolution papers on your desk tonight for you to sign. I won't be back in the office tomorrow." Those words weren't exactly right, but they would have to do.

Wolfe stumbled toward her. "No. Nichelle. Please."

She evaded his touch. "You already said enough." Nichelle left the room, head high, with as much of her dignity as she had left. Behind her, she heard him begin to follow, but she slipped quickly down the hallway and into a guest bathroom to tidy up.

When she was presentable, she snuck out the back door, sending Nala a text when she was in her car, but telling no one else she was leaving. She'd leave it up to Wolfe if he felt like giving explanations. This…thing… they had was over. She couldn't do this anymore. And she meant it this time. There were only so many times she would break her heart for a man.

Even this one.

Chapter 12

Nichelle walked out on the balcony of her rented condo and into the lush heat of a late-summer San Diego. She held the phone to her ear, humming in response to what her sister, Madalie, was saying.

It had been three weeks since she'd left Florida. She hadn't answered a single phone call from anyone at Kingston or from Wolfe's family. Everything she needed to do for the firm she'd done the night before she left for the airport. She'd cut the ties so effectively that she left herself bleeding, too. It hurt.

Nichelle leaned her forearms against the balcony and stared down at the narrow road below and the sandy beach beyond it. At barely two on a Thursday afternoon, there was already a decent amount of people on the beach, many sunning themselves, along with a few swimmers.

"Are you ever coming back?" Madalie asked the same question Nichelle had asked herself nearly every day she'd been in California. Her sister sounded sad over the phone, heartbreakingly so.

"I don't know." Nichelle gave the non-answer with a suffocating heaviness in her chest. "There are just some things I need to work out."

"With Wolfe, right?"

She sucked on the inside of her lip and ignored the abrupt dip in her stomach at the mention of his name. "Yes," she admitted. The afternoon sun pressed soft kisses into her cheek and her throat, while a delicate breeze teased the back of her neck. Although she ached deeply, the weather soothed her in small ways.

"Wolfe is here in Miami. You can't work things out with him if you're all the way over there." Her sister's voice cracked. "We miss you."

Nichelle pressed a fist to her forehead and squinted into the sun. Was she being selfish by running away? "I miss you guys, too, Maddie. I'll be home as soon as I can."

Her sister's watery sigh came loudly through the phone. "Okay."

A sudden knock on her door dragged her attention from her sister's suspiciously thick breathing. Madalie had always been the more independent of her sisters, but she was also the one who felt things the most keenly. "There's someone at the door, Maddie. I have to go."

"Okay, okay. Just come home soon. Okay? Bye." The line went silent.

Nichelle sighed. *Dammit.* At the door, she put her eye to the peephole. A man's tie appeared, something conservative and expensive. She swallowed thickly for a moment before she realized there was no way it could be Wolfe. He wouldn't wear a suit and tie in the heat of San Diego. And he would never follow her to California, even if he knew where she was.

But the man on her doorstep still surprised her.

"Garrison." Wolfe's best friend. "What are you doing here?"

"Visiting you." He gave her one of his restrained smiles, his eyes warming long before his mouth curled up ever so faintly at the corners.

Garrison and Wolfe were the opposite of the other. Wolfe was outgoing and charming, dropping panties with a simple glance while Garrison was more reserved, his looks not exactly magazine-worthy. But there was a restrained heat to him, a subtle sensuality and masculine presence. His new wife had discovered, to her contentment, just how much of a prize he was while the women who'd blown him off in college in favor of chasing the flashier and much more in-demand Wolfe were now crying into their martinis.

"Come in." She welcomed him into the condo with a wave.

He stepped past her with the faint scent of coffee and something else she couldn't identify. "I'm here because you're not answering Wolfe's calls."

Another thing she liked about Garrison, he was always upfront. You never had to guess where he stood.

"There's a reason I'm not answering his calls," she muttered, leading him into the brightly lit living room. "I don't want to talk to him."

"I gathered that much," he said dryly.

In the kitchen, she poured him a glass of sweet tea

without asking, took a glass of water for herself and sat down on the couch across from him.

"He's a wreck over what's happened between the two of you," Garrison said.

"Why is everything always about him?" She tightened her lips. "He said things to me that I never thought would come from his mouth." She arched an eyebrow at him. "Did he tell you that?"

"Yes. He did."

She swallowed in surprise. "Then he knows nothing can be done to fix it. There was no point in sending you—"

"He didn't send me."

This time she couldn't hide her surprise. Garrison, looking debonair and elegant in his pale blue summer-weight suit, crossed one knee over the other.

"Wolfe feels guilty about the things he said, like he deserves to be punished. He knows you better than some subpar tactician with severe talent envy." Nichelle almost smiled at his description of Isaac Franklin. "He's sorry but won't come to you because he's got his metaphoric hair shirt on and is rolling around in it all over Miami. And New York, too, incidentally."

"Good for him." She sneered.

"Nichelle."

"Yes?"

"Forgive him." The faintest hint of a plea crept into his tone.

"I can't. Why should I?"

"He loves you."

"He's got a real nice way of showing it." She drew a painful breath. Everything she'd forced herself to forget in Miami rushed back to her with each word Garrison uttered. It was beyond agony.

"All I'm asking is for you to give him a chance. Answer his call next time. Be open to hearing what he has to say."

"I won't make any promises, Garrison." She bit her lip, crumbling into the sofa, her superwoman facade fading away. "It's been *so* damn hard." Her voice trembled, and she gripped her hands in her lap.

"Jesus." He looked abruptly uncomfortable. But he sank into the seat next to her and settled a hand on her forearm.

"Stop torturing each other with this separation." He squeezed her arm. "Just talk to him."

Tears tickled the back of Nichelle's throat. Her body felt hot and miserable with unhappiness. But it was better than opening herself to be hurt by Wolfe again. He was to blame for what happened this time. But if she allowed him back in, she would be to blame for the resulting heartache.

Nichelle swallowed her tears and looked Garrison full in the face. "Tell him to go screw himself."

Only once he was gone did she allow the tears to run like acid down her face.

Before Garrison came, she had been having a decent week. Never one to wallow in anything, especially not her feelings, she dove into re-establishing her West Coast business connections and plunged into the cool water of the Pacific to wear herself out to the point of exhaustion when that work didn't distract her enough.

But with Wolfe's best friend came doubts about the choices she'd made. Three days after Garrison left, she still couldn't stop thinking about his visit. She reached out to her business contacts, working toward making her relocation to California a permanent thing. But after the phone calls and emails were done, her mind raced back to Garrison and the conversation they'd had.

Wolfe was miserable. He loved her. But not enough to make the journey to California himself. He'd told Garrison everything. But he didn't trust Nichelle. She prowled the condo, only a breath away from tears.

Just stop thinking about him!

Close to sunset, she pulled the front door shut behind her with keys, cash and phone in her jeans pocket. She couldn't stay in the condo any longer. After wandering the neighborhood for nearly an hour, she ended up at the little corner store near the head shop on Mission Boulevard.

The bell over the door jangled as she walked in.

"Ms. Wright." The man behind the counter, more of a boy really, greeted her with his eager smile.

"Hey, Raj."

She already visited the little store too often. Since leaving Miami, she'd developed an aversion to grocery stores, especially the big, bright ones. They left her feeling exposed and alone, waiting for something that would never come. But Raj's corner store with its constant supply of overpriced condiments and pasta and coffee was perfect.

"Things going all right today?" She chatted with him as usual since he seemed always happy to see her, a boy with a crush, which was sweet and helped scrape some of her ego off the ground.

"Yes, ma'am." His face was handsome and eager behind the glass partition. When she looked away in her search for her favorite Ben and Jerry's ice cream, she sensed his eyes on her. She found the Chunky Monkey and took it up to the window to pay.

"Another one, huh?"

She nodded, refusing to get embarrassed about her sadness addiction. Five pints in three weeks. It was a good thing she got up to swim every morning; otherwise she wouldn't be able to fit into her suits by the time she found a new job.

"Just a little something to tide me over until dinner," she said, not sure she was entirely joking.

"It's a delicious flavor," the boy said. "You have good taste." He dipped his head, subtle color touching his cheeks.

"Thank you, Raj." She gave him a smile of her own, then collected her change. "See you next time."

"See you!"

Nichelle swung the plastic bag with the ice cream at her side as she left the corner store and its ringing bell behind. She stepped out in the sunlight and bumped into the person standing near the doorway.

"Excuse me," she said.

"No need to be excused," came a familiar voice. "It was my fault."

She jumped away from the steadying hands, her heart pounding frantically in her chest. Wolfe frowned down at her from his looming height. At least she thought it was Wolfe. This version of him was fully bearded with a thick fuzz of hair on his head and new lines around his mouth. Instead of a suit, he wore black Converse, faded jeans and a plain black T-shirt. Sunglasses shaded his eyes.

She gasped softly at the change in him, because yes,

it was him. With that single touch on her arms, the scent
of him, the brief crush of his broad chest against her,
she knew immediately who it was.

She looked around the street, expecting to see Garrison meandering someplace nearby. Despite the run-
away pace of her heartbeat, she pulled herself together
and took another step back.

"Was Garrison supposed to soften me up for the
kill?" She gripped the plastic bag with the ice cream
against her belly, grateful for the cold, grounding pressure of it on her skin.

"What?" Frown lines etched into Wolfe's brow.

"Don't play stupid with me. I told Garrison I didn't
want to see you. You can take your bad feelings and
shove them up your—"

"Garrison was here?"

"You didn't send him?"

His frown deepened. "Why would I?"

Truthfully, sending an emissary didn't seem like
Wolfe's style. If he wanted to deal with a problem, he
usually confronted it head on, despite any possible consequences.

"It doesn't matter anyway." She gave him a dismissive glance. "You wasted your time coming out here."

"It's not wasted since I got to see you."

She rolled her eyes. "Enough with the bull."

"This is no bull, Nichelle." He crossed his arms over
his chest, both a protective and vulnerable gesture. "I
needed to see you."

"And what, it took you three weeks to get your courage up?"

He looked away, eyes skittering over the storefronts
nearby, the awning of the corner store, the pretty girl

who walked past in her bikini and UGG boots. His forehead wrinkled in confusion when he looked again at the girl, and Nichelle almost smiled.

"It's a California thing," she said. She stepped past him to wait for the light to cross the busy street. He kept up with her. "Why are you following me?"

"I want to talk with you."

"We already said enough the last time we saw each other."

"No, we didn't. I—"

Nichelle stepped out into the street before the light changed. She couldn't listen to another word. She didn't want to hear his excuses for ripping her heart out of her chest and stomping it to pieces under his designer Italian shoes.

A car horn honked. Tires screamed.

Wolfe yanked her out of the street moments before a car plowed through the intersection. His arms lashed tight over her belly, painful and protective. She cried out, frightened, and dropped the ice cream. It rolled into the street. Another car sped through the green light and crushed the carton. Nichelle stared in horror at the pulverized carton still mostly encased in white plastic, banana ice cream and walnuts exploding from the bag and already melting on the street.

"Dammit, I didn't come here for you to kill yourself!"

Wolfe didn't let go. His heart thudded hard against her shoulder blade. But her heartbeat wasn't any calmer. When the crosswalk light changed, Wolfe tugged her across the street toward the narrow path heading down to the beach. Nichelle pressed a hand to her chest, willing herself to calm down. She wiped a hand through the cold sweat on her forehead.

"I'm sorry," she said after her heart stopped racing. "That was stupid of me."

"It *was* stupid." Wolfe tucked her under his arm and fumbled a kiss to her jaw. "But I've done my share of stupid, too."

She bit her lip and relaxed into his embrace, into the sweat-flavored solidity of him. The day was bright with sun, heat pulsing around them, the afternoon wavering like a mirage. Nichelle briefly closed her eyes. Was all of this some crazy dream? Would she wake up in her condo, crying out in grief and loss like she had so many times before?

A pack of giggling girls walking toward them nudged each other, staring at Wolfe, then at her. Their envious looks made her feel self-conscious. She pulled away from Wolfe, although immediately she wanted to curl into him again.

He quietly released her. They walked through the clutter of bikini- and shorts-clad teenagers. It was a Sunday. No school and a packed Mission Beach. Instead of leading her toward her condo, Wolfe steered her with a gentle nudge of his shoulder away from the path toward her place and down to the water.

He paused to toe off his shoes and carry them while she trudged along at his side in the sand. The beach was crowded, mostly surfers and sunbathers, some families with their laughing children, ridiculously beautiful people playing beach volleyball nearby in little more than their underwear.

Nichelle found a quiet spot on the hot sand and sat down. Wolfe settled next to her. She took off her shoes, crossed her arms and balanced her chin on her bent knees, staring out into the water.

"You should go," she said.

"I can't." There was nothing melodramatic in his words, simply a statement of fact. "My mother will kill me if I come back to Miami without you."

"I'm sure you'll manage to recover."

He shifted at her side, his linked arms curved around his bent knees. He stared out at the water, sunlight glinting off his shades. "Nichelle. I was an idiot."

"You've always been an idiot."

A huff of sound, amusement and exasperation, left his mouth. Nichelle bit her lip again. Something about the relaxed ease of him on the sand beside her, the firm warmth of his arm against hers, the pounding of the surf, reminded her how much she'd thought of them like this, lying on the beach in Miami. Just the two of them without any worries. None of his women. No work. Just them and the sun and the weight of their feelings between them. The memory weakened her.

She sighed and dropped down into the sand, lying on her back. He lay with her, tucking his arms behind his head. His big body heaved with a sigh of its own.

"I love you."

She tensed at the unexpected declaration. "You don't accuse someone you love of betraying you. Especially when you know it's not true."

"I *did* know you would never do that to me. Can't I use my rampant jealousy as an excuse?" She heard the faint humor in his voice, the attempt at teasing.

"As if I could ever sleep with Isaac Franklin. He's weak." *And he's not you.*

Wolfe choked on a laughing breath, then stilled. "He

talked about your mole. The one here." He touched her through the jeans. "I just saw red. But instead of taking it out on him, I let my paranoia do the damage." He cursed softly. "I'm sorry. I knew better and I'm sorry."

"You know that anyone who's seen me in a bikini has seen that mole, right?"

"Hell! I know..." His voice faded away. "Once I pulled my head out of my ass, I realized that. Sorry doesn't begin to cover what I feel."

"And you think that should change things back to how they were between us?"

"No, I don't." He rolled to face her in the sand. Bright sunlight reflected off the gold in his sunglasses. She squinted against the glare. After a brief pause, he took off the glasses. And she saw what he'd been trying to hide, the heavy sorrow in his eyes. "I don't want things to go back to how they were," he said. "I want them to be better." He took another breath. "I want..."

For the first time in her adult life, Nichelle saw Wolfe hesitate. He licked his lips, and her eyes grew wider. He was nervous. His hand moved between their bodies, brushing her hip, then her belly. Then his hand emerged with a familiar scarlet box. "I want you to wear this again, but for real this time."

A breath stuttered from her. "What is that?" But her body already knew what it was. She grew warm, happiness heating her from the inside out. Wolfe opened the box, and the canary diamonds winked at her in the sunlight.

"This is an inadequate symbol of my love and trust," he said. "I love you. I trust you, and I can't allow myself to forget that again. This is my promise to you that I won't."

She swallowed. "You don't need to marry me just to keep me in Miami, Wolfe."

"Does that mean you'll come back to me? I want to marry you to keep you in my bed and in my life. I want to make official what everyone's been saying about us for years. And I want to prove to you that I'm worthy of the trust and love you give me every day."

She bit her lip to stifle a smile. "I never said I love you."

His mouth tilted. "You don't have to say it." He took the engagement ring out of the box. "So, will you?"

Yes. Yes! "I'll think about it," she said. "I'm surprised you haven't assumed my answer since you apparently know me so well."

"I have. But I'm giving you the courtesy of allowing you to say it out loud."

She took the ring from him and slid it into her pocket. "Ask me again when we're back home."

A shudder ran through his body, a hiss of relief. He wasn't as confident as he claimed. "God, yes."

She smiled at the vulnerability in his face, the easing of the tightness around his eyes, the way his beautiful mouth softened. His tongue brushed over his full lower lip.

"Nichelle." There was a pleading in his voice.

"Wolfe." And because she knew the man she would soon marry, knew what he needed, she whispered the three words in his ear.

"Then kiss me," he said.

And she did. The press of their mouths together was a sweet welcome that soon became a heated slide of tongue and lips, hands pushing under T-shirts to find warm skin. An embarrassing sound leaked from her mouth, need and relief. Wolfe's fingers curved around her ribs, a thumb stroking the underside of her breast.

Something smacked into Nichelle's leg. She gasped, jerking back.

"Sorry! Sorry!" A slim girl in a bikini grabbed a volleyball near Nichelle's feet, then ran off across the sand.

Wolfe laughed and stood up, the corners of his eyes crinkling with happiness. "We should continue this conversation someplace private, don't you think?" He reached down to help her to her feet.

Nichelle put a hand in his, and he tugged her up into his arms. "Yes," she murmured, a smile as wide as the whole ocean spreading across her face. "We should."

She pressed close to Wolfe and buried her face in his chest, drawing in a deep breath of him that was like home. A place she'd been all along.

Epilogue

"Is she pregnant?"

Wolfe, who'd been buttoning his shirt while his mother's voice blared from the speaker of his cell, grabbed the phone off the bed. He took it off speaker. "What?!"

His mother laughed at his outrage. "Did you knock Nichelle up before the wedding? Is that why you had a quick ceremony on our back lawn less than a week after bringing her back from California?"

Although his mother couldn't see, Wolfe shook his head. He darted a glance toward the closed bathroom door of their hotel and stepped away. He didn't want Nichelle to hear the crazy things his mother was saying. The music of Paris, church bells and faint conversation from a café nearby hummed at him through the open window.

He and Nichelle had arrived in France three hours before, jet-lagged from the journey. But instead of falling into the bed to sleep, they had fallen on each other, passionate and eager to make love for the first time as man and wife.

Nichelle, with laughter in her voice, had asked him several times on the long flight why he'd booked the tickets for immediately after the wedding, knowing they had a nine-hour flight ahead of them and no chance for a true wedding night. But he hadn't been thinking about that when he made the arrangements. He just wanted to finally start the life with her he'd imagined for so long.

So, no. Nichelle wasn't pregnant. But it wasn't for lack of trying.

"Mama, the rush was all mine. But it has nothing to do with a surprise baby."

"If you say so." The sound of a door slamming came to him through the phone. "Get on with your honeymooning then. Thanks for letting us know you arrived safely, although I'm sure you got in long before now."

His neck heated again, but he refused to rise to the bait. "You're welcome."

"I'll tell your father to stop planning for his first grandchild. Too bad, he was getting excited. And I was, too, to tell the truth."

"Mama, I'll talk with you later."

"Yes, my son. Enjoy Paris and your new wife."

He disconnected the call and rubbed the back of his neck. Nichelle carrying his child. The thought warmed him, made him eager to take her to bed again and make it a reality.

"Did I hear something about me being knocked up?"

His wife emerged from the bathroom, flawless in a

royal blue dress and black high heels, mouth red with lipstick. She smelled of the shower and a light citrus perfume, and had changed from the leggings and sweater she'd worn on the plane, or rather the leggings and shirt he'd torn off her as soon as the hotel room door shut. Nichelle was his *wife*. The canary diamond rings once again on her finger proved it. The quick ceremony in his parents' backyard cemented it. And now they were in Paris on their honeymoon, in the place where it all started.

"Yes." Wolfe drew her into his arms. "She thinks I shamefully knocked you up, and that's the reason I ran off to France with you so quickly. My brothers have a bet going, apparently. I told her whoever started that bet had already lost."

The corner of Nichelle's red mouth tilted up in an odd smile. She slid her arms around his neck, sweet breath and sweeter body stirring him all over again. "Well, maybe not."

Wolfe froze, the shock of her declaration tightening his spine. "Do you mean to say…?" He couldn't go on. He stood still in the perfumed sanctuary of her arms, his body torn in two directions as she bit his earlobe and slid her palms over his chest through the half-buttoned shirt.

"No need to tell them now, though," she murmured.

"When—when did this happen?"

"The night before I left for California, I'm guessing." She licked his ear, and he felt the smiling curve of her mouth against his throat. He pulled carefully away to stare down at his wife, soon to be the mother of his child. "Should we even be…?" *Making love?* The shock of her revelation apparently rendered him incapable of finishing a sentence.

Nichelle crossed her arms. "If I thought you'd treat me like spun glass, I wouldn't have told you until we got home." She pursed her lips. "I'm not delicate, Wolfe, just pregnant. And only a little pregnant at that." Then she smiled, dropping her gaze.

Wolfe's heart tripped in his chest at the utter vulnerability on her face. *Jesus.* "Nichelle..." He dropped to his knees and pressed his ear to her flat stomach. "I love you more and more every day."

"Hopefully not because I'm about to add another Diallo to the world." She stroked his face. "Get off your knees, husband of mine. There will be plenty of time for that later. If memory serves, you promised me some French food and music this afternoon."

Wolfe stood up. "You're incredible. You know that?"

"Of course. And you're my well-deserved prize." She smiled up into his eyes and looped her arms around his waist. "I was going to wait until we got back home to tell you about the baby, but..." She shrugged, looking uncharacteristically shy. "As usual, your mother forced my hand."

Wolfe groaned as something suddenly occurred to him. "She's going to think that I lied to her."

"No, she won't. I'll tell her the truth."

The truth that he was going to be a father. A *father.* Wolfe barely knew what to do. He'd made plans for them for the day. But now that he had a child on the way...

"Stop. Stop whatever foolishness you're thinking right now." She laughed at him, dragged him close again and kissed him quickly on the mouth. Her fingers fastened the remaining buttons on his shirt. "Are you ready?"

Earlier they had decided that to increase the likelihood of them getting out of the hotel room that afternoon, they would shower separately. Wolfe went first, taking his twenty minutes in the bathroom before making way for Nichelle to luxuriate under the hot spray and come out of the bathroom looking as if she was on the way to a fashion show.

"Yes." He kissed the corners of her mouth, the tip of her nose. "I've been ready for you forever."

"My charming husband."

They left the room, Nichelle in the protective crook of his arm, the sweet weight of her against him making Wolfe feel lucky with every step.

"*Monsieur* Diallo." The hotel concierge signaled to him as they passed through the lobby. "This arrived for you today." She passed him an envelope. It was eggshell white and thick, expensive paper that smelled faintly of incense.

"Thank you."

Wolfe wondered briefly what was in the envelope. Only Nala, Wolfe's parents and secretary knew exactly where he and Nichelle were. No one else had been told the specifics of their trip.

"What's that?"

"No idea." He turned the envelope over in his hands, then stepped with Nichelle out into the sunny afternoon.

"Open it. Do you think someone sent us a present?"

He chuckled at her childlike excitement, reminded again of the actual child in her belly. His fingers drifted to her stomach. She leaned into his caress, smiling. "Who knew you were such a softie for babies?"

"Definitely not me." He'd only considered children in the abstract before, and only in the context of his promise to provide at least one grandchild to his parents. "But now…"

"Now you're the most excited daddy-to-be there ever was."

And the sparkle and flash in her eyes told him that Nichelle might be the most excited mommy-to-be there ever was. To satisfy her curiosity about the envelope, he paused on the front steps of the hotel to open it. As expected, it was a card.

On the occasion of your wedding.

"Another wedding card for us." Although it was addressed to Wolfe alone.

"But why did they send it here?" she asked. "Is it from our parents?"

Congratulations on making an honest woman out of Mademoiselle Wright. On your way back from Paris, consider a stop in Essaouira with my compliments. May you experience even more joy in your life together. With your partnership secured, I look forward to a long and fruitful relationship with Kingston Consulting.
Best,
Jamal al Din Quraishi

The smile dropped from Wolfe's face.

Nichelle's attention had already wandered from the card to the cobblestoned streets and the beautiful city around them. She walked ahead of him, heels delicately tapping the cobblestones with each step. Her hip-rock-ing stroll drew his eyes, the way the red-soled shoes elongated her legs, flexed the muscles in her calves and made her firm and round bottom even more of a miracle. He no longer had to pretend he wasn't looking. Nichelle walked with the loose stride of a confident and happy woman. She peeked over her shoulder at him, wearing that smile that curled desire in his belly, love in his heart. She clasped her hands behind her, bringing his eyes low to the fire flash of the yellow diamonds on her finger and the full curve of her bottom in the peacock-blue dress. She crooked a finger at him: *Come here.*

"What's distracting you from me?" she asked when he caught up to her.

"The card is from Quraishi. He wishes us well."

"Does he?" She looked surprised. But there was something else, too.

"What am I missing?" he asked.

Nichelle worried her lower lip between her teeth, then put a hand over his heart. "Before I left for Cali-fornia, I told Quraishi the truth. I told him our mar-riage deception was my idea and that I'd resigned from the company. I assured him that Kingston Consulting would still take excellent care of his business interests."

This smaller shock only rocked Wolfe back on his heels a little. "But he never said anything to me. He never asked to nullify the contract. Nothing."

"That's good." Her mouth twitched, a tiny smile of triumph. "I tried to make sure you wouldn't have to deal with the fallout. I guess it worked."

After Nichelle had left for California, Quraishi said nothing to him about dissolving the partnership or even about Nichelle being with the company. The man had simply carried on with their business arrangement as if nothing had changed. Except for a cryptic email in which he'd said he hoped to hear from Nichelle again soon, everything was the same. At the time, Wolfe had been too worried about getting Nichelle back to his side that he hadn't thought much about his business. But it all made sense now.

Nichelle had shielded him with her love yet again. He felt once more the familiar twinge of anger at himself, the regret that he'd allowed doubt to come between them and fool him into thinking she wasn't worthy of his trust.

She dug her fingers gently into his chest through his shirt. A warning. "It's in the past now," she said. "We have the future to look forward to. Together."

Nichelle was right. Still, he'd make up his lapse to her somehow. For now...

"Mrs. Nichelle Wright-Diallo, would you do me the honor of accompanying me to a concert this afternoon?" He smiled down at her, willing all the love he had for her to show on his face.

Faint color moved under her cheeks. "Of course, husband."

Wolfe linked his fingers with hers and they turned as one, walking side by side toward a future they had always shared.

* * * * *

BEST FRIEND TO PRINCESS BRIDE

KATRINA CUDMORE

To Edith.
Thank you for your constant support,
wisdom and friendship.
Love Katrina

CHAPTER ONE

KARA DUFFY HIT the mud with a yelp. Cold muck and pebbles dashed her face. She sagged into the soft earth, every inch of her body aching.

Sucking footsteps, in a fight with the quagmire, approached behind her.

Could this day get any worse?

Not only was she, the poster girl for the charity's first ever fun mud run, going to be one of the last to cross the finishing line, but now one of her volunteer race marshals was having to come and rescue her. She needed to get up. Now. While she had some dignity left.

She pushed with all her might but her hands disappeared into the sogginess and her knees slipped and slid all over the place.

She gave a grunt and flipped over. Swallowing her pride.

But instead of a race marshal, three men, all in their thirties, all muscled and tanned, wearing top-to-toe tight-fitting black clothes, stood watching her. Two were considering her with professional concern, while the guy in the centre was trying desperately to hold back a laugh.

Prince Edwin of Monrosa and his royal protection officers, Domenico and Lucas.

Oh, what? Clamping her hands to her face, she gave a

moan. Between her fingers she spotted Edwin grin. She giggled, relief surging through her, the weeks of disquiet over his lack of contact vanishing more swiftly than the grey March clouds scuttling across the sky behind him.

Lowering her hands, she grinned back at him, all of her work worries, her crabbiness over being so cold, her frustration at lagging so far behind in the field of competitors, disappearing in the face of his entrancing sorcerer's smile.

Edwin's hand reached down and he hoisted her out of the mud, an embarrassing squelching sound accompanying her escape.

With a barely detectable nod from Edwin, Domenico and Lucas moved away in the direction of the two event marshals who were standing at the stone piers at the top of the field that led out onto the return road to the event's tented village.

'You look exhausted.' Edwin paused, that smile still dancing on his lips. 'I'd offer to carry you but I don't want to be yelled at like the last time I pulled you up from a muddy field.'

Puzzled, she yanked her jacket down from where it had twisted around her waist and then she laughed. Of course! He was talking about the first time they had met. She had been seventeen and playing in a rugby cup game and had just been tackled by a prop forward built like a small garden shed. Winded, she had been trying to gather herself when she had been hoisted off the ground. She had expected a teammate but instead she had turned to find a dark-haired guy towering over her, the concern in his golden eyes stealing away her indignation. From the get-go, Edwin had appointed himself as her protector, her rock of good sense…and after Michael, her brother and

Edwin's best friend, had died, despite her resistance he had become her mentor, her modern-day guardian angel.

Now, aching for a shower and hot chocolate at the finishing line, for once she was seriously tempted to take him up on his offer of assistance but of course didn't do so. 'You need to be careful with your back at your age.'

Edwin folded his arms. 'I'm only three years older than you.'

She gave him a sympathetic smile. 'Every year counts.'

He raised an eyebrow, his thumb flicking across the tip of her nose. She shivered at the fierce concentration in his expression. Then, showing her his thumb, now covered in a smear of dirt, he said with his usual quiet humour, 'I'm guessing you don't need this particular memento of today's run,' pausing, he ran his eyes down the length of her mud-encrusted body, 'especially when you are already heading home with a small garden's worth.'

Kara blinked. And stepped away. His touch always made her feel peculiarly vulnerable. 'I need to get to the finishing line—the fundraising team will be regretting persuading me to front up the campaign.' Rolling her eyes at Edwin's grin, she admitted, 'I can't believe I actually agreed to pose for those photos and marketing video of me dashing across the finishing line—I should have known they'd come back to haunt me.'

Turning away, she tackled the mud bath before her. He came and walked alongside her. 'So what has brought you here today? Isn't there some exotic beach or skiing trip missing you?' she asked.

'I decided to forgo my usual Sunday morning haunts to spend some time with you.' Taking hold of her hand again, to help her out of a deep hole she was failing to free herself from, he pulled her out and said gently, 'I know how much today means to you. I wanted to support you, especially as the race is named in Michael's honour.'

An ache for Michael rose up from the pit of her stomach and spread into her chest cavity like a smothering vapour until it wrapped around her heart, the loneliness of it physically hurting even a decade on. She swallowed down that ache to a place deep, deep inside of herself, balling her fists to create the energy to be upbeat and teasing with him. She lifted her head to meet his gaze. The man with the golden eyes and golden heart. 'I always appreciate your backing.' She gave him a wicked smile. 'As does the rest of my team—Kate and Triona were only lamenting earlier this morning the fact that we haven't seen a lot of you in the office in recent months.'

'Where are your team anyway? Why aren't you with them?' Edwin asked.

'I told them to go ahead, I was only holding them up. They needed to get to the finishing line early to thank everyone taking part in the run before they left. We had hoped for a bigger field today and need to persuade as many runners as possible to come back next year. If we can get the numbers right, this run will be a great way to raise funds and promote the work of the charity.'

Edwin's mouth tightened as once again he had to yank her out of the mud. 'Somebody should have stayed with you.' Nodding towards her trainers—well, what was visible of them beneath the inches of mud—he added, 'And equally someone should have told you to wear something more practical.'

She gazed down at his feet and smirked. 'Like your special forces-issue boots, you mean? And don't go denying that you were trained by the Monrosa army—no one goes away, as you claim you did, on a three-month diplomatic tour and returns with biceps that would rival those of a heavyweight boxer.' As expected, Edwin gave his usual non-committal shrug, so she added, 'There was no need for anyone to stay with me for the race. I was doing fine until I came to the incline.'

He made a disbelieving sound. And her heart missed a beat as his gaze continued to hold hers with an unsettling intensity. Only now that he wasn't looking away did she realise just how rarely he fixed his eyes on her for any prolonged period. Disconcerted, she asked, 'Is something the matter?'

For a moment the faint lines around his eyes tensed, but then he turned and, still holding her hand, led her towards Domenico and Lucas, who were waiting for them alongside the course marshals. 'There's something I want to ask you. I need your help. But we can discuss it later.'

She allowed him to guide her out of the quagmire, wondering if this was the first time in all their years of knowing each other that he was asking for her help.

From the first moment that they had met he had helped her, and had shown no sign of stopping. There must have been a time when he had asked for her help…but for the life of her, she couldn't remember one. Yes, she had given him the support of friendship, shared his passion for old black and white movies and mountain trekking, the writing of Douglas Adams, but Edwin, so self-contained, so self-sufficient, so private, had never directly asked for her help. Even in those dark days and weeks after Michael's death, when grief had been chiselled into his face.

Now, as he led her out of the field, she inhaled a shaky breath, her chest tightening. How would she have coped if Edwin hadn't been there for her after her darling, her beloved, her troubled older brother had died? Her parents had fallen to pieces. They had idolised Michael as much as she had. The first family member to go to university.

And Oxford at that. Their pain after his death had been unbearable to witness. Knowing Michael had taken his own life had been too cruel, too senseless, too wrapped in guilt and what-ifs. Kara had stood by and watched her dad try time and time again to reach her mum, searching for support, but her mum had shut him out, disappearing into a world of her own where there was no time or energy for anyone else. She had watched her dad plead, grow angry and eventually shut down. It had crushed Kara's idea of love and relationships to see all of that pain and helplessness wrought on her dad.

As their marriage fell apart and during their eventual divorce Kara had leant on Edwin, needing his support, his encouragement, his advice, his reproaches when she had self-destructively gone off the rails. She had somehow managed to sleepwalk her way through her A levels in the month after Michael had died and gone on to university. But there had been so many bumps along the road, including dropping out of university for a month, until Edwin had made her see sense.

And when she had finally taken her finger off the self-destruct button five years ago, for the first time accepting just how destructive her relationship with her ex-boyfriend Nick was, she had realised that there was one thing she wanted to achieve in life—to set up a charity focused on the mental health of young adults, particularly targeting the difficult years of transition after leaving school. Five years on, the charity had seven centres throughout the UK, ran transitioning and education programmes in conjunction with several universities and provided a twenty-four-hour helpline. But there was so much more that they needed to do. There were so many more young people and their families they needed to help, but the lack of resources was holding them back. The need to do more consumed her.

At the gateway out onto the road, they paused and Edwin shook hands with the marshals, who did a reasonable attempt at appearing to be nonchalant in meeting him, an actual, real-life prince.

When it was her turn to greet the men she pulled them into a group hug. 'Thanks for volunteering today. We couldn't hold fundraising events like this without the support of our volunteers.'

Both men held themselves as stiff as a board and when she released them they eyed her as though they were worried for her sanity and their own safety.

'Kara's the founder and chairperson of Young Adults Together,' Edwin explained with amusement.

Both men relaxed.

One of them, heavily built with long hair and a skull nose piercing, said in a pronounced Cornish accent, 'This morning I was up before dark to come and do my bit.' Reddening, he cleared his throat, rolled his shoulders, and continued, 'My daughter...went through a bad patch last year.'

Kara swallowed at the confusion and fear in his voice. He cleared his throat noisily. 'Your counsellors gave us a lifeline when we didn't know where to turn.'

Kara pulled him into another hug. This time he wrapped his arms around her.

After she had extracted a pledge from both men that they would continue to volunteer for the charity, she hobbled as quickly as she could alongside Edwin on the internal estate road that led back to the tented village which had been erected adjacent to Fairfield House, thanks to the generosity of Lady Fairfield, who, along with Edwin, was a patron of the charity.

Domenico went ahead of them, while Lucas stayed a distance behind.

After graduating, Edwin had worked in the City of London for four years before returning to Monrosa to act as global ambassador for its financial sector. His job brought him to London on a regular basis but for the past month he had remained in Monrosa and his contact with Kara had mainly consisted of the occasional rushed text. 'I haven't heard from you recently—have you been busy?'

Beside her Edwin came to a stop. Kara's heart did a somersault at how troubled he suddenly seemed.

'You're limping.'

Giddy relief ran through her. For a moment she had thought something was seriously wrong. She reached down and rubbed the back of her thigh. 'I think I pulled something.'

Crouching down beside her, Edwin said, 'Show me where exactly.'

Kara pointed to the mid-centre of her thigh with her index finger. 'There.'

His hand touched her mud-strewn thigh, his warm fingers softly tracing over the skin beneath her running shorts. Every muscle in her body tensed as she resisted the temptation to yelp, giggle, move away.

'You've pulled your hamstring. We need to get you back to the finishing line quickly so that you can ice and elevate it.'

His gaze moved up to gauge her reaction.

'Why are you here, Edwin?'

Instead of answering her question he stood and said, 'I'll carry you to the finishing line.'

Kara laughed but she soon stopped. He was being serious. 'I'm fine. And anyway, I have to make my own way there—my sponsorship depends upon it.'

'How much is your sponsorship worth?'

'Close to two thousand pounds.'

For long seconds he held her gaze and Kara's heart gave a little kick. She should look away, make some quip, but now that he was here she realised just how acutely she had missed him over the past month.

'I'll match your sponsorship.' And then, with one of those utterly charming smiles of his, where she felt as if she was the centre of his world, he added softly, 'Now, please let me carry you. You're injured.'

For a nanosecond she actually contemplated his offer. But then good sense kicked in and she walked away. 'I've only pulled my hamstring. And how would it look to all of the other participants if the event organiser not only finished last but also had to be carried over the finishing line? By you of all people.' A safe distance away from him, she turned back. 'You know the media would have a field day if you're spotted carrying me. When are they ever going to accept that we're only friends?'

Edwin came alongside her. 'My father and mother had an arranged marriage. They started off as friends.'

Why was he telling her this? And she couldn't remember the last time he had spoken about his mother, who had died when he was a teenager.

Before she got the opportunity to ask him what was going on, his arm wrapped around her waist and she almost jumped out of her skin. They weren't the touchy-feely variety of friends.

'Your limp is getting worse. If you refuse this help then I'm going to instruct Lucas to carry you to the finishing line.'

Preferring the unsettling effect of being so close to Edwin over the ignominy of being carried by Lucas, who frankly scared her a little with his silent-killer type intensity, she allowed him to support her, but didn't lean as much into his strength as she really needed to.

'My father still misses my mother. They were a good team. Maybe practical marriages are the answer.'

Okay, this conversation was getting odder and odder. 'Answer to what?'

Nodding in the direction of the tented village, which had just come into view, rather than answer her question Edwin asked, 'How much will the mud run raise for the charity?'

Why hadn't he answered her question? 'Close to twenty thousand pounds, which will secure counselling services in Southampton for the first three months of next year.'

'You know I'm happy to provide more funding.'

This was an ongoing argument between them. 'Yes, and I appreciate your offer. But I don't want you funding the charity...there are so many others you support. I want Young Adults Together to be funded by the local communities—it builds a better understanding and ownership of the issues involved, along with helping to de-stigmatise mental health issues.'

He gazed at her with a fondness that burnt a hole right through her heart. 'I'm very proud of you, do you know that?'

Kara shrugged, rolled her eyes, trying not to let her delight, but also alarm, show. When he spoke to her like that, it made her feel totally exposed and fearful as to what her life would be like if he wasn't part of it.

Leaving the dual carriageway and following the main artery into Brighton, a sea of red brake lights appearing ahead of him, Edwin slowed and eventually brought his SUV to a stop.

Beside him, Kara sighed heavily. 'There are road-works ahead. They've been causing traffic chaos for the past week.' Turning to glance at the car directly behind them, she added, 'There really was no need for you to drive me all the way home to Brighton. I feel so guilty Domenico and Lucas are having to drive my car back for me.'

Studying his protection officers in his rear-view mirror, Edwin grinned at their scowls and at how they were taking up every spare inch of space in the front of Kara's tiny car that made him wince each time he saw it, not just because of its canary-yellow bodywork but also because he doubted it would offer her much protection in an accident. She refused to trade it in on environmental grounds. 'I didn't want you driving when you should be resting your leg.'

Kara let out an impatient huff and shifted the icepack he had earlier taken out of the first-aid kit in the boot.

'It's a pulled hamstring and not even a seriously pulled one at that. It's fine,' Kara protested, her nose wrinkling with annoyance, the freckles on her cheeks she usually covered with make-up standing clear and proud.

'I like you without make-up and your hair like that. It reminds me of how you looked when we first met.' He hadn't meant to go out onto the rugby field that day, but seeing her brilliantly dodge endless tackles through intelligent and courageous play the length of the pitch, only to be thwarted at the try line, he had roared in frustration, and then, seeing her inert on the ground, her face buried in the earth, her limbs sprawled, he had raced onto the pitch, the need to get to her, to protect her all-consuming. And to this day that need to protect her was still there. A need that had solidified after Michael's death. Seeing her despair, her loneliness as her family fell apart, he had vowed to protect her, to always support her.

Michael's funeral had been a nightmare. Kara's parents, who were both deeply private individuals, had resented the media attention Edwin's presence had attracted and, already wracked with guilt over whether he could have done more to help his friend, he had listened to Kara say quietly and with a heartbreaking dignity in her eulogy that she had lost her first ever best friend, her inspiration, and he had silently pledged he would always be there for the little sister Michael had adored.

At times, he had struggled. Her pain had mirrored his own grief—not only for the loss of his best friend, but also from losing his mother and the unearthed memories and feelings he wanted to keep buried. But as they had got to know each other over the years their relationship had moved to one of firm friendship, and Kara, with her straight talking and dry sense of humour, gave him balance and perspective and a sense of normality he could so easily lose in a life where people were always way too eager to please him.

Was he about to put their entire relationship in jeopardy? Was he about to compromise the trust between them? Frustration towards his father and fear for the future had him wanting to open the car door and break into a run.

Oblivious to the bombshell he was about to deliver to her, Kara gave him a horrified look, flipped down her sunshade and stared at her reflection in the mirror. 'Are you kidding me? I can't believe I forgot my make-up bag this morning. And as for my hair...' She paused and lifted her long, honey-blonde curls with a grimace. 'Remind me to arrange for there to be a few hair straighteners in the women's changing rooms next year.' She gave a shiver and flipped the sunshade back up. 'I look terrible. I need a serious dose of sunshine—I look like I've spent ten years locked away indoors.'

Admittedly there was the hint of dark circles on the delicate pale skin beneath the sweeping brush of her long eyelashes, but the brilliance of her crystal-blue eyes hid that tiredness from all but the keenest of observers. 'I take it you are still working insane hours.'

Ignoring his comment, she flicked the radio to another station and then another, not settling until she found one playing jazz. She knew he hated jazz.

Ahead there was still no movement in the traffic. Flicking the radio off, he said, 'I saw you hobbling around the refreshment marquee when you were chatting to the runners—my guess is that your leg is a lot more painful than you're letting on.'

She rolled her eyes but then turned in her seat and regarded him with an appreciation that always caught him right in the gut. She followed it with the double whammy of her wide smile that always exploded like a firework in his heart, radiating a lightness inside him that always threatened the protective cloak of royal circumspection he had been taught to adopt from an early age.

'Thanks for coming in to say hello. The runners were thrilled to see you. I think you've guaranteed the success of next year's run. We were inundated with runners asking if they could sign up,' she said.

'I'm sure their interest in participating next year is down to how well the event was organised today and nothing to do with me.'

'Oh, please. You know the huge crowd waiting at the finishing line were there for a reason. And it certainly wasn't to cheer me on. Apparently there was a stampede back to the finishing line once word got around that you were spotted starting the race late—from our female runners in particular.' Nodding in the direction of the car behind them, she added with a grin, 'You and the guys did look rather fetching in your tight running gear.'

When was the traffic going to move again? He had things he needed to say to her. Things that were tying his stomach in knots. He had spent the last couple of weeks with a team of lawyers trying not to be in the position he was now in. What he had to ask of her was huge and unfair. He didn't want to drag her into this mess that wasn't of her making. But there was no one else he could trust. Dryly he responded to her teasing, 'I'm glad we proved to be of some use.' Then, unable to resist teasing her back, he added, 'I reckon it might be safer if you stick to the sidelines next year, though.'

'No way! I mightn't be special-services fit like you but I can hold my own. Trust me, I've learned my lesson and I'll pace myself much better next year.' She gave him a hopeful smile. 'It would be great if you could take part again. I can get Triona to contact your office with the date and hopefully if you are free they'll be able to schedule it into your diary.'

He arched his neck. Being stuck in a traffic jam was not the ideal place for this conversation but he couldn't go on pretending his life hadn't been turned upside down any longer. 'I'm not sure I'll be in a position to take part next year.'

For a moment she frowned but then she visibly paled. Her hand shot out to touch his arm. 'You're not ill, are you? Is that why you haven't been in touch recently?'

Her immediate concern for him only ratcheted up his guilt. He had sworn he would protect Michael's little sister, and here he was, asking her to step into the unrelenting scrutiny of the entire world.

He and Michael, who had both been students at Oxford, had met through the aikido club. As it had turned out, both of them were in Mansfield College studying Politics, Philosophy and Economics, Edwin a year ahead of Michael. On several occasions, Michael had brought him to his family home in London, claiming he needed to be exposed to the reality of how others lived. In London, Michael had taken him to the homeless charity where he had volunteered when in sixth form, and to his local aikido club, where he heard about their programmes to encourage teenagers into sport and away from knife crime. And Kara had tagged along, listening attentively to Michael's opinions, smiling when Edwin and Michael disagreed over some issue. She had visited Michael in Oxford and had gone to parties with them, the only person to ever persuade Michael out onto the dance floor. Kara had idolised Michael and their parents had worshipped him. Edwin used to tease him over it, Michael always shrugging it off until one evening during his second year in Oxford, when they were both at a house party. Michael was drunk and fell and spilt a drink all over someone's laptop. The owner screamed at Michael. Michael just stood there staring at the girl as she ranted at him, not reacting, looking as though nothing was registering with him. And then he disappeared out of the house. Edwin followed him, unsettled by the blankness in Michael's expression.

Edwin finally found him in the gardens of Mansfield. He almost backed away when he realised Michael was crying. Edwin had been brought up to hide his emotions. He didn't know how to cope with someone else's. But he went and sat down next to Michael. And they must have sat in silence for at least twenty minutes before Michael admitted just how much he was struggling to fit in at

Oxford, how apart he felt from student life, his constant anxiety, how he feared disappointing his family, how riddled his mind was with dark, negative thoughts. Edwin listened, tried to help, but he was way out of his depth and ill-equipped to deal with Michael's despair. He encouraged Michael to reach out to the support services in the university and offered to pay if Michael would prefer to go to see someone privately.

And after a lot of resistance, they ended the night hugging, Michael promising to contact the university health services. But in the weeks that followed, Michael shut Edwin down whenever he asked how he was doing. He disappeared off campus or spent days locked away in his room, claiming he was studying and didn't want to be disturbed.

In the run-up to their end-of-year exams, Edwin spoke to the college authorities about his concern over Michael's welfare. Michael learned of his intervention and went ballistic, refusing to speak to him again. Edwin called Michael's parents one night, a call he had agonised over for days, not wanting to betray Michael's privacy or to panic his parents unduly. He spoke to Michael's dad, who responded with disbelieving bewilderment. He told Edwin that, while he appreciated his concern, he was certain he was wrong. For hadn't Michael only told them the previous weekend just how much he was enjoying university life and was looking forward to staying with Edwin in Monrosa over the summer?

Michael failed his second-year exams. The day after he learnt his results he caught a train to the south coast and took an overdose on the beach that night. Early the following morning he was found by a local man.

His parents were away on holiday. Kara was the first to be told.

Kara called Edwin in Monrosa, sobbing and, despite several attempts, unable to tell him what was the matter. It was their neighbour who quietly whispered those words of horror down the phone to him.

Within an hour he was on his way to London. Once there, he held Kara, his heart torn in two by her mute, violent shivering, all the memories of holding his youngest brother, Ivo, the morning of their mother's funeral haunting him, reminding him how Ivo too had shuddered with grief, his fragile bones rattling in his arms.

When his mother had died he had thought that the grief of losing her would simply be about the gut-aching sadness and disbelief—he had never anticipated the ugly swamp of consequences that kept flowing back into his family's lives and swallowing them whole. Their father's angry, authoritarian way of trying to be an effective single parent, Luis's rebellion, which had seen him constantly in trouble with authority, Ivo's avoidance of them all, his own deliberate distance.

Loving someone too much destroyed you.

And in the aftermath of Michael's death, all those emotions had been stirred up again and he had relived the agony of losing someone. Through the shock and grief and guilt he had somehow managed to care for and support Kara, encouraging her to continue with her studies, and to accept her university place, and as time passed they had become close friends, their relationship managing to survive media intrusion and endless arguments when Kara was testing every boundary possible, crying out for attention.

And now he was about to ask her a question that could blow apart the one friendship that kept him sane.

He lowered his window. Drops of drizzle immediately speckled the interior of the car door but he needed some air to clear his brain. On a deep inhale he admitted, 'I might not be able to take part in the race next year because by then I might have succeeded to the throne of Monrosa.'

For long moments Kara stared at him, grappling for words. 'When did this happen?'

'My father has decided to abdicate.'

'And you're next in line.' Looking away, she stared at the still stationary traffic and said distractedly, 'There must have been an accident ahead.' Then, her gaze shifting back to him, she shook her head. 'Wow. I didn't see that coming. But you don't seem very excited. I thought succeeding was what you always wanted.'

In the distance a siren sounded, and it came closer and closer until a police car passed them on the hard shoulder. He winced at the piercing sound. 'Both the royal court and the public will be slow to accept this change in ruler, especially when I push through my reforms to halt the ever-increasing mass tourism to allow for more sustainable development on the island to protect the environment.'

For long seconds Kara studied him, her ability to get to the core of a problem apparent in the reckoning in her eyes. 'You need to sell your vision of the Monrosa you want to rule. Ground that vision in what you already stand for—prosperity for all while protecting both the environment and the vulnerable in society. Look at all the changes you've already made by persuading your father to reform environmental policy. And there are all your ideas on housing and healthcare reform. I know you'll rule with loyalty and compassion while ensuring Monrosa continues to thrive. And the people will come to see and appreciate that too, with time.'

He could not help but laugh at the passion in Kara's

voice. 'Maybe I should employ you as my press officer.' Then, sobering at the thought of the momentous battles he would have in the future, he added, 'Those environmental reforms aren't enough—they are only the start. Changing the mind-sets of the people, especially those heavily invested in the tourism industry, will not be easy. Environmentally responsible tourism and the attraction of other service industries, especially the financial-services sector, has to be the way forward for Monrosa's economy.' He let out a heavy sigh, '*Dio!* We have ruined long stretches of the coastline already with overdevelopment. My father sees no issue with it, but it's unsustainable. I need to succeed to the throne to stop any further development. We need to set in place a twenty-year plan for keeping the economy viable whilst protecting the unique environment of Monrosa.' His mother had been a passionate campaigner for protecting Monrosa's unique microclimates and biodiversity, and Edwin was determined to put the protection of the environment centre stage during his reign.

Kara nodded. 'And you will succeed in putting that plan in place. I know you will.' Then, pausing to bite her lip, she added, 'I'm guessing I'll get to see even less of you once you are crowned. Is that why you haven't been in contact recently?'

'I've spent the past month trying to persuade my father to stay in the role. I'm not convinced he's abdicating for the right reasons.' Seeing Kara's quizzical look, he added, 'He believes it's time for fresh ideas and a new energy in the role.' Then, rubbing his hand over his jaw, Edwin admitted, 'My father also says that he wants to ensure he has grandchildren before he's too old to enjoy them.'

'What has your father abdicating got to do with him becoming a grandfather?'

Edwin inhaled a deep breath. 'My father quietly passed a new piece of legislation last year on succession in Monrosa. From now on, only a married individual can be sovereign.'

Kara tilted her head and gave a small exhale of puzzlement. 'What does that mean?'

Doubt and misgivings and fear stirred like a trinity of foreboding inside him. He wasn't into relationships, never mind marriage—there was too much expectation around the need for love and intimacy. And Edwin's heart was too closed to ever risk loving another person again. Was he really prepared to enter into the minefield of marriage because it was his duty to do so? That question was easily answered. His destiny was to be crowned Sovereign Prince. He owed it to his country, his family, his people. 'I have to marry or my aunt, my father's sister, Princess Maria, will succeed to the throne.'

Kara laid her head against the headrest and let out a heavy, disbelieving breath. 'You're getting married.' She looked away, out to the grey and abandoned-looking industrial estate on the opposite side of the road, her hair obscuring her face.

'That's why I'm here today, to tell you. There's something I need…'

Before he could say anything more Kara twisted back to him, shifting in her seat and giving him a smile that didn't reach her eyes. 'Well, I suppose congratulations are in order. Who's the lucky woman and when is it all going to happen?' Then with a brief laugh she added, 'No wonder you disappeared off the face of the earth for the past month. I thought you were caught up with work and royal duty, not planning the wedding of the year.'

'My father intends on announcing his abdication next

Thursday. The coronation date of the next monarch is already arranged—it will take place on the first of June.'

'So you have to be married by then?' Not waiting for him to respond, Kara said, 'That's just over two months away. So who are you going to marry? Are you already engaged? Is the wedding date set?'

Another police car, siren blaring, passed on their inside. He waited for the sound to fade out before he said, 'Earlier I said I needed your help...'

Kara waited for him to continue. After years of embracing bachelorhood, his brain was still struggling to keep up with the new reality his father had decided to foist on him.

Folding her arms, Kara said, 'Please don't tell me you want me to be your best woman or something like that. I'm sure Luis can manage to behave himself for once and deliver a fitting best man's speech. And if not, I'm sure Ivo could be persuaded. Eventually.'

Did she really think he would become engaged to someone else without forewarning her or at least telling her he was heading in that direction? 'No! Not that. What I want to ask you...' he paused, gave her an uneasy smile that did nothing to diminish her unimpressed scowl '...I want to ask you to marry me. I want you to be my wife.'

CHAPTER TWO

HAD SHE BANGED her head earlier, when she had fallen? She could have sworn Edwin had just asked her to marry him. Was she suffering severe confusion as a result of concussion?

A loud rapping on Edwin's window made them both jump. Domenico was standing there and gesturing ahead, pointing out that the traffic in front had moved on and now Edwin was holding things up.

Nodding, Edwin pulled away.

Kara studied him, and it felt as though she was truly seeing him for the first time in ages. Was this man—this prince, this soon-to-be sovereign—actually asking her to marry him? His concentration was on the road ahead, his mouth pulled into a tight line, a hint of colour in his high cheekbones.

She laughed and said, 'Nice joke, Edwin. Now, why don't you tell me who you're really going to marry?'

He darted a look in her direction, the cleft in his jaw more pronounced than usual. He was seriously hacked off. 'I wouldn't joke about asking you to marry me. Surely you know that?'

Yes, she did. Edwin wasn't cruel. He was honourable and selfless. But right now she was grasping at straws in a bid to try to make sense of this conversation.

'I'm serious, Kara. I'd like you to be my wife.'

'Wow. I never thought I'd be so lucky as to be proposed to somewhere as romantic as a gridlocked dual carriageway on a gloomy Sunday in March.'

'I promise you a nice honeymoon.'

Kara laughed. 'Have you completely lost your mind?'

'Remember the time you rang me in the middle of the night and said that if we both got to thirty and were still single then we should marry?'

Oh, God, she'd hoped he had forgotten about that.

'I was tipsy and emotional at a friend's wedding. I wasn't being serious. I'm not interested in marrying.' In the immediate years after witnessing her parents' marriage implode, she had steered well clear of any relationship that could end so painfully. So she had dated guys who she knew wouldn't hang around, and for a while that had suited her fine. But after graduating, with her family home sold and living alone in Brighton because of work, she had craved stability and closeness. She had thought Nick was the answer to her embarrassing hunger for intimacy and she had embraced their relationship like someone famished. But his early attentiveness had slowly morphed into claustrophobic controlling behaviour and had once and for all firmly convinced her a single life was preferable to the minefield of relationships and the hurt they spawned. Now, folding her arms, she pointed out, 'And anyway, I'm not thirty yet.'

'In six months you are.'

'Thanks for the reminder.' She had a good life, one that was hard fought for after years of uncertainty and grief—supportive friends, a career that gave her meaning, and, most important of all, an uncomplicated personal life that left her free to focus on work, and work alone. Why, then, did hurtling towards thirty leave her with a nagging sense of unease? Was it the frustration of knowing there was an ever-increasing demand for the charity's services both in the United Kingdom and abroad? She desperately wanted to do more. There was so much work to be done in addressing mental-health issues and educating both young people and those who supported them about dealing with matters before they got out of control. Was it this constant feeling of not doing enough that left her unsettled as she faced her thirtieth birthday?

At a pedestrian crossing on a suburban street, Edwin stopped to allow a young man pushing a pram and holding hands with a little girl to cross the road. Kara shared sporadic phone conversations with her parents and usually they were short and revolved around the weather, but a few months ago her mum had surprised her when she asked her what she thought Michael would have been doing by now? Would he have had a career in political activism, as he had dreamed? Would he have been married? Had children? And after the call, she had sat in the silence of her apartment and wondered once again if she could have prevented Michael from dying.

Her gaze shifted to Edwin. He had been her constant, her steadying influence over the past decade. His marriage proposal was not only insane but it was also sending a tidal wave of uncertainty into her life when she had thought she had finally got a handle on it. 'There must be a long line of more suitable women out there—shouldn't you be trying to forge some strategic alliance, or whatever it is you royals do?'

Edwin waited until he had pulled into her street and found a parking space before he answered. 'I need to marry someone I can trust.'

Killing the engine, he unbuckled his seatbelt and turned and regarded her with that regal look of his that spoke of pride and honour. 'And there's no one I trust more in life than you.'

Her heart catching at the sincerity of his voice, she unbuckled her own belt. 'That's not exactly a solid basis for a marriage, though, is it? I'm sure you trust Domenico and Lucas but you're not about to marry one of them.'

Edwin eyed her with a raised eyebrow. 'I can't. They're both married. And there isn't time for them to get divorced. I need to announce my engagement before Thursday; my father is insistent on announcing his abdication then.'

Domenico came alongside the car. Edwin nodded that they were ready to go into Kara's flat. Reaching for the handle of his door, Edwin added, 'I reckon trust is the most important part of any marriage. At least we have that.'

Should she tell him that she didn't want him to come inside? She needed some time and space to make sense of his bombshell proposal. But what was there to think about? There was no way she could marry Edwin.

Inside her basement apartment, she placed her gym bag in the tiny utility room off the kitchen and went and filled her kettle.

Turning to Edwin, she said with a sigh, 'I'm a working-class girl—I have no idea how to be a princess. Even saying the word "princess" feels ridiculous. Me, a princess? No way.'

'The title would be Her Serene Highness, Princess of Monrosa,' Edwin said, removing his black padded jacket and hanging it on her bulging coat rack.

'See—I didn't even know what the correct title would be.'

He shifted the stool he always sat on away from the kitchen counter to allow for the extra-long length of his legs. Sitting, he shrugged. 'You're not expected to know royal protocol. None of that is of importance. What is important is that I have a wife I can trust, a wife who understands that what we'll have is a working marriage. I know how keen you are for the charity to be able to help more people—you could use your status to achieve that.' Rubbing the back of his neck, he said, 'I know what it is I'm asking of you, Kara, and I'm not asking it of you lightly. I have spent the past week agonising over whether to do so, but I think we can make it work. Neither of us is looking for romance…at least that's what you've always claimed.'

His last sentence sounded like a challenge. As though he was testing her constant refrain over the years that marriage was not for her. 'It isn't just a love marriage I'm not interested in, Edwin. It's all types of marriage.' Filling the teapot with boiling water, she added, 'I know this might sound a little rich coming from me, given my outlook on love, but *you* shouldn't discount love—you've never given it a chance. At least I gave it a go. You've always ended relationships way too early.'

Edwin made a grumbling sound and, leaning heavily against the counter, sent a teaspoon clattering across the marble surface. 'I'm happy being single.'

Placing four teacups on the counter, Kara stepped back, folded her arms and raised an eyebrow.

Edwin's gaze narrowed. 'What?'

Kara continued to hold his stare.

'Look, I just like to be careful who I trust. You've done pretty much the same since Nick,' he argued.

'Agreed, but then I'm not the one who now needs to marry. Maybe if you had been more open to those few women you actually dated over the years, willing to trust them, then you wouldn't have to resort to asking your friend to marry you.'

Edwin stood and, pacing the tiny floor space of her

kitchen, raised his hand in exasperation. 'Like how I trusted Salma Rosucci?'

Kara winced. 'I'll admit it was unfortunate that Salma told the paparazzi you were holidaying together in Sardinia.' Biting back a smile, she added, 'On the positive side, the photos they took of you sunbathing cheered up millions of women across Europe.'

Edwin scowled. Then, walking towards her, he placed a hand on the countertop next to her and asked with quiet pride, 'Would marrying me be that bad?'

For a moment something deep inside her wanted to say no, that marrying him would be...would be okay. Better than okay, in fact. She would get to spend her days with him. Would that be such a bad thing? But then logic kicked in. Picking up the teapot, she poured tea into all four cups. 'The media are going to go crazy.'

'Let them. They'll soon come to recognise what an incredible person you are.'

'They'll eat me alive first. I can see the headlines— *"Prince Edwin to Marry Builder's Daughter."* Or how about, *"Why is Kara Duffy Marrying Billionaire Prince Edwin?"* And what will your family say?'

'Luis and Ivo don't care about what I do—they're too busy leading their own lives.'

'And what about your father?'

'He doesn't have the right to an opinion. He may have forced my hand on marriage but he has no say in who I marry.'

Kara buried her head in her hands. 'In other words, he's not going to be happy when he finds out you've chosen me.' At best Kara would have said his father was indifferent to her whenever she visited the palace, and there were certainly times when he seemed to think she was an annoying creature sent to test his patience. 'I know he still blames me for that time I went out racing with you both and cost you the competition because I was so seasick we had to go back to the marina.'

'As I've said before, don't take it personally—my father is cantankerous with everyone. Including his own children.'

'But he rarely speaks to me and the last time I visited the palace he called me Salma...not only does he not know my name but he also mistakes me for one of your ex-girlfriends. Does he know you want to marry me?'

'No.'

A thought snaked its way into her brain. 'Asking me to marry you wouldn't be your way of getting back at your father, would it?'

Unbelievably he grinned at that. 'I hadn't thought of it that way, but it could be an added bonus.'

Shaking her head at the constant tension that existed between Edwin and his father, she pushed a cup along the counter towards him. 'I'd almost be tempted to say yes, just to witness first-hand how you and your father manage the succession; you'll drive each other insane with your alpha-male jostling.'

She carried the other two cups to the front door.

Edwin followed her. 'Alpha-male jostling. Where the hell did you get that idea from?'

She laughed at his indignation. 'It's a constant battle between you two—can't you see that? You and your father are too alike—that's why you clash. You both always want to be in control, the decision maker, the leader.'

He gave her a disbelieving look. 'No, we clash because my father is stubborn and work obsessed.' Indicating the teacups, he added, 'You know, you really don't need to give tea to Domenico and Lucas.'

'So you pointed out the last time you visited, and the

time before that. And several times before that too. I hate the thought of them sitting out there in the cold with nothing to drink.'

Unlatching the door, instead of standing aside to allow her to go outside, Edwin took the cups from her. 'I'll bring them out—you should be resting. And making tea for the protection team will be a definite no when you're a princess.'

'I hate to point out the obvious, but I haven't agreed to be a princess.'

He gave her a grin. 'Not yet. But you will.'

He stepped outside. She called out, 'And you think your father's stubborn,' before going into the sitting room, where she turned on some table lamps against the fading light of the day and then lit the fire before going back into the kitchen to fetch their teacups.

Back in the hallway, she met Edwin on his way back in and she gestured for him to follow her into the sitting room.

She took a seat on the occasional chair beside the fire. Edwin carried a low stool from beneath the window and placed it before her. She lifted her leg onto the stool, wincing at the tightness that gripped her thigh.

Edwin sat on the sofa facing the fire, tucking a leg under himself, an arm running along the back of the navy sofa that was too small for his bulk. The flames from the fire cast shadows on his face. And then his eyes met hers. Silently he waited for her answer.

'I can't marry you, Edwin.'

'Why?'

'Where do I start? My background. What if something goes wrong? I like being your friend. I don't want to lose that.'

He shifted forward in his seat, his eyes holding hers all the time. 'I promise never to hurt you.'

Edwin always kept his word, but what if he couldn't do so in this instance? Sometimes, despite their best intentions, people hurt each other. Not in a deliberate way like Nick, but purely due to human fragility. Look at what had happened between her parents. At first Kara had stood on the sidelines, bewildered and frightened, watching their pain and guilt and dismay over losing Michael destroy their love for one another. They had once loved each other. She was certain of that. But just not enough to counter the tsunami of grief losing Michael had caused. Her dad had looked to her mum for support, but she had pushed him away. Day after day she had watched her mum turn her back on her dad, grow more remote and uninterested in everything, while her dad had become more desperate, constantly trying to get through to her, to make things okay. Eventually, and not surprisingly, her dad had stopped trying, and had become bitter and defensive. It was the speed of it all that still astounded her: within weeks their family life had been stripped away and they were behaving no differently to three strangers living under one roof.

'What are you most scared of?'

She stared into the fire, considering his question, and then studied her ring-free fingers. Nick had given her a ring to mark their anniversary of dating for a year. He used to sulk when she didn't wear it. She hadn't worn a ring for years. The thought of even doing so now made her wince.

She understood why it was so important to Edwin to marry and she hated not being in the position to help him on this one occasion that he had asked for her support, so, despite the tightness in her throat, the wave of vulnerability rolling through her, no matter how sickening it was to have to rake up old memories, the least he deserved was her honesty. 'I'm scared of feeling suffocated, losing myself in a relationship, even in a marriage of convenience.'

'I'm not following.'

She swallowed, the ability to talk suddenly vanishing. 'After Michael...well, you know how crazy my life got for a while...' she tucked her hands under her legs, liking the way her thighs squashed the tingling in her hands at the memory of Nick's ring on her finger '...too much partying and drinking and getting into relationships and friendships that weren't healthy.'

Edwin shrugged. 'You were trying to work things out.'

She exhaled, remembering how much it had cut her to see Edwin's disappointment each time he had learnt of yet another of her long litany of disastrous acts and decisions in the years after Michael's death. Studying him, she bit her lip, wondering if she could dredge up the courage to ask the one question she'd always wanted to ask him, but never had the guts to—why he stuck around. She couldn't bear the thought that it was just because he pitied her. 'You were incredibly patient with me back then.'

Moving even further into his seat, he placed his forearms on his knees, his hands clasped, his gaze holding hers. Her heartbeat rose and rose as the seconds passed. 'You were hurting.'

She blinked. Nodded, her throat knotted with emotion. Was it losing his mother that made him so empathetic to how deeply she had grieved Michael?

'Once I graduated and moved here to Brighton for work, I thought for a while that I had my life under control. Mum and Dad's divorce had gone through and I wasn't having to constantly deal with their arguments. I was enjoying work and I had my own little flat, which I loved. But I knew nobody here in Brighton. And then you moved back to Monrosa.' Picking up her teacup, she held the warm porcelain in her hands. 'With you out of the country I didn't even have someone to give me ear-ache about my lack of judgement.'

Edwin smiled. 'Not earache, guidance.'

With a deep inhale she admitted, 'And then I met Nick. He seemed to be everything I was looking for—really attentive, and he wanted to be with me all the time. Our relationship made me feel safe.'

She shuffled her chair a few inches away from the fire, a burning, embarrassed heat flaming inside her, knowing she needed to continue her explanation as to why relationships terrified her. 'It's hard to explain, but over time I began to realise that he was just too into me. He was constantly texting and calling me. Most evenings he came around here. He'd get angry when I had to work late or if I wanted to go out with work colleagues. He started to call me several times a day. Wanting to know where I was and who I was with. He said he called just to make sure I was okay. And then about a year into our relationship he entered a phase where he'd blow all hot and cold. One day he'd be kind and attentive and the next day he'd totally ignore me. I never knew where I stood with him and it utterly confused me.'

Edwin's nostrils flared.

She could understand his anger.

She rubbed the back of her neck. Would she ever stop feeling embarrassed for being so clueless? Would she ever stop feeling somehow responsible for Nick's behaviour?

'My self-confidence took a dive. I lost all direction and sense of myself. I felt so confused. You probably won't remember this, but you came to visit after you had attended a financial summit in London. You knew something was wrong, so I pretended I was sick and just generally stressed out by work, and you insisted I take some annual leave. You brought me back to Monrosa to stay in your family's villa in the mountains.'

'I remember. You said it was a virus—you never said anything about Nick.'

'I didn't really understand myself what the matter was. I just had this overwhelming sense of panic. So I thought it was something physically wrong with me—some type of stress response to missing my parents and being so busy with work. What I failed to face up to was how destructive my relationship with Nick was.' Kara swallowed at how Edwin's mouth was pulled into a tight line, anger sparking from his eyes.

'Why didn't you tell me?'

Because I didn't want you to know that I had messed up once again. I wanted you to see me as a peer. Not Michael's little sister who kept tripping up in life and needing your help.

'It was during my week in Monrosa that the idea to set up a charity started to form in my mind. I thought about Michael and how he struggled in university. And how I had struggled when I moved to Brighton, away from everything that was familiar to me. I wondered if there could be more support and awareness-building for young adults on managing major transitions and their mental health. I also faced up to the fact my relationship with Nick wasn't healthy, so I broke up with him when I returned to England.'

His eyes narrowing, Edwin asked, 'How did he take that?'

Grimacing, Kara admitted, 'Let's just say it took him a while to accept it.'

Edwin let out an angry breath. 'Did he harass you?'

'I had to block his number.'

Edwin sat forward, rolling his shoulders, his expression perplexed. 'Why didn't you ask for my help?'

'Pride and embarrassment, along with a dash of disbelief.'

Edwin threw his head back and studied the ceiling before returning his gaze to her. 'I wish you had told me.' Then, with integrity burning brightly in his eyes, he said quietly, 'I understand why you'd be cautious about getting into a relationship again and I swear to you I would never hurt you...but I get it, Kara. I'm not going to try to persuade you into something you don't want to do.'

Oh, thank God.

But boy, did she feel guilty.

'Is there anyone else you can ask?'

'There's no one else I can trust.'

She leant back in her chair feeling weak with the simple sincerity of his softly spoken words. 'I know how much this means to you.'

'It's my problem to sort out, not yours.'

'Can you challenge the new law your dad passed?'

'I've spent the past month trying to do just that. He's refusing to budge.' He stood and moved towards the door. 'I need to go back to Monrosa tonight.' Turning, he added, 'Thanks for listening and I hope you can understand why I asked you—people respond to you so positively. Despite what people might like to think, being a royal requires a strong work ethic, empathy and above all the ability to be a strong role model—and you have those qualities in bucket loads.'

Was that how he saw her? Really? Not the chaotic young adult who tested his patience endless times, or the charity CEO with a propensity to over-commit?

'I assume it'll be a temporary arrangement...if you find someone to marry.'

He paused and considered her for a moment. 'I can see no reason why it couldn't be permanent.'

'But what if you meet someone else? Actually fall in love?'

'I have liked being single and not being tied down, but that doesn't mean I won't stay true to my marriage vows. This may be a working marriage but I will respect the marriage even more for that. I will respect that whoever marries me will do so in good faith and deserve my utmost loyalty.'

Thrown, she asked, 'But what of your father's wish for grandchildren? How is that going to happen?'

A hint of a smile lifted on his lips. 'Are you asking me for a sex-education lesson?'

'No!'

'I've told my father he may have forced my hand in marrying but that he has no say in whether or not I have children.'

'How did he react to that?'

'He was surprisingly unperturbed. I can't help but think he didn't want to give away his annoyance that he hadn't included the need for children to be born in the marriage to be part of the succession rules.'

Edwin left the room and, lost for words, Kara studied her hands. They were shaking. How hadn't she noticed that before now? His footsteps echoed on the tiles of the kitchen floor. He came back into the sitting room, shrugging on his jacket. She moved in the chair to stand. He gestured for her not to.

As usual he went to give her a hug goodbye.

But rather than hug her for the normal quick squeeze they usually shared, he laid his hands gently on her shoulders, their warmth seeping into her bones, his cheek brushing against her hair. Pinpricks of awareness bubbled on her skin. An air of sadness, almost vulnerability, surrounded him.

She went stock still. How much must it have taken Edwin to ask her to marry him—this proud, self-sufficient man who never asked for help or support? A whoosh of admiration for him hammered through her. Edwin would have agonised over this and would not be asking her to marry him lightly. He *really* mustn't have another option. She knew what it meant to him to succeed to the throne. All his ambitions for Monrosa. Her head swam with all the reasons why saying no was the only sane thing to do. But how could she turn him down when he had been her lifeline so many times before?

He straightened. Her heart beating like a trapped butterfly, she tried to keep her voice steady. 'I'll give you two years. After that we can divorce. Anything less would seem…unbecoming.'

'Are you saying yes?'

'I think so.'

Edwin pulled her into a hug, his arms holding her tight. Her head swam again. His chest was solid warmth, his scent the usual reminder of the mountain forests of Monrosa.

When he pulled away his gaze held hers. 'I need to leave for my flight. Think about your answer overnight. Call me tomorrow. I don't want you rushing into a decision you may later regret.'

With that he left the room and a few seconds later she heard the front door open and quietly shut. She let out a long exhale and clenched her shaking hands. Her gaze ran around her sitting room. This was her home. Was she really prepared to move away from this life she had built for herself to live in a country where she would know no one other than her pretend husband?

CHAPTER THREE

KARA ATTEMPTED TO join the other early Monday morning joggers as they ran along the promenade, but after a few hobbled steps she gave in to the tightness in her thigh.

It was still dark, a heavy mist dancing around the street lights. She should have stayed in bed. But her jumbled thoughts had needed air.

Last night she had created a pros and cons list for marrying Edwin when she hadn't been able to sleep. On the cons side she had listed in no particular order of importance:

Losing my privacy
Leaving my job and home
Moving to a new country
The media sensation when we marry and divorce
I have no idea what is involved in being a princess
and I'll just mess up
My parents' disapproval—they might like Edwin,
and in truth not show much interest in my life, but
I can't see that stopping them having conniptions
to see their only child agreeing to such a public
and high-profile pretend marriage
Having to fake being in love in public
The damage it could do to our friendship

On the pros side she had put:

It could be fun??

But she had crossed that out for being too frivolous and then had written in capital letters two single points:

It's my turn to help Edwin
It will give me the platform to raise the international profile of Young Adults Together

On a daily basis, the Young Adults Together internet forums received messages from people from all over the world looking for help and support. And the only way to ensure they reached as many people as possible was for local communities to get involved in the charity's work and fundraising.

It hadn't taken her long to realise that the cons side of the list was heavily weighted towards the impact of accepting Edwin's proposal would personally have on her. While the pros side was about her giving back. It was no contest really.

However, there was an extra con she hadn't even been able to write down last night, hating to think that Edwin was anything like Nick, but what *if* he was manipulating her? Just as Nick had used to do. Was he using her to antagonise his dad or perhaps to divert the media's attention away from his succession to the much juicer speculation as to just why he had chosen her to be his bride? She knew she could trust Edwin—for crying out loud, he had done nothing but support her for the past decade...but that nagging doubt was still there.

Cheers, Nick. You've really managed to make me paranoid about everyone's motives.

Hobbling back to her apartment, she knew she had to make a decision. Edwin deserved a final answer from her.

Opening the front door, she went towards the kitchen, where she had left her phone charging last night. By the hall table she paused at the collage of photos on the wall, realising it had been a long time since she had stopped to look at them.

Her gaze sought out one particular picture amongst the dozen others.

Herself and Edwin and Michael, sitting in the beer garden of a pub in Oxford, wearing layers of clothes against the coldness of the winter's night, Michael sitting in between herself and Edwin, his arms thrown around their shoulders, staring into the camera, his expression earnest. Michael had approached life with an intense but passionate seriousness, as though he owed the world a debt. Had university triggered his depression or was it something he had always struggled with?

She blinked as tears washed over her vision, obscuring the photo of her two best friends.

She had lost one.

She wasn't going to lose the other. And she certainly wasn't going to let Nick's behaviour influence her decision either.

Edwin answered immediately. 'Hi.'

His voice was low and husky. Was he still in bed?

Edwin lying in bed... Did he wear pyjamas? Somehow she couldn't imagine him pulling them on. Wait... What exactly would their living and sleeping arrangements be when they married?

Despite her throat being suddenly tighter than her dad's wallet, she said in a tumble of words, 'My answer is still yes. I'll marry you. I'm assuming I'll need to move to Monrosa...but then what?'

There was a pause on the other end of the line. 'I'm glad.'

Her heart galloped at the reserved relief in his voice. She could hear a rustling sound of paper and then the soft tread of footsteps. She had been wrong. He wasn't in bed. Was he having breakfast, in his office? Then he spoke again. 'After we marry we will use the royal apartments within the palace. The south-wing apartments have been recently renovated and will suit us perfectly. There's an office there with a balcony that overlooks the mountains that will be perfect for you.' He paused. She could hear his footsteps again. And then he sighed. 'We'll need to share a bedroom, and a bed —our staff are usually very loyal but sometimes there can be a rogue insider who informs the media about our personal lives.'

Was he serious? Share a bed!

'How big is the bed we'll be sharing?'

'It's an antique four-poster.'

Any antique beds Kara had ever come across were always on the miniscule size. 'How big?'

Edwin cleared his throat, but not before she heard him chuckle. 'I guess you could say it would be a cosy fit for two.'

She huffed. And was grateful he couldn't see her red cheeks right now. 'Order a new bed and make it a super-super-king-size.'

She ended the call to his laughter.

And then she laughed too.

Had she lost her mind?

Wednesday afternoon and the usually tranquil white drawing room of Monrosa Palace, with its walls draped in white and gold silk brocade, fragile French gilt-bronze furniture sitting on handwoven silk rugs, reverberated with impatient mutterings.

'This atmosphere is more akin to that of a funeral than an engagement announcement,' Edwin muttered to Victor, his personal secretary.

Victor eyed the rest of the room. Alongside Edwin's father, who was getting increasingly agitated at the delay in starting the afternoon's proceedings, the Secretary of State, the First Aide de Camp to His Royal Highness, the Chamberlain and various other advisors close to His Highness had assembled for the engagement announcement. And clearly none were happy with his father's earlier declaration in a private briefing that he was going to abdicate the following day.

'His Highness has ruled Monrosa for thirty-five years. We are a conservative society. In time the people will accept his decision,' Victor replied with his usual understated diplomacy.

Turning his back on the room, Edwin studied the news reporters gathered at the far end of the internal courtyard of the palace. The palace, once a Moorish fortress, had been extended and renovated by practically every generation of the Prado family, which had ruled Monrosa for the past six hundred years. His ancestor, Prince Louis II, had erected a low arched gallery supported by three hundred and sixty-five marble pillars around the internal parameter of the courtyard. His father's contribution had been to commission the restoration of the frescoes painted by Miotto and Formano in the south wing of the palace.

Even from the opposite side of the vast courtyard, originally constructed with another enemy in mind, Edwin could sense the media's anticipation that something of importance was about to happen. His father addressed the press every Thursday afternoon. Only something of major significance would warrant a separate press gathering the day before.

It's about to happen.

He balled his hands and breathed deeply into his diaphragm. He needed to ground himself, banish every reason why he didn't want to do this and focus on the succession. Too much thinking and ruminating got you nowhere.

The mumbling behind him had ceased.

He whipped around.

Standing with his aunt, Princess Maria, at the threshold of the room, her hair straightened into sleek waves, her professionally applied make-up emphasising the blue depths of her eyes, Kara stood scanning the room, until her eyes locked with his.

She gave him a nervous smile.

He winced at her unease.

Her forest-green below-the-knee fitted dress had a deep slash from her collarbone to the centre seam, and her hand rose to touch the exposed pale skin of her breastbone.

Her dress was perfect. She was perfect. With her irresistible wide smile and rose blushed cheeks she was what every royal bride was supposed to be.

The only problem was that she was a reluctant bride, only going through with a marriage of convenience in a selfless act of friendship.

Kara's description of her relationship with Nick Green had knocked him for six. He gritted his teeth, once again seething that he hadn't taken the time to unearth why he had never taken to Nick. Instead he had shrugged off that instinct that said there was something insidious about him and had put it down to him just being protective of Kara. He had tried to be chilled about their relationship, pleased for her, when in fact his skin had crawled at the thought of them being together.

But the truth of Nick's controlling personality wasn't the only reason he was so thrown—in Kara revealing the truth, for the first time it had dawned on him that Kara might want greater intimacy between them. What he had thought would be a simple marriage of convenience hadn't allowed for the needs and vulnerabilities that came with any relationship. What if Kara continued to confide in him and expected in return an emotional intimacy he wasn't capable of giving? Just because she had never looked for it as a friend didn't mean that would continue when they were husband and wife.

Michael would have freaked to see his little sister put in this position. Guilt and unease twisted inside him—he knew what he was asking of Kara, the huge sacrifices she was having to make in order to help him to the throne. *Dio*, he hated having to ask for her support—it was selfish, and it felt as though his world order was turned upside down. It was his role in their relationship to be the supporter, the one in control. He didn't want to be dependent on anyone, even Kara. He liked to be autonomous and detached from others. Emotional intimacy terrified him. It was the reason why all of his past relationships had ended. He had always backed away from letting anyone too close. He could never deal with the pain of losing someone he loved again.

Behind him his father called out, 'Maria, I told you not to delay us.'

While the rest of the room, including Kara, was startled at his father's barked reprimand, his aunt gave him one of her serene smiles and, ushering Kara into the room, said, 'The media can wait. Kara and I had some important matters to talk over, including selecting a dress created by a Monrosa designer for the engagement photos.

'What do you think, Edwin? Doesn't Kara look beautiful?' Not waiting, thankfully, for him to answer, his aunt spoke to her husband, Johan. 'Do you remember just how excited we were when we announced our engagement?' Looking back towards Kara and then him, she clapped her hands in excitement. 'Enjoy every moment of this very special time in your lives.'

His aunt, who knew nothing about the truth as to why they were marrying, waited for a response. Only his father, brothers and Kara's parents knew the true reason for their marriage. The fewer people who knew the truth, the better. Struggling to find an appropriate response, he obviously hesitated too long in giving a reaction because his aunt's expression shifted to one of confusion.

Before he had an opportunity to speak his father barked, 'We have much more important matters that need to be taken care of other than worrying about dresses.'

Kara stepped forwards with a conciliatory smile and addressed his father. 'I apologise for the delay, but I do agree with Princess Maria. My choice of dress will send out an important signal of my support for Monrosa.' She tilted her chin. 'It's inevitable, given the speed and nature of our engagement, that things will not always go according to plan one hundred per cent of the time, but I'm sure Your Highness will take that into consideration.'

His father reddened, not used to being challenged, even in such a polite way.

Edwin bit back a smile, proud of Kara's defiance.

Ever so subtly all of the others present in the room slipped to stand behind his father. Only he and Victor remained in the no-man's-land between Kara and his father.

Raúl, Director of Royal Communications, stepped

forward and addressed His Highness with a pained expression. 'Sir, the press are waiting.'

His father eyed Raúl with exasperation and growled, 'Well, what are you waiting for? Go out there and start proceedings.'

Raúl nodded, squared his shoulders. About to leave the room, he doubled back and whispered, 'Miss Duffy, please try to remember your answers from our rehearsal this morning.' Turning to regard Edwin, who had moved over to stand next to her, Raúl added, 'I would suggest His Royal Highness is the one who answers any unrehearsed questions that might arise.'

Kara gave Raúl an uncertain smile. Her job required her to speak in public frequently, but Edwin knew it was her least favourite part of her role and one she was over-conscious and overly self-critical of. The last thing she needed now was somebody doubting her ability.

Edwin cleared his throat and stepped closer to Raúl. 'Miss Duffy is more than capable of answering any questions that might arise.' Edwin tried to eyeball Raúl but the other man's eyes shifted relentlessly in every direction but his. Biting back the temptation to sigh, Edwin added, 'I want some time with Kara alone before we speak to the media. Wait here for another ten minutes before you go out. We will be in the music room and will join you from there.'

Raúl, with a pained expression, peered back towards his father, who was now puce in the face.

'What's the delay now? Edwin, I command you to stop delaying proceedings.'

Edwin turned and approached his father. Those surrounding him remained where they were. A silence fell on the room. Edwin tilted his head and eyed each and every advisor one by one. They all understood he wanted to speak to his father in private. Was this their way of showing where their loyalty lay? Their concerns about his succession? Had he a rebellion on his hands? Seconds passed. He stood his ground. His father went to speak. Edwin shot him a look of warning. This was his battle. Eventually, no doubt realising that Edwin was prepared to wait for the rest of the day for them to retreat, the advisors slowly peeled away towards the back of the room. Edwin could only hope this was the start of the royal court accepting his authority.

Lowering his head, he addressed his father. 'Apart from a brief meeting earlier, I've spent no time alone with Kara since she arrived from London this morning. We need time to speak. I ask you to respect that.'

His father gestured out towards the courtyard. 'The media are waiting and we have important state matters to discuss. You can talk to Salma later.'

Edwin let out an impatient breath. 'You know damn well her name is Kara. And I don't care that you think I should have married someone with better connections and background. We are marrying because you have left me with no other option. But I will not cause any harm or distress to my bride.' As he held his father's gaze, years of frustration with his father's belligerence and uninterest in his family spilled out. 'Kara will soon be part of this family and, whether you like it or not, from now on we're going to act like one—this family has been dysfunctional for far too long. You are to respect Kara and her position. Never force me into a position where I have to choose between her and the crown.'

Whipping around, he guided Kara out of the room, a hand to her back, the need to protect her, to make sure she was okay, thudding through him like some primal beat.

Beneath his hand, her hips swayed as her high heels

hit the marble floor of the anteroom. 'What did you say to your father? He looked even more hacked off than usual.'

She didn't know of his father's unhappiness at his choice of bride and he wanted to keep it that way. 'I apologise for his foul mood. He's anxious about tomorrow.'

Glancing behind her to the silent room, as all those gathered there watched their departure, she frowned. 'Is it always this tense around here?'

'At times.'

'I hope you'll instil a more positive atmosphere when you are in charge.'

'I aim to,' he hit her with a teasing smile, 'but then, you did say that my father and I are alike, so maybe I'll end up just as grumpy as him.'

'Not under my watch you won't.'

He laughed at her warning but there was something in her expression that had him realise that not only would she have his back in her role as his consort, but she would also push him to do the right thing, even if it was not what he always wanted to do. He wasn't quite sure whether to be comforted or alarmed by that.

Moving into the music room, he led her towards the terraced doors, where they were able to watch the media unobserved, thanks to the immense size of the Fountain of Bulls at the centre of the courtyard.

She sighed on spotting the assembled media, a hand unconsciously kneading the side of her neck. She was nervous.

'We'll be okay.'

She turned and studied him. 'Will we?'

His gaze shifted back to the media, remembering the morning after his mother's death. He had joined his father out in the courtyard for his address to the world's media. He had been bewildered and scared, barely able to comprehend that his mother was dead. He had pleaded with his father not to make him accompany him, but his response had been a brief lecture on his duty to the crown and country. To this day he could still feel the force of his need for his mother in that moment, for her words of encouragement and the hug she would give him whenever he had to perform a public duty.

Living your life so publicly was grindingly tough.

'I'll protect you from the media.'

Her hand dropped from her throat to hang by her side. 'It's not the media I'm worried about. It's us.'

Where had that come from?

'What do you mean?'

'For the past few days my calls to my local taxi company have lasted longer than our telephone conversations.'

'As I explained, I've been tied up with legal issues around the succession, and Aunt Maria has been tying me up in knots with her elaborate ideas for the wedding.'

Her pink-glossed mouth flatlined. 'Not *the* wedding, *our* wedding—we should be planning it together.'

'I didn't want to bother you with the details. I knew you'd be busy with your own work.'

That earned him a disbelieving look.

'This may only be a short-term marriage but I want an equal say.'

'Of course you'll have an equal say.'

'So why are you shutting me out?' she asked.

'I'm not shutting you out.' He wasn't, was he? Okay, so maybe he had been distracted in their phone calls over the past few days, but in his defence he was snowed under with things to organise…and there was also the small fact that he wasn't sure how to negotiate their new relationship as an engaged couple.

She raised an unconvinced eyebrow and turned to stare back out towards the media.

He ran a hand along his jaw and grimaced. 'The media will expect us to kiss.'

Her head whipped around.

Her eyes a startled blue, a blush crept up her throat and onto her cheeks.

He should reach out for her, draw her into a hug, tell her everything would be okay…but would it? No matter how much he would like to deny it, them kissing, the physical intimacy of it, was about to shift their relationship from straightforward friendship to a whole lot more complicated.

Kara kneaded her exposed collarbone. 'You don't have to kiss me if you don't want to.'

'I don't have a problem kissing you.'

She gave a tiny snort. 'Are you sure? You certainly don't sound too enthusiastic.'

'I don't want to put you in any situation you are uncomfortable with.' Despite himself he couldn't stop staring at Kara's mouth, the cupid's bow shape of her lips.

What would it be like to kiss her?

He arched his neck, a much too pleasant physical sensation trickling through his body.

Dios! *What was he thinking?*

She backed away from him, her expression flustered. 'I'm sure we can handle a quick chaste kiss.'

'Who said anything about it being chaste?'

She eyed him warily for a moment but then with a laugh, obviously deciding he was teasing her, she added, 'You're all talk—knowing how you like to keep your interactions with the media as brief as is humanly possible, I bet it will be a quick peck.'

'Is that a challenge?'

'No! Just an educated guess. Anyway, based on how badly I fumbled my answers when I had a practice run of questions with Raúl earlier, maybe us kissing will be a whole lot safer than having to answer questions. I have the real potential of putting my foot in it—you know how much I can prattle on when I'm nervous.'

'Be yourself. I don't want you to ever change or feel the pressure to change. You're perfect as you are.'

She gave him an uncertain smile. *Dio!* That had come out all wrong. It sounded like an intimate, flirtatious compliment when it should have been just a statement of fact.

She turned her head to gaze around the room, taking in the antique musical instruments including a pianoforte and harp. 'I can't imagine myself roaming around here dressed in my pyjamas, eating a bowl of cereal any morning.'

'In our apartments you can do what you want.' He paused, and before he could stop himself he added, 'You can even roam around naked if it takes your fancy.'

Where the hell had that come from?

He raked a hand through his hair. Not only was he staring at her mouth in a whole new and inappropriate way, but now he was also inviting her to roam about their apartment naked. What was the matter with him?

She stared at him with her mouth open, but then rolled her eyes. 'I'd just put you off your breakfast.'

'Well, it'd certainly brighten up my day.'

Kara laughed but then, sobering, asked, 'What's going on? Are you trying to flirt with me in case I'm having second thoughts and might back out?'

Was she actually serious? 'Please tell me that you don't believe I could be so manipulative.' Pausing, he added, 'Are *you* having second thoughts?'

'No, but stop acting so weird. It's freaking me out. It's the kind of trick Nick would have tried on. I want to marry you. And how can I possibly not go ahead at this stage anyway, knowing I'd break your aunt's heart if I did? I had thought when she said she wanted to speak to me that it might turn out all Shakespearian and she'd try to persuade me not to marry you in a bid to gain the throne herself, but the complete opposite was true.'

Shaking his head at her vivid imagination, he pointed out, 'There are two important facts you need to know about my aunt—firstly, she hates public life and much prefers to spend her time attending to her gardens on her estate in the north of the island. And secondly, she is an incurable romantic. Planning a wedding is her idea of heaven. I haven't seen her so enthusiastic about anything in a very long time.'

'So I gathered. She also mentioned that your father's planning on moving to the north of the island also after he abdicates. Are you happy about that?'

That was a good question. 'I'll be able to stamp my authority more easily...'

She regarded him and then softly asked, 'But you'd like him to stay here?'

Was he naïve to think he would be able to drag his family back together? 'I know he might be a nightmare to have around but I want us to be a family, work together as a team.' There was a softness, a tender understanding in her eyes. She understood what it was like to have a family blown apart. 'It's what my mother would have wanted.'

Kara nodded and then, leaning against the terrace door, turning her back on what was going on outside, she studied him, her gaze drifting down over his navy suit. Nodding to his gold and purple tie, she said, 'The royal colours for the occasion.' Reaching out, she adjusted his tie a fraction. 'You're looking very handsome today. Your mother would be very proud of the man you have become.'

He swallowed at her words. *Dio*, he could only hope his mother would be proud of the man he was. When she had been alive he had always tried to make her proud and in death that hadn't changed. He wanted to emulate her care for Monrosa and its people. He wanted to keep her alive by his actions.

Out in the courtyard, Raúl hurried towards the media. No doubt under orders from his father to get the proceedings over and done with so that they could continue focusing on all of the issues arising from the impending abdication. 'The announcement is about to get underway.'

Twisting around, Kara watched Raúl. Her hand rubbed against her throat. Her fingernails were painted in a pale pink shade, the sapphire engagement ring he had presented to her earlier shimmering on her finger and disconcerting him with its unfamiliarity. With a wistful smile she said, 'I'm so glad you're going to try to get your family to be closer.'

With a sigh he pulled her in to him. As ever she held herself rigidly. 'I'm sorry your parents wouldn't be here today.' They had invited Kara's parents to be present at the announcement but both had declined, unhappy that Kara had agreed to a marriage of convenience.

She tilted her head so that her forehead rested lightly against his chest, the movement telling him everything he needed to know as to just how disappointed she was, and against her hair he whispered, 'I'll be your family now.'

She pulled back, her eyes glistening with tears. He touched his finger against her cheek, his heart pounding in his chest, emotion catching in his throat, at just how much he really meant those words.

But then with a shake of her head Kara pulled back. 'Please don't say things like that, not when this isn't a real marriage.'

Taken aback by the vehemence in her voice, he asked, 'Why not?'

She twisted away, walked into the centre of the room, as though gathering herself. Whipping around, she answered, 'Because...because I've already lost one family...'

He inhaled deeply, the feeling of being way in over his head hitting him. 'You're not going to lose me.'

'Neither of us can pretend that our marriage is going to be easy. I don't think either of us can say that we'll come out of it unscathed. We need to be careful as to what we promise each other.'

A wave of frustration pushed through him. Kara was right. Wanting to kiss her, thinking they could be family... what was he thinking of? Raising his hands, he sighed. 'You're right.'

'What have you told Luis and Ivo?'

'Luis is in Australia at the moment and Ivo's in Budapest, competing, so I spoke to them both in a conference call this morning.' He paused and frowned. It had not been an easy call. 'Let's just say that once they got over the shock of learning that our father was going to abdicate, they were livid with him for forcing my hand and even more livid with me for dragging you into this mess.' Over the years Luis and Ivo had got to know Kara when they met in both London and Monrosa. Kara and Luis spoke regularly by text, their relationship one of endless teasing and banter, while Ivo was a goodwill ambassador for the charity, promoting its work within the sporting community.

'Wait, are you saying that they didn't know about your father's abdication until you told them?'

'He wanted to wait until tomorrow morning to inform them. I couldn't persuade him to tell them earlier. Things are as tense between him and my brothers as they have ever been.'

'Why won't he accept that they are both professional sports people who compete at an international level?'

'In his eyes they are wasting their time, when they should be here in Monrosa fulfilling their duties.'

She swept her hands over her dress, wriggling to smooth out the material clinging to her hips.

'Don't be nervous,' he reassured. 'You look incredible and I know you'll do great.'

'Aren't you nervous?'

From a young age he had been taught to present a public persona, one that was polite and composed and detached. That persona got him through so many aspects of his public life and was a shield behind which he could hide his true self. 'Why would I be nervous when I'm ready to celebrate my engagement with the world?'

She gave a disbelieving huff. 'Now you just sound corny.'

'Think of all the positives that can come from this—we can run together every morning and we can go hiking into the mountains without having to schedule it months in advance. We can watch movies together rather than just chat about them. And I can finally teach you how to sail.'

'You almost had me until you mentioned sailing. And what of the old adage, familiarity breeds discontent?'

'I think it's contempt, not discontent.'

Kara hit him with a teasing smile. 'I know, but I wouldn't go that far.'

'I want to marry you. And I hope that I'll be a good husband.' His chest tightened, a wave of emotion catching him unawares. 'I want to make you happy. If you are ever unhappy in the marriage then we can end it.'

'Even before the two years?'

Dio! What if she did walk away? Walked away because their marriage had gone horribly wrong? Their friendship destroyed. What if he had hurt Kara when he swore he would only ever protect her?

He clenched his hands. 'If that's what you want.' Opening the terrace door, he asked, 'Are you ready?'

She gave him a nervous smile. 'With you at my side, what can go wrong?' And she stepped out onto the covered terrace.

A lot was the answer to that particularly hopeful question, as Kara soon found out.

As she stepped from the shade and obscurity of the courtyard gallery into the bright spring day and the glare of the world's media, her legs began to shake. All those eyes and cameras. Assessing. Already formulating words and images to describe her, to pass judgement on her.

And Edwin wasn't helping matters with his long stride. Through a clenched smile, she muttered, 'Will you please slow down? And shouldn't we be acting more coupley?'

Edwin came to a complete stop, his expression unreadable. Then, giving her that serious public smile of his that always swelled her heart with pride and affection for this honourable man who took his responsibilities so seriously, he tucked a strand of hair behind her ear and murmured, 'Is this "coupley" enough?'

At the periphery of her vision, reporters jostled each other for a better view of them, one reporter actually pushing another into a flower bed. She nodded frantically, worried Edwin might decide he should do something even more in his pretence of devotion.

He took her hand in his and they resumed their approach towards the reporters, her toes tingling from the sensation of his warm hand enclosing hers with an unnerving gentleness. Keen to distract herself from the endless walk across the vast courtyard, she whispered, 'My dad promised he'd try to watch the announcement on a livestream.'

Not breaking his gaze away from the media, Edwin whispered back, 'Once the abdication is over, we'll go and visit both of your parents. I'm sure we can persuade them to come to the wedding.'

'I've tried endless times during the past few days to talk them round.' Now was probably not the moment for this conversation but the need to offload her worry was too great—especially as she had been storing it up for several days, expecting to share it with Edwin on the phone, but his calls had always been cut short by some crisis or another. 'You know how private they both are—being in the public eye is their idea of a nightmare. And they think what we're doing is crazy—that it will never work. I've tried to tell them about all of the positives that can come from our marriage—raising the profile of the charity, your plans for Monrosa. But they won't listen to me. We'll need to find a suitable explanation as to why they won't be at the wedding ceremony.'

With one easy movement, Edwin pulled them to a stop again.

Standing in front of her, blocking her from the media, he studied her while a silence descended on the courtyard, the assembled media holding their breath at the prospect of a sensational story unfolding.

'The media are waiting,' she whispered.

'Your parents have been through so much—I don't

want to cause them any further distress. We really don't have to go through with this.'

For a brief moment, she was tempted to agree with him. God knew, she didn't want to create even more tension with her parents than already existed, but this marriage and all the publicity it would bring to the work of Young Adults Together was the most fitting way to make sense of Michael's death. She was doing the right thing. And in time, maybe her parents would come to understand that Michael, so passionate about helping others, would have wanted her to do everything possible to help those in need. Seeing the tension in Edwin's eyes, she tilted her head back. 'As I remember it, you've promised me a spectacular honeymoon—you can't back out of that now.'

Edwin studied her for a moment and then with a hint of a smile he turned around and led her towards the waiting media.

In his earlier briefing, Raúl had given her a thorough run-through of the engagement announcement procedure that had included showing her a photograph of each correspondent who would be permitted to ask questions. Sofia Belluci, the royal correspondent for the main state broadcaster, would be the first to speak to them.

'Congratulations, Your Highness.' Pausing, Sofia turned her attention to Kara with a hint of bafflement, and said, 'And to you, Miss Duffy.'

Beside her Edwin said in a clear, neutral voice with no hint of emotion, 'Thank you.'

'Your Highness, after so many years of knowing each other, why have you and Miss Duffy decided to marry now?'

'We've come to realise what we mean to one another.'

Sofia narrowed her gaze, clearly wanting a much more elaborate answer. 'Which is?'

Without missing a beat, Edwin answered, 'Kara is my best friend.'

God, he was good at this. To the point. Unemotional. 'And for you, Miss Duffy?'

She had practised her answer with Raúl endlessly this morning, but, opening her mouth to say all those practised lines, she paused and stared blankly at the media, whose sceptical stares were hardening by the second.

What were her lines...what had she agreed to say?

Tumbleweed moseyed through her brain. And then she blurted out, 'Edwin's my world.'

Oh, what? Why did you say that?

She'd sounded like a gushing teen fan who had just met her boyband idol.

Edwin, looked at her with a bewildered expression for a moment, but to his credit managed to somehow gather himself enough to place his hand tenderly on her cheek and gaze into her eyes, playing the in-love fiancé perfectly.

It was all pretence, of course, but to be gazed at with such unbridled affection had her struggling to breathe.

Edwin turned back to the media, his arm resting on her waist.

The microphone was passed from Sofia to a man in his late sixties, impeccably dressed. Óscar Collado, the major news correspondent from Monrosa's largest selling newspaper. And, according to Raúl, a man with a hound dog's scent for a story. 'How does His Royal Highness your father feel about your announcement...is he as surprised as the rest of us?'

Edwin stiffened beside her. 'Surprised? No. In fact he's pleased that finally one of his sons is settling down.'

Óscar reflected on that answer for a while, clearly sizing up Edwin's tense demeanour and trying to decide if he should repeat the first part of his question, but instead he changed tack and asked, 'And how about your family, Miss Duffy?' Here Óscar paused as though searching for the right words. 'They must be truly amazed.'

It was clear what Óscar was insinuating. Edwin went to speak but she got there before him. With a gracious smile in Óscar's direction she decided to tackle this issue head-on. 'Edwin and I may come from very different backgrounds but our ideologies and outlook on life are very similar. We both value loyalty and friendship and serving others. It's our hope that people will be open-minded and supportive of us.'

Óscar gave an unconvinced smile to her answer. 'How do you think your late mother would have reacted to your engagement, Your Highness?'

Edwin's hold tightened, and he edged her in even closer to him. She swung her gaze towards him, tempted to whisper to him that he should refuse to answer a question that was so unfairly personal and intrusive.

Seconds passed as the media waited for Edwin to answer. Her heart flipped over to see Edwin's jaw working. She placed a hand on his, which was resting on her waist, and threaded her fingers between his. 'I believe my mother would have been delighted to have a daughter-in-law like Kara.'

He spoke with raw emotion in his voice. Taken aback by the sincerity of his answer, she had to force herself to concentrate on Óscar's next question. 'And the engagement ring—is it part of the royal collection?'

'No, it was especially commissioned,' Edwin answered.

She looked down at the sapphire ring Edwin had presented to her earlier that day. It was a stunning ring, an intense violet-blue stone mounted on platinum and surrounded by a cluster of diamonds.

At the media's beckoning she lifted her hand to display the sapphire.

And forced herself to smile.

Don't let the media see you're thrown. So what that he's given you a brand-new ring and not one from the royal collection? It was the sensible thing to do. For a marriage of convenience. Thinking he might not trust you with a ring from the historic royal collection or believe you aren't worthy of one...well, they're just silly thoughts. Aren't they?

When the media had finally had their fill of photographs, it was the turn of another journalist to speak, asking with a bright smile, 'Have you any message for the people of Monrosa, Your Highness?'

'I hope they will enjoy the wedding celebrations, which are currently being planned and will be announced in full in the coming week,' Edwin answered.

The female journalist swept her bright smile in Kara's direction. 'And you, Miss Duffy—do you have a message for the people?'

Oh, just that I'm terrified and not to judge me too harshly when we divorce. Oh, and, yeah—sorry to all of you who will be heartbroken to hear that one of the world's most eligible men is no longer available. Don't hate me for it—it wasn't my idea, honestly. At least you have the consolation that this has nothing to do with love or passion or any of those normal things.

'My message is that I very much look forward to living here in Monrosa and getting to know this beautiful country.'

The woman, in her early thirties, asked enthusiastically, 'And what will your role be when you marry?'

The journalist seemed genuinely interested in her role, and, seeing an opportunity to talk about the charity, she answered, 'I will continue with my work for my charity, Young Adults Together, focusing on expanding its efforts internationally to promote the advocacy and support of positive mental health in young adults. But I also see my role as supporting Edwin at all times...' she paused there, at the point to which she had rehearsed with Raúl, but, seeing the journalist's encouraging nodding, as though willing Kara to say more, Kara found herself saying, 'especially during the transition...'

She stopped, her eyes widening, hot panic making her pulse thud wildly.

I almost gave away the abdication.

She stared blankly at the media as they all shifted forward in their seats with interest, that sixth sense of theirs intuiting a story. What was she supposed to do now? They were waiting for an answer. How on earth did Edwin think she was capable of taking on the role of princess?

Laying his hands on her shoulders, Edwin calmly finished her sentence, 'During our transition to married life. We have both led independent lives but we are looking forward to living together. I know Kara is excited to settle into palace life...' Pausing, his eyes alive with devilment, a smile tugging at the corners of his mouth, he added, 'She has a lot of intriguing plans for life in our private apartments.'

Kara reddened, a nervous giggle escaping.

The journalists gave each other a quizzical look as though wondering if anyone else got the joke.

With a pinched expression, Raúl swept in from where

he had been watching proceedings at the side of the courtyard and spoke to the media. 'Thank you all for attending today's announcement. His Highness and Miss Duffy will now pose for more photographs.'

Edwin pulled her in closer to him. They embraced and smiled.

Maybe this was all they would want. No kissing required.

But no sooner had she had that thought than a chorus of, 'How about a kiss?' rang out from the assembled photographers.

Edwin turned her towards him.

Her stomach took a nosedive.

He leant down to her ear and whispered, 'Do you still think my kiss will be chaste?'

He drew back. She smiled at him nervously. And in return he gave her a wicked grin.

What had she started?

The teasing look on his face disappeared and suddenly he was looking at her with a heart-stopping intensity. This was no longer a game.

Time slowed down.

She fell into the golden depths of his eyes, only now realising there was a solid single fleck of brown in his right eye. What other secrets did he hold? A hunger to know him better swept through her.

Oh, help.

She needed to get a grip. He was her friend, her pretend fiancé.

Stop getting caught up in the crazy pretence of it all. This is not real.

His mouth lingered over hers.

His hands ran down the length of her arms, coming

to rest at her elbows. The warmth of his touch had her sigh ever so lightly.

Something shifted in his eyes. A heat. A masculine heat.

His lips brushed against hers.

Firm and warm.

Light-headed, she swayed against him. Oh…oh…his heat, the hardness of his body, the electrifying rightness of all of him.

This is so wrong, but so right.

He pulled her closer, deepening the kiss, his arms wrapping around her, tilting her backwards.

This wasn't a polite kiss. It was personal. Intimate. His taste, his scent, the heat of his skin against hers was perfectly wrong.

Every cell in her body dissolved to nothing and fire burnt along her veins.

No man had ever had this effect on her.

Oh, please…this can't be happening.

Her pretend fiancé seriously couldn't be the hottest kisser ever. This wasn't fair!

She willed him to keep on kissing her and he obliged by twisting her so that she was hidden from the media, his back to them, and he deepened the kiss even more, exploring her mouth.

Her hands clasped the hard muscle of his neck. Any moment now she was going to burst into flames. They should stop. This was crazy. Beyond madness to be doing this in the glare of the media. But she just couldn't pull away. One more second. One more spine-tingling, head-spinning, belly-warming second. One more thrilling, life-affirming second of hot craving zipping along the length of her body.

Edwin ended the kiss. And studied her up close for a moment, his pupils dilated, heat on his cheeks.

Dazed, she stared at him. Why did he look so different? More handsome, more male…he had always been gorgeous but now there was a raw edge to him that spoke of danger…of lust. Of… Crikey, what was happening to her?

Turning to the media, Edwin gave them a nod before he led her away, much too quickly, across the courtyard.

When they were out of earshot he said, 'You're trembling.' His mouth tightened. 'Forgive me, I got a little carried away proving that I don't do chaste kisses.'

She had to downplay this. She couldn't let him know just how disconcerted she was, how he had just blown her mind.

So tell me, Kara, are you still convinced that you can walk away from this pretend marriage unscathed?

She withdrew her hand from his, gave him a disapproving tap on his forearm, and in the best blasé voice she could muster, answered, 'I could hardly breathe. Thank goodness we won't need to do that too often.'

CHAPTER FOUR

STANDING IN THE hall lined with mirrors, overlooking the formal gardens of the palace, spotting the telltale claret-red patches appearing on her dad's neck, Kara edged closer to him. 'I wonder what Aunt Joan will be wearing today?'

For a brief moment her dad smiled. 'Whatever it is, I'm sure they'll be able to spot it from outer space.'

Aunt Joan liked to wear colour, the brighter the better in her view, to counteract the greyness of so many Irish days. Unfortunately she didn't seem to understand the concept of clashing colours or that sometimes, less was more. Keen to keep her dad distracted in their long wait for Edwin to appear, and in truth looking for something to focus on other than her annoyance with her fiancé, she said, 'It's great that the entire family could make the wedding.'

When had the deep grooves in his cheeks appeared, the greyness in his hair? She hadn't seen him in over two years. Had it been during that time or had they been accumulating for ever and she had just been too preoccupied to notice? Her dad tugged at his shirt collar. 'Sure, wild horses wouldn't have kept that lot at home—this is the most exciting thing to have ever hit the Duffy family.'

Yesterday lunchtime they had finally managed to

squeeze in the wedding rehearsal. Not only had the logistics team had to contend with Edwin's father's schedule, which had him out of the country on a tour to Sweden and Norway from which he had only returned yesterday morning, but also Edwin's ever-changing travel plans.

She had found the rehearsal in the cathedral exhausting. It had taken all of her will not to stare at Edwin, as was her wont recently. Since their engagement kiss she was constantly finding herself staring at him, daydreaming about him in all types of inappropriate ways that certainly didn't belong in a place of worship.

At the rehearsal her dad had trembled as he had escorted her down the aisle. In the hope of relaxing him she had said she and Edwin would join him and the rest of her relatives for dinner that night in the nearby hotel the palace had booked out in entirety to house the Irish Duffy contingent for dinner. She had also invited along her bridesmaids—Siza, her old rugby teammate, and Triona, who was the first employee to join her in Young Adults Together, and was now one of her closest friends—who were also staying in nearby hotels.

She had ended up going for dinner without Edwin. His weekly meeting with the cabinet had apparently become heated when he introduced his plans for designating land zoned for tourist accommodation into a financial centre and nature reserve.

During the dinner she had tried to hide her frustration with Edwin's non-appearance, but when her dad had asked her for a chat after dinner she had expected yet another awkward conversation as to the wisdom of her deciding to agree to a marriage of convenience.

But instead, when they reached his room her dad had shyly plucked out the lightweight suits and crisp shirts he had bought for the wedding weekend. Her heart had melted to see how proud he was of his purchases, and how eagerly he had wanted her approval. He had asked for her advice as to what he should wear for today's garden party and had proudly modelled the grey trousers and pale pink shirt she had picked out. He had self-consciously studied himself in the full-length mirror of the wardrobe and it had hit her once again what it was she was asking of this private man, whose confidence and identity had taken such a battering, to have to step into the glare of the world.

Now with a grimace her dad admitted, 'I think you should know that your aunts gave an interview to one of the main Irish newspapers. I saw it online earlier in the special supplement they've published in advance of the wedding tomorrow.'

Kara groaned.

'It's all very complimentary…honestly, just photos of you growing up and how proud they are of you and how they knew you'd do great in life because you were such a headstrong child.'

Oh, please, someone tell me they didn't use the photos of me on the beach close to Aunt Nina's house with a battalion of cousins.

The photos where her hair was twisted into tight curls and stood on end like hundreds of startled question marks, thanks to a day spent in the sea.

So much for asking that family members wouldn't speak to the media. She didn't want her family or friends to be invested in this marriage. Unfortunately she had forgotten just how much her dad's side of the family liked a wedding, not to mention a royal one featuring their very own niece.

She couldn't even bear to think about just how crushed they'd all be when her divorce was announced. 'Am I right in guessing it was my aunts who eventually persuaded you to come to the wedding?' It was only last week that her dad had finally said he would attend, a fortnight after the rest of their Irish family's acceptances had started rolling in.

Her dad gave a resigned sigh. 'Five badgering sisters would be hard for any man to fight.'

She twisted Edwin's engagement ring, its weight still feeling alien on her finger, regret punching her stomach that her dad was only here because of family persuasion and not to support her in her decision, even if it was not one he approved of. But at least he was here...which was more than could be said for her mum.

'I blame myself,' he said.

'Blame yourself for what?'

He looked her in the eye, the intimacy of it swiping like a blade to her heart. How she missed his easy nature and love of teasing that had used to have her giggling endlessly as a child. 'If we were closer...' He paused, shrugged. 'We've drifted apart, haven't we?' He nodded unhappily towards their opulent surroundings, and then in the direction of Edwin's father and brothers and the various other members of the royal court standing to their side. 'If I knew what was going on in your life then maybe I could have persuaded you not to do this before it all got so out of hand.'

Kara rolled her shoulders and placed her bunched hands in the pockets of her summer cocktail dress.

This morning she had hopped out of bed, thrilled that she had finally persuaded Edwin last night, when he had eventually turned up at her dad's hotel, two hours late, to take an early morning trek with her into the mountains. She had hoped some time alone together would restore the equilibrium that had used to exist between them, that some teasing and banter would fix Edwin back into her world order of regarding him as a friend. But her hope and excitement had soon disappeared when she had gone in search for him. Unable to locate him, she had been forced to interrupt Victor, who had been in a meeting with many of the senior members of the household, to enquire as to Edwin's whereabouts. Curious eyes had studied her, everyone present clearly wondering why she did not know that her fiancé had left Monrosa earlier that morning. She had tried not to let her embarrassment, her disappointment, her confusion show but had backed out of the room, her cheeks stinging with hurt.

And after her make-up and hair had been completed by her team and she had pulled on the strapless dress she had fallen in love with the moment Ettie, a recent design-school graduate and native Monrosian had shown it to her, and stared at her reflection in the mirror, taking in the material printed in layers of pinks and purples and yellows, designed to resemble the colours and pattern of a butterfly's wings, she had stared at the stranger in the mirror and wondered if she could go through with the wedding. But what choice did she have? How could she back out now with most of their guests already here? And on what basis—that Edwin was never around, and even when he was he was constantly distracted by work? With a sigh she faintly said, 'Let's not go over all this again, Dad. You know the reasons why I want to marry Edwin.'

'A marriage without love destroys people.'

She did not want to hear this right now. She had enough on her plate without her dad prophesying doom and gloom for their marriage. She had enough of those niggling doubts herself. 'We might not have romantic love, but there's no one in the world I trust more than Edwin. He has always had my back.' Shifting her head even closer to her dad, she whispered with a fury that rose suddenly and fiercely from somewhere deep inside of her, 'He has never let me down. I owe him this.'

Her dad blinked. And just as quickly as it had risen within her, Kara's fury was quenched, to be replaced with those nagging doubts that had been germinating like a deadly virus inside of her following weeks of Edwin's distraction and distance.

Her dad reddened. 'I wish your mother were here to speak to you. She might be able to get you to see sense.'

Kara shrugged. It hurt like hell that her mum was refusing to take the short plane trip from the south of Spain to Monrosa to attend her wedding, but she was *not* going to admit that to anyone. 'Maybe it's for the best—the last time you two were in the same room it wasn't exactly a pleasant experience for anyone.'

Her dad cleared his throat, stuffed his hands into his trouser pockets, his gaze on the closed double doors out to the gardens. 'You can't spend your days and nights with someone and remain detached. Edwin is a good-looking man… I don't want you getting hurt.'

Her mouth dropped open. Was her dad actually warning her not to sleep with Edwin? Heat ignited in her belly as she remembered their kiss. A few weeks ago she would have been able to laugh off her father's warning, but now she became a physical wreck of hormones whenever she saw him. She fancied him. She really, really fancied him. He was that good a kisser. 'I wouldn't worry if I were you—if the past few weeks are anything to go by, we'll rarely see one another.'

'Victor, where is Edwin? Our guests are waiting for us.'

Both she and her dad jumped at Edwin's father's barked

question that echoed around the cavernous double-height hall ceiling like a helter-skelter in motion.

Victor stepped away from the marble pillar beside which he had been standing and calmly answered, 'His plane landed ten minutes ago, Your Highness. He should be arriving very soon.'

Eyeing Kara as though it was her fault Edwin was late for his own pre-wedding garden party, Edwin's father asked, 'Just how urgent was the business that took him out of Monrosa? Doesn't he realise he's getting married tomorrow and is needed here?'

For a moment Kara was tempted to fire back, *Don't look to me for answers. I've no clue as to what's going on in your son's head. All we've talked about in recent weeks is wedding logistics and succession planning. Heaven knows he's never been good at talking about anything of even a slightly personal nature, but since our engagement he's taken it to a whole different level.*

But instead she gave him a polite smile and answered, 'I'm sure it must be of great importance, as he would not have wanted to keep our guests waiting.'

His Highness muttered something before turning his attention on Luis, who was leaning against the wall, his shoulder touching the gilt frame of a no doubt priceless still-life, flicking through his phone, and snapped, 'Please focus on our important guests this afternoon.'

A grin formed on Luis's mouth. He got the poorly disguised insinuation of his father's words—not to get sidetracked by pretty female faces, as was his wont. 'Don't take your bad mood out on me.' His grin dropping, Luis eyed his father, the roguish prince with a reputation for short-lived affairs with some of the most beautiful women in the world now replaced with the astute professional sportsman who had come close to winning the World

Powerboat Series on several occasions. 'This whole mess is of your own making—no wonder Edwin doesn't want to play ball.'

Every eye in the room swung in Luis's direction, everyone clearly trying to understand the meaning of his words.

Tight-lipped, His Highness stared at his middle son furiously. 'Your constant absence from palace life has caused you to forget the importance of decorum.'

Luis held his father's gaze for long seconds, the heat in his cheekbones in stark contrast to the coldness of his expression. He shot his gaze in her direction. Kara gave him a supportive smile, all the while hoping he wouldn't start an argument that would add even more tension to the day. With a reluctant shrug Luis lowered his head and once again flicked a finger over the screen of his phone.

His Highness let out an irritated breath before turning his attention towards Ivo. 'I've scheduled time in my diary on Monday morning for us to meet.'

Ivo, with his tall, muscular physique, short-cropped hair and sharp features, on the surface appeared confidently aloof, but his low voice told the truth of his gentle nature. 'I'm flying out on Sunday morning.'

'Well, change your plans,' His Highness countered.

With zero emotion showing, Ivo studied his father for a moment. Kara expected him to refuse to change his plans. Ivo might be gentle but he had a stubborn and single-minded streak, which had served him well, no doubt, in his journey to becoming an Olympic rower. After a quick glance in her direction, rather surprisingly, he shrugged in agreement.

Walking towards a window overlooking the gardens, Kara studied their waiting guests down at the water-front, her eyes brimming with tears. Edwin's distance stung even harder in the face of his brothers' understated support.

There were over five hundred guests mingling at the waterfront awaiting their arrival. Along with heads of state and prime ministers, local people and Young Adults Together staff were among the invited guests. She had had to fight hard the resistance of the wedding logistics team to have them invited ahead of corporate presidents and European politicians.

She had had to fight too for her idea to hold this garden party in the afternoon before the wedding. The logistics team had argued that many of the guests, especially those designated as dignitaries, would not arrive until the morning of the wedding and therefore the garden party was unnecessary and would only complicate preparations for the following day. Time and time again, Kara had had to remind them as to why she wanted to host the garden party in the first place—it was Kara's way of including as many Monrosians in the wedding celebrations as possible and her way of thanking those who had taken the time and expense to travel from all over the globe for the long weekend of celebrations.

As it had turned out, many of the dignitaries had opted to travel to the wedding early, and who could blame them for starting their weekend early on a sun-kissed Mediterranean island ablaze with colour, thanks to the springtime blooming of its native wild plants and flowers?

A number of guests had been unable to accept their invitation due to work commitments or personal issues. Only one had not sent an apology, however: her mum.

Kara had spoken to her only once since their engagement photos had been splashed across the front page of every newspaper worldwide. The pain in her mum's voice when she had begged Kara not to ask her again to attend the wedding had torn through her like a sharp blade. Kara knew just how private her mum was but had hoped she would have put that aside for her sake. In the reporting of their engagement, the media had referenced Michael's death, more often than not as a small aside paragraph at the end of an article, as though his death had been nothing but a blip in their lives.

She had gasped when she had seen the photos herself, grown all hot and bothered at the ones showing Edwin passionately kissing her. But it had been one photo—a fluke, a misinterpretation due to the angle at which it had been taken, but unfortunately the photo used by most of the media outlets—that still cut her to the quick. The photo had been taken in the seconds after Edwin had drawn back from their kiss, and the media had chosen to deduce from the intensity of his expression that it portrayed a man deeply in love.

When in truth it was nothing more than the portrayal of a man deeply irritated with himself. He regretted that kiss. He hadn't even been able to look her in the eye since. Which was mortifying, considering the lust it had unleashed in her. And any fears she had had about them sharing an apartment were a joke. Edwin had been away on business most nights since she had moved to Monrosa a fortnight ago. She had tried to shrug off his constant work and royal commitments abroad, burying herself in wedding preparations and in managing the transition of the day-to-day operations management of Young Adults Together in the UK to Marion Parry, her Head of Charity Services, so that she could focus instead on forming an international branch of the charity.

But despite her busyness, and how excited she was at the prospect of helping even more young adults, deep down she was lonely.

Was this how the next two years were going to pan out? Edwin consumed by work, their relationship nothing more than work colleagues who saw each other occasionally? Her spending her nights alone, rattling around their enormous apartment trying not to have sexual fantasies about her indifferent husband? Their friendship lost to the careful dance they needed to perform every time they stepped out to fulfil a public duty, lost to the exhausting toll of keeping up the pretence of being a couple in love, lost to Edwin's ceaseless drive to prove wrong all of the commentators who proclaimed that his succession was happening a decade too early?

His father's abdication announcement had been received with shock and disquiet, the media and public unsettled by what the change in leadership would mean to the country. Ever since, Edwin had been waging a campaign, both at home and abroad, to bring people on board with his succession.

'Edwin, about time.'

Her neck snapped back at His Highness's snarled chastisement. Whipping her head around, she felt her heart leap to see Edwin filling the entranceway, dressed in navy trousers and a white shirt, the top button undone to reveal the smooth, tanned skin of his chest.

His gaze swept towards her. She wanted to look away, to convey her annoyance at his lateness. But instead a rush of relief flooded her body, making her feel weak and light-headed. And then a charge of connection ran between them. A hunger for his company boiled in her stomach and blasted onto her skin.

It's as though he's a different person to the man I saw as my best friend.

She was noticing things about him she'd avoided seeing before—the powerful physicality of his body, the sharp height of his cheekbones, the firmness of his mouth.

He gave her a brief nod of acknowledgement and stepped to the side of the doorway, gesturing towards someone out in the corridor to join him.

And then he was protectively placing his arm around the woman who stood beside him.

Kara swallowed, disbelief punching away all thoughts. In a daze she moved across the room. Her light-headedness worsened. She swayed, her legs threatening to buckle beneath her. The outer edges of her vision darkened. Within seconds Edwin was at her side. Placing his arm around her, he pulled her against the strength of his body.

Together they faced her mother. Kara swallowed air greedily, drawing on Edwin's steadiness.

Her mum remained in the doorway, staring at her with an intensity that stripped her soul bare. Her mum gave a tentative smile that spoke of a bucketload of anxiety and uncertainty. And the years of fighting and disappointments and isolation suddenly didn't compare to the tight emotion in her chest at the joy in seeing her mum.

She held her arms out nervously, wondering how her mum would react.

Her mum drew back on her heels.

Kara winced.

Her mum took a hesitant step forward.

And then another.

They hugged, her mum's embrace so familiar and yet uncomfortable due to its long absence. Kara drew back, the intensity of it all too much to bear.

She turned to Edwin. He had done this for her, had known, without her saying anything, that she wanted her mum at her side when she married. She held his gaze, this man who knew her so well, and blinked back tears.

'Kara?'

She turned back at her mum's soft whisper.

Her mum moved towards her and for a moment Kara was transported to her childhood bedroom and her mum's whispered wake-up call that was always accompanied with a soft stroke of her hair. 'Edwin is right, you know: you *are* going to need me, not just this weekend, but also when this is all over. Divorce is awful. No matter what the circumstances.'

Kara's heart sank. She tried not to wince. On the eve of their wedding Edwin wasn't thinking of their marriage. Instead, he was planning for their separation and divorce.

As one soon-to-be extended family they walked down through the terraced gardens towards their waiting guests. Edwin could feel a headache coming on. They were a family in name at least, but, given the tensions that existed within both his and Kara's families, using the term 'family' was probably an infringement of the Trade Descriptions Act.

This morning he had had to spend way too long persuading Kara's mother to join him on the return flight to Monrosa, telling her that Kara deserved her support even if she didn't agree with her decision to marry him.

That damned engagement kiss.

It had thrown a curve ball into his life, as powerful as a cricket ball whacking him on the head, and had sent him into a month-long dazed existence.

What had been supposed to be a staged kiss had transformed into a primal urge for more…more heat, more connection, more bodily contact.

But the after-effects—seeing how upset Kara had been, the speculative calculation in his father's eyes when they had gone back into the palace, hating his constant urge, even weeks later, to pick up that kiss where they had left off, the conjecture in some of the media that a royal baby was bound to soon make an appearance after such an inflamed public display of passion, the texted messages demanding to know what the hell he was playing at from his brothers…all had led to him withdrawing into himself.

His behaviour was unsettling Kara. He had heard the disappointment in her voice every time he had called to cancel a planned trip to visit her in Brighton, and in more recent days, since her move to Monrosa, her attempts to appear unconcerned when he announced yet another long day of local meetings or another trip abroad.

But the constant questioning of his succession and its impact on Monrosa, the knowledge he had not only dragged Kara into this marriage of convenience but was also in danger of wrecking their friendship irreparably by having senseless fantasies of kissing her—and okay, he'd admit it, those fantasies contained a lot more detail than just kissing her—was spooking him. Fantasies that would wipe out a decade's history of a friendship built on trust and respect. As much as he wanted a more physical relationship with Kara, he knew taking that step would unravel a whole lot of emotions he was incapable of dealing with. He didn't want to compromise their friendship and most important of all he didn't want to hurt Kara. And right now he was trying to walk the exhausting and head-wrecking tightrope balance of not spending too much time with Kara while trying to continue to support her.

Last night, he had arrived late to her dad's hotel and she had bristled with irritation. But when her cousin Alice had sung a duet with her mother, Hilary, that irritation had melted away. The song had been upbeat and funny, the rest of the family howling with laughter, but despite Kara's forced smiles he had seen her loneliness in witnessing Alice and Hilary's close bond.

Now, as he led the party down towards the waterfront, given Kara's monosyllabic answers to his questions enquiring how everything was with her, he wasn't certain that persuading her mother to attend the wedding was the best idea after all.

Her hair was tied in a loose chignon, exposing her bare shoulders. A fragile chain hung around her neck. She was refusing to wear any jewellery from the royal collection and to date hadn't given him a satisfactory reason why.

As had become a recent habit of hers, her thumb was twisting her engagement ring around her finger. *Why does she do that?* Was it to remind herself of its presence? Did it annoy her? He had spent hours with a jeweller commissioning it, wanting to create a ring that was uniquely hers, that spoke of his admiration for her.

Her make-up was soft and subtle, a sweep of mascara on her long lashes, shimmering pink on her lips, but there was a tension emanating from her that said she'd happily tear him limb from limb.

They were only minutes away from their guests. He needed to sort out whatever was irritating her. Now. Before their guests picked up on it.

Keeping his voice low, he leant in to her. 'I thought you'd like having your mother here.'

'Are you trying to offload me onto her?'

Where had that come from?

'I have no idea what you're talking about.'

She tilted her chin. 'My mother told me you believe I'll need her in the coming years—are you frightened I'll go to pieces when our marriage is over? Is that why you went and fetched her this morning?'

'Of course not.'

She gave him a disbelieving look. 'Then why did you?'

'Because a mother should be at her daughter's wedding. And I told your mother that you deserved her attention, not just for the wedding but all of the time.'

She shook her head and as they approached their guests she placed her hand on his elbow, the smile on her mouth not reaching her eyes, 'I'm going to pretend to believe you but I'll tell you this much: I'm certainly not prepared to spend this marriage with you avoiding not only me but also your family. I've no idea what's been bugging you recently but you need to get a grip before you turn into a grumpy emotional hermit.' She paused and grimaced, and on a low sigh she leant even closer to him. 'We both know the consequences of people shutting down.' Bruised, pained eyes met his. 'We have to learn from Michael...'

She walked away from him towards her charity team. His skin tingled with shame and guilt. She was right, of course. Isolating yourself rarely did any good for normal people in normal circumstances, but in the craziness of this pretend marriage keeping a healthy emotional distance was going to protect them in the long run. Yes, there would be short-term pain, but the long-term gains would far outweigh them.

Kara's team embraced her with excited exclamations, bringing her into their fold, until she disappeared from view.

Kara had insisted the garden party was to be an informal affair, much to the disquiet of his father's advisors. But she had stood her ground against their arguments, firm that the party should be a relaxed afternoon where the guests got to wear casual clothes and to mingle informally in a bid to be as inclusive and accessible as possible for *all* those attending, without the pressures dictated by royal protocol.

So without the necessity of formal introductions, his family filed away from him, his father approaching the President of the European Union, almost unrecognisable now in his short-sleeved shirt over linen trousers rather than his usual conservative suits. Luis went and greeted the US ambassador fondly, their old rivalry forgotten now that the ambassador had retired from powerboat racing. Ivo joined Princess Maria and Johan, who were in conversation with a young group of Monrosians all wearing the Monrosa Environmental Protection Agency T-shirts, the charity his mother had founded before her death.

Not only was he getting things wrong with Kara but all of his intentions to force his family to be a tighter unit weren't happening, thanks to the others' uninterest and frankly his own lack of effort. On a number of occasions he had suggested they all meet, but he hadn't pushed the issue when he only got excuses as to why they weren't available in response, or, in Ivo's case, no response at all.

He could blame his workload. His office was tantalisingly close to attracting a major German bank to locate in Monrosa and he was having to lead the final negotiations. And on top of that, there was the management of the wedding and succession planning, diplomatic phone calls that had to be made to international leaders, and daily briefings with the cabinet alongside his father where he was trying to stamp his authority, much to the reluctance of his father's loyalists. And his father's belligerence wasn't helping either.

He had told Edwin he wanted him to take over the day-to-day decision-making in the run-up to the succession, but then proceeded to question every directive he made.

So, yes, his workload was insane. But in truth he

had been avoiding any personal interactions, even turning down Luis's and friends' attempts to persuade him to hold a bachelor party, needing time to get his head straight.

Kara's parents stood beside him, both glancing in the direction of her dad's side of the family, who weren't doing a particularly good job at hiding their surprise at Kara's mother, Susan's arrival. Kara's mother coloured and she turned as if to join Kara and her team but pulled back when the group erupted in laughter. Kara's father stepped towards her, gesturing towards his family. Kara's mother gave a pained smile but, straightening her shoulders, followed him as he led her towards his extended family. Could this weekend be the start of a reconciliation between Kara's parents? He sure hoped so. He was fed up with watching Kara's family letting her down. If they reconciled their differences then maybe they would give her the support and love she deserved.

He had *thought* Kara would be grateful to him for persuading her mother to come to Monrosa. But instead she had twisted his efforts to make it seem as though he had done so for reasons of pure self-interest. And as for Kara's contention that he was heading towards being a grumpy hermit—how was that even possible when he spent almost every waking hour in the company of others?

He stifled a groan.

His old work colleague from London, Laurent Bonneval, carrying his baby son, Arthur in his arms, his beaming wife, Hannah, at his side, was making a beeline in his direction.

After quick hugs, Laurent thrust Arthur into his arms, ignoring Hannah's protests to be careful. Arthur gave him a toothy grin.

Laurent chuckled. 'After all the babies you must have

held in the line of duty, I'd have thought you'd have mastered the art of holding one at this stage.'

Laurent pushed against his arm, forcing him to relax and to allow Arthur's tiny frame to curl against his chest. Arthur chortled and reached for his shirtfront, clinging to him. Edwin stared down at Arthur's tiny hand gripping his shirt, a loneliness, a longing unravelling in his soul.

'Kara, it's so good to see you again.'

His head jerked up at Laurent's greeting.

Kara hugged Laurent—they had met on several occasions in London before Laurent had returned to France to take over his family business in Cognac—and then shook Hannah's hand when Laurent introduced his wife to her. Edwin had attended Laurent and Hannah's wedding last year.

'I always knew you two should be together,' Laurent said, looking at them both with an expansive grin. He threw his arm around Hannah and kissed the top of her head. With a grin that was frankly a little sickening in its serenity he added, 'I'm glad you've finally found your way to one another. Just like Hannah and myself after I almost messed everything up between us by breaking up with her and leaving London for France. It goes to prove that love will eventually win out, no matter how much we fight it!'

Three hours later, and an hour later than scheduled, Edwin marched back up to the palace, his family and Kara trailing behind him.

At the Statue of Hera, he muttered a curse. His father and Princess Maria were still on the lower terrace, studying the wide swathe of agapanthus that grew there and from a distance resembled a stream of ice-blue water.

Had his family lost all sense of urgency?

Luis, idly climbing the wide steps of the terrace below, said something that had Ivo grin and Kara cover her mouth to hide a smile, before all three contemplated him and laughed once again.

When they eventually joined him, Luis gave him a wink before he and Ivo continued their climb back up to the palace.

Kara remained at his side and with a curious look she asked, 'What's the matter? Didn't you enjoy the party?'

'Three times I had to tell Luis it was time to leave.' Edwin blew out an impatient breath. He had had to insist that his family and Kara leave the garden party so that the guests could be encouraged to make their way back to their hotels and homes. Ricardo, the Master of the Household, had personally pleaded with him to bring the party to a close, explaining he desperately needed his serving staff to prepare for tomorrow's wedding banquet.

Kara backed away from him, giving a shrug. 'We were all enjoying ourselves.'

Her eyes were sparkling, her skin glowing, her pleasure at the success of the party twisting inside him so much that he was desperately tempted to push her against the granite plinth of Hera and kiss her happiness, touch his fingertips against the tender skin where her dress skimmed across her breasts.

Her breasts that swelled so perfectly.

Dammit, for years he had successfully ignored them. Even the times when they had gone sailing together and his eyes would burn with the effort of not staring at her when she'd stripped off to reveal a testosterone-surging bikini.

That kiss, and the fact that she was about to become his wife, were messing with his ability to see her as a friend only.

In silence they walked up the steps and into the hall of mirrors, where his brothers were waiting for them.

Luis was fixing his hair in the reflection of one of the mirrors. 'Ivo and I are taking you out for a drink tonight.'

Watching his father and aunt amble up the last set of steps to the palace, willing them to get a move on so that he could say his goodbyes to them, Edwin answered, 'I have other plans.'

Angling his head to better inspect his newly grown beard, Luis responded, 'Well, change them. You can't get married without some form of a bachelor party. Even if it's not a real wedding.'

Their father, now standing at the doorway from the terrace, growled, 'At least Edwin understands the meaning of duty.'

Luis cocked an eyebrow. 'You more or less put a gun to his head. Edwin doesn't want to marry. We all know that. You've given him a life sentence.' Turning, he gave Kara one of his trademark cheeky smiles. 'No offence, Kara, but you know what I mean.'

Kara gave him a half-hearted smile.

Right. He'd had enough. Luis's constant rebuking and bickering with his father was one thing, but this was just plain offensive to Kara.

'Cut it out, Luis.'

Luis twisted around, his arms shifting outwards in question. 'Are you seriously taking his side now?'

Edwin looked from Luis to his father, both angling for an argument, and then to Ivo, who had turned his back on them all to stare out of the window in the direction of the harbour. Aunt Maria appeared from the terrace, cradling a bunch of purple irises in her arms, frowning as she picked up the tension in the air. It was time they all went their separate ways before things kicked off.

He shifted towards the doorway. 'I have work to do.' Then, looking in Kara's direction, taking in once again the sexy slope of her exposed shoulders, imagining his lips on her skin, imagining releasing her hair and coiling it around his fingers, imagining her wearing nothing but the pink sandals on her feet, he backed even further away, his body temperature surging. 'I'll see you tomorrow…at the cathedral. Enjoy your meal with your parents tonight.'

Kara's gaze narrowed. And then she was stalking towards him. Chin tilted, a defiant gleam in her eye, she spoke loudly enough to include everyone in the room. 'I've decided we should have a change of plan. Both your family and mine will dine together tonight.'

She had to be kidding. Did she really want to subject her mother and father to a dinner where his father and Luis would constantly quarrel and Ivo be so detached he may as well be back in Lucerne training for whatever regatta that was currently preoccupying him? Not to mention his own plans for the evening. 'I'm not available.'

Her eyes narrowed even more at his words.

'I've already organised for a private room in the yacht club for myself, Edwin and Ivo to have dinner and drinks,' Luis protested.

Kara whirled around. 'Well, ring and cancel. We're having a family dinner.' And with that she moved towards the door, saying she would go and find Ricardo on her way to check on her parents, who were both staying in the palace tonight in advance of tomorrow's ceremony, to inform him of the change of plan. Before she left the room she glanced in his direction, her arched eyebrows and challenging stare silently reminding him of her earlier accusation that he was hurtling towards being an isolated grump. *Dio!* She really wasn't going to give him an easy time over this. Well, tough. He knew what he was doing. He needed to keep his distance from her. It was for her own protection. He just couldn't tell her that.

His Highness soon followed her, muttering that he had been planning on having a quiet night alone.

Only Princess Maria seemed pleased. Clapping her hands, she exclaimed, 'I'm looking forward to having Kara in the family—it's about time you men were whipped into shape!'

CHAPTER FIVE

A RAP ON her bedroom door had Kara quickly applying her lipstick, spraying on some perfume, standing from the dressing-table stool to make sure her wrap-around dress wasn't revealing anything it shouldn't be, and sitting back down.

Twisting her loose hair behind her shoulders and picking up her mascara bottle, she said, 'Come in.'

Pushing the door open, Edwin propped a shoulder against the door frame and studied her reflection in the Art Deco dressing table's mirror. Pretending to be applying some mascara, Kara waited for him to speak… while trying not to poke herself in the eye.

Would he stop staring at her? And what was with the dark mood?

Wearing a pale blue shirt over navy trousers, he angled his long body as though to deliberately blockade the entire door. 'It's considered bad luck for the bride and groom to see each other the night before the wedding.'

Picking up her hairbrush, she tried to ignore just how deflated she felt that once again he was preferring to spend time anywhere but in her company. 'I think a special dispensation can be awarded to us, considering our circumstances and the fleeting amount of time we've spent together over the past month.'

Moving across the room, Edwin came to a stand behind her, his bulk filling the delicate dressing-table mirror. A wave of awareness spread up her spine. She shifted forward on her seat.

'You're still angry I went and got your mum?'

Kara lifted one shoulder up and then the other, their separate movements indicative of her mixed feelings on Susan's arrival. At least now there wouldn't be endless speculation on her absence, and it just felt right to have her here. But how she wished that she had come of her own volition…and that Edwin hadn't persuaded her by pointing out the fact that this particular bride would need her mum even more than any other bride because of the fallout that was invariably on the cards for this unconventional marriage that would test even the best of relationships. A fallout that was steamrolling towards them at a faster, more intense rate than Kara had ever thought possible when she had agreed to the marriage, thanks to Edwin's continuing disappearing acts and avoidance of all things personal. 'Why don't you want to have dinner with us tonight?'

'As I said earlier, I have other plans.'

She ducked her head to catch his gaze, her heart in her mouth, the horror of his elusive answer stripping away any final pretence of being indifferent to his behaviour. 'A woman?' Nick had never been unfaithful but had subtly, and never favourably, compared her to his past girlfriends and work colleagues. It had seriously rattled her trust that men didn't have wandering eyes.

He rocked back on his heels and came to stand to the side of the dressing table, his eyes ablaze. 'Seriously?'

He was furious. For a moment she felt compelled to apologise but then anger rose in her—it was his evasiveness that was driving these questions and she sure as hell was not going to back down. 'Well, what, then?'

His mouth tightened.

Kara smoothed her hand against her hair, certain it was lifting because of the static tension filling the room.

His eyes narrowed as they honed in on her hand. 'Where's your engagement ring?'

Kara pulled open one of the two walnut inlaid drawers on the top of the table and pulled out her ring. 'I take it off when I'm showering.'

He watched her pull it on.

She grimaced at its weight.

'Don't you like it?'

She studied the sapphire. How could she feel nothing for something so beautiful?

Raising her gaze, she studied the man she was about to marry and answered, 'You're not the only one struggling at the idea of marrying, you know.'

With a sigh Edwin dropped to his haunches beside her. 'There is no other woman. I might be struggling with the whole concept of marrying and how on earth to be an even half-decent husband, but there's no other person in this world I'd rather marry. Please believe me on that.' His serious expression gave way to a light smile, his eyes scanning her for a reaction like a lighthouse beam scanning the oceans.

Well, prove just how important I am...spend time with me. Remind me of all the reasons why I agreed to this in the first place.

She eyed him, her poorly constructed defences crumbling in the face of his now keen attention, at the way his shirt pulled tight across his chest, at the smile on his face inviting her to believe in him, to forgive him.

Am I being too needy? Has Nick's stifling devotion

warped my understanding as to what a relationship should look like? Am I expecting too much?

'It's not going to be easy dealing with my mum and dad—they're both acting like stressed-out quarrelling Tasmanian devils.'

His mouth quivered.

She crossed her arms. 'What?'

He raised his hands defensively. 'Nothing.'

'Well, they are—at the garden party they refused to be photographed together and matters didn't improve when they found out their luggage had been brought to the same bedroom in the apartment they're sharing.'

Standing with a sigh, he said, 'I'm sorry—that should never have happened.'

'It's okay. The apartment has two other bedrooms. My dad moved into one.'

'I'll organise for another apartment to be allocated to him.'

'I suggested that but they both agreed it would be useful to have someone to navigate the palace with. They're both so anxious and intimidated by everything this weekend. I need your help with dealing with them—that's why I suggested we all have dinner together.'

'Maybe you should have left my family out of the mix—they're all like a powder keg waiting to go off.'

She stood and reminded him, 'It was you who had said you wanted for you all to be closer as a family.'

He rolled his eyes and shifted away towards the doorway. 'Sometimes I don't think things through enough.'

'Like our marriage?'

He came to a stop in the centre of the room. 'Not that...' he paused his gaze sweeping down over her '...but I shouldn't.' Again he hesitated, his gaze settling on her mouth. Reaching down, he plucked her silver and gold sandals from where she had earlier placed them on one of the two gilt stools sitting at the base of her bed. Well, her bed for now. Tomorrow her items would be moved to Edwin's bedroom next door.

Passing the sandals to her, he said in a rush, 'We'd better go down for dinner.'

Kara grabbed her sandals. Right, she'd had enough. Skirting around Edwin, she darted across the room and, banging the door shut, she leant against it with all of her weight. 'Right, we're sorting this out now once and for all. What is going on? Why are you shutting me out?'

Edwin moved across the room and, standing in front of her, placed his hand on the door handle and twisted it. 'Let's go—my father is going to be livid if I'm late again today.'

She pushed her weight even harder against the door. 'Not until we discuss this.'

He snapped his hand off the door handle. 'Fine. Give me some examples.'

'Today you arrived late for the garden party—'

'I was collecting your mother—'

'Why leave it till the day before the wedding? And this afternoon at the party, not once did you come to my side. What groom does that? It was embarrassing. And tonight you have some mysterious plans you're refusing to talk about.'

'You know how much I have to deal with right now, with the succession and persuading that German bank to locate here, not to mention all of the changes to the government structures I want to hammer out in advance of my enthronement.'

'There's nothing in that list that would stop you actually talking to me.'

God, how was she going to get through to him?

The urge to touch him, to be close to him once again, had her reach out her index finger to give a single light tap to his temple. 'I have no idea what's going on in there,' a tightness in her throat replacing the burn of anger in her belly, she tapped her finger against his chest, 'or in your heart.'

For a moment his shoulders flexed tight as though he was about to leap away from her. But then they dropped and, bowing his head, he stood silently in front of her. His hair was damp. Citrus mingled with his usual clean woody scent. She pushed herself even tighter against the door, her shoulder blades digging into the wood, for fear of giving in to the temptation of running her hands through the damp silkiness of his hair or cupping her hand against the vulnerable strength of his neck or, most compelling of all, the pull to move towards him and take shelter against his body.

Bruised golden eyes met hers. 'You deserve to have your mother here at your wedding. I wanted to make you happy. That's the only reason why I went and brought her here. But I obviously made a mistake.'

She closed her eyes against the softness of his voice. 'What would make me happy is if we could go back to how we were before all of this—where has our friendship disappeared to?'

She opened her eyes on his sigh.

He shifted to stand squarely in front of her.

Bare inches separating them, he studied her for long moments, a denseness entering the air between them. 'I'm struggling...'

His eyes shifted down to her lips.

Pinpricks of temptation tingled across her skin.

Her hips snaked outwards towards him. She slammed

them back against the door, her tailbone colliding with the wood, making her already unsteady legs tremble.

His head tilted, his eyes remaining fixed on her mouth as though it was a complex problem he was trying to understand.

With a distracted air, he repeated in another whisper, 'I'm struggling,' again he paused, and then his head lifted and his eyes blazed into hers.

Unable to breathe, unable to look away from the intensity of his gaze, hormones washing through her body like a lethal overdose, Kara felt her heart cry out for him to say something, something that would make everything okay, that would destroy the fear inside of her.

'I'm struggling...' he blinked and blinked again and, just like that, the passion, the hunger in his eyes was gone, traded for a wary defensiveness '...I'm struggling with the idea of being a husband.'

The feeling of being robbed of something she didn't even understand had her duck away from him and move into the centre of the room.

'Well, you'd better get used to it because this time tomorrow you'll be my husband—if you still want to go through with it.'

'Don't you?'

How many times had she asked herself that question over the past few weeks, her heart and instinct warning her to tread carefully? But her pride, her need to stick to her word and promises, seeing already the benefit her new position was bringing to Young Adults Together, her desire to help Edwin despite his recent infuriating behaviour, all had her want to see this through. 'On a number of conditions.'

She ignored Edwin's grimace and, holding up her hand counted off with her fingers, 'First condition is that we're going to have breakfast together every morning from now on. Second, we are trekking in the mountains and watching a movie together at least once a week. Third, you promised me a nice honeymoon. I'll accept your schedule is too crazy to allow for one right now, but at some point in this two years of marriage, I expect a holiday, and a spectacular one at that.'

Throwing his hands in the air, Edwin answered, 'Fine.' Opening the door, he added, 'Now can we please go to dinner?'

Coming to a stop where he was standing holding the door open for her, she attempted to hide just how vulnerable she was feeling inside with even more bravado. 'It's not too late to pull out of the wedding, you know— I won't take it personally.'

He smiled at that. His hand lightly touched her forearm. 'Getting married is way more complex than I ever anticipated...' he tilted his head, the tenderness in his eyes melting her heart '...but you're still the only person in the world for me.'

Their main course finished, Edwin caught her eye from the opposite side of the dining table and, looking in the direction of his father and her mother, who were seated to her right, he raised an eyebrow. Kara smiled. Who would have predicted his father and her mother would bond over a shared passion for olives?

Her mother lived alone in a two-bedroom *cortijo*, surrounded by olive groves, in the hills north of Málaga City. Throughout the meal she had described in vivid detail her new life tending to her olive trees, talking about her hopes and fears for this season's harvest. For the first time in years her mother was talking about the future.

The waiting staff reappeared, all five of them in a

gracefully coordinated dance placing a tiny but exqui-
sitely formed trio of chocolate desserts before each diner.

As they backed out of the room, her dad stood up.

Kara held her breath. Her poor father's hands were
trembling so badly the red wine in his glass was slosh-
ing about.

He directed his attention towards Edwin's father. 'I
would like to thank you for your welcome and hospitality, Your Highness.'

He raised his glass even higher, and the rest of the
people at the table reached for their glasses to join in
with the toast, but her dad wasn't finished.

Clearing his throat loudly, he added, 'I ask that you
and your family take good care of my...' his voice cracked
and it took him a few seconds to add, 'my little girl.'

Little girl. God, it was corny and sentimental but she
could not help the feeling of delight and belonging that
filled her heart at her dad's description. For so many
years she had believed he had forgotten that—that she
was his daughter, that she was the same person he'd given
piggy-back rides to around their garden, jumping over
sweeping brushes, pretending they were taking part in
the Cheltenham Gold Cup.

She waited for her father to look in her direction, but
instead his focus remained on Edwin's father. He was
waiting for a response. He had thrown down a gauntlet.
Her dad, a small-time builder, was challenging the sovereign of a small but powerful country. Kara wanted to
burst with pride.

His Highness's frown deepened to a bottomless ravine
transecting his forehead. Kara swallowed. He had done
nothing in the weeks since their engagement to indicate he
was shedding any of his misgivings as to Edwin's choice
of bride.

Sitting back in his chair, he studied her father, then her mother and then finally her, taking his time, a monarch accustomed to people waiting for his considered judgement. Her palms started to sweat.

Edwin said, 'You have our word—'

With an annoyed shake of his head, His Highness interrupted Edwin, his attention now fully on his eldest son. 'My marriage was arranged.' He stopped and chuckled. Kara gave a nervous smile, uncertain what direction this conversation was going in. 'At first my wife and I argued. She actually said I was too arrogant and had to accept that the marriage was one of equals. Of course, she was right, and after a while we became friends. And with time we grew to love one another.' His gaze shifting towards her, he added, 'From the most inauspicious starts, miracles can happen.'

What did he mean by that?

Edwin's father did not wait for her to work that question out. Instead he stood and raised his glass in salute to her father, who was still standing and waiting for a response to his question. 'I will give you my word that we will take care of your daughter as long as she's a member of our family.'

Her father frowned. Kara reddened.

Shooting out of his seat, Edwin raised his own glass, his expression pinched. 'Please be assured, Mr Duffy, that we will take care of Kara *always*.'

Her father's gaze moved from Edwin to his father and back again before he said quietly, 'Thank you, Edwin,' and then took his seat.

Edwin remained standing. He rolled his shoulders and raised his wine glass again. 'To my mother and Michael. We miss you dearly but you will live on for ever in our memories and actions.'

A tangle of emotions lodged in her throat at Edwin's softly spoken and unexpected words. The entire table just stared at him, nobody raising their glasses. A twitch began to beat in Edwin's cheek.

Her mother stood up.

Oh, God, was she about to walk out of the room at the mention of Michael's name?

Raising her glass, her mother waited with a quiet dignity and slowly the rest of the table rose to join her. Only then did she say, 'To Princess Cristina and Michael.'

They all sat down. They had no sooner done so when His Highness added, raising his glass again, 'And here's to many grandchildren in the future.'

Edwin sighed.

Her parents stared open-mouthed at His Highness.

Her mother was the first to gather herself enough to splutter, 'I really don't think so.' Sending a glare in her and Edwin's direction, she added, 'Please tell me you aren't going to be so foolish as to bring a child into this?'

'Of course not,' Kara answered.

In a disgruntled tone, Edwin's father demanded, 'Why ever not?'

Her mother huffed. 'I am not having my daughter left to raise a child on her own.'

Princess Maria, who was seated next to her father, asked with a bewildered expression, 'Why would Kara raise a child on her own?'

'Exactly my question,' His Highness added, staring in Edwin's direction.

Luis gave a cynical laugh and asked his father, 'Are you happy with the mess you've caused?'

'You never specified I have to marry for ever,' Edwin pointed out, lifting his wine glass to his mouth but then lowering it to the table, not having taken a drink from it.

He pushed it away from him as though irritated by the golden-hued wine.

Princess Maria gasped. 'Are you saying—?'

His Highness interrupted with a flick of his hand, 'Of course this is a marriage of convenience. Did you really think Edwin had changed his opinion on ever committing himself to a relationship? I had no choice but to force his hand. This country needs successors. This family needs a new generation.'

With a horrified expression, Princess Maria asked her brother, 'Have you lost all sense?'

His Highness grimaced, but then sat back in his chair, a smile forming on his lips. He glanced in her direction and then Edwin's.

A queasy feeling formed in her belly.

'You saw the engagement photos for yourself. Are you seriously telling me that I was wrong in pushing Edwin to make a choice in his bride?' Edwin's father demanded.

Across the table, her father, red in the face, growled, 'Can I remind you that they are divorcing in two years' time?'

His Highness blanched. And then, leaning forward, he yelled at Edwin, 'Two years? Are you serious? Two years is nothing. You're not even prepared to give the marriage a chance.'

That twitch in his cheek now on overdrive, Edwin answered with poorly disguised fury, 'You do not have a say in this.' With that he stood and muttered, 'I need some air.'

Kara stood and followed him.

Edwin's father called out, 'You can't divorce. We've never had a divorce in this family and we're not having one now.'

CHAPTER SIX

IN THE FAST approaching twilight, a figure ran out onto the road. Slamming on the brakes, Edwin cursed, his motorbike skidding on the gravel surface. The figure, about to be pelted with incoming stones, leapt out of the way.

Tugging off his helmet, he muttered a low curse. Kara was barefoot, her sandals in her hand, her dress, a fine layer of gold and yellow silk material, skimming over the gentle curves of her body. Thoughts on Kara's body, no matter how delectable they were, were not where his focus needed to be right now. 'Being mowed down by a motorbike is a drastic way to get out of our wedding tomorrow.'

She stepped off the grass verge. 'I'm coming with you.'

He pulled on his helmet. 'Stay with your parents. I'm sure they have plenty of things to discuss with you after that get-together.'

Oh, for crying out loud.

Kara went to get on behind him. He reached out to stop her but she slapped his hand away and climbed on. Muttering, he turned the motorbike back in the direction of the palace's garage.

Inside the garage, which had once been part of the palace's own flour mill, he climbed off. And waited for

Kara to follow. But instead she sat there and pretended to ignore him.

He walked out of the garage.

Kara chased after him.

He followed the path towards the pool house and then made a quick divert away towards the sea. Still Kara followed him. 'Are you going to follow me all night?'

'Yes, until you at least tell me where you were going.'

Okay, so he was acting crazily. This was not the behaviour of a grown man, never mind one about to succeed to the throne. But his head was about to explode *and* there was no way he could be around Kara right now. 'Look, I want some time alone—is that too much to ask?'

Gesturing in the direction of the palace, she said, 'Well, you're certainly not leaving me here to face *that* lot alone.' Popping a hand on her hip she added, 'And actually, yes, it *is* too much for you to ask of your fiancée. You should want to be with me.'

Want to be with her...that was the problem: he wanted to be with her, but for all the wrong reasons. And it was eating him up inside. 'What do you want from me?'

Her mouth set hard, her eyes blazing, she answered, 'To not wreck our friendship. We need to talk. Properly. We can't keep burying our heads in the sand and pretending that marrying, your succession, the craziness that's going on around us isn't impacting on us as individuals but also as a couple.' Then with an exasperated gesture with her hands she added, 'At least Nick blew hot and cold...right now you're just blowing cold constantly.'

For long moments she stared at him defiantly but then her mouth wobbled and she blinked hard. His heart sank. There were tears in her eyes. 'I'm really messing up here, aren't I?'

'I can't survive the next two years if you're going to

be this remote. I need your friendship, your support. I need to understand what's going on inside your head,' on a sigh her shoulders lifted, her eyes sad pools of blue, 'because when I don't I feel so sad and lonely. And I didn't sign up for those things. And I know you didn't either.'

He wasn't sad or lonely. Was he?

An uneasiness spread through his bones, bringing a pressing need to end this conversation. But how was he supposed to walk away from those bruised blue eyes holding him to account?

His throat tightened when he realised what it was he needed to do. He had to stop running away into the safety of his own thoughts and isolation. He had to give Kara what she needed and deserved from him. Yes, it might mess with his head, make him deeply uncomfortable and frustrated, but that was his problem, not Kara's. 'I was going for a bike ride into the mountains to clear my head. And, given that you previously said you'd never ride with me again, I assumed you wouldn't want to come.'

She bit back a grin, rightly knowing he was giving in to her. 'I'll try not to scream this time.'

Back in the garage he gave Kara the smallest bike leathers he could find, probably a relic from the time Luis was a mountain-bike fanatic, much to his father's disapproval. For the teenage Luis, the faster and more dangerous the sport, the better.

Then he searched out a suitable-size helmet and boots. He waited outside the garage while Kara pulled on all of the gear.

She emerged a sensual mix of silk and leather. He grinned. 'Great look.' He ducked his head, pretending to be checking the hand clutch. His comment had been supposed to come out as a tease but instead had sounded way too familiar and suggestively carnal. He fired up the engine, trying to ignore the blush on Kara's cheeks.

He drove out of the palace and through the narrow streets of Monrosa City before they began their long climb up into the mountains, the road a series of endless hairpin turns. The sky was rapidly turning from a pink breath of fire to inky blackness. There was little traffic out at this time of the evening, so he was able to drive hard, needing the surge of the breeze against his skin to counterbalance the sweet warmth of Kara's body behind him.

After half an hour they reached their destination. The viewpoint was set high up in the mountain, allowing a clear view of Monrosa City below them. On a headland to the east, the San Gabriel lighthouse flickered.

Kara removed her helmet and threw her head backwards. 'Wow, so many stars.'

Leading her away through the forest, using a torch to guide their way, he brought her to the opposite side of the mountain to a clearing with picnic tables. She gasped and turned around in a slow circle, her neck stretched back to take in the endless night sky that hung over them like a glittering dark blanket just out of their reach.

'It's stunning.'

'There's no light pollution on this side of the mountain. Locally this area is called Angels' Reach. People say it's the closest point to heaven on the island.'

Balancing against the edge of a picnic table, Kara asked, 'It's a special place for you?'

'It used to be, when I was younger.'

'And now?'

Now he wasn't certain what he felt for Angels' Reach. He hadn't visited the mountain for years. 'Are you certain it's not bad luck to see each other the night before the wedding?'

Kara studied him for a moment. 'I'm not sure you can bring bad luck to a marriage of convenience.' She gave a light laugh. 'It's not as though we have to worry about falling out of love or anything like that.'

Silence stretched out between them. Kara tilted her head again to stargaze, eventually asking in a soft voice, 'Is this where you had been planning to visit before I stopped you?'

'Yes.'

'Why here?'

'I like the view. And, as I said, I needed space to think.'

She raised an eyebrow. 'And you couldn't find some space to think in a seventy-room palace?'

He scuffed his boot along the dry earth, remembering what it was like to lie down on it and hear his mother whisper tales from the folklore of her native Aragon. 'I should have brought something for us to drink.'

'You're shutting me out again.'

He started at the anger in her voice. Exasperation, frustration at his own avoidance, his inability to articulate the feelings that were tightly sewn into the fabric of his being and Kara's impossible desire for him to unpick those feelings thread by thread had him respond just as angrily, 'I don't know how to let you in.'

She turned away from him. Went and sat on the bench of the picnic table and stared out into the darkness in the direction of the Mediterranean that the waning crescent moon did little to illuminate.

He went and sat beside her.

She shuffled away, leaning back against the table-top. Waves of irritation pulsated in his direction. 'Start with the small things—it doesn't have to be anything profound. Tell me about the first time you came here, for instance.'

He tossed the flashlight between his hands, a jittery energy entering his bloodstream. 'I can't remember the first time—it was decades ago.'

Those waves of irritation from her moved across to him in even quicker pulses.

Dio, this was so hard. Why did he find it near impossible to speak? Why did it feel like torture?

'My mother used to bring me here to celebrate my birthday. We'd sneak out before midnight and we'd sit here counting down the minutes until it was my birthday.' Something caught in his throat, but he could tell that Kara expected more, so he forced himself to find the words that described memories he had deliberately ignored for years. 'She used to say that she wanted to be the first to whisper *happy birthday* to me.'

Kara sighed. And whispered, 'She sounds wonderful.'

Something large and significant twisted in his chest at the soft wistfulness, the respect in Kara's voice. He held her gaze, his heart tumbling, tumbling, tumbling again and again and again at not just the understanding in her eyes but also the eagerness there, the eagerness to know more about his mother. 'Yes, she was.'

'Tell me more.'

An image of his mother, down on all fours on the palace lawn, chasing after him and his two brothers, pretending to be a grizzly bear, had him smile. 'She was playful, constantly thinking up new things for us all to do, new adventures for us to undertake. One summer we created our own pirate island on the palace's private beach—we even made our own lookout tower using old wine barrels she found in the cellar. And she used to dream up ways to trick the media into not following us, which of course was like something out of a spy movie for us.' He rolled his shoulders, his heart clogged with emotions he didn't want to have to process. 'It's hard to describe but somehow she just managed to make me feel secure, certain about the world.'

Kara twisted towards him. 'You wanted to remember your mum tonight.'

He shrugged.

'I'm sorry she's not going to be there tomorrow.'

A fissure opened up in his heart. 'Me too.'

'I'm sure she wouldn't be impressed with your dad forcing you into a marriage of convenience.'

He laughed at that, imagining his mother's reaction. 'She would have gone crazy.' Then, catching Kara's eye, he admitted, 'But she'd have liked you.'

Kara gave a snort. 'I'm sure she'd have wanted a more suitable bride for you, someone who understands royal protocol and doesn't constantly ruffle feathers, which I seem to be making my speciality.' She let out a sigh. 'Victor isn't happy that I'm refusing to back down on my tour of Europe to raise awareness for Young Adults Together. He wants me to dedicate more time to attending events with you instead. And the chamberlain is putting every obstacle possible in the way of my plans to open up parts of the palace to the public. And as for my proposal to start an apprenticeship programme within the palace for disadvantaged young school leavers... I've never heard so many reasons as to why something won't work. I get that there's a tradition of roles being passed within families— but nepotism like that is just plain unfair.'

He grinned and bumped his shoulder against hers playfully. 'Please don't stop questioning everything. The household needs a shake-up and you're also taking the heat off me.'

Kara pursed her lips and eyed him suspiciously. 'Are you saying I'm your fall guy?'

Did she really have to draw his attention to her mouth like that? It wasn't as though he was ignoring it in the first place. And why was he so damn distracted by her knee touching his thigh?

Her leather jacket was moulded to her curves like a second skin, its zip hanging just at the valley of her breasts like an agent provocateur. Blood pumping through him in hard beats, he placed an arm behind her back. 'Never a guy.'

Her eyes widened. She gave him an uncertain smile.

His hand touched her arm.

She jumped but then settled, leaning ever so slightly towards him, allowing his fingers to curl even more around the soft leather of her jacket. Soft leather. Soft lips. Soft skin.

Silence, darkness, unfinished business.

He eased her closer. She didn't resist.

Her loose hair tickled the back of his hand.

Memories of her scent, floral with an undertone of something earthier, wiped out the forest scent surrounding them.

Her shoulder slotted under his arm, the softness of her body pressed close to where his heart was hammering.

He touched a finger to her chin, tilting her head so that their gazes married. He breathed deep at the heat in her eyes, the parting of her lips. He inched towards her mouth, all thought wiped out by pure physical need. Their lips touched, her mouth even more sensual and lush than before. He tried to hold himself back but that lasted all of five seconds before he was deepening the kiss, wanting to taste, inhale every part of her.

And her hand on his neck pulled him even deeper into the kiss.

Kara was moving.

Panicked, he jerked away, worried he had read this all wrong and Kara was trying to get away.

She pulled him back, her bottom landing on his lap. He chuckled into their kiss and he could feel her lips draw up into a smile. But they didn't stop.

He pulled her hip in against his belly, fire raging through him, her hands raking through his hair.

He fumbled for the zip of her jacket and lowered it, his thumb tracing down over the smooth skin of her breasts.

He groaned again. Her bottom wriggled on his lap.

He wanted to part the material of her dress, expose the lace bra he could feel beneath the silk. He wanted to twist her fully towards him and have her wrap her legs around his waist. He eased away, his head swimming with crazy, destructive thoughts.

But only seconds after he broke their kiss, less than an inch away from her, with a sound of protest she pulled him back, both hands clasping his neck.

Burning, urgent, unthinking need yelled at him to stay there. To lose himself in her. But he had to stop. Before the mess of their impending marriage became an even more tangled chaos of emotions.

He unclasped her hands. Drew back from her mouth.

She stared into his eyes, dazed.

And then with a sound of disbelief she flew off his lap, gawked at him and rocked on her heels before collapsing back down on the bench.

She yanked her jacket zip back up, clamping the skirt of her dress between her legs. 'I hope there's no paparazzi with night-vision cameras hiding in the woods.'

He laughed, glad she was making light of the frenetic intensity of what had just happened.

'Our kisses…they're kind of confusing, aren't they?' she said quietly.

His laughter died. He had no way of explaining them other than as the result of human desire. 'I guess we're both young and healthy and it's been a while since either of us were in a relationship.'

She nodded eagerly. 'And the craziness of our situation isn't helping—maybe subconsciously we think we should be finding each other attractive.' She stopped, her expression growing horrified. 'Not that I'm saying you find me attractive—'

He interrupted her, 'I think we can at least admit to each other the chemistry between us.'

Did she really think their subconscious could be fooling them to that extent? But who was he to argue? If she was happy to believe that, then so was he.

'So what do we do about this attraction?'

Her brow furrowed. 'I don't know. Not beat ourselves up too much when it happens, I guess. And, more importantly, not ascribe too much significance to it…the survival of our friendship is what's important.'

He inhaled deeply. 'I don't ever want to hurt you.'

She nodded. 'I guess it's down to both of us individually to keep everything in perspective—to remember that this is a marriage of convenience thrust upon two people who have no interest in marrying and no desire to marry.'

He pulled his heel along the soft earth, a deep channel forming in its wake. 'Before Nick, did you see yourself marrying?'

She shrugged and scrunched her nose in thought. 'What happened with my parents put me off…but Nick definitely put a solid nail in the coffin of love and marriage for me.' She gave a light shiver. 'I struggle with the idea of trusting someone enough to commit myself to them for ever. I'd hate the vulnerability of that. I'd constantly be watching for a time when they'd try to manipulate me, hurt me. And that's not fair, is it?' Pausing, she considered him. 'You know what, you've never really given me a good reason why you're not interested in marriage?'

He flattened the channel of earth with the sole of his shoe. 'I like my own company. I don't think I'm husband material—I prefer to give my energy to my work.' Then, standing up, he held out his hand to her. 'I'd better get you home.'

She looked at his hand and then looked him straight in the eye. 'Being single suits some people...but only if it's for the right reasons.' Then, standing up too, she tugged him towards the wooden barrier at the edge of the picnic area. 'I think I can hear the sea.'

He leant forward, twisting his head. 'I think I can too. I've never heard it before, even in all the times I came here with my mother.'

She smiled at him, her hand touching his cheek. 'Thank you for bringing me here, for telling me about your mum. It's good to know you better.'

It did feel good to have spoken about his mother. He smiled at how Kara's eyes were dancing with pleasure, a connection, a spark, a sense of place making him intensely happy. But then, just as quickly as that happiness arrived, it disappeared, the intimacy of the moment making him uneasy. Was he making himself vulnerable by being this open? Was he setting them up for a whole load of heartache when this marriage ended by their being too close to one another?

CHAPTER SEVEN

MONICA, THE PALACE's head florist, moved from table to table, adjusting a fraction the elaborate floral arrangements sitting in tall, clear vases at the centre of every table in the ballroom.

On seeing him, she went to leave, but Edwin gestured for her to stay and finish her work.

The doors out to the terrace were opened back, the heat of the day drifting into the coolness of the room.

Beyond the terrace, on the shimmering water, boats in full sail glided through the rolling white-topped waves.

In two hours he would be married. A husband.

He turned away from the golden dome of the cathedral.

The ballroom was a reflection of the view across the harbour. The vast gold chandeliers towering over the tables laden down with gold cutlery and gold-rimmed plates bearing the royal crest mirrored the cathedral's dome, the olive branches in the floral arrangements the green and silver glimmer of the Mediterranean, the pink blush roses the narrow buildings of the old town.

Ricardo bustled into the room. Did a double-take when he spotted Edwin.

'Is everything okay, Your Highness?'

He nodded. 'I want to ensure everything is in place for

the wedding meal later.' From the moment he had woken this morning he had been feeling off balance. Tetchy and nervous, with a side dollop of a tightness in his throat. Was he coming down with something?

Last night, talking beneath the stars, kissing…it had all felt too good, too exhilarating. He hadn't dated for close to two years. No wonder kissing Kara was igniting a fire inside him.

He needed to get through today. Not overthink it. Which was why he was here, unnecessarily inspecting the ballroom like a nervous housekeeper. Anything to distract him. Kara had left their apartment early this morning, as arranged, to get ready for the ceremony in her parents' apartment. Unable to stomach breakfast, he had paced the apartment, ready for the ceremony way too early, and even he couldn't bring himself to work on his wedding day.

Ricardo cleared his throat. 'Is everything to your satisfaction?'

Eucalyptus leaves wound their way up all seven layers of their wedding cake. On top two simple figures crafted from wood stood beneath an arch of intertwined leaves. Kara had asked him if he wanted an input into the cake. He hadn't. The tightness in his throat intensified. The cake perfectly symbolised their treks into the mountains of Monrosa. He turned to Ricardo. 'Everything is perfect.'

Relief washed over Ricardo's expression. 'We want to ensure you and Miss Duffy have a wonderful wedding day. We're all so happy for you. Miss Duffy has been very supportive in the preparations and it will be a pleasure to work for her in the coming years.'

Behind Ricardo, Luis walked into the room and chuckled. 'I'm sure Kara will be a dream to work for in comparison to our father.'

Ricardo flinched, made a non-committal sound and fled from the room.

Edwin sighed. 'There was no need for that.'

Luis shrugged. 'We've been looking everywhere for you. It's time to go.'

Ivo and his father were waiting for them on the central steps out in the courtyard. Ivo was dressed in the same navy-blue officer dress uniform of the Monrosian army as Luis, their father in the red dress uniform of the Commander of the Forces. Today he was wearing the black officer tunic of the Marines, gold cuffs on the sleeves, gold braiding on the shoulders. Across the tunic he wore the red and white sash representing the Order of St Philip, and pinned to the fabric the gold insignia of the two other Monrosian orders.

Without preamble they lined up, equidistantly apart. Edwin stood in the centre beside his father, Ivo to his right, Luis to his father's left.

At the western apartments, horses and carriages were awaiting Kara and her entourage. He closed his eyes, a wave of gratitude, of affection, of respect for her making him dizzy. How many friends would agree to something this enormous, this public, this life-altering? He *had* to make this marriage work.

With a call from their commander, the twelve soldiers flanking them on either side, all in their Sixth Infantry khaki uniforms, led them towards the closed fifteenth-century wooden gates that led out onto the cobbled streets of the city.

It took four of the household guard to open the gates.

A wave of sound rolled towards them. The waiting

crowd cheered and waved their purple and gold Monrosa flags, aided by the warm summer breeze.

The clamour, the close scrutiny, the fevered elation of the crowd sent a sickening sensation through him but he continued to walk at the steady beat that had been drilled into him from the moment he could walk, falling in behind the rest of the Sixth Infantry regiment already waiting outside the palace walls, the Second Regiment falling in behind them.

They walked down the incline that would take them to the narrow streets of the old town and then on to the harbour front towards Monrosa Cathedral, the cheering swelling.

He clenched his hands, the happy calls so at odds with the low weeping and murmuring that had accompanied them the last time they had marched together to the cathedral.

That time, with every step he had taken, his frustration with his father had inched ever higher. Why had he forced them to walk through the crowds to their mother's funeral? Why had he thought it was the duty of three bereaved children to march, just so the public would have the opportunity to express their grief at the passing of their beloved Princess Cristina?

The morning of the funeral, he had held Ivo in his arms and had promised that he would not be forced to march. But, despite his arguing fiercely with his father, his father had refused to relent, forcing Ivo to join them.

That was the day they had lost Ivo to his own impenetrable thoughts.

For his part, Edwin had been so full of anger and disbelief that he soon realised that to survive he would have to detach himself. Shut down all his emotions. Not react when his father had angrily demanded to know why he and Luis had refused to accompany their mother when she had gone out riding that day with Ivo. Not admit his own anger towards Ivo for insisting they go riding even though their mother had complained of vertigo earlier that day.

Now they swept through Plaza Nueva, the thunderous applause startling pigeons from the roof of the Tufail Observatory Tower. A dark-haired girl of five or six, perched on her father's shoulders, waved a cut-out of him and Kara on their engagement day. He smiled at her. She dropped the cut-out, her eyes wide, her mouth a perfect circle of surprise.

His mother would have loved every moment of this. She wouldn't have even tried to hide her pride in her husband and three sons' marching together as one seemingly united family.

How they had all failed her.

They turned a sharp right, the open harbour bringing a strong sea breeze and the sight of waves lapping against the quay walls. People hung from the upstairs windows of the quayside cafes, filming the procession on their phones.

A girl called out her love for Luis. His father sighed loudly.

At Plaza Santa Ana, the Cardinal of Monrosa was waiting for them on the cathedral steps.

Inside came welcome near silence apart from the low whispering from the already assembled guests. Edwin's nose twitched thanks to the heavy scent of incense.

He was about to follow the cardinal when his father placed a hand on his arm. 'You can make this work if you want to.'

He bit back the temptation to laugh.

Did his father seriously think this forced marriage,

already fraying at the edges, could be made to work just to serve his egotistical desire to ensure a future heir?

He walked away, smiled and nodded his way down the aisle, the beaming grins of Kara's family, friends and colleagues punching him in the stomach. How many lies had she had to tell on his behalf?

He took a seat at the top pew.

Tried to breathe.

His mother's casket had sat only feet away from where he sat now.

He had refused to look at it. Instead he had tilted his head and tried to count the number of flowers on the triptych of stained-glass windows behind the altar. But the disbelief kept dragging him back—to the fact that only four days prior his mother had left to take Ivo horse-riding. He and Luis had been supposed to go too but they had become caught up in a battle to win a game of tennis and had refused to leave. He had vaguely waved his mother goodbye. Hadn't replied to her departing call to be kind to one another. Her horse had startled and thrown her off, causing a catastrophic head injury.

Ivo, alone on the isolated trail they had been following within the palace grounds, had raised the alarm on her mobile phone and had frantically carried out the emergency services' instructions on how to help her, a ten-year-old child, alone, carrying the responsibility for saving his mother.

Losing her had destroyed them.

He placed his hands on his knees. Light-headed.

Time stretched out. His father grumbled at Kara's lateness.

Kara was going to walk down the aisle, wasn't she? What if she had changed her mind?

His heart boomed in his chest. Only one person, since

his mother had died, had settled him—Kara. Her acceptance of him as well as astute challenges to his ways of thinking and behaving, her energy, had freed him.

Dammit, where was she?

Cold terror ran through his veins.

Had he blown it? Had he thrown away their friendship for this farce?

Standing at the bottom of the aisle, while Triona and Siza brought her long train under control, her hands resting on both of her parents' arms, Kara felt her legs buckle.

And for a moment a crazy thought passed through her mind at lightning speed.

What if she spoke out? Right here? Right now? Explained that she couldn't be the answer to what the media were terming a new era of optimism in Monrosa? Explained she understood the marriage was creating an unprecedented feel-good factor and was being hailed as an example of hope triumphing after the tragedy of the country losing Princess Cristina, but the media's new near adoration of her, lauding her charity work, describing her relationship with Edwin as the ultimate love story that saw friendship blossom into enduring love, was so far from the truth that she felt as if she was going to burn up in shame?

What if she explained there definitely would be no babies born to them?

What if she made it clear this was only a marriage between friends? One that would end one day, but until that happened she would have Edwin's back and would try her very best to be the princess Monrosa deserved?

What would happen if she said all that, cleared the air?

Chaos probably.

'Are you ready?'

She wanted to say no to her father's question but instead she nodded *yes*. Which was a good thing because there was no way she was going to be heard anyway. The cathedral practically shook as the Bridal Chorus boomed from the pipes of the organ positioned on the gallery overhead, the notes flinging themselves against the vast roof of the even vaster cathedral.

Edwin jerked in his seat, music booming against the stone pillars as the organist began to play. The cardinal and his fellow celebrants on the altar looked down the aisle, a smile transforming each of their up-till-now serious expressions.

Kara had that effect on people.

He shouldn't look back. Not yet.

But he didn't give a damn.

He needed to see her. He needed to see her with a desperation that burned through him and scorched his heart.

He breathed in deeply, stepped even further out into the aisle. Desperate to have her look in his direction, desperate for a connection.

Flanked by her mother and father, her bridesmaids carrying her train, Kara walked towards him, her gaze sweeping to either side of the aisle but not once looking in his direction.

A veil was the only adornment in her tied-up hair. His aunt hadn't persuaded her to wear a tiara after all.

Her full-skirted satin dress with its sweetheart neckline was overlaid with delicate lace that skimmed her shoulders and the length of her arms.

In her hands she carried the same blush-pink roses interlaced with olive and eucalyptus leaves as the displays in the palace ballroom.

There was heat on her cheeks.

She was beautiful.

Look at me.

Her head dipped as though studying the blue and white mosaic tiles on the floor.

Look at me, Kara. Let me know you're okay. I need you...and I don't understand why, but I'm panicking here.

And then finally, only a few steps away, she looked towards him.

Her gaze was heavy with emotion.

His heart pounded.

She gave him a tentative smile.

He blinked away the stinging sensation in his eyes.

She was here.

Standing in the centre of the aisle, powerful, intent, Edwin held her gaze with a burning intensity. Kara's heart turned inside out.

His hair was newly cut. His black, heavily adorned military uniform suited the hard planes of his face, the seriousness and loyalty of his personality.

Her parents peeled away to awkwardly shake Edwin's hand before they took their seats. From the corner of her eye she saw the fond smiles from their guests taking in the fact both her mother and father had guided her down the aisle to their future son-in-law, a family united in their joy of the ceremony about to take place, when the sad reality was that they had only announced this morning that they were both going to escort her down the aisle, united in their ongoing objections to the wedding.

Well, at least they were finally agreeing on something for the first time in a decade.

The music disappeared and silence fell on the cathedral.

This was about to happen. She was about to marry

this man. Her best friend, her saviour, the person who kept her sane, who got her, and with whom she had the most uncomplicated relationship in her life—she was about to marry him and step into a very complicated world.

Edwin continued to stare at her.

She smiled, not certain what to do, not certain how to react to his intensity. 'Hi.'

She waited for him to say something in response.

At the altar the cardinal cleared his throat, and made a gesture for them to approach the altar steps, as they had rehearsed.

But Edwin didn't budge.

He leant down and whispered, 'You're here.'

She swayed at the low tenderness of his voice.

He took her hand in his and led her to the altar.

The cardinal smiled but then frowned in the direction of their joined hands. The joining of hands was supposed to come later in the ceremony.

But Edwin's grasp only tightened around her trembling hand.

She needed to pull herself together.

She was *not* going to crash and burn under the pressure of all this expectation. It was messing with her head and distorting her feelings for Edwin, and she needed to get a grip. She had to stop struggling to keep her emotions in check around him, and as for her body—well, that was off in a la-la world of misguided sexual attraction. As was witnessed last night. She would have happily slept with him. Her legs threatened to buckle under her again. But this time it wasn't terror but a lick of heat in her belly, remembering the dominance of his mouth, the sweep of his hand against her breast.

This was so wrong. She shouldn't be having these

thoughts standing in front of a cardinal, being watched by millions worldwide.

She needed to hold on to the cold, hard fact that this was nothing more than a theatrical performance. A performance that would allow her to champion the work of Young Adults Together.

She dropped her gaze, a stab of loneliness emptying her lungs. Michael would have understood her reasoning. He would have agreed to subvert an institution like marriage to further a good cause. Wouldn't he?

When it came to the exchanging of vows, vows she had written, agonising over every word, not wanting to publicly commit to anything with which they would never follow through, she held her breath and willed herself to remain detached.

But Edwin's intense golden gaze shredded any hopes of her remaining indifferent.

'I promise you my friendship, loyalty, trust and understanding regardless of the obstacles we may face together.' His voice danced along her spine. She tightened her fingers around his, needing an anchor as she made the same simple vows, praying they would survive all the obstacles that littered their future.

And then the cardinal invited them to kiss.

Edwin touched his fingers to her jawline. Her heart kicked hard at the tenderness of his touch. She was doing it again...confusing acting with reality. She straightened, trying to regain some backbone.

She wished he would stop gazing at her as though she was the love of his life and just kiss her. He didn't need to over-egg this. The guests wouldn't suspect this was anything but a love marriage.

But he stayed there, touching her face, reverently, gently.

People began to shuffle in their seats.

His father muttered something.

This was torture. Unfair. Wrecking her heart.

And, fool that she was, she wished they could stay in this moment for eternity. A moment when the past and future didn't matter.

Something cracked inside of her.

I want closeness and intimacy with you. I want to be my true self. I want the freedom, just for a while, to have my heart soar and not be racked by doubts and guilt. I want to be wild and not give a damn.

Inch by inch he edged towards her.

His kiss was gentle. Caring.

Her heart fluttered in her chest.

She leant in for more. But he pulled away.

She wanted to scream. She wanted heat. More of him.

He was smiling when he pulled back.

But frowned as his gaze followed the big, fat tear that rolled down her cheek.

CHAPTER EIGHT

THEY STEPPED OUT onto the cathedral steps to thunderous applause. Kara blinked in the bright daylight, a gust of wind whipping her veil over her face. She scrambled to push it back, heard a chuckle, and then Edwin's strong, capable hands were helping, pushing the fine lace away, his gaze holding hers fondly, his fingertips settling wisps of her hair that had broken free.

Brace yourself, Kara. You can't cry again. Remember this is only all pretend. Don't get caught up in it. Know what is real and what isn't, for the sake of your sanity when this is all over and you have to walk away.

A chorus of 'Kiss! Kiss! Kiss!' rolled through the crowd. Edwin gave a teasing smile and the crowd reacted with good-natured laughter and then even more insistent calls for them to kiss.

Edwin turned to her, those golden eyes burning a path to her soul. An utterly convincing newlywed husband.

He's way too good at this pretence. But then, he was raised to present the image of utterly charming prince to the world. This is all second nature to him. Remember none of this is real.

His mouth touched hers. Her eyes closed, a deep shiver running down her spine.

The crowd erupted, their cheers echoing the boom in her heart.

Dammit. His kisses were perfection.

He pulled away, took her hand in his and led her to their awaiting carriage.

When they pulled away, Edwin took her hand in his and whispered against her ear, 'You look amazing and you're doing a fantastic job. The hard bit is over—try to relax and enjoy the rest of the day.'

How was she supposed to relax with the eyes of the world on her…and when he made her head spin with those kisses? 'You sound as if you're carrying out a work appraisal.'

He raised an eyebrow. 'I must make sure to give you a good bonus at the end of all this.'

Despite everything she felt herself blush, his flirting tone catching her by surprise.

All along their procession back to the palace they were greeted with shouts of goodwill and blessings for their marriage.

At the palace they and their families posed for formal photographs in the Oriental Room, Edwin's steadying hand on the small of her back all the time.

And when they joined their guests for the pre-reception drinks he stayed at her side throughout, and she so wanted to allow herself to drift into a tantalising fantasy world where all of this was real.

A fantasy world that became even more entrancing when, during the intervals between the various wedding banquet courses, acts that Edwin had especially organised for her entertainment appeared on the ballroom stage.

A world-famous contemporary dancer perfectly enacted the words of one of Kara's favourite songs. And before the main course was served a legendary 1970s singer took to the stage. Kara, deep in shock, stared open-mouthed as the backing music to her most famous disco track began to play. Within seconds the entire room were out of their seats, dancing.

After the singer had finally left the stage, having performed three encores, Edwin hugged her, his thumb gently wiping the tears of happiness Kara couldn't hold back.

And then, before the dessert, Edwin stood to make his speech. He formally thanked the guests for their attendance and spoke for a few minutes on his plans for Monrosa, paying special attention to praising the impressive legacy he was inheriting from his father, who gave a brief satisfied nod in acknowledgement.

Then, folding the sheet of paper he was reading from, he waved it briefly in the air before saying, 'I've decided to deviate from the rest of my speech.' Turning, he addressed Kara directly. 'Today, in the cathedral, while I was waiting for your arrival, I began to panic. I thought that you might have changed your mind and wouldn't come.'

She shook her head—that had never been a consideration. Her arrival had been delayed thanks to a dog startling one of the horses along the route.

Edwin shrugged. 'I guess sometimes we need to face the worst possible scenario to fully appreciate what it is we have. You're my best friend. Kara, your loyalty, your intelligence, your humour all ground me. I know we're going to have an incredible partnership.' He paused and those golden eyes melted her heart. 'Thank you for being my wife.'

Then, turning to their guests, he raised his glass and said, 'Please join me in toasting my incredible wife, Kara, Princess of Monrosa.'

She smiled and smiled and acknowledged with a nod all those who rose and toasted her, her cheeks hurting, confusion, disappointment she had no right to feel making her heart thud in her chest.

Friendship…partnership…all the right words to describe their relationship. Had anyone noticed the absence of any mention of love in all of that? Or was it just her?

Changed into a blue trouser suit and white plimsolls, Triona at her side, Kara did a double-take of the now deserted ballroom.

Walking out onto the dance floor where earlier they had danced together, that disturbing chemistry rising between them and causing his heart to thud wildly, Kara said to Edwin, 'Please tell me you didn't end the party early? My dad's side of the family will never forgive you. They don't think it's a proper wedding if they don't get to see sunrise.'

Not waiting to draw breath, she planted her hands on her hips, her jacket parting to reveal an ivory silk camisole tucked into her trousers, her gaze shooting between him and Triona. 'What's going on? Why did I need to change out of my wedding dress?' She lifted her feet. 'And why the plimsolls?'

Triona gave him a look that said this was all on him, muttering she needed some air, and slipped out to the terrace, closing the door behind her.

Kara's suspicious gaze took in the open-necked dark blue shirt and lightweight navy trousers he had changed into.

He needed to make this marriage work. And the only way he knew how to do that was by trying to recapture what they had before he'd ever suggested marriage—a light, fun friendship with laughter and adventure and no complications or expectations.

He followed in Triona's footsteps, coming to a stop by the terrace door. 'I have a surprise for you.'

Her hands dropped from her hips. She edged up onto her toes to try to get a better glimpse out onto the terrace.

He opened the door and stepped outside, gesturing for her to follow.

She squinted out into the darkness and then eyed him with a frown.

But her curiosity obviously got the better of her because she walked towards him with an expression that said this surprise had better be good.

The moment she stepped outside a cheer went up from the awaiting guests who were lining both sides of the walkway down to the waterfront. And, as planned, the guests activated their light sticks in sequence, so that two rows of blue lights flowed all the way from the terrace down to the sea.

Kara screamed, gasped, and finally, thankfully, laughed.

She allowed him to guide her down the cobbled walkway, the guests swaying in time to the band's rendition of Kara's favourite song, 'Sunset Love'.

Kara's hand tightened around his as they made their way down the path of goodwill and celebration of their union. He smiled at Kara's laughter, relieved that so far he had made the right call in planning this goodbye to their guests.

The walkway led them to the palace's private marina and their awaiting families.

Kara dropped her hand from his and stared at *Mistral*, the royal yacht, and its crew, all lined up dockside in order to welcome them aboard. 'Please tell me they're not waiting for us.'

'I did promise you a honeymoon.'

'You said you were too busy.'

'I changed my mind.'

She glanced at all those around them, gave a faint smile towards the crew, and, edging closer to him, whispered, 'You know I get seasick.'

He laughed and gestured to the thirty-three metre boat with its five staterooms. 'I defy even you to get sick aboard *Mistral*. A superyacht is a very different experience to being on a racing yacht. Trust me, you'll be fine, and it's only three days' sailing on the Med.'

She blanched. 'Three days!' She stepped closer to the marina's edge, frowning at the waves. 'Those waves look big…why the hell couldn't we just have gone to some nice hotel or beach? Not that we needed to go away in the first place.'

The sea was choppier than he would have liked, but there was no way he was going to worry her by admitting that. 'You won't feel much movement on board *Mistral*.'

For that he received a disbelieving scowl.

He stepped closer to her. 'I know just how stressful the past few weeks have been for you. You deserve time away, a break.' He held her gaze, his heart swelling with his affection for her, his throat catching. 'It's time we hung out together like we used to, away from the glare of the palace staff and the media.' His throat tightened even more. 'It's time we recaptured our friendship.'

She let out a shaky breath. 'You're right…things have got so confusing.' She swung away to berate Triona, Siza and her parents for keeping the honeymoon secret from her.

Luis was attempting to charm one of Kara's cousins, who rightly was having none of it, so he went over to where his father and Ivo were standing together, not a word passing between them.

His joining them didn't help matters and all three eyed each other warily.

'Best of luck in...' He grimaced, trying to remember where Ivo's next major competitive regatta was to be held. He should have made more time to talk with him.

Ivo studied him and then his father, as though waiting to see if his father knew where his next regatta was.

His father simply shrugged.

'Plovdiv,' Ivo finally answered in a hacked-off tone before he walked away from them.

Edwin eyed his father, who held his gaze unapologetically, a faint tic working in his jaw the only sign of any emotion. He turned away. This whole mess was his fault. He had turned his and Kara's lives upside down.

He went and waited for Kara to join him by the gangway.

She hugged her parents a brief goodbye, but with Triona and Siza she giggled and hung on to them for the longest time.

Why could he never be like that with people? What must it be like to be your true self? Not to feel apart and different?

As heir to the throne, he was always destined to be different. People looked at him differently. Behaved differently around him. People were more of everything around him—more nervous, more gushing, more reserved, more self-conscious. And he had known, for as long as he could remember, that he had to behave appropriately—an inner critic constantly telling him to be careful and proper. An inner critic that over the years had escalated to tight inner control in the aftermath of his mother's death, where he was able to shut himself off from feeling too much for other people.

Kara turned away from her friends.

Rolled her shoulders as though bracing herself.

He rocked back on his heels. A realisation side-sweeping him. With him, Kara *did* hold herself back. It was as though an invisible wall existed between them. Even when they kissed there was a slight reservation, a hesitancy that was right and normal and proper. But it was also the most vulnerable place in the world.

Mistral eased away from the marina wall. Their guests cheered and waved, their blue lights dancing in the air like fireflies.

An explosion filled the air.

Kara jolted and grabbed hold of Edwin.

Gold and purple light filled the air.

Edwin chuckled.

She slapped him on the arm. 'You could have warned me.'

He raised an amused eyebrow. 'Come on, we'll see the display better on the opposite side.' He led her across the upper deck of the yacht, explosions of colours dancing overhead, the gold and purple of Monrosa giving way to the blue and red of the Union flag, and for a while she forgot just how cross she was with Edwin.

But that all changed once they left the natural protection of the harbour and hit the swell.

The boat pitched.

She grabbed the rail. Oh, God, it was only going to get worse once they were really out in open sea.

'I can't believe you thought a sailing holiday would be my idea of fun.' The boat pitched again as they rounded a headland, the swell growing higher. Exhausted from

trying not to let the emotion of the day get to her, terrified she was going to spend the night throwing up, she
added, 'I thought you knew me better.'

Edwin considered her for a moment, clearly trying to
understand where her anger had come from.

Well, good. He could have at least talked this through
with her.

'You're scared. That's understandable.' His mouth
tightened. 'But will you please just trust me on this?'
With that he walked back across the deck and peered towards the building and street lights of the island, which
were increasingly growing dimmer and dimmer.

Her anger deflated like a popped balloon. She felt herself redden. Now she just felt stupid.

Swallowing down her pride, she knew she had to do
the right thing and show some gratitude. She went and
stood next to him. 'How long have you been planning
all of this?' she asked, pushing back the material of her
suit jacket's lapel that had blown forward in the breeze.
The suit was beautifully handcrafted, the silk lining soft
against her skin. 'Who selected this suit? The shoes? Was
it Princess Maria?'

His gaze trained out to sea, he answered, 'I did—
it's that same shade as your eyes. The shoes were the
most practical solution for our journey.' His tone was
distracted.

He chose the suit? *Really?* A shiver ran down her
spine. Here she was worrying about being seasick when
in truth she really should be worried about the prospect of
spending time alone with her new husband. He seemed to
want it to be about them reconnecting as friends, which
she was all up for. But what if they did something stupid like kiss again? Going away together, especially after
last night, was like dancing with the devil. And it didn't

help when he went and did something so cute and adorable and kind as select an outfit for her. One that he obviously had put thought and consideration into. Was he doing all of this just to keep her on-side? She winced at that thought, hating how cynical and wary she had become since Nick. God, she really did have trust issues. Staying well away from relationships really was the best thing for her.

She studied Edwin. What was he scanning the horizon for?

The engine of the yacht cut out. A whirring sound was followed by a splash. Was that the anchor being dropped?

Pointing in the direction of the silhouetted high cliff edges of Monrosa, Edwin said, 'This is where we disembark.'

Disembark? Already? They were miles away from land.

Squinting, she stared in the direction he had pointed in and realised a tiny dot of light was getting ever closer.

She followed Edwin down to the lower deck and then down to the platform at the rear of the boat.

That dot of light turned out to be Domenico and Lucas on board a small boat.

Pulling alongside, Lucas threw a rope to an awaiting crew member, who held the boat tight against the yacht's platform. Domenico held his hand out, gesturing for her to transfer across.

Memories of the blood-curdling heat that had assaulted her insides the time she had been seasick had her hesitate.

A wave hit, pulling the boat away from *Mistral*, a huge gap of black sea opening up just beyond her feet. She stepped back. She was going nowhere.

The crew member and Lucas brought the boat back alongside.

Edwin leapt over onto the boat and held his hand out to her.

'There's no way you're getting me on that inflatable.'

He gave her a bemused look. 'Rib—not an inflatable. And a rib that's used for military patrols worldwide, so it's more than up to the job of transferring us back to Monrosa. When have *you* ever walked with lead feet?'

They were going back to Monrosa? That was a good thing, wasn't it? Was all of this just a hoax? Had he pretended they were going on a honeymoon to avoid speculation as to why they hadn't? Was he playing mind-games with her? Dread knotted in her stomach. Nick had once pretended to be taking her on a trip to Paris, only to cancel it after they had had an argument. She had only learnt he had never even booked their flights when she had broken up with him.

Edwin reached his hand out even further. 'Come on, I'll take care of you. Trust me.'

She studied his hand, both boats rocking in the swell. She trusted him. Of course she did.

'Kara?'

His voice was baffled. He was her friend. She had to trust him. Her feet refused to budge. But he wasn't just her friend any more…he was her husband. And trusting him now took on a whole different perspective. Could she trust him while still protecting her heart, her sanity, her grip on reality?

Enough.

She had to focus on the end game—raising the profile of Young Adults Together and helping Edwin to the throne.

She was allowing herself to get caught up in the emotion and drama of the day again, caught up in the concept of going on honeymoon with her new husband—which didn't look as though it was going to happen anyway, so why was she being such a drama queen?

She grabbed hold of Edwin's hand and leapt, colliding with him, her chest bumping against his. He steadied her, one warm and solid hand on her waist, the other on her back. The heat of his body fused with her limbs. His hold on her tightened. Without thinking she responded by edging her hips against his. The heat of longing fired in her stomach.

He dipped his head, his eyes narrowing as he slowly and silently studied her.

Undone by his nearness, feeling vulnerable under his gaze, she pulled away and attempted to act as though he had no effect on her pulse, which was racing so hard she was struggling to think straight. It felt as though every cell in her body was turned on by him. 'Where should I sit?'

He pointed to a seat at the centre of the boat alongside the cockpit.

Edwin took control of the wheel. She had thought Lucas would resume that duty. He pulled away from *Mistral* at an incredibly slow speed. At this rate they wouldn't reach Monrosa until daybreak.

'You do know what you're doing, right?'

He grinned. 'It was part of my training.'

Got him! 'Your special-forces training, you mean.'

His grin widened and he eased the throttle forward, pulling the rib into a wide arc.

The boat soared over the water. The wind rushed against her, making it difficult to breathe. She gasped. And laughed. The rush of water beneath them, the speed, watching Edwin expertly handle the rib, was exhilarating.

In no time they were slowing as they approached a slipway in an isolated cove.

Two SUVs were waiting for them.

Domenico and Lucas went in one, she and Edwin in the other.

The unpaved road out of the cove was steep and narrow; only a SUV would be capable of accessing the slipway.

At the main road, instead of turning left back towards Monrosa City Edwin turned right. Domenico and Lucas followed behind them.

'Aren't we going back to the palace?'

Edwin threw her a confused look. 'I told you we were going on a honeymoon.'

'Oh, I thought…'

'That I was going back on my word?' He worked his jaw, clearly annoyed. Tense seconds passed, and he shot a look towards her, his expression a horrible mix of disappointment and irritation. But then, with a shrug of his shoulder, he smiled. 'Sorry, but you're stuck with me for three whole days. I'll try to make it as painless as possible for you.'

Forty minutes later, having followed a hairpin-bend-laden road up into the mountains, they passed through the gates of Edwin's family's mountain villa, the sentries on duty saluting.

So this was where they would honeymoon.

She laid her head against the headrest and gave an internal sigh. She was a mountain girl. Walking amongst the towering pines and eucalyptus trees, the only sound coming from the breeze swooping through the valleys, trickling streams, and hidden birds happy to share their voices with the world, restored her. Being surrounded by this landscape that had existed for millennia before her always pulled her up to a sharp stop, grounding her in the reminder of just how transient life was and to be grateful for every day she got to enjoy it. But this would be different. They would be staying in a royal residence with all of its reminders of protocol. What she wouldn't give not to have to be on her best behaviour, to not have to act as if they were a loved-up couple on their honeymoon.

On a turn in the road, the vast royal residence in the distance, Edwin shot off the lit road and onto a narrow lane she had never spotted before.

Studying the side mirror, she said, 'You need to stop—we've lost Domenico and Lucas.'

'That was the plan. We're going to be on our own for the next three days.'

On their own? That was what she had just been long-ing for. Why, then, did it fill her with terror rather than relief? 'Please tell me we aren't going camping.'

He shook his head. 'Why are you being so cranky?'

She gave an indignant huff. But then did a mental eye roll. He was right. She was being cranky…and crabby and grouchy. She hated this side of herself. But being around Edwin nowadays she just felt this defensive force field around herself and it just seemed natural to be surly.

She needed to snap out of it. She held up her hand, her fingers in the Girl Guide pledge position she had learnt years ago. 'I promise to try harder and not moan even when I wake from dreaming of drinking cocktails on some tropical beach, only to find myself in a bug-infested tent.'

He grinned. 'That's more like it—it's good to see the old Kara back: good-humoured with an undertone of sarcasm.'

She snorted.

Edwin's eyes twinkled, and his grin grew even wider. She grinned back, heat infusing her limbs.

They climbed even further up into the mountain. Kara opened her window, the trees of the forest zipping by, and a perturbing mix of fear and exhilaration filled her bones at not only their crazy speed but also at the prospect of being alone with Edwin for three whole days.

The road ended at a set of wooden gates.

Edwin zapped them open.

Beyond the gates the road dipped down in a curve that brought them to a circular driveway.

Edwin killed the engine.

A light shone over a solitary wooden door of a flat-roofed, metal-panelled structure.

'We're staying in a shed?'

He opened his door. 'Well, that promise didn't last long.'

She climbed out of the car and joined Edwin on the gravelled driveway. He pressed a button on his phone. The door popped open.

Inside, the shed was in darkness. Edwin gestured for her to step inside. She folded her arms and refused to budge. 'This isn't where you turn out to be a psycho husband who holds me captive against my will in a shed in an isolated forest, is it?'

He raised an eyebrow, his smile suddenly as sexy as hell. 'It can be arranged if that's a fantasy of yours.' A look of pure masculine heat she had never seen before entered his eyes, setting alight a wild longing in her belly. 'I'm sure there are some ropes in the shed.'

Something very carnal and dangerous melted inside her. She sprang towards the door and leapt inside.

A row of internal lights, domino-style, lit up down the length of the building.

She gasped.

This was no shed.

She walked further into the long and narrow interior, agog at the gorgeous ultra-modern open-plan space. The walls, with the exception of the narrow entrance, were made of huge floor-to-ceiling glass doors. The modern kitchen was made from pale wood, the counter tops the same poured light-grey concrete as the floors. In the living area, two sofas covered in duckling-yellow fabric surrounded a wood-burning stove.

Edwin opened up a row of doors that folded back to reveal decking made from the same wood as the kitchen.

Walking out onto the deck, running the entire length of the building, she said, 'I can't believe that I thought this was a shed! It's absolutely stunning.'

The building was stretched like a bridge between two rocky banks, a stream running beneath the house.

Before them, the forest tumbled down the mountain-side. Kara inhaled deeply, greedily sucking in the heavily pine-scented air.

'Do you like it?'

She turned at Edwin's question. She gestured around her and laughed. 'This is my idea of heaven. Of course I love it.'

'Good. It's my wedding present to you.'

Kara watched him turn away and walk inside, her mouth open.

She rushed after him as he walked towards the far end of the house, which they had not yet explored.

She caught up with him at a bedroom door. 'But all I got you was a set of cufflinks.'

He leant against the door frame. 'You're forgetting the *How To Be a Good Husband* guide that came with them.'

'I hope you took note of point five—"Let her know you realise how lucky you are to have her as your wife".'

'Duly noted. My legal team have the paperwork ready for you to sign to give you full ownership of Villa Kara.'

She swung her arms up into the air in horror. 'Villa Kara! Are you serious? You have to change that name and I can't accept a villa from you. This was never mentioned in the pre-nup. You know I don't want anything when we divorce.'

'You just said you love it here—as I had hoped you would.' He folded his arms. 'Are you saying you're refusing my wedding present to you?'

How did he manage to make it sound as though she was being thoroughly unreasonable and ungrateful? When it was he who was at fault here? 'It's way too generous, and what happens when we split up? I can hardly drive through your family's property to get here.'

'Why not?'

'Because it'll be as awkward as hell.'

His amused expression disappeared. He straightened from his relaxed leaning against the door frame. 'When we divorce...if we divorce—that's still your decision to make—you'll still be an important part of my life.'

She sagged against the opposite wall, suddenly feeling exhausted. She dipped her head, uncertainty and fear sweeping through her, causing her heart to contract as though it was under attack. She should let this go. She knew she should. Just continue pretending they'd resume life as before, pretending their friendship was not already damaged by this whole experience. 'Do you really think we will be able to part so amicably—without any hurt or complications?'

Those golden eyes considered her for long silent seconds. She resisted the urge to cry, to laugh. How had she ended up in the position where she was being torn between the desire to kiss this man and to punch him for not feeling the same confusion and turmoil as she did? Had their kisses had any emotional impact on him?

'It's up to us to make sure we part amicably.' With that he turned and walked into the bedroom.

Like the living area it had floor-to-ceiling windows overlooking the forest. Edwin went and opened one of the two doors either side of the king-size bed, draped in crisp white cotton linen and accented with a green throw and cushions. 'This is your dressing room—your bathroom is on the other side. Your luggage was brought here earlier.'

It was disconcerting to see the faded black jeans she had bought in a shop in Brighton hanging from the rail, a solid crease line running the length of both legs showing that someone had carefully ironed them.

Her gaze moved to the bed. And then back to Edwin.

He cleared his throat. 'My bedroom is across the corridor.'

So they wouldn't be sleeping in the same bed on their wedding night after all. It made sense and would eliminate any awkwardness. Why, then, did it feel like a rejection?

She breathed in deeply. Stepped back to make space for him to leave. Smiled. 'It's been a long day—I need a shower and sleep. A lot of sleep. I'm exhausted. Worn out.'

She stopped. He had probably got the point the first time.

He nodded and moved towards the door.

She breathed in hard when he passed her. Was about to exhale, but he came to a stop a footstep beyond her. He turned. 'Please tell me you'll accept Villa Kara? It's important to me.'

Her entire body tingled from having him stand so

close by, by the appeal of his gaze that was utterly focused and determined. 'Why?'

'Because it will mean that you'll still want to be in my life.'

She closed her eyes, uncertainty, confusion, sheer bewilderment over the beautiful intention of his words clashing with her fears for the future of their relationship.

She opened her eyes. 'The first thing I'm going to do is change its name—Villa Kara is one hundred per cent cringe.'

CHAPTER NINE

Sitting on the stone ledge, her feet dangling in the stream, Kara tossed her head back to catch the rays of sunlight breaking through the overhead tree canopy. Her denim cut-offs suited her perfectly and her white halter-neck… well, as much as he hated to admit it, it was troublingly sexy. It was just a piece of simple white cotton after all, but the way it pulled on her chest, its cut exposing all but a few inches of her shoulders, got to him in a way it shouldn't.

The sun caught the platinum shades in her hair, the ends brushing against the dusty surface of the ledge.

How was he going to cope with sharing a bed with her when back in the city? When they returned to the reality of their lives away from this oasis of escape?

They had spent three days trekking in the mountains by day, cooking meals together and playing poker at night, Kara cheekily refusing to admit she tried to cheat every single time. Three days of conversation and teasing. Three days of pretending she wasn't getting under his skin. Yesterday he had become obsessed at the idea of undoing the pearl buttons of the blue embroidered blouse she had been wearing and had even burnt himself when distracted as they had been preparing dinner, scorching the tip of his finger on a hot pan. Three days of resisting the urge to kiss her, of averting his gaze from her bottom when she trekked ahead of him. Three days of resisting the urge to hunker down to retie her laces, which she never knotted properly, knowing that if he knelt before her his fingers would trail against the now lightly tanned skin of her legs, trace over the small brown birthmark at the back of her right knee. Three days of his heart dancing to hear her laughter, to see her blue eyes widen in amazement when a red kite swooped close to where they had been picnicking, her hand reaching for his. Three days of quickly ending their celebratory hugs when they reached the summit of their climbs.

And two nights of her closing her bedroom door to him.

Two nights of sitting out on the terrace staring at the stars, unable to sleep, listening to a nightjar filling the air with its constant song.

Two nights of journeying through that labyrinth of hopes and fears and thoughts in the middle of the night, of wondering if the chemistry, those fleeting looks that electrified him, were all in his imagination or if she bore their curse too.

Dio! To think that a week ago he had actually considered cancelling his tour to Asia. Now it was his lifeline. In two days' time they would make their first appearance together as a married couple when they attended the opening of a new conservation centre in Monrosa's protected wetlands, named in honour of his mother. And the day after, he would leave for Asia. Ten days away would clear his head, give him the space to get back on track with this marriage of convenience.

They had one more night alone before they returned to the city. He *had* to continue keeping his distance from her.

He dropped the picnic blanket to the ground. Her eyes popped open and she smiled. 'Hi.'

He nodded back, unfurling a picnic blanket beside her, trying to steady his pulse. When she was so obviously delighted to see him it did crazy things to his heart.

Kara edged onto the blanket and he sat beside her, dipping his own bare feet into the stream. Maybe the icy water would cool the heat in his body.

Lifting her feet from the water, she wriggled her toes. 'You'll be glad to hear my feet are no longer aching.'

Her toes were long, her feet narrow with a delicate arch. She lifted her feet even higher, circling them. Her ankles were slim, her calf muscles toned.

What would it be like to have her legs wrapped around his?

He grabbed the champagne bottle from the basket, popped it open. He passed her a glass.

She sighed. 'This is heaven.'

For the next half an hour they drank the champagne and nibbled on the fresh bread they had baked together that morning, using an olive-oil-based recipe Kara swore by. The sun was gentle, the birdsong and sound of the water pressing over the boulders in the stream hypnotic. A lazy sense of calm had his body grow increasingly heavy, his thoughts drowsy.

Champagne finished, Kara lay back on the blanket with a sigh and he joined her, the hard stone beneath him a welcome solidness. They lay with their feet side by side, drying them on the edge of the rock ledge.

Kara swayed her bent knees side to side, her hands on her belly, her gaze in his direction, a wide smile on her mouth. 'I think the champagne has gone to my head.'

'Mine too,' he admitted. 'I guess the long trek and lack of lunch probably didn't help.'

Above them a buzzard soared in the thermals.

His heart rate upped a gear. Without looking he knew Kara was staring at him. He closed his eyes. He was *not* going to look in her direction. He should make some excuse and leave.

'I'm very jealous of your long eyelashes, you know.'

He opened his eyes and turned to her. Her eyes held a soft, dewy tone. Her lips glistened as though the champagne had seeped into them. Gentle heat infused her cheeks.

Her hand shifted off her belly and onto the blanket between them. 'I'll miss you when you're away.'

He sucked in some air. *Dio!* He really should head back to the villa. 'And I'll miss you.'

Why had he said that? Because it was true.

Qualify it... Don't go down a road that will be hard to come back from.

'Touring can be boring—it would be nice to have you there for company.'

She looked away from him but not before he saw the disappointment that dispatched her smile.

She bit her lip for a moment before saying, 'And I have the Pink Heart's charity ball to attend. It will be my first official duty on my own.' She looked back at him, gave a shrug. 'I'll miss having your guidance.'

'I've asked Princess Maria to travel with you to the ball and sit at the same table.'

She gave a fleeting smile. 'Thank you.'

His hand found hers on the blanket.

Her eyes widened. He held his breath, waiting for her reaction. Her fingers threaded through his.

A question appeared in her gaze.

'I guess it's understandable that things might get a

little muddled between us at the start of the marriage,'
he said.

'Muddled?'

'The emotion of the wedding, being alone, neither of
us having been in a relationship for a long time...our hormones, our feelings, are getting muddled up.'

She nodded eagerly. 'And the champagne isn't helping either.'

Why is this...this...? Dio! *Call it what it is. Why is this
flirting so damn enjoyable?*

He cleared his throat, his eyes glued to her mouth,
memories of what it was like to kiss her heading straight
to his groin. 'I want to kiss you.'

She shifted onto her side. 'Good.'

He released her hand. Moved onto his side too, edged
up to her. Ran his hand through her hair. It was warm.
As was her cotton top. Even the denim of her shorts held
the heat of the day. He placed his hand on her bottom.
Pulled her even closer. Found her mouth with a groan.

They kept it soft and exploratory for the whole of ten
seconds.

Then her hand clasped against his skull, her mouth
opening for him.

He rolled onto his back, taking her with him. And saw
stars when her body rocked against his. He held tight,
his arms on her back, one hand cupping her bottom, the
other a sharp shoulder blade, wanting to meld her to him.

Within a minute things were seriously getting out of
control. Kara was moaning against his mouth, her legs
twisted around his. Her chest pressed against his was the
sweetest, most dangerous, most tempting thing that had
ever entered his life.

His thumb stroked the side of her breast. Her body
shuddered.

Her mouth shifted away from his and began to trail down his throat, her lips scorching the skin beneath his open-neck T-shirt.

Her hands trailed even further south.

Pleasure blasted through him. With a groan he pulled her back up towards him, cradling her face in his hands. 'We can't.'

Her expression shifted from unseeing desire to frustration to disappointment and finally acceptance on a long inhale of breath.

She rolled off him.

He held her hand. 'Are you okay?'

'In a few minutes I will be.' She rolled her eyes. 'These blasted hormones—they have a lot to answer for.'

He sat up, allowed his blood pressure to settle and stood up.

He yanked off his T-shirt and then his shorts.

Kara gawked at him, a hand covering her mouth.

He spun around and jumped into the deep pool of water beyond a large boulder, a spray soaring upwards as he plunged beneath the cold water.

Even submerged, he heard Kara's shriek.

CHAPTER TEN

THE CENTRAL COURTYARD of the Senator Hotel had been transformed into a Viennese ballroom. Chandeliers hung from invisible wires, and a full orchestra played on the temporary stage. Dancing with Javier Ventosa, a paediatrician consultant at Monrosa's University Hospital, Kara tried to focus on her steps and turns, her head spinning at the quick rotations, only too aware Princess Maria was following her every move, just as she had done all week when she had supervised Kara's dance lessons.

Mastering the steps of the Viennese waltz had been excruciatingly slow, she had tripped over her dance teacher, Horacio, more times than she could count and she had used the feeble excuse that she was more of a rugby girl to explain to Princess Maria her lack of progress when in truth it was her nephew who had stolen her concentration away.

They had been so close to making love. And a week on, her focus was still shot and a throb of unfulfilled lust was making her rubber-boned. A week on and she still couldn't strip him from her mind, that image of him yanking off his top and shorts and plunging into the stream, soaking her in the process, playing on a constant loop. He had emerged all wet, glistening muscle, frustration etched on his face.

In silence he had walked away from her and she had collapsed back onto the ledge, weak with the need for more.

Dinner that night had been tense. Their conversation had been halting and awkward and full of things unsaid.

When he had left for Vietnam, his hug goodbye had been brief and she had watched him get into the car taking him to the airport and had winced at the relief that had swept over his expression.

He had wanted to get away.

Mortified by his relief, she had thrown herself into work, into settling into her new life in Monrosa, taken dance lessons in advance of tonight, and spent her evenings walking the interior of the palace and grounds, trying to familiarise herself with her new home.

A few times she had considered travelling to Villa Kara, driven by the need to find some antidote to the constant confusion settling into her bones. Confusion driven by his infrequent calls to her, which were full of facts but absent of any real truth between them.

The mountains usually brought her peace and in the private isolation of Villa Kara she might have been able to eke out some calmness. But memories of their stay there had kept her away. Memories of how Edwin had looked every morning when she had opened her bedroom door to find him freshly showered and preparing breakfast in the kitchen, his good-morning smile managing to ignite a furnace of happiness inside of her. Memories of his deep laughter when she had got stuck when rock climbing, but then his calm words of encouragement in guiding her back down.

Trying to create a new life in a new country, the pressures of royal life, trying to map out precisely how she was going to turn Young Adults Together into an effective global charity, were all making her vulnerable… and if her past history was anything to go by, when she was stressed and confused she was prone to making bad decisions. Very bad decisions. Decisions like sleeping with Edwin even though it would torpedo any hopes of their maintaining their friendship when this was all over. Some people managed to remain friends with their exes but there was no way she could do it. She simply didn't have the emotional toughness for it. She would find it impossible not to feel exposed and heart-sore knowing what once had been there.

See, this was why she wasn't cut out for relationships— she just became an emotional mess when embroiled in them. She was better off in the safety of singledom. She needed time to adjust to her new reality. Time to let the emotional fever inflamed by what the media had called a fairy-tale wedding ceremony and the promises they had made in public, die away.

The music came to a stop.

Javier bowed his thanks to her for accepting his invitation to dance. He was an incredibly attractive man… and single too. But not one cell in her body seemed capable of responding to his dark looks and charming smile.

She accepted his hand and offer to escort her back to her table.

But then she dropped his hand, the hairs on the back of her neck standing to attention.

Javier stepped back and bowed to someone behind her.

And backed away.

A dovecote-full of fluttering exploded in her stomach.

'I never knew my wife could dance so well.'

Longing pure and unadulterated flushed through her body at his low whisper.

She swung around. She wanted to throw herself into his arms but caught herself in time.

Instead she smiled at him goofily, heat blasting her cheeks. 'You're home.'

All through her dance with Javier, whom he had first met when opening the new children's wing of MUH, Edwin had stayed in the shadows of the courtyard watching Kara as she glided across the floor in Javier's arms. Lust and jealousy had him barely clinging to his sanity. He had wanted to march onto the dance floor and interrupt the dance midway, demand the right to dance with his wife.

His wife. His beautiful wife. *Dio!* Her ballgown was the sexiest thing he had ever seen. It was a dress that summed up her personality—the pale blue, close to silver tulle skirt overlaid with floral appliqué, cute and lovely just as she was, the plunging front and back the hidden side of her that was all heat and passion.

'You're home.'

Had words ever seemed so sweet, so right, so layered with danger?

He searched for some light-hearted response, but the delight shining in Kara's eyes stole every word away.

He held out his hand and invited her to dance with him.

Around them, other couples who had already begun to circle the dance floor smiled fondly at their reunion.

She stepped into his arms. He longed to be able to pull her close, anchor her to him, but the waltz demanded an exasperating distance be kept between their bodies.

'Why are you home early?' she asked.

'There's still a lot of work that has to be done in preparation for my succession.'

And I missed you.

'How was Hanoi?'

'Hot and chaotic but very beautiful. I loved it there.'

He *had* loved Hanoi, but he had felt flat there. He had longed to have Kara by his side, experiencing the infectious chaos of the city and the stunning beauty of the surrounding countryside. He had missed her laughter, the appraising sweep of her blue gaze, the way his body tingled when she was in the same room. *Dio*, he was so sick of pretending his feelings for Kara had not changed, when they had. She was no longer just a friend. She was his wife. Lying in his hotel bedroom two nights ago, he had finally admitted to himself that he wanted her. As a husband wanted a wife. He wanted to sleep with her, mouth against mouth, breath against breath, skin against skin.

The pretending had to stop.

'I missed you,' he said.

Her gaze shot up to meet his. She frowned as though she was trying to decipher the true meaning of his words.

Her lips parted. Those glorious soft lips… Thoughts of what they were capable of had tormented his dreams for the past week.

The music came to an end. Instead of stepping back, Kara touched her fingers against the skin above his shirt collar, an intimate move that had relief and raw need buckling his knees. 'I missed you too.'

He gathered her closer. Placed a kiss on her neck, just below her ear.

They stayed on the dance floor until the orchestra played the final song of the night. They said their goodbyes to the event organisers and he led her out of the private exit, where Álvaro and Marco, their assigned protection officers, were waiting for them. Domenico and Lucas had made a poor attempt at disguising their delight when he had announced he was cutting his trip short. Their eagerness to get home to their families had sent his head into a spin. Why was he jealous of something he didn't want?

He had told them to take the next three days off work.

They drove in silence through the streets of Monrosa. Tourists and locals, leaving the restaurants of the old town, stopped to stare as the outriders passed them by, grabbing their phones to snatch a photo as their SUV driven by Álvaro swept past.

He held Kara's hand, her fingers clasping his tight.

Back at their apartment, he instructed both Simone his valet and Cecilia, Kara's dresser, who were awaiting their return, that their services weren't needed.

He brought her into the drawing room, knowing he was at a fork in the road that was his life.

He gestured towards the drinks cabinet but Kara shook her head.

This would be their first night of needing to share a bed.

The decisions he would take, *they* would take, in the next few minutes could alter their lives for ever.

But they were both adults. Capable of handling uncharted territory.

He cleared his throat. Lost for words.

Kara touched her hand to her breastbone, giving him an uncertain and fleeting smile.

'Tonight...' he faltered.

She moved forward from where she had been balancing her fingertips against the side table filled with gold and silver framed family photographs towards the marble fireplace. 'Yes?'

There was a new framed photograph on the side table. He went and lifted the heavy silver frame. It was a signed photograph from their wedding photographer, Patrizia

Mauro, of them waving to the crowd as they had emerged from the cathedral. Kara's eyes were sparkling. The perfect image of a bride overcome with emotion. He cleared his throat again. 'Tonight...we'll be sharing a bed.'

Kara inhaled deeply. 'Yes.'

He winced at the dread in her voice. 'I can sleep on the floor...'

'No! Of course not.'

It really was time for the pretending to stop. He bunched his hands.

But would the truth destroy everything?

'If we sleep in the same bed...'

He lowered the frame to the table, catching a glimpse of his parents' wedding photograph. They had had a good marriage despite its having been arranged. Could Kara and he come to some sort of arrangement that would work for them?

'I'm attracted to you and I've missed you. I want to kiss you again. And I'd prefer for it not to stop there.' Unsteadied by his admission, he paused. Had he just made the biggest, most embarrassing blunder of his life?

He waited for Kara to say something, but instead she walked past him and out into the corridor.

He followed her, unsure what was happening.

In their bedroom, she stood at the near edge of the bed, her back to him. 'Cecilia was going to help me undress, so I'll need you to unbutton my gown for me.'

A lick of desire travelled the length of his body at the huskiness of her voice. He fumbled with the button holding the material tight to her waist, his fingers beating like nervous bats against her lower back. The button, once he got his fingers under control, gave way easily. He shifted his head down to her ear. 'I'm guessing you could have easily undone that yourself.'

She shivered, her neck tilting away from his breath. 'Yes, but there would have been no fun in that, would there?'

He touched a finger to her spine. She arched her back. 'I've spent the entire week away thinking about you.'

She twisted her head. Her eyes, even in the faint light cast by the single lamp in the corner, glittered. 'In a good way, I hope.'

'I'm afraid not.' He liked her groaned response. A lot. His fingertip bumped over the knots of her spine and then his whole hand fanned out to sweep across the edge of her shoulder blade, his skin tingling at the soft warmth of her body.

He edged the material of her dress off her shoulders. She drew her head back and whispered, 'Tell me what you've been thinking.'

He touched his lips to her collarbone. 'Our kiss, the pattern of your ribs,' he edged closer to her neck, he nipped her skin between his teeth, chuckled to hear her moan, 'your sighs of pleasure when I touch somewhere tender.'

She turned to him, her hands holding the material of her dress from falling down. Fire and energy radiated from her. 'Tell me what you want.'

'I want to make love to you.'

She nodded. Dropped her hands. Her dress fell to the floor.

She stood before him, naked except for pale blue panties.

He drew in a breath. She was more beautiful than he had ever imagined.

She arched her back and, reaching up, released her hair from its coil. It tumbled down over her shoulders.

He undid his bow tie. Pointed to the buttons of his dress shirt. 'Your turn.'

CHAPTER ELEVEN

CRUSHED SHEETS. Aching and deliciously heavy bones.

Kara grinned and twisted onto her side. Sleep called to her, but just out of reach gorgeous memories wound their way through her dazed brain.

She sighed.

'Your sighs of pleasure when I touch somewhere tender...'

Her eyes shot open. The room was in darkness. Water was running in the bathroom.

She curled the top sheet over her head and groaned. What had she done?

Had she really done those things with Edwin? She flung the sheet back, struggling for air.

Everything was going to be okay.

This was still a marriage of convenience. Their relationship might have shifted off centre from friendship but the roller coaster of emotions, the power play, the constant threat of heartache that came with a full-blown relationship wouldn't apply to them.

The water was switched off. Shadows moved on the white marble floor of the bathroom.

She sat up in the bed, yanking the sheet up to her shoulders. Would she have time to dash into the dressing room? No! She couldn't bear the thought of him seeing her naked.

Why didn't you care last night, when it mattered? Because you were lost to the joy of seeing him again? Lost in the intimacy of his words, his touch? Lost to the chemistry that experiencing the powerful act of marrying had unleashed on you?

She had to play it cool. Not freak out. Not overthink all of this.

The bathroom door swung fully open.

Edwin stood there, a towel tight on his narrow hips, beads of moisture on his chest.

He gave her a devastating, satisfied smile that slowly morphed into a tender, almost bashful grin. He tilted his head, ran a towel over his hair and walked towards the bed. 'Good morning, my lovely wife.'

A storm of panic passed through her.

'We made a mistake.'

His smile evaporated.

'What?'

His hair was all tousled and sexy. But his expression was one hundred per cent perplexed.

She shivered despite the fact that her insides were scorching, churning chaos.

'We shouldn't have slept together.'

He flicked a hand over his hair, fixing it into position, his mouth tightening. 'Why?'

She didn't know why. She just knew she was drowning in panic. What was the matter with her? Why was she saying these things? Her panic rose like a tide that would never recede. 'You know why. It's just going to make our divorce more complicated.'

He flung the towel towards the bathroom. It hit the door frame and smacked onto the wooden floor of the bedroom. 'Are you saying you regret sleeping with me?'

She closed her eyes. 'No.'

'So what are you saying?'

Put some clothes on. I can't think straight, remembering how my hands, my lips, touched every inch of you. How I refused to stop even when you begged me to. I needed to know every inch of you. I wanted to know you... I've spent a decade wanting to know you. I've spent a decade wanting to love you.

Unable to breathe, she blinked.

I love you. Oh, God, I love you. This can't be happening. I'm messing everything up. And if you find out I'll just want to die. Will you feel sorry for me? Will you find excuses to walk away? Or will you, like Nick, use it against me?

She lifted the sheet even higher, gathering the edges around her neck. 'Don't you think it was a mistake?'

His mouth tightened even more. He turned away, grabbed the towel from the floor, disappeared into the bathroom for a moment, returned and then went into his dressing room.

An agonising time later he emerged, flicked on her bedside lamp and studied her. He had changed into a dark grey suit, silver tie and white shirt. Brooding and hacked off.

He knows! Her cheeks flamed. 'I'm sorry.'

His mouth tightened. And then with a sigh he sat down on the bed beside her.

She wanted to leap out of the bed, escape from him, but she was naked, and she and her shredded dignity couldn't handle the thought of him analysing every imperfection of her body as she wobbled towards the bathroom.

He dipped his head, his hand moved as though to touch her leg beneath the sheet but he grabbed it back. They had made love endless times during the night, drunk on physical release. Drunk on whispered words of discovery, of tenderness between two people who knew each other but whose souls, whose secret internal selves were a mystery they were just discovering.

He looked back up, his expression closed. 'Last night wasn't a mistake. We're attracted to one another.' He paused and shrugged as though that fact was of little significance. 'These things happen when two people are in close proximity. Let's keep it in perspective. It was one night.' He stood up, his expression emotionless. 'It doesn't have to happen again.'

She faked a smile, while her heart was on the floor. 'I guess we got it out of our systems.'

He shrugged again, and, taking his phone from his pocket, he checked the screen and frowned. 'I have a cabinet meeting I need to attend.'

Halfway towards the bedroom door, he turned around. 'Will you be okay?'

She heard the concern in his voice. She nodded. 'Of course.'

He left the room and she closed her eyes, curling onto her side, inhaling his scent on the sheets.

She was in love with him. She was in love with her husband.

She closed her eyes, hating the vulnerability of that. Hating that it weakened her, made her susceptible to so much pain and humiliation and disappointment.

She jerked the sheet back, sprang out of the bed and in the bathroom switched on the shower. Her diary was full for the day. If Edwin could walk away from last night so easily, then she sure as hell was going to do the same thing. How many times had she seen her dad reach out to her mum, only to be rejected and humiliated? How many times had she tried to please Nick, only to encounter a snide comment or whatever mind game he had decided to indulge in that day?

She was not going to humiliate herself. She was going to behave with dignity and pride both within this marriage and when it was time for them to separate.

And just maybe, with the passage of time and aided by Edwin's interpretation of last night as having been of no particular consequence, she might be able to stuff her feelings for him so deep inside of her, even she would be able to disregard them.

Edwin's father glared at the organisation chart he had just distributed to the cabinet so intently Edwin wouldn't have been surprised if it spontaneously combusted.

'These changes aren't necessary. You're overcomplicating things. Why on earth do we need a social-media team, a technology minister?' His voice growing ever louder, his father added, 'A diversity and equality minister? What on earth will *his* contribution be?'

'*Her* contribution, you mean. I have already selected a candidate for the role—Sofia Dati, Professor of Equality Studies at Monrosa University.'

Pausing, he studied the cabinet he was inheriting from his father, the majority of whom were men who had been in their roles for far too long.

'It's my intention to reshuffle this cabinet too. Reassign roles. Change the nature of each department's responsibilities to reflect the challenges we face as a country—our need to be more responsive and responsible to the environment, the changing diversity of our population and the need for a more advanced communication infrastructure that will attract even more companies to our business hubs.'

His patience thin, his ability to concentrate even thinner, he cut across his father before he could utter a word of objection, 'We've covered enough ground for today. I'm calling an end to this cabinet session.'

The ministers were regarding him with a variety of expressions from nervous to aghast and outraged. He couldn't afford to alienate them, not with their experience and influence within the country, which he would need in the coming months. He had to bring them with him on this journey of change, even if it meant dragging some of them kicking and screaming into the twenty-first century. 'I will meet with each of you individually to discuss aligning your experience and interests with the new structure. Change can be daunting, but we have to embrace it to ensure we are meeting the needs of our people. We have an exciting future ahead of us.'

At least a few of those around the table smiled at his words—albeit nervously.

He left the cabinet room, his footsteps the only sound. Even his father seemed to have been stunned into silence.

He walked in the direction of his offices. He had a call with the Swedish Trade Minister in an hour. Then a meeting with his own Finance Minister and his team, where discussions on budget reallocations would undoubtedly get heated. A meeting after that with the succession-ceremony logistics team.

He needed to remain focused and present. And not give in to the disbelief pounding through him.

He entered his outer offices, Victor's team all turning in his direction. Maribel, his travel coordinator, stood up, holding a pile of documentation in her grasp.

He couldn't do this. He couldn't discuss his trip next month to Washington.

He backed out of the room.

Out in the corridor he flung open the nearest door into the gardens.

He bolted down the terraces, ignoring the curious glances from the gardening team, until he came to the waterfront.

He sucked in air greedily but the tightness in his chest refused to give.

He cursed, the thin layer of denial that had got him through the cabinet meeting melting. To be replaced by the sharp kick of shame.

He had let himself down. He had let his country down. And, most importantly of all, he had let Kara down. She had agreed to their marriage in good faith. She hadn't signed up for him to seduce her.

No wonder she had immediately regretted it, considered it a mistake.

What had he expected? That she would have been happy with the fantasy he had imagined in the shower this morning of them sleeping in the same bed every night and fulfilling each other's needs?

He had walked out of the bathroom intending to wake Kara by kissing the length of her spine, and instead had faced her bruised eyes and horrified expression.

Maybe he should be grateful that at least one of them was thinking straight and saw it for the mistake that it was rather than feeling as though someone had punctured his ego and kicked it down the street like a rusty old can.

He had to make this right. Do the correct thing after a night of making the wrong decision over and over again.

He found her in her office, staring out of the window towards the internal courtyard.

Was she thinking of their engagement announcement out there? Their first kiss?

He called out her name.

She startled and whipped around. Wearing wide-legged pink trousers and a white blouse, her hair tied back in a ponytail, the crispness of her appearance was in sharp contrast to the tiredness in her eyes.

He worked his jaw, hating the unease between them. 'We can separate.'

Her head jerked back. 'Is that what you want?'

No, what I want is to kiss you, to bring you back to my bed and lose myself in you like I did last night. I want to go back in time to when our relationship was easy and straight forward. When I hadn't been pulled under into a world of chaos by the chemistry that our first kiss, out there in that courtyard, unleashed.

'What I want isn't of importance.'

Kara's expression tightened. 'I asked you a question Edwin, do you want to separate?'

'If it will make you happier.'

She folded her arms. 'It was a yes or no question.'

He cleared his throat, frustration bubbling up inside of him. Why was she making this so hard? He should lie, make all of this easier. But the least she deserved was his honesty. 'No I don't want us to separate but after last night—'

'Why?'

He swallowed and blurted out, 'Because I want to somehow make this right, and if we separate now it probably won't ever be right between us again.'

She winced and on a long sigh she considered him. Her eyes were so terribly sad.

He had really got this all so wrong.

'What do you mean by "make this right"?'

'I want things to go back to where they were, when we were friends.'

Seconds passed. She studied him with a perplexed

expression. She went and stared down to an open diary on her desk. 'I have a teleconference call in ten minutes with a Greek mental health charity who are interested in rolling out the Young Adults Together model as part of their work.' Her gaze swept up to meet his, her expression cool. 'I'd like to think we are both mature enough to put the importance of our work before any regrets.'

CHAPTER TWELVE

THE SCRAPE OF a door handle turning. Silence. Eyes closed, she waited for the mattress to compress. But there was only a stillness. She opened her eyes. The bed beside her was empty. She darted a look at the door, listened for a sound from the bathroom. Nothing. Had she imagined the door opening?

Her hand moved out, patting the cool sheets, the vast emptiness.

Where was he?

Disorientated but knowing it was some time in the early hours of the morning, she grappled to turn on the bedside lamp. Then fumbled for her phone in the bedside locker drawer.

Her hands shook. He had *never* not come to bed in the two weeks since they'd slept together.

She typed out a message.

Where are you?

Waiting, desperate for the phone to ping, she imagined him in an accident. Had he gone out on his motorbike? What if he was with another woman? No. He wouldn't do that.

Her phone pinged. She jolted, the chime an invasion of the silence of the room.

I'm in my office.

She hurled the phone across the bed. The bed where they had explored each other's bodies. She sprang off the mattress and, pulling on her dressing gown, she bolted out of the bedroom and across the corridor.

Her dress, on a silk padded clothes hanger, hung from the dark wood freestanding mirror of her old bedroom, which nowadays functioned as her hair and make-up room. Later this morning a team would once again magically transform her from Kara Duffy to Her Serene Highness, Princess of Monrosa.

Transform her on the outside. Inside she knew she was a fraud. Pretending to be a princess. Acting out, in an ever so careful and measured way her love and devotion for her new husband, desperately hiding the truth of her real, visceral love for him. Especially from him.

And today was what it was all about. His enthronement. The first day he would reign as Monarch of Monrosa.

She eyed her dress for the ceremony again. It was a dress that simply was. It made no demands. No statement. Below-the-knee length with cap sleeves, the ivory cotton tweed shot with threads of gold, it was elegant and understated. It conformed. It was a grown-up's dress in the serious world of power and politics and duty and service.

It represented everything she had to become.

She touched the soft tweed, tiredness washing over her. She should go back to bed. Today was going to be exhausting with both the enthronement and the celebration ball afterwards to attend. An entire day of public scrutiny where she had to act the dutiful and proud wife and hide her constant heartache, her real, authentic, frantic, soul-destroying love for her husband.

She turned, her steps immediately faltering.

Edwin was standing at the door.

She pulled the lace edges of her dressing gown together, feeling exposed in her nightwear while Edwin was dressed in black trousers and a lightweight black cashmere jumper. Gorgeous in a tired and crumpled way.

For a nanosecond she felt tenderness for him. She wanted to hold his hand and lead him to their bed. Hold him while he slept.

But then a wave of anger, of fear, of raw vulnerability swept through her. 'If you decide not to come home, at least have the courtesy to tell me.'

He blinked at her fury. 'We need to talk.'

He wasn't only exhausted, he was also nervous. Was he about to end their marriage? Their friendship? Was he too worn out by the pretence of their marriage?

She lifted her chin. Determined to be dignified. She would *never* let him even glimpse her devastation.

He held up the ivory sheet of paper in his hand, the crown's gold insignia on the top. 'My enthronement pledge. I'd like to read it to you.'

Where was this conversation going? She wanted to say no. She was in no mood to talk about his enthronement but, seeing how his hand trembled as he held out the heavy page towards her, appealing for her to say yes, she nodded.

'I do here solemnly swear to govern the people of Monrosa in accordance with the laws and customs of our country. I promise to rule with fairness and integrity, serving to the best of my ability, always with the utmost honesty.'

With a sigh he lowered the paper. 'With the utmost honesty.' He grimaced and inhaled another breath as though starved of oxygen. 'How can I promise to serve with honesty when I'm not honest with either you or myself?'

His voice was husky, as though it was taking a huge effort even for him to speak.

She swallowed hard, her fingernails biting into her closed fists. It was all over, then.

She moved towards the door, her gaze focused on the dark corridor behind him. The media would camp outside her Brighton apartment. 'I need to call my dad.'

His hand reached out as she neared him. 'It's five in the morning.'

She pulled her arm away so that he couldn't touch her. 'I can slip out of Monrosa before everyone wakes. We can go to my Aunt Nina's house—it's in the middle of nowhere. The media will have a hard time tracking me down there.'

His hand shot further out, blocking her from leaving the room. 'Hold on. Why would you go and stay with your aunt?'

Remain dignified. Don't cry, don't plead. Don't think you can change his mind. Don't do any of the things that stripped Dad of his pride and self-worth.

'You can say I'm ill…or whatever excuse you want to use for me not attending the enthronement. I'm guessing there's nothing your father can do once you've acceded to the throne.'

Edwin stood squarely in front of her. Pale and horrified. 'You're leaving?'

She winced at the distress in his whisper, her threatening tears turning to ones of pure confusion and anger. 'Isn't that what you want?'

He stepped back, and then strode into the room, raking a hand through his hair. 'Of course I don't want you to leave. *Dio*, Kara!' His voice was rising all of the time, his horror replaced by dismay. 'I have told you time and time again that I would never want to separate from you. Why won't you believe me?'

'Why won't I believe you? Oh, give me a break, Edwin. We both know you're only in this marriage to succeed to the throne.' She threw her hands up into the air.

Stop it. You said you wanted to leave with dignity.

Well, I don't care now. I want to lash out. I want to be angry. I'm so fed up with pretending and being nice. I'm too upset and heartbroken to shut up.

'We both know it makes you deeply uncomfortable— we barely speak, you can't bear to look at me and at night you turn your back on me.'

Turning away, she ran into their bedroom and then into her dressing room next to it. She flung back the sliding door of the wardrobe where her weekend bag was stored, wincing at the sight of her wedding dress, which was being stored there temporarily. The national museum wanted it for a special display to celebrate their wedding. They wouldn't now.

'It's not the marriage that's the problem, it's me.'

The bitterest, most cynical laugh she had ever made erupted from deep inside of her. She whirled around to face him. 'Oh, please—not the *It's not you, it's me* line.'

Why was he looking so upset? He had no right to be. She grabbed some T-shirts and bundled them into her weekend bag, burning humiliation torching her skin. She was failing everyone. Failing the charity. Failing Michael's memory. Failing all of the people who relied on the charity. Failing everyone who had come to their wedding in good faith.

'I never wanted to fall in love with you.'

Her hand stalled where she had grabbed a pile of underwear. The white, pastel, bright red and pink colours of her underwear blurred together. He had never seen her wear any of them. How many wives could say that of their husband? She closed her eyes. Pushed down on the hope that stirred somewhere deep in her stomach, disappointment making her feel faint and nauseous. She placed a hand on the frame of the wardrobe to steady herself, reality and memories fortifying her. 'I'm sorry to tell you that I'm well versed in *I love you* being used as a get-out-of-jail-free card. It was a speciality of Nick's any time I tried to break up with him. He would suddenly transform from being indifferently cruel to being the most loving and thoughtful boyfriend a girl could wish for. He was a master of manipulation. What had you expected, that you would waltz in here this morning and we would have a nice little chat about being honest and I would just say okay and agree to staying in a marriage that was destroying me?'

White noise crowded his head. Panic crawled beneath his skin. Why did it physically hurt so much to talk, to express everything that was swarming inside of him?

Making an angry sound, Kara hurled some underwear into her suitcase, the light cotton landing like confetti. Then, yanking at her hand, she shoved her engagement ring towards him. 'Here.'

Dio! She really was serious about leaving.

'No…it's yours.'

The brilliance of the blue stone caught in the sharp light of the recessed lighting. He had spent hours working with Alberto Enciso, the head designer at the royal jewellers, Frechilla & Rouet, designing the ring and picking the exact shade of stone to match Kara's eyes.

'It will never belong to anyone else.'

Her mouth tightened, her eyes blazed with disdain.

'Oh, yeah, I'd forgotten that it would never be part of the royal collection. A fake ring for a fake marriage.'

'It's an eight-carat sapphire! There's nothing fake about it.'

Her nose wrinkled, her mouth twisted. 'That's not what I meant. My point is it's not from the royal collection.'

Lost, he stared down at the ring she was still thrusting towards him. Her hand was shaking, her fingertips white where she was grasping the ring. He had thought his choice of ring would symbolise to Kara his desire to create something unique just for her. Instead she had clearly seen it as a form of rebuttal. *Dio*, he had got so many things wrong. 'Why did you refuse to wear jewellery from the royal collection?'

Her nose wrinkled even more, her cheeks grew hot. 'Because I thought you wouldn't want me to.'

Aghast, he leant against the door frame, ran a hand against the screaming tightness in his temples. 'You don't believe that I see you as part of this family now, do you?' It was as much a question to her as a realisation to him.

Her bottom lip trembled for a split second before she whipped around and tugged open another drawer in her wardrobe. This time, sweaters in her favourite colours of cobalt blue, bright red and pure black hit the suitcase.

He was so tired of living a lie. Tired of being terrified of losing her. So tired of being terrified by emotional intimacy because of the potential pain of growing close to a person and losing them. So tired of closing his heart, of hiding himself from her in fear of appearing foolish, of failing in his promise to protect her.

He opened his mouth, a hot sensation running through his body. 'I have things I need to say to you,' he paused, lost for words, 'things about me and my life I've never shared with you before. Or with anyone else.' He gave a mirthless laugh. 'You see, that's the problem—there hasn't really been anyone else in my life except you for the past decade. You have been the star around which my life has revolved.'

She turned with a sneer, folding her arms.

She wasn't buying it. And he couldn't blame her. Not after Nick's games. And especially given just how closed he had been with her throughout their friendship and especially since they had made love.

He ran a hand through his hair, frustrated and scared he was going to get this wrong. 'I swear I'm not trying to manipulate you. I've been living a lie for so long, and I'm tired of it.'

She made an impatient sound before brushing past him. Out in the bedroom she pulled back the curtains to the early morning sky and went and sat on the sofa in the sitting area. She crossed one leg over the other, her dressing gown parting to reveal her thigh. Seeing his gaze, she tugged the material back in place. Folded her arms and waited for him to speak with a cynical eyebrow raised.

He sat beside her but after a few seconds stood again, needing to move.

He paced the room, his shoulders on fire from tension. He rolled them but found no relief. His skin burnt. He came to a stop, forcing himself to sit and talk to her at the same level, eye to eye, even though he felt sick with the thought of having to open himself up to her. 'I'm in love with you. Not as a friend. As your husband.'

She winced. 'Why should I believe you?'

He glanced at their bed, his chest tightening. 'The night we made love...' He paused, the horror, the slamming disappointment of her words the following morning, coming back to him. He cleared his throat. 'I thought we spoke then, not in words but in our lovemaking. But the day after, you said it was a mistake.'

Kara shifted forward in her seat, her arms dropping to her sides. Stared at him.

Dio, she had seen his tears.

He wanted the ground to swallow him up.

'Edwin.' She said his name as a sigh. She ran a hand down her cheek, closing her eyes for long moments before opening them again. 'It *was* a mistake because it shifted my love for you from being a friend to being your wife.' She sighed deeply, shook her head. 'I don't know why I'm saying these things, but I get it when you say you're tired of lying. So am I.'

What was she saying? Was she saying she was in love with him? He worked his jaw, the adrenaline of panic sending his pulse into a frenzy. He opened his mouth, closed it again.

Dammit, just ask her.

'Are you saying you love me?'

Her hand, trembling, moved against her mouth, her cheeks flaming. 'I'm in love with you...' his heart soared, but crashed to the floor at the pain etched in her eyes '...but I can't stay in this marriage.'

'Why...if you love me and I love you?'

'But they're just words. I love you, Edwin. I love your honour, your sense of duty, your drive to do the best for your country, your inherent decency. But I'm lonely. I'm lonelier in our marriage than I have ever been in my entire life. You feel so distant from me.' A large tear dropped along her cheek, and she gave an unhappy laugh. 'I swore I wouldn't do this. I can't live in a marriage where I don't feel safe, and I don't feel safe with you because you shut me out.'

Her words cut him in two, their honesty searing his

heart. His throat was on fire. It felt like a monumental task to even open his mouth to speak. Years of silence and denial had made him psychologically mute. But he *had* to speak. Or else he was going to lose her. 'I'm terrified of losing you, but the crazy thing is I shut you out because I'm scared of the pain that would come if I did lose you—it's this crazy circle of avoidance that feeds itself and it's out of control.'

Her hand trailed over the soft lace edges of her dressing gown. 'You won't lose me.'

He smiled at that. 'You were just packing your bags.'

She gave a guilty smile. 'I was running away, embarrassed by my feelings for you. I wasn't really thinking, but deep down I was hoping we'd stay friends...that maybe with time and a small miracle we'd be able to go back to where we were.'

He held her gaze. The blue-eyed gaze that had spat fire all those years ago when he had plucked her off a muddy pitch. 'I don't want to be your friend. I want to be your husband. And not just in name.'

Such beautiful words. Words that could turn a world upside down. But meaningless if they weren't backed up by action and truth and real connection. Her parents' marriage had been destroyed by a lack of truth and connection.

If their marriage had any hope of surviving then they both needed to speak the truth, expose what was really in their hearts. She felt faint and, no matter how hard she tried to breathe in, she wasn't capable of dragging in enough air to feed the panic pushing her heart to near exploding point. 'I'm in love with you, but relationships, marriage, terrify me.' She wanted to stop but knew she needed to continue and blurted out without drawing breath, 'Losing Michael, my parents' marriage imploding, my relationship with Nick have all made me wary of trusting that people will be there, will be truthful and honest with me. And so far in our marriage it doesn't feel like we've had any of that.'

Grimacing, Edwin shifted his gaze away from her. He bowed his head. Studied his clasped hands. A long silence followed. Her heart raged in her chest. He was doing it again, closing down on her. She wanted to weep with frustration. He had spoken his oath to her, saying he wanted to be honest with her. And yet he kept shutting her out, as though he didn't trust himself, or simply want, to fully open his heart to her.

'I learned at a very young age that I have to present a mask to the world. When my mother died I was scared and angry, I wanted to rebel, to walk away from everything. But how could I? I was the heir to the throne, the oldest son. I *had* to be responsible. I had to be the one who remained in control while Luis went crazy and Ivo went silent.' He clasped and unclasped his hands, tension radiating from him. 'And the mask I had learned to pull on when in public soon became a private mask too.' He cleared his throat and stared unseeingly at a point beyond her shoulder. 'I used to think I could hear her footsteps outside my bedroom door. I was certain I caught glimpses of her walking around corners of the palace. I thought I was going crazy. I felt so weak. I could barely function. Princess Maria tried to help me, but I couldn't bear to talk. I was afraid that if I did start talking everything I was holding in would spiral out of control.'

Her heart broke to hear his bewildered pain. He looked at her and inhaled a long, deep breath full of remorse. 'With Michael, I should have helped him. I should have been a better friend but I was so closed to my own emotions I just panicked. I didn't know how to help him.'

A tight band squeezed her chest. 'You did help. You spoke to the university authorities and my parents.'

He shrugged away her comment.

Her stomach churned and her throat was raw. She dug her nails into the palms of her hands.

Ask him! For God's sake, ask him!

'Was it because of Michael that you stayed friends with me?'

Those golden eyes burnt into hers. 'No, you had already got under my skin.'

Her heart tumbled, emotion clogged her throat. She dipped her head to meet his gaze and whispered, 'We all feel guilt. We all wish we could have done more for him. I don't think that regret will ever leave us.' She paused, struggling to find the right words. 'You haven't been the only one hiding. I have too. I've been hiding even from myself.'

His hand reached out to rest on the cushion between them. 'What do you mean?'

'For far too long I've been too terrified to accept my feelings for you because I thought it would destroy our friendship. I was too proud to be honest about my feelings because I never wanted to be humiliated. I guess I need to learn from that. And the best way we can honour Michael is by trying to lead truthful lives ourselves, where we don't hide our pain.'

'Losing my mother, witnessing Ivo's pain, the way my family has floundered ever since…shutting down was the easiest way to cope.'

She nodded in understanding. 'Before our engagement, I thought I was okay with the fact that you were so private and closed off. It suited me that we had distance between us. But being married, being around you all of the time, the intimacy of it all, that distance went from being okay to just being very alone and uncertain and insecure.'

He shifted closer to her, those golden eyes searing into hers. He was only inches away from her, both of their heads bowed as though in confession. 'Do you believe me when I say I love you?'

'I don't know… It's so strange to hear you saying you love me after all these years,' she whispered back.

He moved even closer, his mouth close to her ear. 'But it feels completely natural for me to say it. I love you. I love you, Kara Duffy, with your sexy laugh and glittering blue eyes. I love that you always try to beat me to the peak of every mountain we climb. I love your chatter all the way up and down that mountain. I love you for your optimism and humour and imagination. I love that you treat me like a normal human being, never pandering to me.'

She tilted her head, dizzy with the intimacy of his whispers, dizzy with the desire to believe him.

His hand touched against the silk material covering her leg. She pulled away from him, doubts suddenly crowding in.

He moved back towards her, a quiet determination in his eyes. 'When we slept together, it was the most right and real night of my life.' His voice was low, tender. She wanted to weep in relief. 'There was a truthfulness and honesty there that I desperately wanted to ignore, desperately wanted to pretend I didn't crave. That's why, despite it feeling like a kick in the teeth, I tried to pretend to myself that I agreed with you that it was all a mistake, when in fact it felt like the best thing that would ever happen in my life.'

'Are you really saying all of this because you love me—or is it due to the enthronement?'

He studied her with a quiet determination. 'I won't succeed to the throne in order to prove to you my love. Princess Maria can succeed instead.'

She leapt out of her chair, her mouth working like a goldfish's before she finally managed to spit out, 'You're kidding me. You're not about to give up the throne, the role you were born for.'

Edwin shrugged, his expression deadly serious. 'I want you in my life. I want to be your husband. I want to spend every single day proving to you just how much I love you.' His voice cracked. Pinched lines appeared at the corners of his eyes. 'I will walk away from the crown to prove that to you.' Taking his phone from his pocket, he added, 'I can call my father now and tell him of my decision.'

'No!' She took the phone from him, threw it onto their bed. Faced him and said in low voice, 'You do love me.' She whispered those words as much for herself as him. Needing to hear the most amazing realisation of her life out loud.

His expression transformed into gentle delight and tenderness.

She blinked and said, 'Love is pretty terrifying, isn't it?'

'Yes, that's why I think we should ease into this.'

'What do you mean?' she asked.

'We skipped a whole lot of important stuff, like date nights.'

She eyed him. 'We've known each other for more than a decade.'

He took her hand. 'A decade where I've been trying to deny my feelings for you. I've stood on the sidelines and watched you become this incredible woman with endless passion and empathy. A woman I hugely admire. A woman who makes every day worthwhile.'

Her heart about to beat its way out of her chest, she softly whispered, 'I love you. And I want to be your consort.'

Leading her to their bed, kicking off his shoes, he lay down on the mattress and opened his arms to her. She placed her head against his chest, his hand stroked her hair, and he told her a story of a misguided prince, too scared to love his wife until he found the courage to let her into his heart.

And later that day she stood at his side when he was crowned Sovereign Prince of Monrosa, her heart overflowing with pride and love.

EPILOGUE

GABRIELA'S TINY NOSE WRINKLED. She let out a mewl of protest as the cold holy water trickled down her forehead. But she immediately settled back into her deep sleep the moment Edwin drew her against his chest, a small smile lifting on her pink Cupid lips.

Kara reached out, laid a finger against her daughter's cheek. How could skin be so soft, so perfect? She shared a look with Edwin, the wonder in his eyes matching her own amazement. After three long years they finally had their much longed-for baby. At times, she had thought it would never happen for them, her arms aching with the need to hold Edwin's baby.

The cardinal blessed Gabriela and walked away towards the main altar of the palace's private chapel. Handing Gabriela to her godfather, Ivo, who studied his niece with intense pride and adoration, Edwin took her hand and lead her towards the altar too.

Confused, she turned and looked behind to their families. But they were following behind them. Her mother and father walking side by side, their annual trips to visit her in Monrosa for Christmas and during the summer helping to heal the wounds between all three of them. And now they were united in their adulation for their firstborn grandchild. In front of them, Edwin's father seemed to be swallowing back tears. He too knew just how desperately they had wanted Gabriela. Retirement hadn't suited him, but now that Edwin had convinced him to be the island's environmental ambassador he was thriving in his new role.

Edwin brought her to stand before the cardinal.

Touching his hand to her cheek, he said quietly, 'I thought this would be a good time to renew our vows.'

Really? She still looked pregnant, her boobs were sore and she sobbed at the drop of a hat. She eyed her husband, her rock, her life, her calm reassurance when yet another blue line would fail to appear, and nodded *yes*.

He smiled, his eyes pulling her into that private, intimate space they disappeared to when alone.

Then, handing her a white card, his looping handwriting on one side, he said, 'I thought I should write our vows this time.'

At the cardinal's invitation he spoke his vows first. Not once did he look down at the card. Not once did he falter in his delivery. He knew the words as though they were etched onto his brain.

When it was her turn, she laughed when Edwin handed her a clean handkerchief embroidered with his initials—he knew her so well—and, swiping away her tears, through a voice choked with love and hope, she spoke the words her husband had written for them both. 'You are my best friend, my ally, my safe harbour in life. I promise to give you my trust and honesty, my truthful love. I promise to take risks for you. I promise to be always there for you. You are my heart. Dance and laugh and love with me for ever.'

* * * * *

FOUR BRAND NEW STORIES FROM
MILLS & BOON MODERN

The same great stories you love,
a stylish new look!

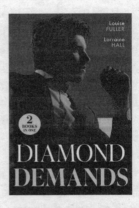

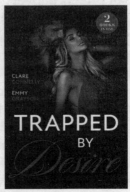

OUT NOW

MILLS & BOON

Afterglow Books is a trend-led, trope-filled list of books with diverse, authentic and relatable characters, a wide array of voices and representations, plus real world trials and tribulations. Featuring all the tropes you could possibly want (think small-town settings, fake relationships, grumpy vs sunshine, enemies to lovers) and all with a generous dose of spice in every story.

♪ @millsandboonuk

◎ @millsandboonuk

afterglowbooks.co.uk

#AfterglowBooks

For all the latest book news, exclusive content and giveaways scan the QR code below to sign up to the Afterglow newsletter:

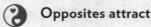 Opposites attract

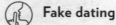 Fake dating

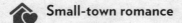 Small-town romance

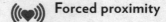 Forced proximity

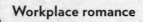 Workplace romance

 Spicy

OUT NOW

Two stories published every month. Discover more at:
Afterglowbooks.co.uk

OUT NOW!

3 BOOKS IN ONE

Rebecca HUNTER

Julie DANVERS

Clare CONNELLY

Workplace ROMANCE

IRRESISTIBLE ATTRACTION

Available at
millsandboon.co.uk

MILLS & BOON

OUT NOW!

Available at
millsandboon.co.uk

MILLS & BOON

LET'S TALK
Romance

For exclusive extracts, competitions and special offers, find us online:

f MillsandBoon

X @MillsandBoon

⊙ @MillsandBoonUK

♪ @MillsandBoonUK

Get in touch on 01413 063 232

For all the latest titles coming soon, visit
millsandboon.co.uk/nextmonth

MILLS & BOON

THE HEART OF ROMANCE

A ROMANCE FOR EVERY READER

MODERN
Prepare to be swept off your feet by sophisticated, sexy and seductive heroes, in some of the world's most glamourous and romantic locations, where power and passion collide.

HISTORICAL
Escape with historical heroes from time gone by. Whether your passion is for wicked Regency Rakes, muscled Vikings or rugged Highlanders, awaken the romance of the past.

MEDICAL
Set your pulse racing with dedicated, delectable doctors in the high-pressure world of medicine, where emotions run high and passion, comfort and love are the best medicine.

True Love
Celebrate true love with tender stories of heartfelt romance, from the rush of falling in love to the joy a new baby can bring, and a focus on the emotional heart of a relationship.

HEROES
The excitement of a gripping thriller, with intense romance at its heart. Resourceful, true-to-life women and strong, fearless men face danger and desire - a killer combination!

From showing up to glowing up, these characters are on the path to leading their best lives and finding romance along the way – with plenty of sizzling spice!

To see which titles are coming soon, please visit

millsandboon.co.uk/nextmonth

MILLS & BOON
A ROMANCE FOR EVERY READER

- **FREE** delivery direct to your door
- **EXCLUSIVE** offers every month
- **SAVE** up to 30% on pre-paid subscriptions

SUBSCRIBE AND SAVE

millsandboon.co.uk/Subscribe

GET YOUR ROMANCE FIX!

Get the latest romance news,
exclusive author interviews, story
extracts and much more!

blog.millsandboon.co.uk

MILLS & BOON
MODERN
Power and Passion

Prepare to be swept off your feet by sophisticated, sexy and seductive heroes, in some of the world's most glamorous and romantic locations, where power and passion collide.

Eight Modern stories published every month, find them all at:

millsandboon.co.uk

MILLS & BOON

HEROES

At Your Service

Experience all the excitement of a
gripping thriller, with an intense romance
at its heart. Resourceful, true-to-life
women and strong, fearless men face
danger and desire – a killer combination!

Eight Heroes stories published every month, find them all at:

millsandboon.co.uk